STRANDS OF
THE WEB:

THE SHORT STORIES OF
HARRY STEPHEN
KEELER

STRANDS OF THE WEB:

THE SHORT STORIES OF HARRY STEPHEN KEELER

Edited by

Fred Cleaver

RAMBLE HOUSE

ISBN 13: 978-1-60543-198-7
ISBN 10: 1-60543-198-2

Cover Art: Gavin L. O'Keefe
Preparation: Fred Cleaver, Francis M. Nevins
and Fender Tucker

TABLE OF CONTENTS

STRANDS

Harry Stephen Keeler has a deserved reputation for long intricate novels packed with both plot and frequent plot digressions. He practiced the skills needed to build his elaborate webworks in an apprenticeship writing short stories.

Starting when he was 22 he wrote two dozen short stories in a four year period including 17 stories in 1914. All this time he had his eye on the future. While he was mastering the short story he started writing short novels and serials with a goal of book publication. When the serials started selling to better markets the short work was abandoned.

He didn't forget the early efforts when he started publishing books. He often incorporated the stories into his novels—many times without regard to the stories' relevance to the novel. Sometimes there were wholesale changes to the main character or the point of view. He was also able to overcome what he saw as the principle weakness of the work by stretching the length to the edges of a reader's endurance.

I first learned of Harry Stephen Keeler and his crazed world sometime in the 1970s through the pioneering work of Mike Nevins in *The Armchair Detective,* a mystery fanzine available at the University of Colorado. The university library was once run by a mystery fan and there were many Keeler novels on the shelves. But an intriguing part of his career that eluded me for years were the short stories that had been cobbled together to make his first books.

I began to find these stories as obscure magazines showed up on eBay. Eventually I found Keeler's first story in a bound volume of *10 Story Book* at the Library of Congress. Other rarities were published by Richard Polt in the newsletter of the burgeoning Harry Stephen Keeler Society.

This book owes a lot to Mike Nevins presentation of Keeler's writing journal in a year by year list published by Polt. Keeler recorded when the stories were written and how much they sold for. The stories in this book are presented in the order in which they were written according to this journal and with Keeler's original titles.

The journal doesn't say who bought the stories and there are a few I know nothing more about. Some of these are in the journal as never having sold although it is possible they were published. At least some of these marketplace failures were published under various pretenses in the Editor's column of the *Chicago Ledger*. A few others sold and simply haven't been found. They could be in any number of obscure and uncatalogued publications.

Keeler made major or minor revisions to most of these stories. I have chosen the earliest version I could find. They also had an afterlife in the decade after their publication when they were syndicated to newspapers and republished in other magazines, mostly magazines edited by Keeler.

Keeler's first sale, "The Spender," was to the magazine *10 Story Book* and published in the October 1913 issue. *10 Story Book* had been published in Chicago since 1901 and paid $6 for each story whatever the length. Editor John Stapleton Cowley-Brown liked Keeler's work and he became a regular contributor. One version of events Keeler told Writer's Digest in 1930 is "I wrote two short stories while waiting for an engineering connection. *10 Story Book* bought them straight off. Fired with enthusiasm, I dashed off ten others and in self defense they made me editor." I can't make those numbers add up and in later years Keeler said he became editor after Cowley-Brown was fired for possibly defaming a litigious department store owner.

Whatever the truth, Keeler became the new editor in 1916. Despite a couple of resignations during the first few years Keeler remained editor until the magazine went out of business in 1941. He didn't contribute new fiction after 1920 as the magazine redefined itself by mixing the stories with photos of scantily dressed women but his anonymous presence can be seen in occasional bursts of outlandish Keeler humor.

The one exception to the fertile period of 1913-1917 is "A Telescopic Romance." It was written in 1910, apparently before Keeler's mother committed him to an asylum for a few years. This story inspired some of the more unusual influences from Keeler's work. Ken Keeler (no relation) considered using the much longer book version "A Strange Romance" for an episode of his television series Futurama. Two young filmmakers were inspired by Ken's DVD commentary for that episode to make their Youtube feature of the story without reading it.

"The Hand of God" was contributed to a Mystery Writers of America anthology in 1951. It is apparently based on an early story—I believe it is the lost fragment "Dream Girl" but have found no evidence to back that up.

The obvious influence on the stories are the plot twists associated with O. Henry. The first sale was a story about a tramp named Soapy, one of three featuring a name made famous in the O. Henry story "The Cop and the Anthem."

Naming the four "most interesting writing men on record" in a 1919 Chicago Ledger editorial Keeler started with O. Henry. What impressed him weren't the clever stories but the large sums O. Henry could demand for a story. See "A Check for a Thousand" for Keeler's yearning to make more than $6 a story.

Two other writers Keeler cited were dime novel authors Colonel Prentiss Ingraham and William Wallace Cook. These are men known more for quantity than quality. He admired Ingraham's speed and Cook's volume. Cook wrote well into the pulp era and had work published in *Top Notch Magazine* alongside Keeler. Keeler is famous for keeping large files of newspaper clippings to work into his novels. In his 1912 pseudonymous memoir *The Fiction Business* Cook goes into great detail about how he organized his extensive clippings.

The other man Keeler admired was Swedish dramatist August Strindberg. I will leave it as an exercise for the reader to find the influence of Strindberg on these stories. A hint someone else might find useful: Keeler chose a Strindberg story to feature on the cover of a 1931 issue of *10 Story Book*.

There are two items which reach out to stage and screen. I have used the order Mike Nevins gives from the notebook and have placed the short story "The Services of an Expert" before the play of the same title. Some Keeler statements indicate he wrote the play first and the story after his efforts to market the play were unsuccessful. The play was eventually staged in Chicago by a community theatre group in the late 1920s.

I know even less about his photoplay "Soapy's Trip to Mars." Short comedy sketches were standard for films of the day and Keeler's story certainly has more slapstick than logic.

One story is a collaboration. A friend from the days before Keeler's marriage who we know a little about is Franklin Lee Stevenson. Stevenson moved to Chicago from Wisconsin. He worked on newspapers and had ambitions to write poetry and fiction. The fiction was not successful despite a few pieces his friend Keeler published in *10 Story Book*. In a work of anonymous verse about a dinner party of uncertain date chez Keeler:

And there's Professor Stevenson, a doctor of short-story
At old De Paul. He cures 'em up—insipid, weak, or gory.

Other sources state Stevenson taught journalism at De Paul. He
had moved to Michigan when he found his niche in the poetry
world in 1924. He built a business selling verses to funeral home
directors to pass on as memorial verses to grieving families. His
obituary in *Time* magazine labeled him "the undertaker's poet
laureate." Keeler credited himself with only 6¢ of the $6 payment
for "Sidestepping Ryan." When he reused the story in a novel
Stevenson wasn't named.

The last story, "Goodbye, Coppers!", was a bit of therapy that
helped break the writer's block Keeler had after the death of his
first wife Hazel in 1960. It helped him to get back to the novels he
worked on until his death in 1967.

It should be noted that the racism in some of the novels can be
a sticking point for many. It is a strange irony that the most racist
story in this book, "Sunbeam's Child," is set in Barack Obama's
Chicago neighborhood of Hyde Park.

If I had to pick one favorite in this collection it would be
"Babes in the Wood." This tour of Chicago's red light district
from the tawdriness of Dearborn Street to the swanky clubs has
realism that matches historical accounts (compare *Sin in the
Second City* by Karen Abbott) with a story of pure Keeler
coincidence.

I would like to thank Fender Tucker for all he has done to bring
Keeler back into print including his patience with this book. Mike
Nevins who introduced me to Keeler and still has the enthusiasm
to worry over Keeler's wayward commas. Richard Polt sets the
standard for Keeler scholarship with his devotion to the Harry
Stephen Keeler Society and the indefatigable *Keeler News*. Thanks
to Chris Mikul for sharing Keeler rarities. Morgan Wallace
supplied valuable information on obscure corners of publishing.
And my own Mrs. W-H for tolerating Keeler in the house and
spending vacations in libraries looking for more Keeler.

Fred Cleaver
Colorado 2009

STRANDS OF THE WEB:

THE SHORT STORIES OF HARRY STEPHEN KEELER

A TELESCOPIC ROMANCE

Y FATHER—I dare not mention his name—was one of the foremost astronomers in America. His publications regarding his researches in stellar space had long kept the world agog previous to his death. In his last scientific paper, written when I was a young man, he had broached the subject of his latest discovery, namely: A telescope lens of such great refracting power as to unfold to man all the hidden mysteries of celestial space. He had told briefly of his discovery of the changed properties of quartz crystals which had been subjected to rapid mechanical vibrations of a peculiar sort. The nature of these vibrations he did not divulge, but stated that the entire molecular structure of the material was altered when vibrations were applied in certain directions and with particular frequencies according to a recondite mathematical law known as yet only to himself.

In that paper, furthermore, he broadly asserted that before another month he would give to the world corroborative evidence that the celestial bodies known as fixed stars were really suns not unlike our own. The great problem that he hoped to solve, he had said, was whether or not some of these suns were surrounded by planets. If these latter bodies showed signs of life upon their surfaces, then proof of the multiplicity of world systems was at hand.

Consequently, scientific and uneducated people alike had waited with intense expectancy for the revelations that were soon to come from this eminent student, my father. When his death was announced a week before the time he had appointed for the great test, disappointment, I dare say, filled the breasts of many who feared that his labors had been uncompleted.

My mother had been dead for a number of years and I, William, was the only son. After graduating from college, not caring for the life of solitude and study that my father had led, I departed for a neighboring city and there took up the carefree existence of many other idle young men. This was made possible by a generous check sent me every month by my indulgent father, who, having sufficient wealth inherited from his own paternal parent, saw no reason, probably, why he should pecuniarily stint me, his only child.

When a telegram reached me that my father was dying of pneumonia I caught the first train to his home city in my haste to reach the bedside before it should be too late. Arriving at my destination, I was met at the station by Burke, the old family servant, who had cooked the meals and taken care of my father for a number of years. The look on the servant's face told me plainly that my father had passed away. As we walked slowly down to the house, Burke related to me, in full, the incidents that preceded my father's death.

"Your father," he said, "was all wrought up about his new discovery. After he received the telescope lens from the grinders he was up day and night working on it. Sometimes, long before dawn, I'd wake up and hear the vibrating machine humming away for a minute, then stopping for a length of time and then starting up again. After several days and nights he had the lens in the proper condition and then laid it away careful as anything in a box that he had made for it. He told me to be mighty careful of that box, for if it got handled rough or jarred the new properties of the lens might be utterly changed."

He then continued: "Your father then tore up all his calculations. He had a brain that scarcely ever forgot things, and I suppose he figured that he could keep in mind all that he needed. The last night he was up he got the telescope ready for the lens; he must have caught cold, for he complained of feeling sick and went to bed. By the next night he was dying of pneumonia and the doctor couldn't do anything to save him. You know the rest of the story yourself."

My father was buried; his funeral was small and unpretentious. It was the evening of the funeral day and for the first time since my arrival I stood in the little observatory idly looking over the huge telescope and the remaining astronomical contrivances in the room. I noticed an opening in the former instrument and rightly surmised that it was intended for the reception of the lens whose making had so engrossed my father's last days. A sudden inspiration seized me to be the first one to whom the mysteries of the heavens should be revealed.

Upon looking around more carefully I spied over in the corner a rosewood box, and at once decided that therein lay the ground quartz crystal discussed in my father's last scientific paper. Going over to it I tried several keys among those upon the bunch turned over by Burke to me on the day of my arrival. I found at last a small key which unlocked the cover. On raising the latter I saw, reposing on a soft velvet cushion, a large transparent disc with highly-polished convex sides. For a moment I gazed at it, marveling as to how it could be in a state of molecular strain and yet appear so clear and transparent; finally I lifted it slowly out, carried it carefully over to the telescope and deposited it in the opening so obviously intended for its reception.

For a few seconds I stood looking at the small patch of sky which was directly in line with the huge telescope; then I lowered my head and sighted along its brass top and saw that it was pointed at a small cluster of indistinct stars in the region of the Great Dipper. I now drew up a small stool, seated myself upon it and with some trepidation placed my eye to the eyepiece of the instrument. An involuntary cry of amazement broke from me at the sight that met my eye. There in the field of vision was a scene from a far-away planet belonging to some distant sun!

On close inspection I saw that I was looking down in a garden luxuriant with foliage of a violet hue. Scarcely twenty feet distant did it appear to be. Here and there were what seemed to be blooming flowers with petals of deep purple. It appeared to be late afternoon, for the shadows cast by the sunshine, which itself appeared to be of a reddish gold hue, were long in comparison with the objects causing them. Across the garden frolicked a small light-colored woolly animal, not unlike a dog in appearance, with the exception of a small horn protruding from its head between its two eyes.

A huge gaudy butterfly sailed gracefully back and forth, sending the small animal into apparent paroxysms of anger; the latter stood stiffly on its legs and emitted what appeared to be short, sharp barks, but which, of course, gave forth no sound.

I noticed that since I had first looked upon this scene it had shifted by almost two-thirds of its length. Carefully noting one of the edges of the field of view, I saw that the scene was slowly but regularly passing across my vision from right to left. At once my mind grasped the cause. The earth, upon which the telescope was of course fixed, must in its ceaseless rotation on its own axis cause the telescope to sweep slowly across the sky as the night progressed. As a result, any view in the instrument must by degrees be supplanted by another view which, in turn, must slowly give way to the encroachments of a succeeding one. Intensely interested by the panorama passing before my eye, my attention was suddenly riveted by the sight of a young girl, clad in a cream-colored garment, sitting in what appeared to be a seat hewn from a large rock. Some distance behind her a door appeared to lead into the large garden. This entranceway was built in a dwelling place, only a part of which was as yet visible, that seemed to be made of a gray stone in which here and there small red and green crystals sparkled.

The girl seemed to be reading from a scroll of parchment; suddenly, as though weary, she dropped it to her lap and leaned her head back on the rounded top of the stone seat. As a result she appeared to be looking into my eyes. Her hair was a shimmering yellow and her cheeks were colored with the same delicate pink that is characteristic of beautiful girls on the earth. Her eyes, however, attracted me the most. They were deep violet, not unlike the color of the foliage, and had long dark lashes that swept her cheeks when she closed them for an instant. Judging by terrestrial standards her age did not appear to be over twenty years. "The most beautiful creature I've ever seen," I said, after looking long and rapturously at her.

Suddenly an idea crossed her mind that caused her red lips to break into a smile. For an instant my heart stopped beating, for she seemed to be smiling directly up at me. I felt that all I need do was to spring to my feet, take a few steps forward and be at her side.

In these few moments, however, the earth had moved to such a new position that the girl was now on the edge of the telescope disc; in a few seconds the scene had changed by such a small increment that she was no longer a part of it.

With disappointment written on my face I rose to my feet. My first inclination was to manipulate the moving mechanism of the telescope so as to move it back a short way, but a moment's consideration showed me that to do so by the smallest angle must undoubtedly sweep entire oceans and continents with lightning rapidity past my gaze. If the telescope's direction should be in the least altered I realized that I might never again be able to direct it to the spot where this wonderful girl lived—the spot which Chance had so fortuitously thrown in my way. As I stood gazing at the small portion of sky, in some infinitesimal corner of which lived a girl who had unconsciously thrown a complete enchantment over me, a new idea smote me. I pulled out my watch and noted carefully the time. There had come to me the realization that if the telescope should remain absolutely undisturbed in the meantime, it must on the following evening sweep out the same path across the heavens.

I saw, therefore, that if I should be posted at the eyepiece on the next evening at a few minutes before the present time, the same scene must again pass before me.

With all interest in this distant world gone for the present, I slowly turned out the lights in the observatory, leaving everything else untouched. After carefully locking the door I went to my room, disrobed, and jumped into bed. All night long I tossed back and forth, unable to sleep. I had indeed fallen deeply in love. A vision of a girl with golden hair and violet eyes haunted me until morning.

The following day was clear and bright, with not a cloud in the sky. I moped in the house all day, wondering why the hours passed so slowly, and inwardly praying that the sky would remain free from clouds. By evening I was worked up to a high degree of mental excitement; joy at being again able to see the object of my affections conflicted with fear that at the particular moment during which the garden would pass across the view of the telescope she would be either away or else inside of the house studded with the red and green crystals.

Promptly at ten minutes before the time at which I had first gazed on the preceding evening, I was seated on the stool with my eyes glued to the telescope. Rapidly there appeared to pass before me a stretch of country; first a river and then a wood with violet foliage crossed my vision. Here and there strange animals in herds cavorted up and down the banks of the rivers. Now and then a hut built of gray stone and studded with sparkling colored crystals appeared to move by me.

Soon I saw that I must be gazing at the outskirts of a village or town, for the huts were now much larger and closer together. Suddenly, however, the edge of the garden came into view and I soon recognized it as the same one that I had seen the night before. As more of it became visible I saw with disappointment that no one was in it; even the little woolly animal with the small horn between its eyes was absent. Just at this moment some one appeared in the doorway or opening in the gray stone habitation and I saw with delight that it was the violet-eyed girl. Slowly she walked through the garden, looking straight ahead. As she turned to retrace her steps, I scarcely breathed, so near she seemed. Soon, however, she was on the receding edge of the disk, and as she passed from view she turned her face upwards for an instant and I secured another sight of her features.

Still not daring to move the telescope lest I should lose her altogether, I sadly arose, extinguished the light in the observatory and went out, locking the door behind me. From weariness at not having slept the night before I slumbered fitfully until dawn, dreaming of the girl who had caused me so much mental perturbation. As I opened my eyes and looked out of the window I jumped to my feet in dismay. The entire sky was overcast with clouds and rain was pouring down in heavy sheets. All day long it rained, and I shook my fists at the sky and cursed the meteorological conditions. By night the rain had stopped, but the clouds remained and served to screen away the heavens. As a result I went to bed after the critical moment of the two previous evenings had passed and tossed back and forth until again overcome by troubled sleep.

Again I woke early with the depressing feeling of not having seen the wonderful girl for a long time. Not a cloud, however, now floated in the sky. Throughout the day I patiently sat and waited with my chin in my hands, thinking and thinking; vainly I tried to reason myself out of this mad infatuation for a girl with whom I knew it was impossible that I should ever become acquainted.

By night time I sat at the table in the observatory while the minutes dragged slowly by. Again and again I looked at my timepiece. Finally it lacked by seven minutes of the time when the telescope should sweep over the wonderful garden again. At this juncture Burke entered the observatory through the open door in order to inquire as to some purchase of supplies that he thought should be made. Inferring that I was merely about to scan the sky for points of interest, he decided evidently to give gratuitously a little astronomical information, of which he must have picked up considerable in his twenty years of service.

"I see, William," he said, "you've got the tube pointed up exactly at a group of what your father used to call the Sirian Stars. Their distances, he was telling me, as calculated from their small parallax, is so great that it takes light from different ones everywhere from a hundred years up, to reach the earth."

Hearing these words I sprang to my feet.

"Merciful heavens!" was my first thought. "Light—traveling a hundred years—the Sirian Stars! Then—then I am seeing this girl as she was over a century ago when the light waves that comprise her appearance first started out into space." I sank my head in my hands. "And instead of being a young and fair maiden now, she has already passed middle age, probably been an old and grizzled hag and is now a moldy skeleton."

In a sudden mad rage at having been tricked by Fate I stepped to the opening that contained the lens, jerked it out and threw back my arm preparatory to hurling it with all my might on the floor and smashing it into fragments. Burke, astounded at my actions, evidently anticipating what I was about to do, jumped at me and caught my wrist. "You young fool!" he cried, "do you want to destroy one of the greatest discoveries ever made?"

At this juncture the lens slid from my fingers, dropped on its edge to the floor with a resounding bump and toppled over on its side unbroken, unharmed, and as we stood glaring at each other, it gently rocked back and forth on its convex side.

Full of shame, I saw what I had almost done. Although realizing that I was in love with a phantasm, a nothing, a thing which no longer existed, an overwhelming desire filled me to gaze upon my love again. I stepped away from Burke, and looking at my watch, noted that I had still two minutes left me. "I was a fool, Burke," I said simply. "You—you didn't understand the circumstances, though." With haste I picked up the lens and reinserted it into the telescope. I then quickly placed my eyepiece and peered out into the night.

Nothing whatever met my eye but a dark patch of sky in which was a cluster of faint stars that seemed to blink and twinkle down ironically at me. The wonderful crystal lens had turned to glass!

THE SPENDER

S OAPY" HARRIS, so named by his brethren of "the road" on account of his allegiance to soap and water, peered forth from his vantage point behind a clump of bushes.

He was observing the antics of the gay automobile party which was having a picnic lunch in the grove at the side of the road. Their huge red car standing unattended in the roadway had first attracted him to the locality; now he was patiently waiting for them to depart that he might possibly find some uneaten sandwiches.

He perceived, both from the profusion of empty wine bottles scattered about the grass, and the maudlin shouts that met his ear, that the six people whom he was watching were well on the way to a state of bibulous exhilaration; he also recognized from their appearance that they belonged to the class of which he knew little— the idle rich.

"Soapy" glanced at the sun low in the west and waxed impatient for them to go; then he chuckled as he saw one stout man with a large diamond pin in his tie, trip unsteadily over a protruding root and fall prostrate.

Presently, they gathered up their silverware and walked with uncertain steps to their machine. In a moment they were whizzing far up the road and "Soapy" emerged from his place of concealment and sauntered over to where several soiled napkins and various empty bottles indicated the site of their repast.

As he was gazing around in the fast gathering dusk he suddenly became transfixed with surprise. Staring up at him from a tuft of weeds was a yellow slip of paper with the figure "500" in the upper right hand corner. As soon as he recovered from his astonishment his hand swooped down upon it and a closer inspection showed that he held a government note for five hundred dollars in his fingers.

His palm caressed it lovingly; he observed in spite of all his stupefaction how smooth and crisp it was.

Nervously he looked around him; seeing no one in the vicinity he placed it hastily in his pocket and walked out to the road. Here he turned and pursued his way rapidly until he came to a railroad crossing. Again he turned and was soon making his way along the track.

After he was some distance from the intersection with the road he drew out the note and read each side slowly. Then he replaced it with care and began to try, as he walked along, to comprehend the good fortune that had come his way.

He remembered how just five years ago he had left the little factory town in the East on the account of the hopelessness of ever becoming able to gather enough money to marry Amy Bridges. He had gone West and she had told him that she would wait for him. He remembered too, how in the West he had fared no better than in the East. At the end of a year he had accumulated nothing. During the second year he had gone from pillar to post, out of employment half of the time. By the end of the third year he had found himself "beating the road" in the search for work and he had in time stopped searching altogether, for his was one of those natures that usually takes the path of least resistance. In time, his associates in trampdom, amused at constant possession of a cake of soap, had given him the "monicker" of "Soapy"—and it began to seem as though "Soapy the hobo" he would remain for the rest of his days.

A year ago he had written Amy a letter, friendly but ambiguous, yet conveying nevertheless the impression that he was not doing well in the West; he had enclosed his address as "general delivery, Denver." Passing through that city a month later with another tramp, he had called at the post office delivery window and had had handed to him a little letter addressed in a dainty handwriting to Mr. James W. Harris. She had ended with the words—"I know you'll make good, Jimmy, and save some money—and I am still waiting for you. With all my love to you, Amy."

And now Fate had smiled on one of her own victims.

As he proceeded along in the darkness he began to think about the future and to devise certain plans for using the yellow-colored bill that nestled in his pocket. First, he told himself, he would catch a freight that very night and be at Omaha, only a hundred miles away, by morning. There, after he had washed himself and improved his appearance as much as possible, he would deposit the bill at a local bank and draw half of it out at once. If the teller should question him he would say that it represented the savings of two years—that he had been carrying it in that form for safety.

At least, he knew, there would be no one who could disprove such an assertion.

Then, after securing a shave, a bath and a much needed hair cut, he told himself, he would purchase a tan leather suitcase and black leather traveling bag. For these he would pay about twenty dollars. He would secure two well made suits of clothes, one black and one grey; for them both he would expend about fifty dollars. He would buy shoes, shirts, collars, and other articles of wearing apparel.

He would purchase a diamond scarf pin for his tie and a diamond engagement ring for Amy. For the pin he would disburse about fifty dollars—and for the ring at least a hundred.

When he had done these things and had withdrawn the remainder of his money, he would acquire a ticket for "back home" and go bravely back to the little Eastern town, arriving "on the cushions"—clean and well dressed. His friends would see him and would know that he had done well in the West. He would go to Amy at once and place the ring on her finger. Together they would pick out a tiny cottage and he would arrange for its rental. He would furnish it new at an expense of about a hundred and fifty dollars and then they would be married.

He totaled up all these expenditures in his mind and found that over a hundred dollars would yet remain for a nest egg.

He would go to work and be a man among men again. With a home, a bank account, a new wardrobe, the respect of his friends—and last and best of all, Amy, he could and must make good again. All that he had ever needed, he had decided long ago, was a start; now he had it. And perhaps later, he assured himself, there might be a little child to twine its arms around his neck—a little child that should never know that its daddy had once been a ragged tramp.

He had completely lost his slouching gait. He walked with shoulders squared and head erect—like a man to whom a new vista of life had been opened. The world was his now, he felt, for no one back home would ever be able to surmise that he had once been "Soapy" Harris.

Unexpectedly his ruminations were brought to an abrupt stop, for his further progress along the track was arrested. In front of him ran a ravine across which a railroad bridge had formerly existed. By one of those queer mischances that even bridge builders do not fully understand, the dirt in one embankment had sifted away due to the vibration of some passing train, and as a result one

of the bridge supports had suddenly given way also and now the
entire structure lay crumpled and demolished in the bottom of the
gully.

It took him several minutes of peering around in the darkness to
comprehend the situation. When he had fully satisfied himself as
to the extent of the damage, a long drawn out whistle escaped his
lips. All at once, as though in answer to him, the far reaching
whistle of a locomotive sounded out on the air.

He wheeled sharply and gazed down the track. Visible now
only as a tiny spot of light, he distinguished the headlight of the
engine. He listened carefully and detected the "chug, chug, chug"
that told him it was a heavily loaded freight train. Then he kneeled
down, placed his ear to the rail and listened for the vibrations that
were caused by the heavy engine driving-wheels passing over the
joints in the rail. Their rapidity satisfied him that it was approaching at high speed.

He understood quickly the fate that must overtake the engineer
and fireman if the train should run over the embankment and into
the gully in the darkness; he saw too, that he alone must warn
them if it were possible.

Hastily he looked around and discerned a post looming up in
the darkness at the side of the track; hanging from a protruding
hook was a dilapidated lantern. He grasped it at once, knowing
from experience that it would have a chimney of red glass.

He sought in his vest pocket for a solitary match that he had
been carrying all day in the hope of getting something to smoke. A
sigh of relief escaped him when he found it.

Kneeling on the track he raised the chimney with his left hand,
with his right he struck the match carefully on the sole of his shoe
and inserted the lighted splinter of wood into the interior where the
wick should be. When no answering flame met his gaze he inspected it more closely and discovered the reason—there was no
wick left. Wildly he shook the lantern and knew from the sound it
contained no oil. He jerked the chimney free and cursed fervently,
as with a well-directed kick he sent the metal framework spinning
far into the gully.

As the match was still burning in his hands he had another re-
source to fall back upon. All he needed, he was fully aware, was a
strip of paper that he could crumple up, ignite in the flame of the
match, and thrust blazing into the interior of the glass chimney.
During the fraction of a minute that it should continue to burn, its

rays would be changed to a red color and might warn the coming trainmen that grave danger awaited them.

The headlight of the engine appeared larger now and the rails sang as though filled with a thousand violin strings. "Soapy" glanced at the road bed and saw that he must look to himself for paper as nothing but sand and gravel met his eye.

The flame of the match was becoming unpleasantly hot to his fingertips. He hurriedly set the glass chimney down on the rail and his free hand raced through his pockets in search for paper and in one by one found—nothing. With a sinking feeling in his heart he realized suddenly that he had cleared his pockets that morning of all the trash they had contained.

And then the sinking feeling in his heart became more intense, for in his last pocket his fingers came in contact with something that was smooth and crisp.

~ ~ ~ ~ ~

The engineer of Freight No. 34 noticed a red light come suddenly into existence far down the track in advance of his engine. It burned for almost a quarter of a minute and died out as mysteriously as it had come. He shut off his steam and applied his brakes. Then he jerked the whistle cord twice to indicate that he had received the signal.

As he did so a solitary figure struck across the fields in the search for a place to sleep.

VALLEY EXPRESS ON TIME

O LD RONALD BAER, president of the Cherry Valley Interurban System, drummed on his desk with his fingers; this was his usual method of signifying that as far as he was concerned an interview was ended.

"No, Holly," he repeated, with a tone of finality, to the young man just arising from his chair, "I haven't any objections to you, personally, but I've had in mind for a long time different plans concerning Natalie.

"As I've already remarked, you must strive to remember, my dear sir, that as power foreman of the Cherry Valley Traction Company at a salary of only a hundred and fifty dollars per month, you are hardly in a position to provide for a girl who has been reared as my daughter has. Doubtlessly, in her youthful optimism, she feels that she is willing to undergo all sorts of deprivations and losses of luxuries—but frankly—I've seen Love's young dream fade, under those conditions, in too many cases already."

Robert Holly gloomily pushed his chair back to the wall and started for the door of old Baer's office. Half way across the floor he turned and came back.

"I'm suddenly reminded, Mr. Baer," he remarked, "that there were really two important matters on which I wished to see you. The first, relating to Natalie, you've evidently settled. The second touches upon the men at the power plant. One month ago, I believe, a signed request was sent to you by them, asking for a twenty per cent increase in wages to apply to all employees of the Cherry Valley electric lines. So far, no answer from you has come. You must readily admit that all of them—stokers, engineers, dynamo operators, as well as section hands, linemen, and even conductors and motormen—when compared with men in similar lines of work in other sections of the country, are grossly underpaid. Unfortunately they haven't any redress. They are settled here in Ashdale—and in different parts of the surrounding territory—with their wives and children; in fact, they were settled here long before the Interurban Company linked the towns of Cherry Valley with its lines."

He paused for a moment to see what effect his words were producing.

"They cannot easily pull up stakes and move to other places. Yet, in spite of this, a strike is impending and has been impending for a month—and unless something is done it might take place before long. I consider it my duty to tell you that if such a situation arises I shall feel compelled to go out with them all. For the last two years I've worked with these boys, and, candidly, my sympathies are with them. Consequently, if this strike should ever take place, I will have to follow the rest—and in that event you must of course consider my resignation as handed in."

Old Baer glowered.

" 'In that event'—quoting your own words, Holly—there are enough strikebreakers in the East to run the Cherry Valley Interurban Company. However, this is Monday. I'll prepare an answer to the men's demands this week."

After the power foreman had left, old Baer sat and reflected for a long while. After all, he thought, Holly was a clean-cut young chap, out of the Tech School only a few years. Natalie could easily do worse for a life partner. And he wondered, vaguely, what he could say to her when she herself should ask him, looking at him with those great brown eyes that were so like the eyes of her mother, gone these twenty years.

But when his mind turned on the threatened strike his face grew black as a thunder cloud. So the men were dissatisfied, were they? And they were menacing the income of the company with a possible strike. And Holly, his power foreman, hand in glove with them, too. Well, what if they were underpaid? Surely, a man has a right to hire labor as cheaply as he can get it.

He thought of the generous dividends that Cherry Valley Traction stock had paid in the last years since he had acquired 51 per cent of the existing shares, since stockholders' meetings, with all their useless wranglings, had been discontinued on account of the futility of the voters of the other 49 per cent; since he, Ronald Baer, had assumed the absolute dictatorship and had ruled affairs with an iron hand.

Then, because he found himself getting more and more incensed, he proceeded to divest his mind of all thoughts regarding the entire matter.

By Wednesday he was still undetermined as to what answer he could render to the men; by Saturday, however, he had almost decided to offer them a wage increase of 5 per cent.

After lunch, therefore, having had in mind for some time a personal trip to inspect a new safety device he had installed a few days previously on the main line a few miles out of Ashdale, he donned a short outing coat and left the office, prepared to weigh the pros and cons of the affair as he walked along.

At the time the Cherry Valley lines had been first constructed, the engineers in charge had encountered a hill composed of a hard, flinty, red stone. Rather than run the track over or around this obstruction, they had bored through it and had come out on the other side, leaving a short tunnel of about forty feet in length. This bore, known to the employees and passengers as the Red Rock Tunnel, was situated out in the country, yet within an hour's walk of Ashdale.

A few months before the present time a heavy interurban trolley car, in speeding through the underground passage, had left the rails. As it scraped along one of the rocky walls a part of one of its sides had been torn off. The passengers had been rudely shaken and some of them greatly terrified, but none had been injured.

Nevertheless a number of damage suits had been instituted against the company; these had to be settled. This did not at all appeal to old Ronald Baer, so he had taken steps to guard against a repetition of such an accident.

After forty-five minutes of vigorous walking along the track, breathing in great lungfuls of the fresh country air, he reached the mouth of the bore. He had quite resolved by this time to allow his last decision to stand unaltered.

For a moment he paused to fumble for a match; his eyes, accustomed to the outside light, were unable to pierce the gloom of the tunnel. With light in hand he picked his way carefully inside. There near the middle was the mechanism he wished to examine.

A lever, erected at the side of the track, he saw, could be moved a short distance. By means of conceding bars at the bottom, two movable rails, placed between the regular rails, could be drawn to such a position that they cleared the latter by only a few inches. In this same position the flanges of the wheels on a car tending to leave the track would be caught by them and the car, as a result, kept in its correct path. When repairs to the roadbed were necessitated, the lever could be opened to such a point that the guarding rails cleared the main ones by an essential distance.

Old Baer stepped back and forth between the ties in the half darkness, working the lever to and fro, and wondering at the same time why it had not been secured to the iron hook in the side of the tunnel by means of the chain and padlock hanging conveniently near. Mentally he made a note to discipline the track foreman, upon the latter's return to the office.

Then, having seen all he wished, he threw back the lever against the wall and wound the small steel chain several times around it; after passing the chain thru the hook a few more times he padlocked the ends tightly together. Then he prepared to leave.

To his consternation he found he could not move his right foot.

He struck another match and gazed downward. The cause was evident. Thoughtlessly, he had stepped between the track rail and the guard rail when he had locked them within a few inches of each other. As a result, the portion of his foot above the ankle passed between their edges; his ankle, he found, however, he could not withdraw. Longitudinal motion, he discovered at the same instant, was prevented by the two adjacent ties.

This was a fine thing, he thought, for the chief executive of the Cherry Valley Traction Company to do—to lock himself up in his own safety device. Should the fact ever leak out, he would be the laughing stock of everyone.

He pondered for a few seconds and then felt in his clothes for his pocket-knife. Finding it, he opened the small nail file that it contained and commenced filing at one of the links of the chain; in about a minute he found with much relief that he had already made a slightly perceptible cut.

For a little while he filed steadily away; he felt for another match, and, discovering it to be his last, nevertheless ignited it, since his eyes, now accustomed to the darkness, were able to see with some degree of accuracy by the diffused light coming in from the mouth of the passage. He perceived that he had cut half through the link and so decided to rest for a few moments before finishing his task.

Then it was that a sudden thought, coming in on his consciousness without warning, caused him to grow sick with fear.

He had forgotten the northbound express!

Every afternoon at 2:45 it left Ashdale, and, barring usual delays caused by passengers mounting at different streets in the town, was scheduled to flash through the Red Rock Tunnel at 3 P.M.

With trembling lands he felt for his watch. Drawing it out, he held it so that the light from the outside fell on its face.

Its hands pointed exactly to the hour of 3!

Panic-stricken, he tugged with might and main at the steel chain. It would not give. He wrenched, twisted, turned and pulled at his foot. It caused him much agony but steadfastly refused to be drawn from between the two rails. As he had on low shoes that did not reach even to his ankles, he knew in an instant that removing his foot-gear would avail him nothing.

A sudden tremulous vibration of the ground, coupled with a light humming noise from the trolley wire above his head, caused his face to whiten, his arms to drop almost paralyzed at his sides, and his heart to beat with a horrible thumping sensation that seemed to reach every point in his body.

For once, the northbound express was on time!

Looking far out along the track, he saw it coming over the hill—a ponderous, yellow car; he saw the sun glint from the brass controller handle as the motorman threw it over to full speed.

And he, Ronald Baer, was imprisoned in a tunnel whose black interior was invisible from the outside; imprisoned out in the country where shouts for help would reach no ears; held in the path of a car that carried no headlight and whose motors created such a din that conversation, among even the passengers themselves, was rendered inaudible.

Fascinated, spell-bound, with icy terror gripping his heart, he watched it speeding closer and closer—400 yards—300 yards—200 yards——

He crouched down and covered his face with his hands.

The good citizens of Ashdale whose domestic duties had prevented their venturing out on that memorable Saturday afternoon, first learned the news when the glaring headlines of the Ashdale Gazette confronted them at the supper table:

TRACTION SITUATION COMES TO A CRISIS
Employees Walk Out at 3 P.M.

The employees of the Cherry Valley Interurban Traction Company, hopeless of receiving their demand, walked out en masse this afternoon.

At 3 P.M. every electric switch in the power house was opened and the fires then drawn from beneath the boilers.

As a result of the power going off, cars were brought to a standstill all over Cherry Valley.

The first intimation received by the Gazette was from several disgruntled passengers, who, in company with the car crew, were compelled to dismount and walk back to Ashdale when the 2:45 northbound express slowed up and came to a stop a few hundred yards this side of the Red Rock Tunnel.

At 4:30 P.M. a notice, granting the employees all the terms of their demand, and signed by President Baer himself, was posted on the door of the power house.

It is rumored that President Baer's sudden change of attitude is caused by a general run-down condition, resulting from overwork, and necessitating a trip to the South for rest. It is also rumored that Robert Holly, power foreman at the plant, will be left in full charge of the company's affairs.

And the rumor that had reached the omniscient Gazette was quite correct.

President Baer did leave for the South that night to give his shattered nerves a chance to recuperate. And he did leave young Holly in charge of the affairs of the Cherry Valley Traction Company; and what is more, he left in the care of the same young man, his daughter Natalie, who was, of course, a more important charge than all the traction systems in the world.

WHEN THE RIVET FELL

About four stories ... careless workman ... anyone might get the same ... stand back, ivery one of yez an' gi' th' man air ..."

With these dissociated phrases sifting in on my consciousness, I opened my eyes and sat bolt upright—with the result that I discovered I was on the sidewalk. A curious crowd, held in check by a blue-coated police officer, stood around me in a circle. At my side knelt a little man with a short pointed beard who, I learned a few moments later, was a doctor.

He placed his hand on my arm and helped me to regain my feet. The crowd, their morbid interest now gone after seeing an apparently dead man return to the land of the living, swiftly dissolved, and the police officer returned to the corner to continue his duty of regulating the heavy downtown traffic.

I turned to the little man at my side who was gazing at me all the while with manifest interest. "Wh-what's happened to me? I can't just grasp matters," I managed to articulate.

"Very simple to explain," he answered. "You see this steel skyscraper here, in process of erection? You were passing along the sidewalk at the same time that one of the rivet tossers on the fourth floor made a miscalculation in throwing a hot rivet toward the bucket held by a helper of one of the steam hammer operators. As a result, the rivet flew out toward the street and, in descending, struck you on the head, putting you down and out, so to speak. I happened to be on a passing car. Being a physician, I jumped off and came over to where you were lying. My examination failed to reveal any fracture of the skull, but I feared a possible case of brain concussion, until a moment ago when you regained your senses. As long as you're on your feet now, evidently not much the worse for your experience, my advice to you is go home, take it easy the rest of the day—and in future, stay away from uncompleted steel structures. They're dangerous. Good day."

He nodded to me and, picking up a small black satchel at his side, disappeared among the scurrying people.

I continued my way down the street. After I had covered a few steps I noticed that all the objects that met my eye looked unfamiliar to me—street carts, street signs, buildings, advertisements—in fact, everything. When I had traversed a block I stopped short in my tracks. The doctor had advised me to return home. Where, in heaven's name, was my home? What city was I in? Who the deuce was I, anyway? When I failed to find an answer to this last self-propounded query, I leaned up against a lamp post, sick at heart with the realization that something both terrible and mystifying had befallen me. It required but a few more moments thinking to render the fact plain.

My mind, so far as the events of my life before I regained consciousness on the sidewalk were concerned, was a total blank!

Catching sight of a little stretch of grass-covered ground, over which benches were scattered here and there, and which I learned later was named Grant Park, I hastened over to it and, finding a secluded seat, tried and tried to recall some fact from my previous existence which would enable me to gain some inkling as to where I was and who I was.

It was at this juncture that the idea first occurred to me to look through my pockets—and I lost no time in acting on it. The contents of each one I emptied on the bench which I occupied; my search, however, was meagerly rewarded. A timetable of a railroad named the Chicago and North-Eastern, a bunch of keys, twenty-two dollars in bills, and a pasteboard square, numbered 177, together with some small change, were the only articles that, with the exception of my clothes, were on my person. A later search for any marks of identification on my wearing apparel proved equally fruitless, although I obtained a pair of plain gold cuff buttons which I was afterward forced to pawn.

A small, grimy faced urchin, with a bundle of newspapers under his arm, passed my bench, looking inquiringly in my direction. I thrust a coin in his hand and seized the paper that he held toward me. I commenced a perusal of its first page with desperate eagerness.

From it, I ascertained that I was in Chicago, that the date was October 25, 1908, and from the various headlines that I skimmed over, I learned that a financial stringency was on, and that thousands of men were out of work.

Was I, then, a citizen of Chicago, or had I just arrived from some city on the Chicago and North-Eastern railroad?

There were two courses open to me—that was quite palpable. I could go to the nearest police station and tell my story, in which case, as victim of a peculiar type of mental malady, I would be sent by due process of law to the horrors of a State insane asylum, there to await the return of my memory—possibly for a day—perhaps for life.

On the other hand, I could rent a small room, procure daily the newspapers of Chicago, Cleveland, Buffalo, and New York, which seemed, from the map in the Chicago and North-Eastern folder, to be the largest ones on its line, and if I should be fortunate enough to read of my mysterious disappearance, communicate with my relatives or friends, whoever they were.

The latter course I adopted.

I rented a room in a small hotel near the heart of the city, proffering as an explanation of my absence of luggage, that it had been lost through a mistake of the railroad; an unpretentious but clean restaurant near the hotel I patronized for my meals. And each day, from a news stand situated in the business district, at which papers from places other than Chicago were sold, I purchased the chief news publications of the cities I have already mentioned.

A week passed.

Absolutely nothing appeared in any paper concerning any disappearance. And each day my store of money grew less and less—and my spirit grew more and more troubled.

~ ~ ~ ~ ~

Since the memorable day that I had turned out the contents of my pockets at Grant Park, in the vain attempt to obtain some information concerning myself, a month had flown by. I was no wiser today than I had been then.

I no longer resided at the quiet little hotel that I had first selected. In fact, I now had no permanent place of abode, unless a bench in Grant Park could be called such.

For the last few nights I had been sleeping on the floor of a lodging house on West Madison Street, known among its inmates as "Harrigan's Flop." The cost of accommodations for one night at "Harrigan's Flop" was nominal, being the sum of five cents, since each guest brought with him his own newspaper to spread beneath him in lieu of a mattress.

Neither did I dine any longer at the restaurant where I had formerly eaten all my meals. For the last week I had been one of the most regular customers of an eating-house on South State Street, the streaked plate glass windows of which bore the crudely painted letters, "BALTIMORE JOHN'S PLACE." A rough wooden counter, along which numerous high stools were lined up, together with a wooden cigar box serving as a cash register, provided the principal fixtures of the place. At meal time such a crush of men existed within its doors that a line of three or four extended behind each stool; it was not at all unusual to hear the different members of these waiting lines burst into profanity when the occupant of any stool appeared to be utilizing more time than was necessary in consuming the meal that "Baltimore John" provided.

The order that was chiefly in demand was priced at a nickel, and was known as "coffee and"; this consisted of four stale rolls, together with a large bowl of an insipid tasting, coffee colored liquid whose only redeeming quality was its heat.

The reason for my new mode of living was nothing other than the fact that my cash had dwindled to the point where it consisted of only a few nickels and dimes.

Vainly I had tramped the streets in the search for work when it had first become apparent to me that my store of money would not be of infinite duration. At all the mammoth department stores that towered above State Street long lines of discouraged looking men reached from the employment offices on the second floors, down the stairways and out to the streets.

At almost all shops and factories, signs had been hung out reading "NO HELP WANTED." The city newspapers carried a few scattered advertisements of firms that desired a man for this or that position. To answer any one of these advertisements in person brought one invariably face to face with a horde of other men—all there with the same object—to secure that position at any cost.

In two instances only had I even the good fortune to be able to have an interview with that mighty potentate—a possible employer.

The first instance occurred at a West Side foundry that had advertised for a man to check castings. The usual swarm of applicants were there, and I had had the exceptional luck, if luck it were, to secure the first place in the line by arriving at the establishment at five o'clock in the morning.

After my last rebuff I gave up the search completely. Competition was too keen, and my handicap, as I now discovered, was too great.

It was a cold, raw day, with a drizzling rain falling as I walked northward along Michigan Avenue with my coat collar turned up and my hands deep in my pockets, fingering the last dime I possessed. My shoes, worn through the soles by the fruitless search for work, oozed moisture at each step and seemed to emit a sound not unlike, "sqush-sqush, sqush-sqush."

I had no particular destination. One has to walk, and walk briskly at that, to keep warm on a bleak November day. I chose the direction of "north" for the reason that I had already covered every other possible direction in the downtown district.

It was not long before I found myself tramping along Lake Shore Drive, which I learned subsequently was known from one end of the city to the other by the more common name of "Millionaires' Row."

I daresay I felt rather bitter toward the owners of those magnificent homes, who were able to ride about in carriages or motor cars, while I, chilled, hungry, tired, disheartened, and with memory partially gone, was forced to walk the streets, knowing that for but one night longer could I enjoy even the protecting roof of "Harrigan's Flop."

An open window suggested a course of action to me.

Why not equip myself with a pointed bar of iron, return that night to Lake Shore Drive, force an entrance through a window in one of these many residences, and possibly decamp with a pocketful of valuables. My conscience had become more or less deadened in the last few days. I need expect no qualms from it, at any rate.

And if I should be captured, then from what I had read, of late, concerning prisons, they were more hospitable places than the street—and they at least fed you there, giving you at times bean soup and brown bread. Glorious combination! The thought of it made determination more firm, for, as I reasoned then and there, I could not possibly lose, one way or the other, by turning burglar.

At once I began to survey the mansions of "Millionaires' Row" a little more attentively—and with a professional eye—the eye of a cracksman.

One small house, in particular, appealed to me, since, on account of its situation, it afforded less likelihood of my being detected during operations. It stood far back from the street and had a large front yard along the edges of which ran an ornamental iron fence, about seven feet high.

I looked it over carefully. Whoever the owner, he was indisputably a man of warped mind, so far as architectural taste was concerned. It presented a consortium of curves, spirals, turrets, angles, and gargoyles, mixed in such profusion that in comparison with the more sedate mansions on either side of it, it was rendered ridiculous in spite of its expensive materials and construction.

In its front yard, a fountain, surmounted by a group of stone nymphs, played merrily in company with the rain. On each side of the driveway reposed a huge, bronze tablet, bearing in bold hammered letters the name, ALGERNON VAN DER PUYSTER.

On seeing this indication of the owner's crass egotism, I gave vent to a derisive laugh. How any man, the possessor of such an appellation, could placard the public highway with it, like any common burlesque-show comedian, was beyond my understanding.

With another cautious look over the premises, I retraced my course till I reached Grant Park. From here I stepped across the street to the Public Library and proceeded to the general reading room, where I sat down at a reference table and busied myself, ostensibly making out a list of books, but in reality fortifying myself in preparation for another siege with the inclement weather outside.

In a nearby rack devoted to civic affairs a book entitled "Photographs of Prominent Chicagoans" attracted my attention. I stepped over and, as an experiment, turned over the pages where those people whose names began with the letter "V" were grouped. Just as I had expected, I found a photograph and a brief notice which described the man who I had already decided was to be the victim of my robbery of the coming night.

"Algernon van der Puyster; graduate of Yale, class of 1900; holds amateur polo championship of the United States; bachelor; residence 206 Lake Shore Drive." Above it was the picture of a more or less ordinary looking young man with a somewhat effeminate expression on his face.

So this was van der Puyster! And a polo champion, eh? All the better. Possibly a few gold medals would be lying about in his home. One ought to be able, I felt, to hammer up a gold medal, sell it, and buy not only vast quantities of coffee and rolls, but even bean soup and brown bread.

As soon as I had absorbed enough warmth at the municipal expense, I slipped from the library and made my way over to Randolph Street, where a number of hardware and plumbing establishments were located. Here I walked casually down an alley tablishments were located. Here I walked casually down an alley until I came to a rubbish heap, which gave sufficient promise of supplying me with the article I required. After rummaging around a few moments, I secured a short, pointed iron rod, a piece of lead pipe about seven inches in length, and the tail of a candle. The iron bar I wrapped in a piece of newspaper and carried in my hand. The remaining two articles I dropped in my coat pocket, which at once assumed a suspicious sag.

Fortunately, at six o'clock the rain had ceased to fall so I trudged slowly over to the North Side and found a bench in a small public recreation garden in Washington Square. I was not alone, however. The benches were full of other derelicts like myself, some showing no evidence of having had a shave for several weeks, many collarless, others sitting dejectedly together, flaunting in the line of vision of the passers-by the bare toes that emerged from the cracks in their shoes. One topic of discussion seemed to be of paramount interest, namely—Socialism.

At as near to ten o'clock as I could determine, inasmuch as none of the few loiterers who had remained shivering in Washington Square seemed so wealthy as to boast a timepiece, I left and walked rapidly east several blocks until I again found myself on "Millionaires' Row."

Here I paced up and down until the street appeared to be totally devoid of cabs and automobiles. Then, with considerable trouble and exertion I climbed over the iron paling that separated the van der Puyster grounds from the street, wondering vaguely what I could do in case I should be compelled to make a hasty and unceremonious exit to avoid capture, should such a thing impend later.

For once, Fortune was with me. The upper stories of the house were quite dark, only the basement, presumably the servants' quarters, being illuminated. I crossed the grass and came to the casement of one of these windows. Standing on this, I inserted the pointed end of the bar between the sill and lower edge of one of the first floor windows; then I bore down upon it with all my weight.

The lock broke with a sudden snap. I waited a moment with my heart pounding so forcibly that I could feel it in every portion of my body. Then, as nothing more happened, I raised the window quietly, clambered up on the sill, and dropped lightly in on the floor of the room. I tossed the "jimmy" out on the lawn, lowered the window, and drew down the shade. Then I ignited the wick of candle that I had brought with me.

As its flickering rays lighted up the room, I looked about me. Evidently I was in the bed-chamber of van der Puyster himself, since two large, peculiarly shaped sticks, which I surmised to be polo sticks, were fastened cross-wise on the wall. Directly beneath them, on a marble mantel that was covered with framed photographs, reposed a heavy, engraved cup, made of silver.

On the floor was a rich rug, similar to those I had seen displayed in the various store windows as "oriental"; its size was such that it nearly covered the room, leaving a small strip of highly polished hardwood around its edge.

Drawn up to a grate directly beneath the mantel, in which, however, there was no fire, was an easy chair. I saw then that the pleasant warmth that I had felt on entering was emanating from a steam radiator on the opposite side of the room.

In one corner stood a massive, shining, brass bed; in the other, a heavy, oak bureau. To this last article of furniture I immediately turned my attention.

In its right upper drawer I found four scarf pins—one a diamond—stuck in a small velvet cushion. The whole set I dropped in my pocket.

In the left hand upper drawer I came across a small bracelet watch, such as sportswomen wear on their wrists; four diamonds were imbedded in its rim. An attached card bore the written inscription, "A happy birthday to Edith—from Algernon."

For a moment I paused, fingering it with uncertainty. I disliked very much to spoil "Edith's" birthday, but a sudden mental picture of a steaming hot bowl of bean soup and a gigantic loaf of brown bread caused me to add it to the four scarf pins.

It was at this point I heard footsteps in the room above us. Panic-stricken, I blew out the candle and tossed it, still smouldering, under the bureau.

The footsteps still continued but appeared to be slowly descending a staircase toward the floor on which I, myself, stood.

Groping through the almost impenetrable darkness with which I had so foolishly enveloped myself, I attempted to regain the window that had served as my means of ingress. But the task was far more perplexing than I had supposed. I was completely turned around.

Zounds!—what an impact my much abused cranium made with the corner of the marble mantel. To state that I saw stars is no exaggeration; for a few seconds, impressions of moons, comets, as-teroids, and every other species of astronomical body traveled over my optic nerve. Just then my hand came in contact with the back of an easy chair and I dropped into it without any delay, to wipe away the tears that had started to my eyes with the severe momentary pain.

But the long deferred miracle had occurred.

With the bump that had come to me in the darkness, my memory had returned at the same time. By a few quick trials, I found that I was again able to recall the incidents of my past life.

I was overcome with joy to such an extent that I became oblivious to everything but that one fact.

I remembered with exceptional vividness how I had gone to the Chicago and North-Eastern depot to board a train for the East; how I had acquired a timetable and, finding that I was an hour too early, had started for a bank where I was known, in order to draw more funds, first, however, checking my hand baggage at a nearby counter and receiving a pasteboard slip numbered 177; how I had left my watch at a downtown jewelry store to be repaired; how I had paused to gaze at a building being erected—then blackness—followed by the events I have already related.

The footsteps were coming rapidly down the hall—the door opened with a rush—and a hand groped around the wall for the electric light switch.

Click!

The room was flooded with light.

The servant clad in blue livery, who stood in the doorway, gave a sudden start of surprise. His lower jaw dropped and his eyes opened wide. Then he bowed low and spoke.

"Ah! How you startled me," he said. "If I had known you were returning a week sooner than you had intended, I would have had the house lighted for you. May I take the liberty of asking as to whether you enjoyed your trip, Mr. van der Puyster?"

MISSING: ONE DIAMOND SALESMAN

T HE CHIEF LEANED back in his swivel chair.

"Baumann," he said, "this thing is a little too much for me. All I can do is to have his description telegraphed to every port in the country. As to his letter—there's something odd—something wrong. Tell you what I'd like to do. There's a character in this big city of Chicago that's a regular shark on the Sherlock Holmes business. If anyone can unravel the knot in that postscript, he can. I'd like to hand these two papers over to him."

"Call him in," said his visitor briefly.

The chief pressed a button at the side of his desk. A blue-coated police officer responded instantly. "Send Nichols or one of the other men down to Harrigan's lodging house, and find Mackleby Hawkins and tell him to report here immediately."

He turned to his visitor again and continued speaking.

"This Mackleby Hawkins is a queer one. He's what you call a tramp. His hang-out, when he's not gallivanting around the country on the bumpers of a freight, is Harrigan's lodging house. Talks well—carries himself like a man that's had a college education—but no one knows anything definite about him. How the department got acquainted with him—that's a story in itself—but suffice to say, he's done some mighty clever work for us in the past few years. Seems to have a natural faculty for the game. I've offered him a steady job with the force on several different occasions. All he does is to laugh and refuse, and sail out on another bumming trip. Whenever he—"

The swinging door to the chief's office opened.

The figure of a man about thirty years old stood framed in the doorway. His hair was raven black; his eyes of the same dark hue had a piercing look that was in keeping with his sharp aquiline features. His clothing comprised a neatly patched pair of trousers, a coat with badly frayed cuffs, and a blue flannel shirt held together at the neck by a bandanna handkerchief. Shading his face, which was covered by a several days' growth of beard, was a gray slouch hat.

"Did you want to see me, Chief?" he drawled. "Just got in off the grit an hour ago."

"Come in, Hawkins. Take a chair. This is Mr. Baumann of Baumann and Rheingold, retail jewelers. Mr. Baumann, suppose you tell Hawkins yourself just how the land lies."

Old Baumann adjusted his eyeglasses on his nose. He surveyed the newcomer critically. This was certainly a peculiar looking specimen to hand over for some detective work. Still—the chief would hardly have recommended him unless— Well, he might as well follow the old chief's advice if he wished to find out anything at all.

"Well, Mr.—er—ah—Hawkins, here's what we're up against. Last Friday, Skeering—the millionaire harvester machine man of New York—stopped off in our store on his way from the West to look over several diamond necklaces for his daughter's birthday gift. His choice narrowed itself down to two—one valued at thirty thousand dollars—the other at thirty-five thousand. We offered to send one of our salesmen, Murgatroyd, to New York in time to arrive on the daughter's birthday and allow the young lady to select the necklace which appealed to her most. The arrangement was satisfactory.

"Murgatroyd took the jewel case containing the necklaces out Saturday afternoon. We had already purchased for him a through ticket to New York and had reserved a berth on the eight o'clock train that night. Monday was the birthday of Skeering's daughter.

"Murgatroyd was to telegraph me Sunday night on his arrival. Sunday night came—but no telegram. Monday morning came—and still no telegram.

"We communicated with his boarding house at 106 Walton Place. We ascertained that he had packed his suitcase, entered the cab that he had ordered by 'phone, and which was drawn up to the curb at seven o'clock, and had driven off in the direction of the New York Central Depot. That was all they knew.

"On making inquiries of the railroad, we found that his berth had been occupied: showing, of course, that he had followed the procedure we had laid out for him."

"Just a moment," interrupted Hawkins. "How long has this Murgatroyd been in your employ?"

"Twenty years. We trusted him implicitly, although of late, rumors have come to our ears that he's been running around with some burlesque show actress."

"I infer then, that he's a single man," said Hawkins, "since you state he lives in a boarding house and that he's been mixed up with this actress. What's the name of this woman, and what theatre has she played at?"

"She goes by the stage name of 'Daisy Dalrymple.' The last theatre she played in was 'The Folly.' "

"Good!" remarked the seedy Hawkins. "Go ahead with the story."

"Well," continued old Baumann, "yesterday, which was of course Tuesday, came—and still no telegram—but a letter signed by the missing Murgatroyd himself." He reached over to the chief's desk and took up two papers. "Here it is."

Chicago, Ill., 1913
Baumann and Rheingold,
Retail Jewelers,
Chicago
Dear Sirs:—

I daresay you've discovered by this time that you're out two necklaces valued together at sixty-five thousand dollars. Of course, as you've already surmised, no one else but your former slave, J. H. Murgatroyd, is the proud possessor of these gems. By the day you receive this letter, courteously mailed by a friend back in Chicago, I expect to be safely on board a steamer bound for South America. I will not take up any more of your valuable time.

Yours very thankfully,
J. H. Murgatroyd

P.S. As per your request of last week, I enclose on a separate sheet a complete list of my customers for the last year (my private record) with which to check up your books.

Old Baumann paused. With one hand he removed his eyeglasses; he leaned over, and with the forefinger of the other, tapped Hawkins on the knee.

"And here's the most incomprehensible, mystifying thing in the whole affair," he said impressively. "The list of names that Murgatroyd encloses contains not one person that has ever been a customer of our firm!"

He proffered Hawkins the penciled list.

The latter waved it back. "Just read off the first ten or fifteen of these so-called customers."

"Well," returned the jewelry merchant, clearing his throat, "they run as follows: Edward C. Larson, William P. Lacey, Frank R. Sayre, George B. Regel, William C. Nolan, Mrs. Jennie A. McCauley, Mrs. Mary G. T. Nelson, Thomas I. Sachs, Rev. Frederick Robinson, Mrs. Willard Lawrence, Mrs. Dwight Merriman, Benjamin F. O'Malley, James G. Philben, Mrs. John O. Perkins, Lee Wing Quong, Mrs.—"

"That's enough," interrupted his listener. He turned to the chief. "Chief—do you notice anything out of the ordinary about those names?"

"Just ordinary names," grunted the veteran police head. "I happen to know two or three of those people myself. Those are bona fide residents."

Hawkins turned to the jewelry dealer. "Mr. Baumann," he asked, "did you ever make a request of Murgatroyd to hand in an account of his past customers?"

"Never. The records of our firm are absolutely complete."

"Is it a customary thing at your store to consummate a sale as high as thirty thousand dollars or more?"

"No. Very rarely do we sell an article worth over a thousand. We don't go in much for the expensive trade."

"Is this letter and list in Murgatroyd's own handwriting?"

"It is—without any doubt."

Hawkins arose.

"Just give me the two documents," he commanded. He tucked them in the pocket of his dilapidated coat. "I'll probably be able to put you in line with some specific information in say—twenty-four hours. I'm going back now to Harrigan's palatial hostelry, dig up an old trunk of mine that's down in his basement, rescue from oblivion my civilized suit of clothes—my boiled shirt and my razor—and then scout around a bit. Good day, gentlemen!"

He stretched himself, yawned, and walked leisurely out. At the door he stopped to roll a cigarette.

"That's his way," said the chief grimly, after he had passed out. "But he gets results!"

It was the afternoon following the interview between Baumann, the chief and Mackleby Hawkins.

The chief lay back in his chair trying in vain to rest comfortably and keep awake at the same time. It was very hot. Outside, in the street, a few horses plodded wearily by, their lazy footsteps sending up clouds of fine dry dust that settled thickly on every article in the room. A few flies droned languidly back and forth.

He awoke suddenly with a start. A familiar figure, clean-shaven and well-dressed, stood in the doorway, smiling broadly.

The chief was usually very grouchy when he was caught napping. "Well, Hawkins," he inquired gruffly, "how are you coming out on yesterday's little problem?"

"Oh—that? That's all solved. Nothing much to it. It's up to you now. Your missing diamond salesman is locked up in a garret room down in the Italian settlement."

"Eh!—what—what's that?" shouted the chief, sitting bolt upright and becoming suddenly wide awake. "Locked up? Who took him in custody?"

" 'Taken in custody' is a poor phrase in this instance," returned Hawkins. "He happens to be the unwilling prisoner of four Italians—or I might modify the statement and make it three—since one's in New York just now. I might also state that one of these three gentlemen is a master of English. The whole trio is holding Murgatroyd in the effort to make him disclose the whereabouts of the two necklaces. Fortunately, however, he's been too foresighted to place them in the usual jewel case. They've cut up his clothes and ransacked his suitcase as well.

"Now, Chief, I know what the blackhander and the rest of his tribe are. I've hit the road from 'little old N'York' to the Golden Gate with all types of men; and in the final analysis the crooked Italian shows a yellow streak from his ear lobes to his toe nails. Just send up about four of your best men, give these fellows a liberal exhibition of firearms, and they'll all collapse. The number of the house, by the way, is 762 Milton Street. You'll find your man locked in the attic."

"Well, by all that's holy—Hawkins—where did you—? Wait!" The chief hurriedly pressed a few buttons; when men appeared in answer to his call he gave a few sharp, decisive orders and directions. Presently, four stalwart plain-clothes men hastened down the broad stone steps of the building. At the sidewalk, they separated and hurried off in different directions.

"And what else have you got to tell me, Hawkins? Here, don't stand, have a seat." The chief drew up an extra chair to his desk.

"Well, Chief, there's not a great deal more to tell you. I might proffer a little advice to Baumann, through you, and that's as follows: tell him he'd be doing a sensible thing if he discharged the

uniformed Italian who opens the heavy swinging doors at the store
for customers. It's poor policy to employ a man who can't keep
from discussing the big deals of his house with his countrymen."

"Where did you get all this dope?" asked the chief.

"I read Murgatroyd's letter—a little closer than the rest of
you—that's all."

The chief scratched his head. "Letter? I don't see yet that Murgatroyd told you all this in his letter. And say, why did he give
Baumann a false steer, anyway?"

"He didn't—voluntarily. Murgatroyd telephoned for a cab.
When he innocently marched into the one that drew up to the curb
in front of his boarding house that Saturday night at seven o'clock,
he wasn't aware that three other men were going to spring out of
an alley several blocks farther down the street, force their way into
it, gag him and tie him up. He didn't know that the driver was one
of the gang—that the cab was a special one secured for the purpose. Naturally he wasn't cognizant of all this, since he had ordered a cab from a reputable concern that employs drivers who are
beyond suspicion.

"He didn't know either, that one of the gang was all in readiness to make the trip East on his ticket in order to make it show on
the Pullman car records that lower berth 14, car 4, train 175, assigned to one J. H. Murgatroyd, had been occupied. Neither should
he have been expected to know that he would later be compelled,
most likely at the point of a gun, to write a letter to his employers,
branding himself as a thief who was bound for South America
with his firm's property.

"But—he must have expected from the first moment of his cap-
tivity that the gang that held him tight would make some sort of an
attempt, through a false communication, to ward off the possibility
of any search being made for him in Chicago—so he did the best
he could under the circumstances.

"He utilized the long hours of his solitary confinement in producing a little letter on his own account—one which the leader
was only too glad to allow him to enclose, since, from its business-
like aspect, it made the main letter seem so much the more genuine."

"Chief, I read that list of names pretty closely, and a good many
times. Then I discarded the hypothesis that this man had fled the
country either alone or with this actress, Daisy Dalrymple, for I
had already discovered something about that list that you and
Baumann had entirely overlooked."

"And what was that?"

"Simply this: Every surname in the group begins with a letter that falls in the portion of the alphabet that lies between L and S inclusive! Here's a slip of paper containing the first fifteen with their prefixes and given names omitted. It's not necessary to bore you with all the rest.

Larson
Lacey
Sayre
Regel
Nolan
McCauley
Nelson
Sachs
Robinson
Lawrence
Merriman
O'Malley
Philben
Perkins
Quong

"What then does that indicate, Chief? Nothing other than this: that list was compiled from the available portion of some sort of an alphabetical index—for some sort of a reason—which we'll see in a few minutes. Now what's the most common form of alphabetical arrangement of names? The Chicago City Directory of course!

"I made for a city directory, where I commenced to look up these names. I saw in two minutes that I was on the wrong track. Of the first fifteen alone, the names William P. Lacey, James G. Philben, and Lee Wing Quong were missing from the directory. I didn't yet have the correct book—that was obvious.

"What other forms of indexes are common to Chicago citizens? Why not the Subscribers' Directory of the Chicago Telephone Company? I got access at once to the latest one out. Here I had better luck. The names William P. Lacey and James G. Philben showed up—but the elusive Oriental, Mr. Lee Wing Quong, was still unentered. Evidently, I was not yet in possession of the right book.

"So I started out for the Chicago Telephone Company's main office. On the way, I stopped off in the vicinity of Murgatroyd's boarding house on Walton Place, where I spent several profitable hours. I located four livery stables within a radius of half a mile. Of each, I made the same inquiry—whether a conveyance had been ordered any time last Saturday afternoon for J. H. Murgatroyd of Walton Place. I met with a peculiar and similar narrative in every case. A polite voice, it seems, with the faint trace of a foreign accent, had put the same question, over the 'phone, to each livery office in turn, Saturday night at six o'clock. On meeting with a negative answer in three instances, the voice had merely murmured: 'Beg pardon; my mistake,' and had rung off.

"But in the fourth instance it so happened that a cab actually had been ordered for J. H. Murgatroyd of Walton Place. On obtaining an affirmative response, the polite voice had replied: "Mr. Murgatroyd has altered his plans. Kindly cancel the order for his cab. Good bye.' The livery establishment immediately nullified the order on the books.

"So I hied myself over to the main office of the Chicago Telephone Company, where I made a request to be allowed to examine the directories that have been issued at intervals of every three months for the last twenty years. They handed me a curt refusal. That was the time they 'phoned you at my bidding; after they got you on the wire, however, everything was fine and dandy. They conducted me at once to the old files of subscribers.

"In the directory that just preceded the one in use today, several more names on my list failed to materialize, so I searched further and further back until, in the directory of January-March, 1908—six years back, I succeeded in locating every name that Murgatroyd had written. This then, or one of the same edition, containing Chicago's old system of exchanges and numbers, was the book from which the list had been compiled.

"I glanced over the addresses that corresponded to each name. Those of the first five ran as you see on this slip of paper:

625 Cornelia Str.
1304 E. 57th Str.
6544 S. Paulina St.
700 N. Kedzie Ave.
848 Lakeside Pl.

"But assigned to the sixth name was no address at all—merely the following notation:

   ... toll ...

"Now, as anyone knows, the word 'toll' in the telephone directory indicates that the party resides in some village or town of Cook County outside of Chicago, and that a long-distance wire is necessary; at any rate, it does not constitute an address. So I discontinued any further study along that line and turned my attention to the telephone exchanges and exchange numbers, of which the first fifteen ran as you may notice on this next slip of paper:

	Lake View	2033
	Hyde Park	850
	Wentworth	1891
	Garfield	550
	Edgewater	538
toll ...	Oak P'k	973
	Edgewater	2076
	Hyde Park	172
	Midway	1234
	North	1926
	North	591
	Kenwood	1479
	Edgewater	2033
	So. Ch'go	126

"Now, Chief, the exchanges as they run down the list present nothing unusual nor satisfactory—only a frequent repetition of the common ones—'Edgewater' and 'North'—but the exchange numbers, ah! they were the key to the mystery!

"It's not necessary to show you all the processes that I put them through—how I added 'em, multiplied 'em, took the first digits, and the last digits, and tried everything I could think of—till I finally struck it.

"You'll observe that if you erase the last two figures on each exchange number you'll have left in some cases, one digit—in other cases, two digits. For instance—2033 with the last two figures erased leaves just a 20; and 850 under the same operation leaves just an 8; and 1891 treated in the same manner leaves just an 18. Now, I have here a separate sheet of paper with the left-hand column showing the first fifteen exchange numbers; the right-hand column shows the same numbers with the two right-hand figures erased.

2033	20
850	8
1891	18
550	5
538	5
973	9
2076	20
172	1
1234	12
1926	19
591	5
1479	14
2033	20
377	3
126	1

"You'll again observe, if you examine carefully, that none of these numbers in the right-hand column exceeds 'twenty-six.' From that simple fact alone, we must suspect a simple code message, since the simplest code between letters and numbers is, of course, the one where 'A', the first letter of the alphabet, is represented by '1', where 'B', the second letter of the alphabet, is represented by '2', and so on, through the twenty-six letters.

"Now, our first figure in the right-hand column is '20' and the twentieth letter in the alphabet is 'T'; our next figure is '8' and the eighth letter of the alphabet is 'H'; the following figure is '18' and the eighteenth letter is 'R.' Substituting in each case the letter of the alphabet that corresponds numerically to it, our column of figures presents a column of letters, the first fifteen showing as follows:

20	T
8	H
18	R
5	E
5	E
9	I
20	T

1	A
12	L
19	S
5	E
14	N
20	T
3	C
1	A

"At this point, I knew without any further doubt that Murga-troyd was in some sort of predicament, that he had attempted to get a few words to us by a code and, as it appears, all he had was the middle portion of some antiquated telephone directory.

"Carrying the substitution process through the entire column of numbers that we obtain from the whole list of names, and arranging these letters alongside of one another, we get the following jumble:

THREEITALSENTCABHELDPRISTOPWHITEFRAMHST WOCHMSNOGFBHVCTCLOSALSOSEARCHDSTCSHUR-RYHELP

"By splitting this jumble up and inserting a few letters and punctuation marks where it appears necessary, we get something more coherent. Here it is:

THREE ITAL(IAN)S ENT(ERED) CAB; (AM) HELD PRIS(ONER) (AT) TOP (OF) WHITE FRAM(E) H(OU)S(E) (WITH) TWO CHIM(NEY)S; NO. G-F-B; H(A)V(E) C(U)T CLO(THE)S, ALSO SEARCH(ED) S(UI)T C(A)S(E); HURRY HELP.

"Now one obscurity remains: 'No. G-F-B.' By merely leaving the original numbers in place of the senseless letters G—F—B, we have '7—6—2.'

"Now, where would three Italians, or four including the driver, with a bound man in a cab, be likely to have imprisoned him for several days while they made a thorough search of his clothing and belongings—while they interrogated him again and again as to the location of the jewels, and received but one explanation, which they would not believe? Why—no place else than down in Little Italy; for you know, yourself, Chief, they couldn't get away with it elsewhere.

"So I've spent all morning taking in the Italian settlement from the elevated railroad west to the river, and from Chicago Avenue north to Division Street, looking for houses numbered '762.' I've met with all sorts of 'em—green houses and red houses; even Italian churches and empty lots, until suddenly, at 762 Milton Street—a narrow, dark, badly-paved and ill-smelling thoroughfare—I ran square into a white frame house with two chimneys, and with attic windows tightly boarded up.

"Back I went, hot foot, to the Telephone Company. Their installation and removal records show that in the spring of 1908, a telephone was removed from 762 Milton Street—which accounts for the presence there of such an old phone directory as one of that date. From the company's offices—"

The telephone on the desk jangled sharply. The chief raised the receiver to his ear.

"H-e-l-l-o—hello—that you, O'Rourke?—nabbed the three of 'em, you say—good—and—Murgatroyd—he's O.K., is he?—pretty bruised?—too bad we can't fix the beggars for that—of course they wouldn't show fight—they never do—and the diamonds?—what! Well, I'll be—all right—all of you report to my office at once—good-bye."

The chief turned towards his visitor. "O'Rourke tells me that the diamonds—"

"Were safe all the time," interrupted Hawkins. "I forgot to tell you about that. Murgatroyd lost his nerve Saturday afternoon; didn't want to take a chance on carrying sixty-five thousand dollars worth of diamonds over a twenty-four-hour trip, so he carried 'em to the office of one of the big express companies and expressed 'em as an insured package—insured at their actual value. He counted on having old Skeering identify him at New York.

"His landlady kindly consented to my going over his room yesterday afternoon. Tucked down in the bosom of one of his newly-laundered shirts I found the express company's receipt. Here it is."

The chief looked at Hawkins for several minutes; then he spoke. "Hawkins, you're an ingenious chap, and at the same time you're a blanked fool. Are you going to be a tramp all your life? There's a place on the force for you anytime you want it. Do you want to start in tomorrow as one of the regulars?"

"Say, Chief, did you ever go flying through the night on the blind baggage of a sixty-mile-an-hour flyer, or swinging your legs out the opening of a 'side-door' Pullman—and full of the joy of living—and freedom—and speed? Did you ever—sh-h-h!" He held up a warning forefinger. His eyes took on a far-away look. "Can you hear it, Chief?"

The chief strained his ears. Then he stepped to the window and peered out. He heard nothing—nothing except a weird, long-drawn-out whistle, followed by the staccato 'chug-chug-chug' of a freight train pulling out of the railway yard near the station. So he turned back to his desk.

But his visitor was gone.

BABES IN THE WOOD

TO THE DWELLERS in the fashionable Northminster Apartments of Chicago, demure little Miss Gladys van Sutten was more or less of a mystery.

With her maid only, she occupied the second floor corner apartment. She dressed becomingly, paid her bills promptly—and lived a life of the greatest propriety. That she was charming to behold was evidenced by the sniffs of the feminine element of the Northminster Apartments, whenever the masculine members, in their conversation, enthusiastically referred to her.

She had but one caller, Mr. Horace-Percival Chesterton, who invariably on Wednesday and Sunday evenings at eight o'clock drew up to the curb in a taxi-cab—who remained chatting in the little parlor until 10:45 in full view from the boulevard—and who then departed.

Horace-Percival was understood, by those who were slightly acquainted with him, to be one of those most fortunate beings, a scion of a wealthy and aristocratic family. As certain rumors had it, he had studied for the ministry until a sudden generous inheritance had placed him beyond the necessity of arduous labor as well as any ministerial duties.

One thing was certain. He resided uptown in a fashionable club, dressed expensively but conservatively—and no longer worked for a living.

On this particular Wednesday evening Miss Gladys van Sutten sat in her parlor sewing on a bit of fancy work—and pausing occasionally to listen for the slam of a taxi-cab door. Now and then, however, she varied her procedure by stopping to admire a large solitaire ring that reposed on her left hand. As the onyx clock on the mantel chimed eight, she laid away her fancy work and rose to her feet. The bell rang.

The maid stepped into the room and bowed. "Mr. Chesterton," she exclaimed.

"And just how is my little yellow haired sweetheart tonight?" said Horace-Percival as he entered.

"Just bored to death, Horace. Life's just one round of dull events. Fancy work, reading, an occasional matinee, a visit from you twice a week—and that's all. I'll be glad when we're married, Horace. I'm going to make you take me to lots and lots of places that I couldn't see by myself."

"For instance?"

"Oh, you men," she returned with a little pout. "You can go to Chinatown; you can visit these places they call 'gambling-dens'; you can even walk through the wicked vice district where—Oh! Horace—to little ignorant me who has spent all her girlhood in a convent school—these things would be interesting beyond everything."

"Well, dear," he replied, "I confess I'm as ignorant of these things as your own precious self is. I'm afraid I would hardly know what to do—or where to take you—unless I made inquiries myself. However, we don't have to wait until our marriage. If you really think it would interest you—and I'm sure I should like to have a good square look at the vice district myself—I'll call next Sunday evening as usual, and instead of staying in the house we'll go down and have a peek at the underworld—just you and I—a couple of babes in the wood."

Gladys clapped her hands with delight. "I shan't be hardly able to wait until Sunday night, Horace. That'll be splendid—such fun. Don't forget your promise now!"

And Horace-Percival didn't forget.

On Sunday evening he and Gladys were seated on a South State Street car bound for Eighteenth Street. He showed her a slip of paper on which was written, "Armour Avenue and Twenty-second Street," "Huxbaums," and "Sleiburg's Dance Hall."

"There," he remarked. "I've been making enquiries about the chief points of interest in the Underworld. We must take them all in."

At Eighteenth Street they dismounted and walked westward two blocks until they reached Armour Avenue.

A long and very narrow street lit up by numberless red incandescent bulbs met their sight. Slowly they walked southward, gazing enquiringly at the windows and brilliantly lighted entrances of the different houses.

As they proceeded, painted women clad in low necked short skirted costumes of pink and purple and yellow peered curiously out at them.

The huge men who idled casually, one in front of each resort, scrutinized the pair with a half smile on their faces.

From every house came the sound of a jangling mechanical piano, punctuated at irregular intervals by shouts of ribald laughter or fragments of a song, sung in harsh feminine voice.

Here and there, drunken men, with their arms twined around each other's necks, lurched in pairs from the doorways, singing popular songs with the words quaintly slurred and run together.

As the two sightseers neared the Nineteenth Street crossing, a beer bottle crashed from a third story window and broke into a thousand fragments on the street pavement.

From many of the windows they passed which were devoid of illumination, came a monotonous sound of 'tap-tap-tap'; from others came stage whispers and low whistling calls.

At Twentieth Street they came upon a Salvation Army band that stood near the sidewalk, exhorting the few stragglers that stood around them in a circle "to forsake the path of sin and come into the fold."

They noticed how certain houses had automobiles, cabs, and carriages drawn up to the curb, two deep; how others seemed to be totally deserted.

Here and there they spied colored girls hurrying along the street, bearing in their hands trays covered with snowy napkins.

At Twenty-first Street a window was flung violently up; a woman thrust out her head and laughed raucously, bibulously. "Children, children," she screamed, "does your mama know you're out?" She closed the window with a bang.

Around the corner of Twenty-second Street they came upon a radiant establishment, outwardly ornate with shining brass and bronzed decorations, and with a sign above reading in massive gilded letters, simply, "Huxbaum's."

They entered.

Seating themselves at a small table near the entrance, they gazed with interest through the haze of cigarette smoke. In gold frames, large gaudy canvases of women hung on the walls. Hither and thither, waiters scurried like cockroaches, taking orders and bringing trays on which stood delicate little wine glasses with long stems.

At the piano stood a colossal Ethiopian, clad in a dress suit, twanging a banjo; the snowy immaculateness of his shirt bosom was rivaled only by the gleaming whiteness of his teeth when he smiled broadly in answer to the applause at the end of each selection.

To the waiter who stepped up enquiringly to their table, Horace-Percival gave his order—"two crêmes-de-menthe." For a number of seconds the waiter stared at them dumbly, sadly; then he hastened off with his empty tray.

"Are you enjoying the experience, Gladys?" asked Horace-Percival.

"Just interested to death, Horace," she replied.

When their waiter returned, Horace-Percival shoved a shining fifty cent piece towards him. "Waiter," he said, "we're a couple of just plain greenhorns cruising around down here for an adventure. This I understand is the notorious 'Huxbaum's.' What sort of place is it, anyway?"

The waiter pocketed the half dollar with avidity; the pitying expression on his face vanished; then he leaned over and whispered hoarsely:

"Well, sir, dey call dis joint d'gate to d'underworld. All dese goils y'see in here a' settin' around here wid dere gentlemen frens 's jus' beginners at d'game. Dey makes big money—an' if dey saved it dey could retire well off in a few years—but dey don't—none of 'em. In about a year or two de booze—an' d'dope—puts 'em over dere on Armour Avenoo where dey makes much less an' even den has to split wid d'house; den dey goes down and down until—psst!—dere goes de bell. I'm wanted at d'bar. I'll be back in a few minutes an' tell youse two more about dis place."

For a while Horace-Percival and his companion sat at their table sipping their cordial and watching the many girls, dressed in the height of fashion, all painfully young—the majority very pretty, who sat at the different tables plying their "gentlemen frens" with wine to get them in a condition of sodden compliance.

Then since the waiter seemed to have disappeared, they rose and left.

"Isn't it interesting, Horace?" said Gladys, her cheeks quite pink.

"I'm glad I came," answered Horace-Percival. "Always wanted to see what this land of wickedness was like. We'll go on now and rummage around until we bump into this—" He paused to consult his slip of paper. "—this 'Sleiburg's dance hall.' "

They crossed State Street and walked slowly up Twenty-second. The sudden sound of a band breaking into an orchestral din above their heads caused them to pause and glance upward. They saw from the dingy overhanging sign that they stood on the threshold of 'Sleiburg's'.

They climbed the long steep stairs and with Horace-Percival in the lead pushed through the red velvet curtains that hung at the head of the brass railing. Once inside they secured a small table near the rear of the hall and again ordered the same as before—"two crêmes-de-menthe."

For a few moments they watched the dancers, women with rouged faces, with darkened eyelashes, with long willow plumes of various hues and lengths going with male escorts through the many barbarous phases of the "22nd Street Tango."

When the dance stopped, a young girl clad in red, and with hair clipped in short black 'bangs' stepped out in front of the musicians' rail where she sang in a shrill falsetto, a sentimental ballad—"When the Sands of the Desert Grow Cold."

Through the dense cigarette smoke that filled the hall back of Gladys, Horace-Percival suddenly caught sight of a stout man with a suitcase entering the immense room, puffing and perspiring.

The stout man gazed with perplexity from table to table. Horace-Percival rose suddenly. "Excuse me for a minute, Gladys," he said. "I've got to telephone on a business matter." Hastily he made his way over to where the stout man stood, waiting for him. His voice was authoritative. "What's wrong, Slykes?"

"The whole gang's in dutch, Slim," said the stout man speaking rapidly and in a low voice. "I've got the straight info from Pete's lad what's workin' in the District Attorney's office as an office boy. You 'member that country gal you fetched in from Burlin'ton, Iowa—the one I married to you on a phony bible—you know—the last one we got—the one we put in German Annie's joint on Armour Avenoo. Well, bo—that's the most expensive $500 this bunch ever divvied up. It seems she croaked herself night before last with a bottle o' ear ache medicine—laudanum, I 'spose—but before she kicked off she got a letter out to the District Attorney sayin' she couldn't stand the life—an' givin' him the names and places. He pinched German Annie. She squealed. Result—! He's got the dope on all our gals—an' there's a warrant out for ev'ry one o' us an' they're goin' to serve 'em tomorrow morning. Ev'ry one's skipped but you an' me. I'm taking the 11:45 for the Yoonited States Line—an' unless you want to do a stretch o' ten on the Mann Act—my advice is—beat it in a red hot hurry. S'long, old pal." He picked up his suitcase and waddled swiftly from the hall, still puffing, still perspiring.

H. Percival returned to his table. His face was drawn, tense, weary. "Gladys," he said hurriedly, "I didn't want to spoil your evening by telling you earlier—but I'm leaving town tonight on a business trip. Come dear, pick up your wraps and I'll bring you home. I'm taking the midnight train for—for—for Canada."

The music had started up again. Once more the dancers were whirling around and around. Painstakingly the pair picked their way across the polished floor, through the gliding couples.

Leaning against the side of the entrance, plainclothesman McGuffy, of the Pittsburgh Detective Bureau, escorted by Chesterfieldian "Bill" Morgan, of Chicago Detective Headquarters— watched the pair as they came towards the doorway. His eyes followed Gladys from toe to bonnet. At the conclusion of his inspection he scratched his head and frowned. Then he repeated his action of scratching his head.

"Holy mackerel," he exclaimed to himself, "I got a notion to chance a bow to that dame. Why, she's a livin' likeness of Goldie Henderson, last year's queen of the Pittsburgh Tenderloin, what blew the town an' ain't been heard of since."

He uncurled his legs, removed his hat, and nodded towards her smilingly.

Gladys glanced quickly at her escort. His moody gaze was riveted on the floor. Then with a face from which all color had suddenly fled, leaving it a ghastly white, she nodded back to Detective McGuffy.

THAT ELUSIVE FACE

I T WAS AN absurd thing to devise in the first place—that system of mine for remembering every face that I wished to remember.

But it was a more than absurd extreme that I allowed myself to be carried to, three years later, when I became utterly obsessed by the game and then discovered—

But you shall judge for yourself.

It started with my reading a detective story. In the last chapter the wily sleuth, after a series of rather brilliant deductions, had become confused by the somewhat similar appearance of two persons.

I had leaned back in my chair then, idly wondering as to whether or not some scheme could be originated for recalling and placing faces that presented an air of familiarity. And as I thought on the matter I remembered having read in some psychological work that one unconsciously associates the sound of certain words with certain happenings, times, or places, even so much as years afterward.

Why, then I reasoned, could not the features of a face be expressed as a word, nonsensical or otherwise, and be stored up in the memory and held, so to speak, at the end of the tongue?

So I had seized paper and pencil and had sketched out a possible plan for achieving the result I have mentioned.

The most important features, and those least subject to alteration through the addition of glasses, mustaches, and the like, were, of course—taking them in some logical order:

THE EARS
THE FOREHEAD
THE EYES
THE NOSE
THE CHIN

Then why not, I thought, divide each of these features into five different types, assigning to each type a letter which by virtue of itself and its position in a keyword should indicate the appearance of that feature?

And here was the very scheme itself as I afterward perfected it. For each kind of ears I distributed consonants in the following manner:

Close-lying ears	B
Outstanding ears	C
Large ears	D
Small ears	F
Lobeless ears	G

And for each type of forehead I distributed vowels:

Bulging forehead	A
Receding forehead	E
High forehead	I
Low forehead	O
Wrinkled forehead	U

Continuing in the same manner, I assigned to the eyes:

Wide-set eyes	H
Narrow-set eyes	J
"Squint" eyes	K
Large eyes	L
Small eyes	M

And for the five different kinds of noses the vowels once more:

Pointed nose	A
Drooping nose	E
Retroussé nose	I
"Hump" nose	O
Flat nose	U

And finally to the five different chins the following allotment of letters:

Square chin	P
Pointed chin	R
Receding chin	S

Protruding chin	T
Double chin	X

Now, as I reasoned, with this system any face which I desired to remember could be expressed as one word—for instance, that of Bisbee, my partner in business, a man with

(1)	Ears, lobeless	G
(2)	Forehead, high	I
(3)	Eyes, "squint"	K
(4)	Nose, drooping	E
(5)	Chin, square	P

as the word, meaningless except perhaps to myself, of G-I-K-E-P.

And inasmuch as no two faces on earth are exactly alike, and since also it was evident that my arrangement of letters permitted of three thousand different combinations, then without doubt I had room for many, many people.

Therefore, if I should meet any man anywhere, for my business demanded considerable travel, who seemed familiar and whom I desired to recall—then all I need do was to express his face as a word—associate the sound of the word with whatever time and place it should bring to mind, and thus instantly know the circumstances of our first acquaintance.

But this was three years ago.

To show you the working out of the plan I need describe to you the incidents of one night alone.

Let me take, for instance, the evening that I helped my bachelor son, Jack, to move from our home far up on the North Side, out to South Chicago, where his recently acquired position with the Illinois Steel Mills demanded that he reside, in order that he could more easily go back and forth between the mills and the company's down-town offices.

After we had unpacked his trunk and he had got comfortably settled in his new room, I left and prepared to make the long journey back to the North Side—some fifteen miles all told. This was about nine o'clock.

As I started to ascend the steps of the elevated railway at Sixty-Third Street a man came hurriedly down, skipping three steps at a time. He collided violently with me, and as I am a man nearly fifty years of age and not of very great build, the impact threw me up against one of the supporting pillars of the entrance. As I endeav-

ored to regain my balance I ran hastily over his features from force
of habit.

Outstanding ears—C; low forehead—O; small eyes—M; flat
nose—U; double chin—X;—

"C-O-M-U-X, comux, comux—" I repeated to myself. An inci-
dent two years past popped into my mind. Then I spoke aloud and
sharply:

"See here, my dear sir, do you always go through life bumping
and smashing into other people? You did that same trick to me
some two years ago at Hannibal, Missouri, on the corner of Main
and Third Streets."

"Good Lord!" he ejaculated, staring. "What a memory you
must have! I was in Hannibal just two years ago and—"

But I was angrily pushing my way up the elevated stairs, brush-
ing my clothes as I climbed.

Arriving down-town after an hour's tedious riding, I stood on
the corner of Randolph Street, waiting for a surface car to take me
northward. A stranger—at least a stranger until I placed him—
approached me and requested a match for his cigar. As the light
from the match I handed up lit up his features I spelled them out—
couldn't resist it any more than a hungry man could resist a beef-
steak.

"Large ears—D; wrinkled forehead—U; large eyes—L; 'hump'
nose—O; pointed chin—R. D-U-L-O-R, dulor, dulor—"

"I see," I remarked to him, "that you've taken to smoking cigars. When I last saw you, nearly three years ago in the cigar store
on Valley Street, Burlington, Iowa, you were trying to get a special brand of cigarettes."

But I had started for the center of the street since my car had
drawn up to the crossing.

As I searched for my fare on the back platform I looked the
conductor over casually. Small ears—F; receding forehead—E;
small eyes—M; drooping nose—E; protruding chin—T.

"F-E-M-E-T, femet—" I said to myself. Suddenly I recalled the
very occurrence, with its shout, its ringing of bells, and its crowd.

"I trust," I said, handing him a nickel, "that you didn't lose
your position with the Indianapolis City Traction Company on
account of your jerking the bell-cord too quickly that day at Me-
ridian and Washington Street—the day the old gentleman got
dragged several rods. Pretty busy corner there. That was about
eighteen months ago, wasn't it?"

His eyes opened wide. Then he answered me:

"Holy smokes, was you on the platform? You got it c'rect, stranger. I got canned for that little piece of hastiness. Then I came on to Chicago and got this job."

I entered the car. The only seat vacant was one across from an old gentleman, reading a paper. Having nothing with which to occupy my attention, I did as I always did—commenced to spell out faces—and took his for a starter:

"Close-lying ears—B; wrinkled forehead—U; narrow-set eyes—J; flat nose—U; double chin—X; B-U-J-U-X, bujux, bujux—ah, yes! That Western trip, of course!"

I leaned over and tapped him on the knee.

"Don't want to interrupt you," I remarked, "but the last time I saw you was last winter in Minneapolis, near the junction of Hennepin and Nicollet Avenues. You were asking me if I could direct you to a car that would take you over to St. Paul. I presume you got the right one?"

"I got it," he replied, "but how you ever placed me is a mystery. Your face is just barely familiar—but I wouldn't know in a thousand years where I'd seen you."

And so we talked all the way until I dismounted at Buckingham Place, where I and my wife reside.

It was several weeks after this—or, to be exact, six days ago—that my faith in my memorizing system received its first blow—when I came across the face that eluded my every effort to place it—and yet was familiar to the extent that I was sure I had seen it before.

I was hurrying back to my office after lunch in very good humor, since I had just successfully identified a beggar that had accosted me on the street as being the same one that had accosted me in Buffalo six months previously. As I turned a corner a few moments later I caught sight of a face whose possessor was entering a large dry-goods store. An immediate sense of familiarity compelled me at once to spell it out.

Small ears—F; high forehead—I; wide-set eyes—H; pointed nose—A; square chin—P. F-I-H-A-P.

"Fihap, fihap, fihap," I said over and over to myself. The keyword seemed to suggest nothing—seemed to bring up no associations whatever, and yet I was certain that I had somehow or somewhere seen the face before.

During the remainder of that afternoon I fretted over the matter. That night my sleep was somewhat disturbed.

For the next few days I succeeded in dismissing it to some extent from my mind, since a large tide of business affairs provided other matters on which to concentrate.

Then, just three days latter, I saw it again.

This time the possessor was stepping into a car at Adams and State, at about three o'clock in the afternoon. For an instant I stopped in my tracks; then I quickly collected myself and proceeded, while the face was yet partially in view, to check up my original data. Small ears—F; high forehead—I; wide-set eyes—H; pointed nose—A; square chin—P. F-I-H-A-P was undoubtedly the correct keyword.

"Fihap, fihap, fihap—" Where in Heaven's name had I seen this individual before? Under what circumstances had we met?

I did no more work that afternoon. I was depressed, abstracted, worried.

Not for an instant did I close my eyes in sleep that night. I lay awake for bedtime until dawn, pondering, figuring. Small ears—F; high forehead—I; wide-set eyes—H; pointed nose—A; square—but was it a square chin? Could it be really considered a protruding chin? In that case it would be under the letter "T," and the keyword would then be FIHAT; but, no—the chin was neither protruding nor receding—it was just a square chin—"P" was right—FIHAP—fihap—fihap—

I was up against a stone wall. I was baffled. I was maddened.

Next morning I merely nibbled at my breakfast. My wife murmured something about my seeing a doctor. I telephoned to my business partner, telling him that, due to a little attack of *la grippe*, I would not be down to work for several days.

The truth of the matter was—that I had decided to find the owner of this face if I had to spend the rest of my days on the corner of Adams and State, searching.

The entire day I stood on that corner, watching the crowds for the face. I did not bother to classify people any longer. I was searching for but one physiognomy—the one that refused to respond to my association test. In short, however, it did not show up.

Naturally, I did not sleep that night, either. My mind was working ceaselessly on the riddle. Small ears—F; high forehead—I; F-I—F-I—FIHAP, fihap—To insure my freedom from mental torture, to save my very sanity itself, I must find the owner of this face and beg him to tell me where he had met me before.

The following morning I was again posted on the same corner. To-day, though, I varied my procedure by occasionally walking around the block.

At precisely five o'clock in the afternoon, just as the sidewalks began to be jammed with crowds of home-going workers, I caught sight of the elusive face that had caused me so much worry and perturbation; this time its owner was carrying a peculiarly shaped, brand-new valise, black in hue.

I rushed forward.

In the same second a stout woman stepped squarely into my path. During my delay the owner of the face swung himself upon a moving streetcar.

When I reached the track I was too late. The car was a half block down the street. So I sprang upon the next one and secured a position on the front platform, where I watched carefully every person that dismounted from the car a block ahead of me.

For a long while no one carrying a black leather satchel stepped off.

After a considerable lapse of time, however, I caught sight of the man and the black valise alighting. As ill luck would have it, a coal-wagon then became firmly planted on the track in front of my own car. So I, too, dismounted quickly and half walked, half ran toward him.

Suddenly he disappeared up a flight of steps that were too far in advance of me to enable me to make out their exact location.

As I arrived near the locality where he had vanished I saw for the first time that I was in my own neighborhood. Well, that was some consolation. I would interview my wife at once and ascertain as to whether she had noticed any strangers carrying black valises in our neighborhood that day.

When I reached home I drew out my latch-key and opened the front door of our flat. As I stepped into the front hall I nearly stumbled over a black valise that sat directly in my path.

Some one standing near it in the gloom looked up and spoke:

"Hello!" he said, "I've been permanently transferred to the downtown offices. So I've come back, dad, to live with you and mother."

THE SERVICES OF AN EXPERT
—THE STORY

T WAS CLOSE upon midnight.

I had just placed my silk hat on the rack that hung at the side of the room when I heard the slight sounds coming from the direction of the fire escape. Then I detected the shadow on the window pane.

I paused in the act of removing my gloves, and felt quickly for my back pocket. My revolver was there.

So I stood very quietly in the darkness and watched the man on the iron framework outside as he fumbled a moment and then raised the window. Since a small patch of moonlight, now outlined on the rug, acted as a weak source of illumination, I drew further back in the shadow of the door.

After thrusting one leg over the sill, the intruder drew in the rest of his body. For an instant he stood, glancing with uncertainty at the raised window back of him.

Then it was that I slid my right hand carefully along the wall until my fingers came in contact with the electric light switch. With my left I drew out the small, nickel-plated revolver that I have always with me for cases of emergency.

"Hands up!" I said calmly—and snapped on the incandescents.

He thrust his hands instantly above his head and stood blinking in the sudden flood of light. I had opportunity then, for the first time, to survey him from head to foot.

He was a small and rather stockily-built individual, clad in a checkered suit; his face could be aptly described by the phrase "roly-poly." On his head reposed a derby hat, and dropping from his collar was a gorgeously red tie that lent the final touch to his general appearance of flashiness.

"Well," I remarked, advancing toward him with weapon still extended, "what's your game, my man?"

He seemed to be yet dazed by the sudden turn of affairs for him. After a pause, he spoke.

"My game? Well—to tell you the truth—I don't just know. A minute ago I was sliding in that window back of me ... and now

. . . I seem to be . . . well . . . just waiting . . . for something to happen."

"Don't worry," I answered grimly. "It'll happen." I stepped toward the 'phone that stood on the table, watching him all the while. He didn't blink an eye. So I stopped.

"I suppose you're one of these fly-by-night birds they call second-story men, eh?" My voice took on a more sarcastic tone. "Or perhaps you're only walking in your sleep now. In a short while you'll wake up and declare it's some terrible mistake. Or possibly you've stumbled into the wrong house by error?"

His upraised arms were losing their rigidity. To satisfy myself as to whether he was armed, I stepped over to him and inserted my hand into each one of his pockets in turn. He had no weapons, however.

"All right," I said. "Let 'em down." I went over to the window, closed it, and drew down the shade. Then I returned to the table and dropped into the swivel chair, beckoning him at the same time into the straight-backed chair that stood directly across. "Sit down," I commanded. "Before I turn you over to the police I'll have a little talk with you. Do you know where you are? Do you know whose apartment you're in?"

"Well," he replied, "the name on the doorbell downstairs says Mr. Peter J. Dawson."

Probably I was goading him with my remarks far more than was necessary as I answered:

"You're quite observing, I'm sure. I presume then, that you really dropped in because you happened to read in the Chicago Suburban News that Mrs. Dawson left yesterday for the East, and that Dawson himself was to leave the city this morning for a few days in Cincinnati. Put a little too much faith in the newspapers this time, didn't you? Did you make sure, by telephoning first, that the servant was away too—Heaven knows where?"

He bit out his reply in short, angry words. "Say! If you're going to turn me over, hurry up an' do it. I'm not going to sit here an' listen to all your gaff."

"Here, here," I said, "don't get huffy, my good sir. I'm a good fellow—a very good fellow at times—in fact, this is the one time of your life that you want to cultivate my friendship, of all persons." I watched him narrowly. Then I continued quizzing him.

"Confess, though, now . . . you just strolled in, as it were, to see whether any of the famous—or infamous—Dawson diamonds, that were so accurately described in the newspaper account of the big dinner party last week, were lying around loose. How about it?"

His answer was non-committal, to say the least.

"I'm not confessing anything of the sort. Ring up the cops and be done with it." He laughed an odd little laugh. "All the good cells 'll be filled up with drunks in another hour. It's midnight now."

The more I thought of our unusual situation, the more I felt that this man could possibly prove very valuable to me. My questioning now took on a definite trend.

"What's your particular specialty, if I may make so bold as to inquire? It's a rare treat to talk with a real second-story man; or are you perhaps a porch climber? or a lock-picker? or a stick-up man? Or maybe even a safe-blower?

"For example," I went on, "assuming that the jewelry you're looking for is over there in that iron box," and I pointed toward the massive safe that stood in the corner of the room, "just what, may I ask, was your method of procedure to be?"

"For the last time," he said wearily, "I'm telling you I'm not talking."

I was quite determined, though, to continue along the line on which I had already started.

"Ah, yes!" I remarked soothingly, "but you must talk. I feel a rather charitable impulse running through my veins this evening—an impulse that prompts me to be a trifle lenient with you. What do you know about safes?"

For the first time he betrayed a little interest.

"Oh, I know a little about 'em," he replied. "For instance—that one—over there—" He motioned toward the corner of the room. "I could tell you a few things about it—just from where I sit. That's one of the earlier ones put out by the International Burglar-proof Safe and Lock Company. That's their type—" He wrinkled his brow and pondered a moment. "—36 B."

Things were shaping up better than I had expected. My voice must have shown the satisfaction I felt. "Good. You *are* quite an educated fellow in your line. Now that safe belongs to my wife. Not a soul knows the combination of it but herself. I frankly confess I don't. Is a safe like that really burglar-proof? Could you open it, all alone, unaided?"

He crossed his legs. "I daresay I could," he returned, gazing at me through eyes that had become mere slits. "It's all in the way you spin your dial around and listen for the tumblers dropping into place." He inserted his thumbs jauntily in his arm-holes and commenced to whistle a gay little tune. "But I don't intend to try," he added.

Obviously, this was the man I required. I dropped my tone of banter and spoke seriously.

"Now—as a sporting proposition and because I've never seen such a person as yourself work—if you could demonstrate your ability by opening yon strongbox in—say—five minutes—not a second more, you understand—I'd be careless enough to shut my eyes and let you walk out of here through the same fire escape window you came in."

Exultantly, he rose to his feet. "Say—are you dead in earnest? Are you on the square about that proposition? D'you mean it? Will you let me walk out o' here if I can jiggle that combination open?"

"Certainly," I assured him. "Of course I mean it. Can you do it?"

"I can make a try at it," he said, walking toward the safe. Then he glanced over it.

The silence was suddenly broken by the sharp ringing of the telephone bell.

I ignored it.

Then it rang a second time.

The little man returned to the table and stood waiting, with his hands in his pockets. "Going t' answer?" he inquired.

"Let it ring," I replied curtly.

He watched me closely, his face breaking slowly into a grin. Then he levelled his forefinger directly at me and launched forth into a scathing speech.

"Huh!" he exclaimed. "I'm a little next to you now. You're afraid to answer that 'phone. May I ask just why you don't want anybody t' know you were home in the flat t'night—on the night of June the twenty-fifth—while the lady o' th' house is in the East—while you're supposed to be on a train going to Cincinnati? Eh? What's coming off here t'night? What's your game—Mr.—Mr.—Dawson?" At this point he evidently ran out of either breath or denunciatory ideas.

That cursed 'phone then rang for the third time. I was not only quite flustered now—but angry as well. "That's enough from you," I growled.

His accusing forefinger was still pointed at me as the 'phone bell rang for the fourth—and what proved to be—the last time. He must have taken great delight in making me squirm, for he started off again.

"You've got something shady scheduled here for t'night. You don't dare answer that phone. When you get ready t' let me into your little game, then maybe I'll do your dirty work. Not until." He sank into the straight-backed chair and stared at the window in back of me.

I glanced apprehensively behind me, realizing that this rascal was perhaps playing for time. A suspicion crossed my mind that possibly a confederate was posted near the grounds. But we were quite alone. For about a minute I thought on the matter. This man had arrived at a crucial moment for me. Without doubt, it seemed best that I render a detailed explanation to him if I wished to placate him—especially in view of the fact that the telephone had complicated matters as it had. So I leaned back in my chair and began, picking my words with care.

"I'm going to let you in on a family secret now. Of course, I'm quite safe—and, likewise, I don't have to do it. If I wish, I can turn you over any minute and the little tale you might tell I could brand as a lie, pure and simple. But in some respects you're a valuable man to me tonight. You can do me a big service. In return, I do you the bigger service—of saving you from five or ten years in the Joliet Penitentiary.

"Now pay attention," I commanded. "I'm up against the wall. In other words, I'm broke. I've had financial reverses—I'm busted—ever since a week ago. If I had fifty or sixty thousand I'd be a rich man again in a year. But I haven't it. How about my wife?

"No doubt," I went on, "you've often read in the papers of P.J. Dawson—the race track bookmaker—the man that made killings a year before last at Latonia and Juarez. And you must know, too, that almost all gamblers, when times are good, salt their money away in diamonds. Well—I was no exception to the rule—but I made one fatal mistake. I gave all of mine, as fast as I bought 'em, to my wife. It's all she cares for—all she can see."

He was paying strict attention to my words, so I continued, punctuating my remarks with emphatic gestures with my clenched fists.

"She loves diamonds better than she ever loved me. As a result of the last ten years, she's got a hundred thousand dollars' worth in rings and gee-gaws—got 'em hoarded up in that safe of hers like a miser. She's sticking to 'em tighter than a barnacle sticks to the bottom of a mud scow.

"But that don't help me," I added. "If she knew I was down and out—she'd start divorce proceedings in a jiffy. Luckily, I know my wife pretty well by this time. I guess, however, you grasp the situation all right.

"She left this morning for a short trip East. That part of the statement in the Chicago Suburban News was correct. The servant went to visit a sick sister. And I—well—I'm on a train bound for Cincinnati . . . nix! . . . are you wise now?

"Instead, I'm back here in the apartment tonight, reconnoitering—looking over the land—figuring out whether I could procure tools, come back tomorrow night, and drill, saw, hack, punch or chisel my way into that strong-box. And then, by the most happy chance, along comes yourself—an expert in your line. Do you see now what I need you for? Can you help me out? If you can, you're a free man." I leaned back and mopped my forehead. I had talked for five straight minutes.

If I had expected sympathy, however, I failed woefully in my expectations. He was coldly calculating—nothing more.

"I'm talking business, now," he said. "What's there in it for me?"

So far as I could see, there was no necessity for me to dicker with this fellow, since it was quite evident that I had the upper hand. So my reply was short and to the point.

"Not a red cent."

He seemed still inclined to argue. "Pretty hard bargain, I call it."

I was becoming impatient. The unpleasant thought of a possible confederate, in the hope of whose assistance he was delaying matters, again entered my mind. "To my way of thinking," I remarked, "it's a pretty easy bargain."

"Well," he returned, "what guarantee have I got that you'll let me go if I do th' job—that is—if I can?"

Really, the man's stubbornness was aggravating. "Numskull," I said, restraining myself with difficulty from shouting at him, "—if I can get at that property, which all came from my own pockets in the first place, it's to my decided advantage that you, the mysterious burglar, gets away. And likewise, it's to your undeniable benefit to keep a quiet tongue in your head afterward. Then, too, haven't you my promise—my word of honor?"

He did not lose the opportunity to deliver a thrust.

"A lot o' faith,' he jeered, "I'd put in the word of honor of a guy that'd steal from his own wife. If this wife is the kind of woman that I think she must be—that I think any wife must be— she'd hand over all she's got to put her husband back on his feet. Say," he finished with a leer, "ain't you what they call Indian-Giver?"

This was going just a little too far. I commenced to feel withered, so I determined to use up no more valuable time discussing the offer. "We're wasting precious moments," I said sharply. "What do you intend to do?"

Evidently he realized that he was hardly in a position to do otherwise than comply with my wishes.

"Make the best of it," was his reply. "Friend—you're a mighty hard man to deal with—and if anything goes wrong—don't blame it on anybody but yourself." He paused. "Well—here's where I get down to work. I never use tools. Too crude."

He removed his coat.

I watched him with interest, wondering how on earth he could open a supposedly burglar-proof safe without an instrument of any kind. He seemed, however, quite self-confident.

He folded up his coat and deposited it on the chair which he had occupied. Then he unfastened each cuff and turned it back, clear to the elbow. He glanced at me. "Say, friend," he queried, "if I can do it, don't I get one little jewel for myself—say a little half-carat ring?"

Seeing the preparations he had already gone to, I had not been inclined to yield jot nor tittle. His persistency, though, had exhausted my patience.

I plunged my hand into my pocket and brought forth my last bill—a crisp, yellow fifty—which I flung on the table without a word. He seized it cheerfully and tucked it in his vest-pocket.

After all—what did it matter? The difference between his remuneration and mine was too great.

He walked slowly over to the safe and rapped on its sides and top with his knuckles. Then, with great mysteriousness, he wet the tips of his fingers, one at a time, on his tongue, and wiped them on his rolled up sleeves.

He stooped over.

Then he went through a series of puzzling actions. At times he spun the dial. At other times he worked it slowly, pressing his ear close to the iron door, and listening with a far-away look on his

face. Occasionally he glanced in my direction out of the corner of
his eye.

For nearly a minute I watched him. Then, since it was summer
time and the room had begun to feel stifling, I stepped casually
over to the window, raised the shade, and opened it to its full extent, letting in a refreshing breeze from Lake Michigan.

This accomplished, I turned around to see how my expert was
coming along with his task.

Great Caesar's Horn Spoon!—

While my back was turned he had quietly succeeded in swinging open the door of the safe and had extracted therefrom a huge
blue-steel revolver which, in less than a second, he had raised,
pointed in my direction, and fired with a thundering report great
enough to wake twenty neighborhoods.

I dropped flat to the floor and lay still as a log.

Hurt? Not a bit of it! He probably missed me by a mile—but I
was taking no chances of receiving another broadside from that
villainous-looking weapon. While I lay prone, never moving, he
stood stock still for a quarter of a minute. Then, with four giant
strides, he cleared half the room and landed in the swivel chair
with his back to me.

Cautiously, I raised my head. Silently, I regained my knees and
feet. I tiptoed backward a step to the window and out on the fire
escape, where I crouched down, watching the little man in the
swivel chair.

Excitedly, he was jerking the receiver hook of the 'phone up
and down. Finally he must have roused Central, for I heard him
say: "H'llo—h'llo—'lo—North Shore Station please—"

After the lapse of a few seconds he must have obtained his
connection for he shouted into the transmitter: "Station? Station?
Police station? Send an ambulance or a doctor or an officer or
something in a red-hot hurry to 725 Franklin Road—the second
flat—the Dawsons' flat. I've wounded 'r killed a man. Nope, don't
know him—lost my latchkey—missed my train to Cincinnati—
came in by fire-escape—found him here—yes! yes! yes!—this is
Dawson himself speaking—sure—yes, Peter J. Dawson—"

I had heard enough. I slid silently down the fire-escape ladder
and hastened forth into the night, my last two dimes jingling as I
ran.

THE SERVICES OF AN EXPERT – THE PLAY

CAST:

Peter J. Dawson — A racetrack bookmaker

Pyles — A sneak thief

PLACE:

A room in Peter Dawson's second floor apartment in a Chicago suburb.

TIME:

Near midnight.

SCENE:

The scene will show, after the stage has been illuminated (since at the rise of curtain everything is in darkness) a well furnished room containing near the front of the stage a library table on which rests an electric lamp, a portable telephone, and a number of scattered papers. To the left of the table is a swivel chair; to the right is an ordinary straight-backed chair.

At the rear of the stage in the center is a door, on one side of which stands an upright coat rack; in the other side is a small serving table holding a decanter of liquor and several glasses.

At the left of the stage (as seen from the audience) is a fireplace (containing no fire) and a Morris chair; on the right of the stage is a bookcase.

At the rear (to the extreme left) is a window which opens out to a rear fire escape. In like manner, at the rear (to the extreme right) is a large solid-appearing safe with black exterior and polished dial.

At the rise the stage is in total darkness, with the exception of a certain amount of diffused moonlight entering through the window curtains. As to whether any one is in the room cannot be ascertained. Absolute quietness reigns.

A shadow appears on the pane. It pauses for a few seconds. It fumbles on the sill. Apparently the window is not fastened for, with a tug, the man on the fire escape succeeds in raising it. He thrusts one leg over the sill. He then draws in the rest of his body.

He lowers the window quietly and stands for a few seconds in the moonlight.

With a sharp click the lights are suddenly turned on, illuminating the stage. Standing at the wall snap-switch is a figure clad in a white dress suit with white shirt front and white tie. His silk hat hangs upon the hat stand. On his hands are gray gloves. His features are sharp-cut. [The author, for clearness, takes the liberty of representing him in dialogue by "WHITE-TIE".] His hands hold a small nickel-plated revolver leveled directly at the intruder.

WHITE-TIE.

(At the instant he snaps on the lights.)

Hands up!

(The man at the window thrusts his hands quickly above his head. He is seen to be a short, stockily-built, "roly-poly-faced" individual clad in a rather loud checked suit of the ready-made type. He wears a flaming red tie. [The author for clearness, represents him in the dialogue by "RED-TIE."] On his head is a derby hat. His whole general appearance betokens flashiness.)

WHITE-TIE.

(Advancing to center of stage with weapon still extended.) Well? . . . What's your game, my man?

RED-TIE.

(Staring for a few seconds.) To tell you the truth . . . I don't just know . . . A minute ago I was sliding in that window back of me . . . and now . . . I just seem to be . . . well . . . just waiting . . . for something to happen.

WHITE-TIE.

Oh! Yes! I see. I suppose you're one of those fly-by-night birds they call "second-story men" . . . eh? . . . (sarcastically) Or perhaps you're just walking in your sleep now. In a minute you'll wake up and declare it's some terrible mistake . . . or maybe you just stumbled into the wrong house?

(Steps in the direction of the phone. Stops and watches his captive.)

Here, come over here.

(RED-TIE approaches him with hands upraised. WHITE-TIE with one hand still holding revolver inserts his free hand into each of RED-TIE's pockets. He finds no firearms.)

All right. Let 'em down. Come over here . . . Sit down. Before I turn you over to the police I'll have a little talk with you.

(He steps backward to the window and draws down the shade. He returns and sinks into the swivel chair. The short stout man drops stiffly into the straight-backed chair across the table and places his hands on his knees.)

WHITE-TIE.

(Continuing) Do you know where are? Do you know whose apartment you're in?

RED-TIE.

Well . . . the name on the doorbell downstairs says Mr. Peter Dawson.

WHITE-TIE.

You're quite observing, I'm sure. I suppose, then, you really dropped in here because you happened to read in the *Chicago Suburban News* that Mrs. Dawson left yesterday for the East . . . and that Dawson himself was to leave the city this evening for a few days in Cincinnati.

Put a little too much faith in the newspapers this time, didn't you?

Did you make sure by telephone first that the servant was away, too? . . . God knows where.

RED-TIE.

Say! If you're going to turn me over, hurry up and do it. I'm not going t' sit here an' listen t' you rub it in.

WHITE-TIE.

Here . . . here . . . don't get huffy, my man. I'm a good fellow . . . a very good fellow at times. In fact—this is the one time of your life that you want to cultivate my friendship.

Confess, tho, now . . . you just strolled in, as it were, to see whether any of the famous—or infamous—Dawson diamonds, that were so accurately described in the newspaper accounts of the big dinner party last week . . . were lying around loose. How about it?

RED-TIE.

I'm not confessing anything of the sort. Ring up the cops and be done with it. (Laughs.) All the good cells 'll be filled up with drunks by 1 o'clock. It's midnight now.

WHITE-TIE.

I'll do that presently . . . perhaps . . . It's a rare treat to talk to a real second story man. (Laughs derisively.)

What's your particular specialty, if I may be so bold to inquire? Porch-climber? . . . stick-up man? . . . or even safe-blower?

Now ... for example ... assuming that the jewelry you're looking for ... is over there in that iron box (points toward safe) ... just what, may I ask, was your method of procedure to be?

RED-TIE.

(Wearily.) For the last time, I'm telling you I'm not talking.

WHITE-TIE.

Oh, yes. But you must talk ... or act. I feel a strange, charitable impulse running through my veins ... an impulse that prompts me to be a trifle lenient with you. (Pause.)

What do you know about safes, you poor, miserable, red-tied, check-suited specimen of humanity?

RED-TIE.

(Looking vindictively toward his tormentor.) I know a little about 'em. For instance ... that one ... over there ... (flicks his finger in the direction of the safe) ... I could tell you a lot about it just from where I sit ... That's one of the earlier ones put out by the International Burglar-proof Safe and Lock Company ... that's their type ... (wrinkles his forehead) ... 36 B.

WHITE-TIE.

(Surprised.) Well ... I declare ... you are quite an educated fellow in your line.

Now that safe belongs to my wife. Not a soul knows the combination of it but herself. I frankly admit I don't.

Is a safe like that really burglar-proof?

Could you open it ... all alone ... unaided?

RED-TIE.

(Crosses his legs.) I daresay I could.

It's all in the way you spin your dial around an' listen for the tumblers dropping into place. But I don't intend to try. (Puts thumbs jauntily in arm-holes of vest. Whistles gay tune.)

WHITE-TIE.

No? ... Now as a sporting proposition ... and because I've never seen such a genius as yourself work ... if you could demonstrate your ability by opening yon strongbox in ... well, say ... five minutes ... not a second more, you understand ... I'd be impolite enough to turn my back and let you walk out of here by the same fire escape window you came in.

RED-TIE.

(Rising to his feet.) Say, are you dead in earnest? Are you on the square about that proposition? D' you mean it? Will you let me walk out o' here if I can jiggle that combination open?

WHITE-TIE.

Why—sure I mean it. Can you do it?
RED-TIE.

I might make a try at it. (Walks back toward safe and glances over it.)

(WHITE-TIE remains seated.)

(The silence is broken by the sharp ringing of the telephone bell on the table.)
WHITE-TIE.

(Looking stupidly at it.) Hell fire! (He makes no move to answer it. It rings a second time. RED-TIE walks back from the safe and stands with his hands in his pockets waiting for WHITE-TIE to lift the receiver. The latter still makes no move.)
RED-TIE.

Going to answer it?
WHITE-TIE.

The devil with it. Let it ring.

(RED-TIE watches him closely. His face breaks into a grin. He points his finger at WHITE-TIE.)
RED-TIE.

(Pointing.) Say! I'm a little wise to you now, You're AFRAID to answer that 'phone. May I ask just why you don't want anybody t' know you were home in the flat t'night—on the night of June 20th—while the lady o' th' house is in the East—while you're supposed to be on a train going to Cincinnati? Eh? What's coming off here t'night? What's YOUR game, Mr. Dawson?

(The 'phone rings for the third time.)
WHITE-TIE.

(Flustered and angry.) That's enough from you.
RED-TIE.

(Still pointing has forefinger at him, as the bell rings for the fourth and last time.) You've got something already scheduled here for t'night. You don't dare answer that 'phone.

When you get ready t' let me into your little game—then maybe I'll do your dirty work. Not until. (Sinks down into the straight-backed chair.)
WHITE-TIE.

(Ponders.) Well . . . suppose I let you in on a family secret. Of course—I'm quite safe. Don't think for a minute, though, that I have to do it. I can turn you over any minute and the little tale you might tell I could brand as a lie, pure and simple. But in some respects you're a valuable man to me tonight. You can do me a big service.

In return I do you the bigger service—of saving you from five or ten years in the Joliet penitentiary.

Now pay attention.

I'm against the wall. In other words, I'm broke . . . I've had business reverses . . . I'm busted . . . ever since a week ago. If I had fifty or sixty thousand I'd be a rich man again in a year. But I haven't it.

How about my wife?

No doubt you've often read in the papers of P.J. Dawson, the racetrack bookmaker—the man that made the big killings year before last at Latonia and Juarez. And likewise you must know, too, that almost all gamblers, when times are good, salt their money away in diamonds. Well—I was no exception to the rule— but I made one fatal mistake. I gave all mine, as fast as I bought 'em, to my wife. It's all she cares for—all she can see.

She loves diamonds more than she ever loved me. As a result of the last ten years she's got a hundred thousand dollars worth in rings and gee-gaws . . . got 'em hoarded up in that safe of hers like a miser. She's sticking to 'em tighter than a barnacle sticks to the bottom of a mud-scow.

But that don't help me.

If she knew I was down and out . . . (snaps fingers) . . . the divorce court for her in a jiffy . . . Luckily, I know my wife pretty well by this time.

I guess you grasp the situation all right.

She left this morning for a short trip East. That part of the statement in the Suburban News was correct. The servant went . . . that is . . . yes . . . went to visit a sick sister. And I . . . well . . . I'm on a train bound for Cincinnati . . . nix! . . . . are you wise?

Instead, I'm back here. In the apartment tonight, reconnoitering . . . looking over the land . . . figuring out whether I could procure tools, come back tomorrow night, and drill, saw, hack, punch or chisel my way into that strong box.

And then . . . as I was leaving . . . along comes yourself, an expert in your line.

Do you see now what I need you for? . . . Can you open the safe? . . . If you can you're a free man.

(Mops forehead after his long speech.)
RED-TIE.

I'm talking business now. What's there in it for me?
WHITE-TIE.

Not a red cent.

RED-TIE.

Pretty hard bargain, I call it.

WHITE-TIE.

To my way of thinking it's a pretty easy bargain.

RED-TIE.

Well . . . what guarantee have I got that you'll let me go if I do the job . . . that is . . . if I can?

WHITE-TIE.

Why, you poor fool . . . if I can get into that safe . . . get my hands on that stuff that all came from my pockets in the first place . . . it's to my decided advantage that you . . . the mysterious burglar, gets away. And likewise it's to your undeniable benefit to keep a quiet tongue in your head afterward.

Then besides . . . haven't you got my promise . . . do you want my word of honor?

RED-TIE.

A hell of a lot o' faith I'd put in the word of honor of a guy that'd steal from his own wife. (Laughs sneeringly.)

If this woman you mention is the kind of woman that I think she must be . . . that I think any wife must be . . . she'd hand over all she's got to put her husband back on his feet again.

But instead . . . you creep around like a snake in the grass . . . sniveling something about a divorce . . . afraid to face the music.

Say, ain't you what they call an Indian-Giver? (Smiles.)

WHITE-TIE.

(Sharply and angrily.) We're wasting precious moments. What do you intend to do?

RED-TIE.

Make the best of it, I 'spose. Friend . . . you're a hard man. But if anything goes wrong . . . don't blame it on anybody but yourself.

Well . . . here's where I get down to work. I never use tools. Too crude.

(Takes off coat. Folds it carefully and deposits it on chair. Unfastens left cuff. Turns it back to elbow. Unfastens right cuff and repeats the operation.)

(Glances toward WHITE-TIE and sits down on coat.)

Say, friend . . . if I can do it, don't I get one little sparkler for myself? . . . say a little half carat ring?

WHITE-TIE.

(Wearily.) Well! You are a persistent beggar. After all, I suppose it's worth it. Here—here's a nice yellow fifty. It's new and it's crisp and it's genuine. So see that you earn it.

(Produces a yellow bill and flings it on the table. RED-TIE seizes it, tucks it in vest pocket and bows.)

(He [RED-TIE] walks over to the safe. He taps it on the sides and tops with his knuckles. He then wets all ten fingers on his tongue, one at a time, and also wipes them one at a time on his rolled up sleeves. WHITE-TIE looks on curiously and alertly.)

(RED-TIE crouches down. WHITE-TIE steps over nearer, where he can watch operations better, still keeping the gun loosely in his hand. RED-TIE works at safe very mysteriously. At times he spins the dial. At other times he places his ear close and listens as he manipulates it slowly. All in all, he spends a full minute working at it.)

(Now he turns it back and forth, eyeing it more carefully. He suddenly makes a small adjustment. Then, still stooped over, he steps backward a foot and swings open the door of the safe.)

WHITE-TIE.

(Lightly clapping hands.) Bravo!

(Quickly RED-TIE reaches within and as quickly withdraws his hand. He wheels sharply. His right hand holds a heavy blue-steel revolver.)

(He fires instantly.)

(WHITE-TIE staggers, drops his pistol, falls heavily to the floor and lies quiet.)

(RED-TIE rushes to the table, stepping over the body and drops into the swivel chair. He grasps the 'phone and excitedly rattles the receiver hook up and down, speaking into the transmitter.)

H'llo . . . h'llo . . . North-Shore Station, please.

(Five seconds pause.)

Station? Station? Police-station? All right. Send an officer at once to 725 Franklin Road—the second flat—the Dawsons' flat—I've killed a man . . . Nope—don't know him . . . lost my latchkey . . . missed my train to Cincinnati—came in by the fire escape—found him here—yes! yes! yes! This is Dawson himself speaking . . . sure . . . Peter J. Dawson—

CURTAIN.

WHEN TIME RAN BACKWARD

IT WAS A peculiarly shaped bottle made of dark green glass. Its base, round and covered with corrugations, rose to a tapering neck. In appearance it was not unlike what is known as a Venetian flask. Inside was a liquid of the same color, so I discovered later, as absinthe—but not nearly so viscous. A pasteboard tag, tied to the neck, bore the mystifying printed words:

"Turns Time Backward."

I had just moved into my newly rented quarters at the boarding house of Mrs. O'Hara on North State Street. Under ordinary circumstances, I would have become very wroth at finding an article left behind by some former lodger, but in this case I was too perplexed and too full of wonder at those cryptic words to give way to any anger.

My first impulse, of course, was to summon my landlady and give the bottle over into her keeping.

"Turns Time Backward." What on earth did it mean? Was it some kind of a joke?

That the gentleman who had rented the rooms before I moved into them was a peculiar chap, I gathered from one of Mrs. O'Hara's bursts of loquaciousness at the time I paid my first deposit. It seems that in addition to being a student of the occult, he was an ardent collector of strange articles from the Orient.

Again I studied the words on the card, "Turns Time Backward." Was it possible that he could have stumbled upon a secret that would—

I drew the cork and sniffed at the contents. The sweetish odor emanating from the liquid within showed that it could not be wholly unpalatable. Although a teetotaler, I had always gloried in the fact that at some time or other in my life I had at least tasted every fancy and mixed drink known to civilization. Therefore, I reasoned, I ought, at least, to become familiar with some of this "turns-time-backward" wine, now that the opportunity had presented itself.

My eyes roved over the dresser in search of a small glass. Not being a habitual toper, that article was, of course, lacking. My gaze, however, fell upon the large tumbler that usually holds my toothbrush. Good enough. I drew the cork again and filled the glass nearly to the brim.

"No use of being stingy with another man's goods," I remarked genially to myself. "Might as well give Time a good reversal."

"Apprehensive of the approaching suppertime, I glanced at my watch and found it to be five-thirty, P.M. Then I downed the tumbler's contents.

Now I feel quite certain that those same contents could never make a world-wide reputation for themselves as a beverage. Yet, on the other hand, they were not half bad, once they were down. They seemed to present a combination of odd flavors such as I had never tasted before.

Nothing unusual occurred, though. I dropped into the easy chair by the window and drummed with my fingers upon the arm pieces, waiting expectantly to see what effects, if any, should be produced.

The only thing noticeable was a sudden surge of heat that seemed to spread instantly to the tips of my fingers and the ends of my toes. These last-named members began to feel as though they were radiating warmth and life through millions of miles of space. I felt slightly weary, and yet a trifle elated. For a few seconds my head swam. Then things cleared up.

With the consciousness that I had hoaxed myself, I gazed out of my window which faced Chicago's great West Side. Then I rubbed my eyes in amazement.

The sun, that not two minutes ago was touching the horizon, had climbed back and now stood several degrees above its former position. Such a thing was unheard of. Then again I rubbed my eyes. It was unbelievable.

Hastily I rose to my feet and seized my hat. I felt that I must get outside at once and join the immense throngs that would be watching this strange phenomenon from every street corner.

Fortunately, I met no one to delay me as I made my way downstairs to the front door. Arriving on the front steps, I stood paralyzed, my mouth wide open.

The mechanics of the universe were running in the wrong direction.

I could see people everywhere calmly walking up or down the street backward, with as much unconcern as though they were doing it in the ordinary way. Street cars, automobiles, grocery wagons—all ran in a direction opposite to that which they normally pursued.

I glanced at my watch again. Its hands pointed to five o'clock. Almost at the same instant, the bells of St. James's church nearby chimed distinctly five times. I must get down at once to the club on Michigan Avenue, interview Caruthers, my life-long friend and companion, and ascertain the actual cause of this revolutionary state of affairs.

I hurried to the corner. Here I perceived a stout man, grasping a newspaper in his hand, gallop up to a newsboy, taking strange backward jumps not unlike those of a kangaroo. The boy took the paper from him, handed him a cent and then went down the street himself, hoppity-skip, backward.

I mounted a car, taking good care to board one which, although it was headed north, was, in reality, retracing its way south.

As the conductor's broad back loomed up in front of me, I watched him. He suddenly jerked a bell cord. The register, which up to the time had shown a total collection of one hundred fares, dropped suddenly to ninety-nine. Then the blue-coated official turned and gravely handed me a nickel.

What else could I do but accept it? I found myself now to be only a poor human atom to whom no course was left but to take matters as I found them. No doubt, Caruthers would explain everything.

The ride downtown was itself uneventful. My heart rose continually in my mouth lest we meet with a collision, since the motorman stood upon what was for us the rear platform and carefully studied the stretch of track which we had already passed over.

At Madison and South State Streets I dismounted. The clock on the Marshall Field building showed the time to be a quarter of four.

For a moment, I paused to peer in the windows of the basement pressrooms of the "Chicago Evening Vulcan." Imagine my surprise to see thousands of newspapers, that were neatly stacked in bundles, being fed into the folding machines, passing through the presses, and coming subsequently out in the form of rolls of clean white paper which were instantly carted back to the storerooms.

I hurried to the club. I felt certain that I would find Caruthers in the card room playing his inevitable game of poker—and I was not disappointed. He was seated at a square table with three others whom I knew slightly and he nodded absent-mindedly to me as I stood looking on.

He had a great pile of unstacked chips in front of him. Just as I arrived on the scene he shoved them forth to the center of the table. "Gentlemen," he grunted, "in a friendly game such as ours, I could never prolong the betting when I hold an invincible hand. I have here that rare bird, the Royal Flush. The pot is mine."

Blakely, to his right, never blinked an eye at such extraordinary news. "I call Whitson," he said, and forthwith proceeded to abstract ten red chips from the pile in the center.

Whitson, to the right of Blakely, leaned forward and he, too, removed ten red chips from the rapidly decreasing heap, remarking quietly, "I call Barberry's ten."

Barberry, at Whitson's right, drew out the remaining ten colored disks, which left but a few scattered white ones in the center of the table. "I'm betting ten reds," he stated, "on the hypothetical strength of three big aces."

Whereupon I fled precipitately.

Could it be possible, I thought, that I was losing my reason? My watch now showed the time to be only five minutes past three. It was very warm. Perhaps the heat had been affecting me. A brief sojourn among the cooling breezes out at the South Shore bathing beach would undoubtedly restore me to my natural self again. Perhaps a cold plunge in the lake would help to right matters.

The beach was crowded. Numberless bathers slipped from the tiny dressing rooms at the rear of the beach and made their way backward into the waves. But the most remarkable thing—they were dripping wet before they entered the water. Those who emerged from the lake, particularly the women, did so very gingerly, an inch at a time, sending up shriek after shriek—but as they reached the sands they were perfectly dry.

With despair in my heart, and curses against the glass of green liquid that I had so foolishly imbibed, I left the beach without taking a plunge. I was beginning to realize that things were really as they seemed. I saw now, when it was too late, that I had precipitated an extremely unfortunate state of affairs either for myself or for the world in which I had lived, by meddling with something that had not concerned me.

By noon time I was seated on a bench in Grant Park, wondering how to adjust myself to these conditions.

For nearly five long hours I sat there. My ruminations came to nothing. The sun crept closer and closer to the eastern rim of Lake Michigan and, when the factory whistles blew the announcement that the hour of 7 A.M. was at hand, I realized with a start that there was nothing I could do but return to my rooms and make the best of things as they now were.

Fumbling in my clothes, I found the stub of a cigar. I remembered knocking its ashes off yesterday and slipping it into my vest pocket for future use—a reprehensible habit, to be sure. Lighting it, I gloomily puffed away at it. The more I puffed the longer it grew. When, of its own accord, it finally went out, I examined it. My fingers held a perfect Havana. So I flung it bitterly away, knowing now that in this topsy-turvy world, as a complete cigar it had entirely lost its utility.

I did not search for a car to take me home. I walked slowly along North State Street toward my rooms. The streets became more deserted until, finally, only a few nocturnal fishermen, lugging heavy strings of fish, could be seen making their way backward to the lake.

As I marched along, my hands thrust deep in my pockets, I saw window-shade after window-shade in different houses suddenly drawn down. Immediately after the lowering of each one, an alarm clock would strike sharply—then all would be silent.

Last night had returned.

Noiselessly, I let myself into my boarding house. I reached my room and, in the gray light that usually precedes the dawn, flung myself in the easy chair and dozed off. When I awoke I had a headache such as I never hope to have again. My throat was parched and dry, giving me a thirst that seemed infinite in magnitude. Rising to my feet, I lighted the gas and peered at my watch. Its hands were both touching the XII. Then I gazed in the direction of my dresser.

The green flask stood where I had left it, but the breeze from the window had whipped the tag over. From where I stood I could read:

One Quart of
JENKS'S PEERLESS SCALP TONIC

MAKES TIME GO BACKWARD BY
PUTTING **HAIR** ON **BALD** HEADS

COMPOSED OF BENEFICIAL VEGETABLE
OILS DISSOLVED IN
50 PER CENT OF **PURE ALCOHOL**

THE SEARCH

THAT DE LANCEY had been highly successful in the undertaking which he had described to me when last we parted in New York, seemed clearly proven by the account I had clipped from a New York paper on the second day of July. It read:

MAN ARRESTED IN PARIS

(cable) Paris: July 1. An American, said to be of French parentage, named E. M. De Lancey, was arrested here today in connection with last night's robbery of Simon et Cie, 14 Rue Royale, in which two of the most well-known diamonds in the world were stolen.

The stones, known as Castor and Pollux to the trade, are similarly cut and weigh eight carats apiece. The total value of the two, considered by English experts to be well over £12,000, is due to the fact that one is a green, and the other a red diamond. Although certain circumstances point to De Lancey's complicity in the crime, the jewels were found neither in his possession nor at his rooms, and since sufficient definite proof in other directions is lacking, the authorities expect to be compelled to release him within a few days.

A few of the people who are known to have been with him the morning after the robbery are under surveillance, and it is hoped that the stones may ultimately be recovered from one or another of them.

Clever old De Lancey! How invariably he made a success of everything to which he turned his crooked abilities.

As for myself, I had, of course, expected to be of assistance to De Lancey merely in getting the two stones into the hands of old Ranseer at his farm near Morristown, New Jersey, after which our pay would be forthcoming and would be divided up according to our respective risks in the proceeding. This was the method which we always pursued.

Had the clipping itself, however, been insufficient evidence that De Lancey had scored one on the French police, his letter, which reached me a week and a half later, made everything clear.

The communication, which was, of course, in cipher, when translated ran as follows:

                                            Gay Paree, July 4.
T. B.
_____ Str.
New York.

Dear Old T. B.: —Was it in the New York papers? Must have been. Pulled it off as slick as the proverbial whistle. The blooming beggars kept me locked up three days, though. But they were shy on proof—and besides, they were too late.

T. B., there is to be a new man, a German, in our crew after this. Never mind where I picked him up. I firmly believe he is the only man in Europe who will be able to get those gems across the pond. His name is Von Berghem. He called at my rooms this morning after the coup. I passed the stones to him, each one wrapped in a little cotton package and tied with silk thread.

Now, T. B., he's bound for New York, taking the trip across England in easy stages as befits a gentleman traveling for his health, and according to our plans, should embark on an ancient tub named the Princess Dorothy which leaves Liverpool on July 6th and arrives at New York nine days later. Immediately upon landing, he will call at your rooms.

As we have already arranged, you will have two of Ranseer's carrier pigeons (nesting birds, by all means) in a dark covered basket. Secure one stone to each pigeon so that if anything should go wrong, you could liberate them instantly. With their known ability to cover as much as 500 miles, at a speed of 30 miles an hour, they would be able to reach the vicinity of Morristown in less than two hours, even taking into consideration darkness.

As soon as things blow over, yours truly, De Lancey, will slide on toward your famous old N'Yawk, after which—heigh-ho, boy—the good old white lights and ease for a time.

A last word as to Von Berghem. He wears glasses, has gray hair, and carries a mole on his left cheek. He will be accompanied by his fifteen-year-old son, as sharp a little rascal as ever spotted a Scotland Yard man fifty yards away.

                    Yours jubilantly,
                            De L.

So Von Berghem seemed to be the only man in Europe who could get those two sparklers across the pond?

Surely, if he had to get them out of Europe before the eyes of the police, and get them into the States before the eyes of the customs authorities, he would have to be sharp indeed, especially in view of the fact that a hue and cry had already been raised.

Everything was in readiness, though. The pigeons were cheeping in their covered basket. On the mantel were two small leather leg bags ready for the loot. I looked at my watch and found that it was after nine o'clock.

Strange that Von Berghem had not arrived. I had called the steamship offices by telephone at six o'clock and had learned that the Princess Dorothy had docked an hour before.

Then I fell to wondering why he had encumbered himself with his son. Unquestionably, he must have realized that in dealings such as ours, every extra man, constituting a possible weak link, meant just so much more chance of failure.

The clock struck ten.

Where had De Lancey found this fellow—this Von Berghem? I found myself asking myself. Was he sure of him? Did he understand the game as we did?

Everything that De Lancey did was perplexing. He seemed to know every crook between the equator and the poles and to understand just what part to assign him in any undertaking. Without doubt, he must have known what he was doing this time.

So he was the only man that De Lancey believed capable of—

The clock struck ten-thirty.

I heard the slam of a taxi-cab door down on the street below.

A second later, the bell of my New York apartment tinkled sharply.

I hurried to the front door and opened it quietly. In the outer hall stood a tall man wearing glasses—and a mole on his left cheek. At his side was a boy of about sixteen.

"This is T. B.," I whispered.

"Von Berghem," he answered, and stepped inside with the boy, while I closed the door behind them.

I passed down the narrow inner hall and threw open the library door. "In here," I said, and snapped on the lights. "How did you make out?"

Von Berghem seemed to be ill. The whiteness of his face and his halting gait as he leaned heavily on the shoulder of his son, signified either sickness or—

Failure! Ah—that must be it. My heart seemed to stop beating. Von Berghem must have been unsuccessful in his mission.

He sank heavily into a chair that the boy brought forth for him. The latter dropped down on a small footstool, nearby, and remained silent.

In the interval, I studied Von Berghem and perceived for the first time the horrible expression on his face. His eyes had the same haunting look that I had once seen on the face of a maniac in the state insane asylum.

"Met with considerable trouble," he stated laconically, after a pause.

"Tell me about it," I said, half sympathetically and half suspiciously. His gaze, which had been roving aimlessly around the room, he directed toward me again. Then he commenced to talk.

"I called on De Lancey the morning after the robbery. He gave the two gems into my keeping at once. The lad was with me. He's a coming thief, is the lad. We took a cab at once for the station. Three hours afterward, De Lancey was nabbed.

"The lad and I boarded a train that morning for Calais. We reached there at one o'clock in the afternoon and spent the rest of the day in a hotel. From the hotel we made the boat safely that evening and got into Dover at midnight. So far, everything ran without a hitch. We stayed at a hostel in Dover till morning.

"No use to bore you telling you of our crawling progress across England. Only three hundred miles, but we spent four days covering it. Of course, we were just a gentleman and his son traveling for pleasure.

"But things began to liven up for us. We had hoped by this time that we were not being looked for after all, but apparently we were wrong. As we got off the train in the station at Liverpool, on the evening of July 5th, the lad, little lynx that he is, spots a man in a brown suit carelessly watching all the passengers. He nudges me quickly.

"Now comes luck itself. A crazy emigrant, farther down the platform, pulls out a gun and commences shooting through the roof. Hell and confusion break loose. During the the big rush of people that takes place, the lad notices a little door leading out to a side street. 'Quick, Daddy,' he says, 'we'll slip out this way.'

"Outside, he flags a cabby in a jiffy and we drive to a little dirty hotel on a side street, where we spend the night, wondering whether the man in the brown suit was looking for us or for someone else.

"However, we're on our guard now. We don't feel quite so easy. Next morning we make the pier and board the Princess Dorothy, which boat, I may add, is one of the few that do not touch at Queenstown or any other point but New York, once she leaves Liverpool. Yes, friend T. B., every detail was figured out long in advance by De Lancey himself.

"As soon as we get aboard, I lie down in the stateroom and let the lad remain on deck. I'm not a well man, friend T. B., and traveling under the conditions and handicaps that we traveled under is hard on me. The following is the boy's account.

"As he says: No sooner had the ship pulled out from the docks and was headed about for the open water, than a motor car comes rushing pell-mell up to the landing. Out jump four men—and one of 'em is our friend in the brown suit. The lad whips out the binoculars and watches their lips. 'Damn—too late—wireless—' is what our brown-suited near-acquaintance appears to say.

"Well, in spite of the fact that we're equipped with wireless, nothing happens to us on the boat. But at no time do I forget the existence of the Atlantic Cable. All the way across I take my meals in the stateroom and the lad prowls around deck trying to pick up some information. But, as I said before, everything's as peaceful as the grave.

"It's a mighty long nine days for us, friend T. B., but late in the afternoon of the fifteenth, we find we're within one hour of the Battery—and we realize now that things are very doubtful for us.

"As we step from the gangplank together, each of us suddenly finds a hand on our shoulder. In front of us stand three men, two of 'em fly-bulls with stars, the third a customs inspector. 'You're Von Berghem,' says one of 'em. 'Want you both to step in this little house at the end of the pier for a couple o' hours. When we get done there won't be any need of a customs inspection, for the inspector himself here is going to help us out.' He laughed unpleasantly. 'Yep—we got a warrant,' adds the other in answer to my unspoken question.

"Well, my friend, I, Von Berghem, know my limitations. I didn't take the trouble to deny anything. Smilingly, I admitted that I was Von Berghem and that this was my son. Then I asked them what they intended to do. 'Just want to look you and your boy and your two suitcases over,' admits one of them.

"In that little inspection house they locked the door. They drew down the shades and turned on the lights. They commanded us both to strip. When we had done this, they made us stand stark naked up against the wall. They began by examining our mouths, taking good care to look under our tongues. Then they combed out our hair with a fine-tooth comb. After a full fifteen minutes, in which they satisfied themselves that the jewels were not concealed on our bodies, they started on our luggage. 'This is an outrage,' I grumbled.

"They dumped out the clothing in our suitcases and placed it in one pile, together with that which we had been forced to discard. Then they commenced with our underclothing, which they examined seam by seam, button by button, square inch by square inch. Following that, our garters, our socks, our suspenders, were subjected to the same rigid examination.

"As fast as they finished with an article of clothing, they tossed it over to us and allowed whichever one of us was the owner to don it. In that way, we dressed, garment by garment, always protesting stoutly at the outrage.

"In the same manner they went through our neckties, most of which they ripped open; our shirts, collars and vests followed next.

"When they came to our outer suits, not content with an exacting scrutiny, they brought out hammers and hammered every inch. Our shoes—look for yourself, friend T. B.—are without heels; they tore them off, layer by layer. Our felt hats underwent similar treatment, for they removed the linings, replacing them later, loose.

"Our suitcases were examined at buckle and seam, rivet and strap. At every place of concealment they pounded vigourously with their hammers, using enough force to smash steel balls, let alone brittle diamonds.

"Friend T. B., we were in there three and a half hours, and had we had trunks, we might have been there yet. They left nothing unturned. Everything, though, has to come to an end. In disgust, they finally threw away their hammers. 'That lead from Liverpool's a phoney one,' said one of the three to the two others. 'You're free, Von Berghem and son,' his companion added. 'It's a cinch you've not got the proceeds of the Simon Company's burglary at Paris. You and your boy can go.'

"This was about two hours ago. We have had no supper, for we took a taxicab and, with the exception of a couple of breakdowns on the way, came straight here in order to tell you of the situation in which we found ourselves."

I was very bitterly disappointed. And I told Von Berghem so.

"It's a shame," I said. "De Lancey stakes his liberty on a bit of dangerous and clever work—and then sends a bungler across with the proceeds. Of course, man, they've got 'em by this time. It doesn't matter where in the stateroom you hid 'em—the wood-work, the carpet, the mattress—they've found 'em now. Well— we'll have to put it down as a failure—that's all."

He heard me through before he uttered a word. Then, dropping his glasses in his coat pocket, he answered me sharply.

"Failure? Who has said anything of failure? You do me a great injustice, friend T. B. Are your pigeons in readiness? All right. Von Berghem never fails. Look!"

He pressed his hands to his face. For a moment I thought he was going to weep, for he made strange clawing motions with his fingers. Then lowered his hands.

I sprang to my feet, suppressing a cry with difficulty. Where his eyes had been were now black, sightless sockets. On each of his palms lay a fragile, painted, porcelain shell—and in the hollow of each shell was a tiny cotton packet, tied with silk thread.

THE GODDESS IN THE CAMERA

T HE BOOKS DEVOTED to the technique of the Short-Story all state that the modern reader has become so astute that he almost invariably scents the denouement of a tale before he reaches it, thus minimizing or nullifying the effect of the "punch."

Of which declaration having delivered ourselves, we, the author, realizing the deploredness (yea, there is such a word) of the situation, desire nevertheless to set forth the narrative concerning Jimmie Calthrope; his friend, "Bill" Morgan of the Central detective bureau; Daphne, the dazzling damsel of Benziger's bathing beach; and The Young Man With The Tan Shoes.

A connoisseur of feminine beauty was Jimmie Calthrope, furniture salesman for one of the most prominent nest featherers on West Madison Street. In his bachelor suite on the North Side, in the city of rustle and bustle, yells and smells—

Chicago, did you say? You've guessed it the first time, gentle reader. But, seriously now, the exercise of this astuteness must cease at once. We strenuously object to being anticipated. Again we commence.

In his two-room suite on the North Side he had hundreds upon hundreds of pretty girls. (No, he was not Bluebeard the II. These were photographs.)

Dark girls and strawberry blondes, fat girls and elongated ones, smiling girls and serious ones, all gazed down from their positions of vantage on the walls.

But by no means is it to be inferred that Jimmie Calthrope was a trifler. Nothing like that at all. He was an amateur photographer.

And his specialty, as before mentioned, was collecting specimens of feminine pulchritude.

Some of these photographs he had taken himself—and knew the originals well. Others were copies that had been entered in the contest by enthusiastic friends. Still others he had purchased in stores, where pictures of prizefighters, actresses and famous murderers were always on sale.

And he even subscribed to a matrimonial paper, by means of which he secured many of his choicest specimens.

But in spite of his many years of ardent collectorship, he had not yet secured the picture of the perfect girl—the picture that was to be a great sun to which the many others should seem as mere asteroids. Although he remained constantly on the alert, the p. g. did persist in eluding him. Hopefully, though, he had reserved a large, empty space above his reading table for the enlargement of this face whenever he should be fortunate enough to run across it.

The scene shifters will now prepare the scene at Benziger's bathing beach. Jimmie is shown at Upper C. lounging on the sands, watching the rhythmical ripples of Lake Michigan, shown at R. C. and L. Rear.

Not far from R. I. E. is shown The Young Man With The Tan Shoes, also lounging on the sands—but with his camera lying at his side.

Time: 2 P.M. on a Sunday afternoon in July.

At this point "she" enters the scene at L. U. E. "She" is strolling along the sands in company with a flashily attired gentleman, twirling her parasol. (Maledictions on the Phoenicians and Egyptians for perfecting written language. Of course, she, not the gentleman, is twirling the parasol. Should we endeavor to be any more explicit, we fear that we might give the impression that she's twirling the gentleman.)

Jimmie turns his head and catches sight of her features.

Ah! Countenance of countenances! The perfect face at last! Magnificent violet eyes, with long, dark eyelashes sweeping her cheeks. (See paper edition of the Flora Series, No. 142,139—Page 6.) Hair of hue like the five-dollar discs struck off by the mint at Philadelphia. Cheeks that openly dare the proof of a moistened forefinger drawn across them. Teeth that rival those of the swan— just a minute, please—the circuit must be grounded. Neck that rivals that of the swan in alabaster whiteness. Teeth as straight and even as the line-up of the band at an Italian funeral (going toward cemetery).

They stop.

The gentleman points out toward R. R. We suspect he wants only to display that scintillating polyhedron on his fourth finger. "Do you see," he remarks, "that white sail just disappearing below the horizon, Daphne?"

Daphne! What a fitting name for the perfect face! Suggests sylvan dells, water sprites, nymphs and naiads, doesn't it? Only be sure and pronounce the "n."

Daphne glances languidly at the sail. Then they commence to resume their stroll. She catches sight of The Young Man With The Tan Shoes—also his camera.

"Wontcha take my picture?" she inquires coyly.

Business of inward cursing by Jimmie Calthrope. Five cameras and seven kodaks at home—but not one for the fateful moment!

More inward raging. The editors buy these stories by the word, you know.

The Young Man With The Tan Shoes springs to his feet and makes a Chesterfieldian bow, with the palm of his right hand directly over his left ventricle. "Tickled to death, lady," he answers. Now you know, without being told, that he wears a red necktie and a green hatband. "Just got 'er loaded with a new fillum," he announces.

The flashy gentleman stands apart, amusedly watching the performance.

The Young Man With The Tan Shoes steps off several feet till Daphne occupies just the proper position in the finder for a bust photograph.

"Now, lady," he commands, "just turn your head a trifle, so's to ketch the glint of the sun on your earring. There, that's enough. Now tip your head up just a little—there—that's O.K.—that gets the shadow off your face. Now watch the little blackbird come out o' th' canary box." At this mirth-provoking sally a beatific smile o'erspreads her physiognomy and he snaps the shutter. "Glad to mail you a print, lady," he says, "if you'll give me your name and address."

Evidently this phase of the question had not yet occurred to her. Pondering for a moment, she draws from her purse a jeweled pencil and, after borrowing a scrap of paper torn from the notebook of her escort, she scribbles something thereon and smilingly hands it to The Young Man With the Tan Shoes.

Then she resumes her promenah-ah-ahd.

The thread of mercury in the thermometer stretches itself like the houn' dawg that sleeps in front of the depot at Hannibal, Missouri. More and more people procure bathing suits for fifteen cents and rush madly into the drink that stretches across to Michigan City.

The Young Man With The Tan Shoes—also our disgruntled hero—decides to help raise the level of the lake.

The Young Man With The Tan Shoes repairs to a checking-booth at the rear of the beach, where he checks his camera, receiving a pasteboard square, reading in pencil:

```
GUS, THE CHECKMAN
NO. 270
FIVE CENTS REQUIRED
ON RETURN OF
ARTICLE CHECKED
```

Fourteen seconds later Jimmie hands over the counter his brand new three-dollar cane and receives a pasteboard square bearing the penciled words:

```
GUS, THE CHECKMAN
NO. 271
FIVE CENTS REQUIRED
ON RETURN OF
ARTICLE CHECKED
```

Exit from the scene The Young Man With The Tan Shoes.
Enter—impinging directly on Jimmie's cerebrum—an idea.
To-wit:
With the aid of a pencil, the "271" on his check can be altered to "270" by describing a suitable curve from the top of the "1" to the bottom.
However, we're sure you grasp.

*   *   *   *   *

Above device representing the passage of time, in this case, one-half hour.
Up to the checking booth steps Jimmie Calthrope, inwardly quaking lest the perspiring Gus hold too good a remembrance of his patrons' faces. He flings a check on the counter bearing the number—well, by George—he actually had the nerve to do it—as sure as we live—number 270.

"My camera," he succinctly states. He conceals his nervousness by laying down two nickels instead of one.

But Gus is no student of the portrait-parlé system. He is a paranoiac to a certain extent, for his mind revolves continually about one fixed idea, namely: "Lager beer: how much will I be able to drink tonight?"

Farewell, brand-new three-dollar cane.

Our hero walks off with the camera instead.

Some coup. These collectors are something fierce. Say—we once knew a stamp collector that—But that's another tale, as Kipyard Rudling says.

It's by far too pleasant a day to go home. So Jimmie wends his way several blocks southward to Lincoln Park, where he spends the remainder of the afternoon amid smeary infants and Cracker-Jack.

About four-thirty he hears thunder, and apprehensively thrusts out his hand to feel whether any preliminary drops are dropping. But it's a false alarm, so to speak, for a more rigid investigation discloses the fact that the keepers are dealing out the porterhouses in the Zoo nearby.

Time hanging somewhat heavily on his hands, he picks up a newspaper several days old which some previous occupant has left on the bench, and, not having had sufficient leisure during the past week to acquaint himself with the world's happenings, glances over it.

An account of a happening at the State's prison takes a fifty per cent Nelson on his optic nerve.

The account reads:

DIAMOND DUFFY ESCAPES JOLIET.
STATE PENITENTIARY LOSES ANOTHER BOARDER.

Edward T. Duffy, known in police circles as Diamond Duffy, just commencing a second sentence of ten years for the burglary of several necklaces from Mrs. Potted Palm's residence on the Lake Shore Drive, made a successful get-away from the State penitentiary at Joliet last night.

By means of saws, presumably smuggled in by outsiders, he cut through the bars of his cell in the outer house and dropped to the yard. A rope ladder found hanging to the prison wall, together with reports made by surrounding residents of hearing an automobile chugging in the vicinity about midnight, indicates plainly the method of his escape and proves conclusively that he was aided by friends.

No trace of him has been found so far.

Now, after reading it, our hero promptly throws the paper away and forgets about the whole matter until later, when the Fate Sisters Three, in their great perpetual vaudeville act entitled "What Next?" twist together two of their skeins and thus place "Bill" Morgan in the setting.

But of this, more later.

The bar mechanism on our typewriter which bears the asterisk having just suffered a compound dislocation of its second vertebrae, we are compelled to resort to the expedient of turning the clock ahead verbally.

Seven P.M.

The shades of night have fell—er—fallen. Jimmie rises and leaves the field of the afternoon's activities, now strewn with the ghastly corpses of millions of former packages of Cracker-Jack, and returns to that afore-mentioned lonely suite.

There, just turning from the door, stands his old friend "Bill" Morgan, one of the low-candlepower lights of the Central Detective Bureau.

"Just dropped in on you because I happened to be in the neighborhood," states Mr. Morgan.

"Come right in, 'Bill,' old horse," says Jimmie. "I'm going to do a little developing in the darkroom and then make a gas-light print for an enlargement. You can sit and tell me all the news."

So they retire to Jimmie's improvised darkroom, where Sleuth Morgan, lighting a big black cigar as a counter-irritant to the pungent chemical odors, explains how he happens to be near Jimmie's domicile.

"S'pose you read in the paper about Diamond Duffy making his get-away last Tuesday night from the Joliet pen," queries Morgan. "I was down in your neighborhood tonight, following up a little lead—but it turned out to be a false one. Chief, up at headquarters, is raising Cain because nothing's been accomplished so far."

"Funny thing," he continues, as Jimmie ransacks a cupboard, looking for soap and towel, "about myself and Diamond Duffy. Went through the same boys' high school together, down in McHenry. Why, I know the skate like I know my own brother—used to juggle sines and cosines together in Trig—but, believe me,

Jimmie, I've got no love for him. He was a sarcastic devil, and bullied every one he could.

"But, say—he used to make the dandiest girl at the annual class play. Made up pretty as a picture; never had more than the slightest down on his face. Why, he was such an artist that he even had his ears pierced once and bought a pair of quaint gold earrings shaped like little beetles; used to wear 'em on all these occasions."

"And, Jimmie," continues Bill, after a pause, "I'm as certain as anything that that nervy crook is back in Chicago among his pals of the underworld, enjoying his freedom, laughing at the police— and dressed as a girl!

"But the worst part of it's this—if he is—then the rogues' gallery pictures ain't worth a tinker's dam. All we can watch out for now is a pair of gold, beetle-shaped earrings—which tip the boys have, of course, received from yours truly. But rats! We'll never get him on that clue. What we need is a photo of him dressed as a girl—earrings and all." And Sherlock Holmes Morgan falls to chewing savagely on the end of his cigar.

Now, esteemed reader, we fear that we've bungled our tale. We glimpsed that look of enlightenment that just flashed over your face. Personally, we think it's a darn shame that we can't tell a story without the reader beating us to our climax.

But, nevertheless, we'll not quit in the sulks after hammering out one thousand nine hundred and eighty eight words.

Of course, Jimmie turns out the gas and lights the ruby lamp.

And, of course, he fills a glass tray with water and dumps into it a developing powder, which he stirs well with a glass rod.

And, of course, he places the printing frame in a convenient spot and turns on the small battery fan in order to have a good drying breeze.

And he snaps open the catch on the hinged back of the camera, with the result that he finds neatly packed therein: Three ham sandwiches, two hard-boiled eggs, one piece of layer cake and fifteen diminutive sweet pickles.

Voila tout.

VICTIM NUMBER 5

Eddie the Strangler was broke again. It seemed as tho nothing could be done to relieve this condition of impecuniosity—except, of course—another "job" like the previous ones. After all—why work for a living? It was so easy for one to come silently thru the window, approach the bed in stocking-feet, and then quickly fasten one's long steel-like fingers about the neck of the sleeper. To be sure, it required steady nerve—particularly during the short struggle that always ensued in the darkness—but there was little chance for one to fail if one took sufficient pains to get one's thumb in the proper position on the windpipe. Then, too, although becoming less so each succeeding time, it was still rather unpleasant to have to view the purplish-black face of the dead person after the "job" was completed, the tiny pocket light turned on, and the search for the valuables begun. However, one had to endure these little trials for the sake of the recompense, since always—if one did not take it upon oneself to endure them—loomed up the dread possibility of having to earn one's bread by manual labor.

Thus reflected Eddie the Strangler as he leaned against a convenient lamppost with his hands sunk deep in his pockets and his hat pulled down over his forehead, waiting expectantly.

Apprehensively his eyes glanced toward the clock, visible thru the glass panel of the corner near-beer saloon door. Eleven P. M.! She certainly ought to be along soon. It was here that he had first seen her, a number of evenings before, as she strode briskly home from some place or other.

Finally she passed. Again Eddie looked her over critically. Not only the diamond hanging from each ear lobe, but the rings on her hands as well, showed conclusively that she must possess other jewelry of value. Well—it might as well be tonight as any other time. No use of following her night after night.

A half block behind her Eddie fell in step. This would be the last time that he need trail her to the place where she lived. His previous shadowing had shown him that she invariably proceeded to a rear room on the first floor of a theatrical boarding-house up near Washington Square. By making his way quickly to the alley, after she closed the front door behind her, and watching her windows as she turned on the lights, he had learned that she lived alone.

This pink-and-white girl would be an easy victim. The very first one of those that went before had been a woman. She had died with but a few impotent thrusting motions of he soft white arms. The next three, tho, had been men. They had required more skill, more coolness, especially that huge German ex-bartender out in Englewood. However, one ought not to confine one's attention to the masculine sex alone; one should be more universal in one's calling. This handsome creature would help to even things up.

As she ascended the front steps and shut the door behind her, Eddie shrugged his shoulders and laughed aloud. Long before this time tomorrow the newspapers would be out with their glaring headlines, reading: "The Strangler Works Again" and "Young Woman Found Murdered in Bed. Valuables Missing." And he, Eddie, the cause of the extra editions, would be laboriously figuring out the value of the haul at so much per carat, in his tiny room in that great jungle, Chicago's West Side.

Swiftly he departed for the alley where he secured a position of vantage between two ash cans and watched her while she entered the room, switched on the light, and drew down the shades. Then he waited patiently until he saw the lights suddenly go out, the shades raised and one window opened wide to admit the cool breeze from the lake. That, in itself, was luck. He had liked that phase of the situation from the very first moment, a week before, that he had begun to collect data on the coming affair. It obviated the necessity of bringing along a glass cutter and a cumbersome ball of putty.

An hour passed.

It must be the right time now. Before removing his shoes and climbing up on the fence that separated the two back yards he exercised his fingers vigorously for a few minutes. One's fingers must not be stiff at the crucial moment.

It required but a few seconds to climb from the fence to the sill and to step lightly in thru the open window to the floor of the room. For a very short while he stood motionless, listening to the regular breathing of the sleeper.

Then it was he heard footsteps coming down the hall. Bah! Some fool perhaps about to knock on the door, awaken the girl on the bed and ruin everything.

Well—there was no need for everything to be ruined. With cat-like tread he crossed the floor to the opposite wall.

Good! It was exactly what he had made it out to be in the semi-darkness—a square trunk. He raised the cover and as he did so a tiny block of wood tumbled to the carpet. With his hand he groped within. Excellent! No tray—and empty as well. This would be a safe refuge while the fool outside should either knock or go on about his or her business.

He stepped in with his right foot and followed with his left. Then he sank to his knees and allowed the cover to drop slowly till an opening of only an inch in height remained. He listened.

"Rap-rap-rap," came from the panel of the door. Then a voice exclaimed, "Estelle? May we come in a minute? Have you gone to bed yet?"

No answer.

"She's asleep," continued the voice to some one else. "We'd better not disturb her. It's late."

The footsteps left the region of the door. "Better to wait two or three minutes," thought Eddie, "till everything's quiet again, before tackling the job. These fools might change their minds and come back." He let the heavy lid rest on his shoulders and altered his position a trifle.

"Click!" went the spring fastening on the "trunk" as the upper half of the mechanism came in contact with the lower half and the cover shut.

"Oh—Oh—God!" screamed Mademoiselle Estelle Le Comte, snake charmer at the Hippodrome, next morning as she went to examine her newest python and found him coiled tightly around the neck of a little man whose face was unrecognizable on account of its purplish-black hue, its bulging eyeballs, and its protruding tongue.

A CHECK FOR A THOUSAND

JOHN BURTON THORNE, writer of short stories, read with exceeding care the notice printed in *Chesterton's Magazine*:

Here, then, was a chance for his latest tale, "Hennesy's Luck," as soon as it should be finished. A thousand dollars! Think of it! Perhaps—After all, one never can tell. John Burton Thorne, winner of the one-thousand-dollar prize offered by *Chesterton's Magazine*. It would mean prestige among his friends. It would secure recognition for him in editorial circles. And last, but not least, for one like himself, who had no relatives and who lived in a boarding house, it would bring absolute freedom from financial worries for a year while the Great American Novel should be written.

A thousand dollars! That would no doubt cause more or less competition. To secure such a prize would require a trifle more than the usual good fortune. However—A thousand dollars— Well, it was certainly worth trying for.

> The Editors of *Chesterton's Magazine* are in immediate need of good short stories and for the best one received within September and October will pay $1,000.00. All others accepted will paid for at their usual rates.

John Burton Thorne worked more diligently than usual during the following week. Not merely content with rewriting "Hennesy's Luck," to adapt it to the general style of *Chesterton's Magazine*, he polished it until, in a literary sense, it shone.

A thousand dollars! If through the remotest chance he should be so fortunate as to obtain it, then future stories from his pen would command higher rates from other editors. It meant, too, that all those sneering acquaintances who took such pains to discuss him and his work behind his back would be at last compelled to admit that in adopting such a precarious livelihood as literary work he had merely stepped into his proper element—and, likewise, a success in that element.

Why not stop writing for a while and take a rest? He placed his materials in the bottom drawer of his bureau and proceeded to spend the days sitting in Washington Square, smoking and dreaming of the possibilities that lay in the winning of the thousand-dollar prize.

At night he began to remain awake longer than usual, forming conceptions of what one's feelings must be upon opening an envelope and extracting therefrom a thousand-dollar check. For the first few nights he pictured it as being salmon-colored like the nominal—very nominal—ones he had received in the past. But this was to be a check such as he had never yet received. So he decided, a few nights later, to picture it mentally as being blue. And to this color he adhered from that time on. It was to be blue, and written, of course, on smooth glazed paper.

But, unfortunately, John Burton Thorne, in his capacity of a mere author, could not possibly know, as he dreamed daily, that the editorial desks of *Chesterton's Magazine* were stacked high with unread manuscripts, of which many were of exceptional merit; manuscripts sent in by the so-called "top-notchers" as well as by obscure and amateur writers; manuscripts in such profusion that several extra readers had been engaged to sift the grain from the chaff.

So, being ignorant of all this, John Burton Thorne sat each day in Washington Square, thinking, wondering, anticipating, hoping and holding foremost in his mind the picture of a narrow slip of paper bearing the printed words, "Pay to the order of—" and "One thousand dollars."

Several weeks later, Mr. William Green, more commonly known as Bill Green, a hardworking grocery clerk, passed through Washington Square on his way home from a strenuous day's activity in weighing and wrapping butter, sugar, potatoes, and sundry other staple commodities. Happening to espy some one whom he knew, lolling on one of the benches, he seated himself and opened a conversation.

"Well, Thorne, how's that there writin' game o' yours goin'? Are you takin' in much coin?"

John Burton Thorne turned and gazed straight into the eyes of his interrogator.

"Say, Green, suppose I should tell you one of these days I carried off a one-thousand-dollar prize offered by *Chesterton's Magazine*. Would you call that 'much coin?' "

"Gosh," replied Bill Green, "that there is certainly some prize!"

Four more weeks passed, swiftly for Mr. Bill Green, whose spare moments were occupied in ascertaining the likes and dislikes of captious customers, but slowly for Mr. John Burton Thorne, who sat through the entire day in Washington Square.

He had heard nothing from his manuscript. Of course he could not possibly know that there were still many stacks of unread stories lying on the desks of the engaged readers of *Chesterton's Magazine*.

And it happened that just four weeks after his first conversation with John Burton Thorne, Mr. William Green, more commonly known as Bill Green, the hardworking grocery clerk, again passed through Washington Square on his way home from a strenuous day's activity in weighing and wrapping butter, sugar, potatoes, and sundry other staple commodities. And in the same manner as before he espied some one whom he knew, lolling on one of the benches. So he seated himself and opened a conversation.

"Well, Thorne, how's that there writin' game o' yours goin'? Are you takin' in much coin?" He paused. He surveyed Mr. John Burton Thorne a little more closely. The professional wielder of the pen looked rather tired, worn perhaps. His eyes too appeared somewhat odd. Then Bill Green asked a further question. "By the way, Thorne, did you ever hear anything about that there one-thousand-dollar prize you were a-tellin' me of when we was talkin' last?"

John Burton Thorne turned and gazed straight into the eyes of his interrogator.

"Yes, I did," he replied. "I won it, Green. I'll show you the check—I haven't cashed it yet."

His fingers explored an inner pocket for a few seconds and then brought forth a slip of blue paper, smooth and crisp.

~ ~ ~ ~ ~

"A very deplorable case," said Dr. Abbott of the Kankakee State Hospital for the Insane to his assistant, who had just returned from a vacation. "You can see him sitting down there at the other end of the ward. Thorne's his name. He was a writer. His fixed delusion consists of the belief that he won a thousand-dollar prize for one of his short stories. The usual case of a psychopathic individual with too much thinking upon one subject. Harmless variety of paranoia, of course, but hopeless on account of the secondary delusions which sooner or later set in. The bank turned him over after he tried to cash a blue cigarette coupon. There—look quick—

he's showing it to our new patient—that case of dementia praecox that was just brought in this morning."

~ ~ ~ ~ ~

"Odd thing," said the editor of *Chesterton's Magazine* to his assistant, as the letter addressed to J. B. Thorne returned to the office bearing an official notice stamped at the bottom in red ink: "Not residing any longer at above number. Address unknown. Return to sender."

He slit open the end and tossed the envelope into the wastebasket. Then he made room in one of the pigeon-holes of his desk for a narrow slip of blue paper bearing the numeral "1,000."

PACKAGE 22,227

RARELY HAD CURIOSITY been so intense in the main office of the International Express Company as it was after the fact had been definitely established that Package 22,227 was acting in a most mysterious manner—a manner totally unlike that of the twenty-two thousand two hundred and twenty-six packages that had preceded it in the month of July.

Doubtless, you will ask what an inanimate thing such as Package 22,227 was doing that could create such an interest among the employees.

Well, I dare say, now that the old International Express Company is defunct—forced to the wall by the advent of the government's parcel post—and, I am, therefore, no longer in charge of the main office, which has long since ceased to exist, I may with impunity relate the facts of that puzzling affair.

Thompson, the head clerk, was the first to discover it. On the morning of July 19th he stepped over to my desk, scratching his head and looking somewhat perplexed.

"Mr. Bennett," he said, addressing me, "there's something here that's shown on the incoming express sheets from the depot as weighing two pounds. I just put it on the scales and it stands a little over three. Probably an error at the depot, don't you think?"

"Very likely," I replied, going over to Thompson's desk and glancing at the "package"—for such is the term we were accustomed to apply to every separate item of express.

It was an odd looking thing. It was not even wrapped. It consisted of a small wooden box, painted blue, about a foot long and possibly five inches in both width and depth. On each end was screwed a metal handle such as one finds at times attached to heavy boxes of freight. Across the top was pasted a written label bearing the inscription:

To:—Mr. John Chester Carlyle,   From:—Peter Clucas,
12 W. Elm Str.,   776 Olive Str.,
Chicago, Ill.   St. Louis, Mo.
VALUE:—$1.50.

Across the bottom of the label was chalked, in black crayon, the month and serial number which was assigned to every item that entered the Chicago depot—in this case, "22,227 (July)." The most peculiar thing about it, however, was the fact that the box did not lock with a key, but bore a small combination dial on the front of it.

Assuming that an error had been made, Thompson and I dismissed the matter from our minds until next day, when before letting it go out on the North Side delivery wagon, he threw it upon the scales again. Then he called me over. It now registered five and a half pounds.

So it was hardly surprising, considering our bewilderment, that we suggested to Bill Jenkins, driver of the North Side wagon, that he casually inquire of Mr. John Chester Carlyle as to the contents of the box.

At noontime the drivers returned with their wagons to the barns near the main office. Shortly after, Bill Jerkins came stamping in, carrying the blue box under his arm.

It seems that he had called at 12 W. Elm Street. The landlady had informed him that a Mr. John A. Carlyle had formerly resided in her house, but had died from heart trouble several months before. He had always stated in his conversations with her that he possessed no living relatives whatever, and this statement, she said, was borne out by the circumstances which followed his death. Absolutely no relatives or friends had come forward either to claim or identify his body, even in response to an advertisement which she had inserted at her own expense for a week in a leading Chicago newspaper. As a result, the county had been compelled to bury him—and that was all she knew. This was the information that Bill Jerkins brought back to us.

By nightfall we were further astounded at finding that the weight of Package 22,227 had risen to six pounds. It had stood on shelf 80 all afternoon. So far as we knew, no one had been near it.

That evening we dispatched an official letter to the sender, Peter Clucas of 776 Olive Street, St. Louis, asking him as to whether we should return the box to him or hold it until further orders.

By the following day the thing weighed nearly seven pounds. Then it was that a bright thought occurred to me. I remembered that when the company leased its downtown quarters, the building had been lighted by a private plant in the basement. The generator, with its strong field magnets, must be situated directly beneath us. Unquestionably, Package 22,227 entailed something that was made of soft iron and was being attracted by the electrical apparatus below us.

I lost no time in apprising Thompson of my brilliant deduction. Down we went to the basement. My explanation immediately ceased to be any explanation at all, for we found that the private lighting plant had been discontinued several weeks before, the machinery moved out, and the lighting circuits connected up with the Commonwealth Edison's central-station system.

Next morning I knew from the self-satisfied look on Thompson's face that he had been putting some hard thinking on the matter and had, himself, arrived at an explanation. Before I had time even to throw back the cover of my roll-top desk he came over.

"I think I see the whole modus operandi o' th' durn thing now," he remarked. "Just as you surmised, Mr. Bennett, it's magnetism—only it's this way instead of your way. Inside of Package 22,227 there must be an electro-magnet, a battery, and a complicated clockwork for gradually allowing an increasing current to flow through it. This building, like all the other big downtown buildings, has steel beams holding up the floor. Consequently, the attraction occurring between the floor and the package makes the weight each day greater than it should be."

"Very good, Thompson," I replied. "Before stepping to the head of the class you might step out with me into that empty lot next door. Bring the scales and I'll bring Package 22,227. Inasmuch as there are no steel beams holding the earth up, there'll be no attraction and the box will resume its original weight of two pounds."

Over we went to the empty lot, while a few pedestrians regarded us quizzically from the sidewalk. But Package 22,227 now registered between nine and ten pounds.

We even purchased a pocket compass from a nearby optical store. We waved it over, and under, and around the box—but the compass needle remained absolutely undisturbed. Thus did our latest hypothesis die a natural death.

That night we wrapped the blue box, tied it, and sealed the junctions of the cord. We didn't propose to be the victims any longer of some practical joker in the office who evidently knew the combination and was surreptitiously adding lumps of lead to the contents.

Next day, the package stood in its usual place on shelf 80; its wrappings were obviously untouched, its seals intact, but its weight—an even fifteen pounds! It had increased as much during that night as it had in the three days preceding.

By noontime I felt instinctively that we were about due for another scintillating idea from Thompson. And I was correct.

"It's got some deliquescent powder in it," he stated. "Something that absorbs moisture from the air."

"Very clever," I retorted sarcastically, for the thing was beginning to get on my nerves. "The original contents of about one pound, since the box and handles have an appreciable weight, absorb fourteen times their own weight of moisture." I laughed and seized a pencil and pad. For a short space of time I figured. Then I showed Thompson my results. My computations showed that if the box, which was 12x5x5 inches in volume, was full of actual water at the recognized density of four one-hundredths of a pound per cubic inch, its weight even then would be less than we had actually found it to be.

Nevertheless, to satisfy Thompson, I placed it in the window, where the fierce rays of the July sun baked it all afternoon. If there was any moisture inside of Package 22,227 at the beginning of that solar session, it's a certainty that it was considerably reduced by evening, for the sun actually blistered the paint. By evening, though, it had merely taken on another two pounds.

There had never been anything in Thompson's demeanor or conduct around the office that would lead me to believe that he could be the perpetrator of a hoax. Notwithstanding, I decided to eliminate that remaining possibility. So that evening I broke a rule of the company. I took Package 22,227 home with me.

After supper, being a widower and living in a boarding house, I retired to the privacy of my own room. But before doing so I procured from the cook a spring fish-scale, a broom, and a handful of stout twine. The broom I placed across the backs of two straight chairs and suspended the fish scales in the middle of it. By means of a twine sling I attached the box to the hook of the scales. Then I sat down in a rocking chair and proceeded to watch it so that I might discover whether any change should take place by midnight.

When I commenced my vigil at eight o'clock the pointer on the scales stood at "17 lbs." on the brass index. By ten o'clock I was so sleepy that I daresay I couldn't have read the face of a clock. At midnight, when I awoke with a sudden start and found that I'd fallen asleep somewhat earlier, I peered carefully at the index. The pointer had now traveled slightly beyond the mark, "18 lbs." And my door was still locked—with the key on the inside.

Bewildered and angry, I went to bed.

Why go into further details regarding the daily upward progress of its weight? Suffice to say that whether placed on spring or beam scales the results obtained invariably checked each other. The most acute ear in the office failed to detect any ticking or other sound whatever coming from it. When it was shaken nothing rattled but the handles. And everyone, from myself to Maisie, the stenographer, and Red, the errand boy, found ourselves unable to think of anything but Package 22,227.

Anxiously we awaited an answer from Mr. Peter Clucas of 776 Olive Street, St. Louis, in the hope that he would drop some hint in his reply that would clear the mystery up.

Finally, late one afternoon, the letter we had sent came back, reaching us, in fact, on the day that Package 22,227's weight approached close to forty pounds. From the appearance of the envelope, the letter had evidently been traveling all around St. Louis and its environs. Written or stamped in red ink across the face of it in various places were the following notices:

No such number on Olive Str. (Vacant lot.) Addressee not known in neighborhood. Name not appearing in St. Louis Directory. Try East St. Louis, Ill. No such address at East St. Louis, Ill.

Upon the return of our letter a great whoop of joy went up from the force. Why? Well, simply because among the different stipulations printed on the back of all our express receipts was one which specifically stated that:

Sec. 5.—In the event of any error in addressing, loss of shipment tag, or similar event the office holding a package, parcel, box or crate, may at its own discretion open same to get information, even though the wrappings or contents shall thereby be damaged.

A great load was taken off our minds, for we knew now that there was no chance for "Mr. Peter Clucas of 776 Olive Street, St. Louis"—obviously a fictitious name and address given by the sender—to demand the return of his box. We now had a perfect right to open it and examine whatever should be within.

Fascinated, everybody stood around while Thompson brought a saw. As I rolled up my sleeve preparatory to sawing off the end of the blue box I happened to glance at the clock. Twenty minutes past five! Going-home time already arrived. Since, on account of our wretched traction system, it was impossible to secure a seat either on an elevated or a surface car after five-thirty, there was nothing to do but replace the blue box on shelf 80 and postpone the opening until morning.

Usually I was the first to leave the office. Thompson was invariably the last, as the duty of turning out the larger lights devolved upon him. This night, however, I remained a few minutes to remind him to call up the American Safe and Lock Company the first thing in the morning and ascertain how soon our new vault was to be installed. An epidemic of safe-robberies had broken out in the last few weeks through the efforts of a group of crooks spoken of in the newspapers as "the auto-car gang." So we had deposited the six thousand dollars, constituting next day's pay-roll for all the employees of the company, in the bank over night instead of following our usual custom and leaving it in the safe.

When we opened up in the morning we found reason to congratulate ourselves on our foresightedness of yesterday. The "auto-car gang" had unwittingly played a joke upon themselves, for they had called in the night by way of the alley, had bound the watchman hand and foot, and, in the belief that they were getting away with next day's pay-roll, had by means of a block-and-tackle lugged off our old empty safe in their automobile.

But it was not entirely empty, though. That confounded Thompson, at the last moment before leaving, had taken a sudden notion and had locked Package 22,227 in the safe.

SOAPY'S TRIP TO MARS

SOAPY'S TRIP TO MARS.
A short photoplay burlesque on the modern
"South-sea-adventure" tale.
By
JOHN JONES.

I—SYNOPSIS.

Soapy, a tramp, carelessly selects the top of a freight car bearing the sign, "GIANT POWDER, USE CARE IN SWITCHING," on which to nap. After a short nap he lights a cigarette and absentmindedly flings over his shoulder the burning match, which drops through a chink in the car roof.

On account of the terrific explosion, Soapy is hurled through inter-planetary space and lands upon a street on Mars. He is instantly captured by a small band of black, grotesque people and carried to the palace of King Marto the XXXXII, who, upon learning the circumstances, decrees that Soapy, as an undesirable, shall be boiled in oil. At this juncture, the princess La-La, a horrible looking creature, falls in love with Soapy and demands him for a husband. Soapy is, therefore, made prime minister of Mars.

On the wedding day the King becomes interested in a flask which Soapy carries. As a result of drinking the contents he falls into a drunken stupor. Soapy steals the keys to the palace arsenal, gets access to that room, and, just after the Martians discover the sleeping King and the theft of the keys, lights a match and blows himself earthward.

The Martians shoot arrows at him as he flies away from their planet, and, as he twists and squirms, he suddenly awakes and finds a group of brakemen pelting him with lumps of coal.

2—CHARACTERS.

SOAPY . . . . A Tramp
MARTO XXXXII . . . . King of Mars

PRINCESS LA-LA . . . The King's Daughter
Martians and Brakemen.

3—SCENES.

4—SCENARIO

1—Leader:

SOAPY SEARCHES FOR A PLACE TO SLEEP.

Scene: A railroad yards. Various boxcars are seen standing on spur tracks. One in particular has painted upon it, "GIANT POW-DER, USE CARE IN SWITCHING." Soapy, a dilapidated tramp, ragged, unshorn, and carrying the inevitable tomato can, appears. He yawns and gazes around from car to car. This one seems to appeal to him, so he slowly climbs the ladder bolted to the side of it.

2—Scene: Top of boxcar. Soapy yawns again and lies down to take a nap. Presently he sits up and fumbles in his pockets for to-bacco, matches, and papers. Upon finding these materials he rolls a cigarette and lights it. Carelessly, he tosses the match over his shoulder. A look of horror then comes over his face. He turns to see where the match has fallen.

3—Scene: Close-up and enlarged view showing match poised on the edge of a chink in the roof of boxcar and still burning.

4—Scene: Explosion, represented by a flash of red.

5—Leader:

SOAPY LANDS ON THE PLANET MARS.

Scene: A spot or street on the planet Mars. Odd-looking, black men with long noses and white rings around their eyes are passing to and fro. Something (a dummy) suddenly drops from the skies. It picks itself up and brushes off its clothes, proving itself to be Soapy, still smoking his cigarette. Dumbly he stares about him. The Martians surround him and take him prisoner. A wooden chariot drawn by two of their number is brought up and Soapy is bundled into it. Accompanying the chariot they all hurry off.

6—Leader:

SOAPY IS CARRIED BEFORE KING MARTO THE XXXXII.

Scene: The courtroom of King Marto the XXXXII. The King, wearing a crown, is seen sitting on a throne in a large bare room (with preferably a few columns visible). The crowd of Martians enter with their chariot bearing their prisoner. They lift him off and remove the chariot. The King steps down off his throne and examines Soapy more closely. He then ascends the throne and raises his hand. In answer to the command a Martian brings forth a quill and a scroll of parchment. The King writes a few words on it.
Cut-in leader:

"EARTHMAN, YOU ARE AN UNDESIRABLE. I SEN-TENCE YOU TO BE BOILED IN OIL."

Cut-back to scene.
Soapy at once throws up his arms and appears to collapse. A tall angular female Martian, black in face, long nosed and bearing the usual white rings painted around her eyes, enters the court-room. Upon seeing Soapy, her face breaks into a grin. She wrings

her hands with delight, showing she is greatly enamored of the captive.

Cut-in leader:

PRINCESS LA-LA: "FATHER, I LOVE THIS EARTHMAN. HE SHALL BE MY HUSBAND."

Cutback to scene.
Soapy is instantly released and the grotesque Princess La-La throws her arms about him. The Martians all applaud.

7—Flash up on screen a close-up and enlarged picture of the Princess La-La.

8—Leader:

SOAPY, PRIME MINISTER OF MARS, FINDS THE DAY HAS ARRIVED FOR HIS MARRIAGE TO THE PRINCESS LA-LA.

Scene: Courtroom of Marto XXXXII as before. Soapy is seen sitting at a small table covered with writing materials, situated at the side of the throne. Only he and the King are present in the scene. Soapy draws from his pocket a flask, at the contents of which he gazes wistfully. The King becomes interested at once and steps down from his throne. Taking the flask from Soapy he sniffs at the contents. He tastes it. Then he drinks it down.

9—Flash up on screen a close-up and enlarged picture of the King, showing pleased expression on face.

10—Cut back to courtroom scene.
The King ascends his throne, yawns, and drops off to sleep. Soapy peers cautiously around, ascends the throne, and removes a large bunch of keys that hang from the King's belt. Then he steals from the room.

11—Scene: Corridor leading to the palace arsenal. (Columns should be visible if possible.) Soapy is seen making his way on tiptoe along the corridor. Reaching a door at the end, he inserts his key and enters, closing the door behind him.

12—Scene: The palace arsenal. This is a dusty, cobweb cov-ered room containing two clumsy-looking mortars and eight or ten kegs which contain explosive material. Soapy hastily stacks the kegs in a pyramid, first, however, removing the head of one of them.

13—Cut-back to courtroom.
The Martians, together with the Princess La-La, dressed in a bridal veil, are seen arriving in the empty courtroom and, discover-ing the King asleep, they immediately search for his keys and find them missing.
Cut-in leader:

"THE MAN FROM EARTH HAS STOLEN THE KEYS TO THE ARSENAL."

Cut-back to courtroom scene.
The Martians are discovered making a rush for the corridor.

14—Cut-back to arsenal and show Soapy peering through the keyhole of the door.

15—Scene: Keyhole view of the corridor leading to the arsenal showing the Martians running toward the door.

16—Cut-back to arsenal showing Soapy mounting to the top of the pyramid of kegs.
Cut-in leader:

"I'M USED TO THESE EXPLOSIONS NOW."

Cut-back to arsenal scene.
Soapy is seen lighting a match and watching the door. Just as the door tumbles in, he drops the lighted splinter of wood into the opened keg.

17—Scene: Explosion, represented by a flash of red.

18—Scene: The palace yard. The Martians are pointing at some object in the sky and are busy shooting arrows upward.

19—Scene: Inter-planetary space. (In which Soapy is surrounded by painted moons and stars.) He wriggles, twists, and turns, being struck at intervals by arrows coming from the angry citizens on Mars.

The view slowly dissolves into a —

20—Cut-back to boxcar top. Soapy is seen gradually awakening while pelted with lumps of coal, thrown by a group of laughing brakemen on the ground below.

QUICK CUT OFF

THE RUBE

PERHAPS THE Rube's years numbered twenty-four. His face was innocent and child-like. His hair was the color of the autumn wheat. His neck was sunburned to a bright cherry hue. His hands were big and clumsy—and calloused. His suit was new and tight at the legs.

So much for the external appearance of the Rube. Neither you nor I would have had any difficulty in picking him out for what he was. We might not have guessed, however, that in his right hand coat pocket reposed a roll of bills constituting the sum of two hundred and sixty-five dollars, the savings from twelve months of plowing, raking, hoeing, cultivating, milking, woodchopping, currying, harnessing, potato-bug spraying, hay tossing, shock turning—and what not else.

And neither could we have known that in his vest pocket, underneath that tightly buttoned, brand new coat, was the massive gold watch with the diamond-studded Masonic charm, left him by his Uncle Ezra—which article, it was rumored in the Rube's family, had set Uncle Ezra back two hundred dollars.

With open mouth the Rube stared at the gilded entrances of the hoochy-koochy shows, the palaces of "living art models," the medical waxwork museums "for men only," and the three-for-a-quarter-finished-while-you-wait photo postal galleries that lined Chicago's great cosmopolitan strand, South State Street, from the Polk Street depot to the Elevated Road.

As he passed a doorway, lighted only by a flickering gas jet, he noticed a young girl with very dark eyelashes and very pink cheeks. Down at Elmo Junction, Illinois, where the Rube came from, all pink cheeks were the gift of Nature. Let us assume these were. Anyway, they have frosted globes on the cluster lights of State Street now.

" 'Lo kid," she exclaimed.

In amazement, the Rube stopped in his tracks. Here he, a stranger in Chicago, a mere nobody in a great whirling pandemonium of humanity, had been singled out for a cheerful greeting by a pretty girl with dark eyelashes and pink cheeks.

"H'llo," he replied, in the absence of any definite ideas of conversation.

"Where you going?" she inquired boldly.

"Jest walkin' along."

"It's an awful hot night. Let's you and I go and have a drink."

"Sure." The Rube suddenly thought how good a glass of cold soda-pop would taste.

Together they proceeded, under the leadership of the girl, through a side door on Van Buren Street, under the shadow of the elevated structure. Once inside, the girl led the way to a tiny private room with two doorways. There they seated themselves at a sticky table.

"What'r you going to drink, kid?" she asked, scrutinizing him cautiously

"Oh, ginger ale 'r sody-pop, I guess."

"Aw, kid," she urged, "you're in Chicago now. Didn't'cha ever taste a cocktail?"

The Rube fumbled in his right-hand coat pocket. Presently his hand emerged, his fingers holding a bill, a two-dollar bill, which he flung on the table with a devil-may-care air. While she pressed a button imbedded in the wall, she surveyed the Rube carefully.

"I've hearn tell o' them there things—them cocktails," said the Rube. "I allus wanted t' taste one. I'm a hell of a feller, girlie; I don't stop at nothin'. I come here t' see Chicago an' I'm going t' see th' hull blame works. I knowed you jest natchelly liked me 'r you wouldn't hev spoke t' me—me bein' a stranger t' you. Say, girlie, will you go to a nickel show with me w'en we go out o' here? 'S all on me."

"That'll be splendid," she said nervously, yet not forgetting to lean over and pat the back of his hand, lovingly, in accordance with the role that had been thrust upon her by this naive individual from the country. "That's just the idea—we'll take in a nickel show together, when we leave here."

The Rube caught site of one of the two doors which opened on the private room. A sign above read, in crudely daubed letters: "WASH ROOM." He stood up suddenly, gazing shamefacedly at his soiled hands.

"Say, girlie, I'm goin' t' wash up—ain't been offen th' train over f'teen minutes. You get two o' them there cocktails an' you see 'at th' waiter gives you th' right change from that there two dollar bill. I kin trust you, girlie. Don't let 'im give you any lead nickels. Jest ring 'em on the table."

"Go ahead, kid, and wash. I won't let him put anything over on me. And 'member, we're going to that nickel show shortly."

"You bet," he echoed jubilantly, as he disappeared through the small swinging door.

The waiter, carrying a limp and soiled towel hanging from the crook in his elbow, entered the room.

" 'Lo, Nell," he said in a low voice. "How's biz?"

"Punk. Bring two manhattans, one for me and one for the gentleman in the washroom. And rush 'em, will you, Jack?" Covertly, she glanced toward the washroom while he disappeared.

In less than a minute the waiter reappeared, conveying a badly scratched and battered japan tray on which stood glasses, each containing a pinkish liquid with an anemic cherry wobbling from side to side in the bottom. After placing them on the table with geometrical precision, he counted out one dollar and seventy-five cents, which he piled in a little heap at the side of one of the glasses. Then he quietly withdrew.

The girl again glanced quickly in the direction of the washroom. The clatter of a roller towel was plainly audible. With celerity she reached down into her stocking and withdrew a slim phial, which she uncorked and held over the glass that stood opposite to her own. One drop, two drops, three drops, four drops. She paused, considering. Then the fifth drop. Hastily, she corked the phial and re-inserted it in her stocking. Then she commenced to powder her nose.

Fifteen seconds later, the Rube appeared. His face shone from the liberal application of soap. His hair was neatly parted in the middle and plastered down with water. He seemed like a living replica of the wax dummy that stands in the show window of Weinstein's clothing store across from the Polk Street depot.

When he had seated himself, the girl raised her glass. "Here's looking at a good-looking boy," she said.

The Rube was a bear at scintillating repartee. For the half of a minute he pondered; then he evolved a brilliant retort.

"An' here's lookin' at a good-lookin' girl," he replied.

"You know," he continued, after he drained his glass, through the expedient of tilting it almost upside down, and had smacked his lips several times, "travelin' cert'nly tires a feller out. W'y girlie—would you b'lieve it—I come all th' way from Elmo Junction, Illinois—I've rid a hunnerd an' twenty-fi' mile this afternoon!"

"Go on," she replied in mock amazement. "You don't mean to say so."

"Hones'." He placed his head on his arm, which latter member lay outstretched upon the table. "Gee gosh, I'm tired. I c'd jest go t' sleep an' sleep fer a year." He closed his eyes. "I'm s' tired—so durn tired—'at I—'at I—so tir—" His voice trailed off into incoherence.

Immediately, she rose to her feet and crossed to the opposite side of the table. She shook him gently by the shoulder.

"Hey," she called experimentally.

But he didn't budge.

Whereupon, taking each in quick succession, she went through his outside pockets, with the deft fingers that had become so by previous practice. This accomplished, she unbuttoned his coat and went through his vest pockets.

Then, not forgetting to take with her the $1.75 which still adhered to the table top, she picked up her skirts and fled out to State Street.

Nine o'clock came.

Ten o'clock also.

Then eleven.

The waiter poked his head in the door and studied the snoring Rube.

"Hey guy, wake up," he croaked. "Dis ain't no flop. Dis is a respeccerable booze joint. Wake up. Yer lady fren' beat it t're hours ago."

Stupidly, the Rube opened his eyes. Uncomprehendingly, he looked about him. Bit by bit, the events of the earlier evening began to come back to him.

Let's see—there had been a girl somewhere. Oh, yes—a stunning little girl—such pink cheeks. And let's see—they had gone someplace or other and sat down at a table. The Rube stared at the table top. His head pounded. His face burned. Of course, this must be the table. And then—they were—they were—they were—oh, yes—they were going to go a nickel show; maybe the girl had gone to the nickel show by herself.

He gazed down at himself. His coat was unbuttoned. Likewise his vest. Odd! He dropped his hands into the coat pockets; then he gasped. Empty! What time was it, anyway? Uncle Ezra's watch—eh?—gone?

The Rube's eyes fell on the daubed sign. Memory at once began to be much clearer. He rose with difficulty and staggered into the washroom.

In a dark corner stood an empty scrub pail covered by a dry scrub cloth. He stooped over and tossed the rag to one side. He lowered his hand to the bottom of the pail and, a second later, withdrew it, holding a roll of bills and a massive gold watch and charm.

Then the Rube passed out to State Street.

JOHN JONES'S DOLLAR

O N THE 201ST DAY of the year 3214 A.D., the professor of history at the University of Terra seated himself in front of the Visaphone and prepared to deliver the daily lecture to his class, the members of which resided in different portions of the earth.

The instrument before which he seated himself was very like a great window sash, on account of the fact that there were three or four hundred frosted glass squares visible. In a space at the center, not occupied by any of these glass squares, was a dark oblong area and a ledge holding a piece of chalk. And above the area was a huge brass cylinder toward which the professor directed his subsequent remarks.

In order to assure himself that it was time to press the button which would notify the members of the class in history to approach their local Visaphones, the professor withdrew from his vest pocket a small contrivance which he held to his ear. As he moved a tiny switch attached to the instrument, a metallic voice, seeming to come from somewhere in space, repeated mechanically: "Fifteen o'clock and one minute—fifteen o'clock and one minute—fifteen o'clock and one min—" Quickly, the professor replaced the instrument in his vest pocket and pressed a button at the side of the Visaphone.

As though in answer to the summons, the frosted glass squares began, one by one, to show the faces and shoulders of a peculiar type of young men; young men with great bulging foreheads, bald, toothless, and wearing immense horn spectacles. One square, however, still remained empty. On noticing this, a look of irritation passed over the professor's countenance.

But, upon seeing that every other glass square but this one was filled up, he commenced his talk.

"I am pleased, gentlemen, to see you all posted at your local Visaphones this afternoon. I have prepared my lecture today upon a subject which is, perhaps, of more economic interest than historical. Unlike the previous lectures, my talk will not confine itself to the happenings of a few years, but will gradually embrace the course of ten centuries, the ten centuries, in fact, which terminated three hundred years before the present date. My lecture will be an exposition of the effects of the John Jones Dollar, originally deposited in the dawn of civilization, or to be more precise, in the year 1914—just thirteen hundred years ago. This John Jon—"

At this point in the professor's lecture, the frosted glass square which hitherto had shown no image now filled up. Sternly he gazed at the head and shoulders that had just appeared.

"B262H72476Male, you are late to class again. What excuse have you to offer today?"

From the hollow cylinder emanated a shrill voice, while the lips of the picture on the glass square moved in unison with the words:

"Professor, you will perceive by consulting your class book, that I have recently taken up residence near the North Pole. For some reason, wireless communication between the Central Energy Station and all points north of 89 degrees was cut off a while ago, on account of which fact I could not appear in the Visaphone. Hence—"

"Enough, sir," roared the professor. "Always ready with an excuse, B262H72476Male. I shall immediately investigate your tale."

From his coat pocket the professor drew an instrument which, although supplied with an earpiece and a mouthpiece, had no wires whatever attached. Raising it to his lips, he spoke:

"Hello. Central Energy Station, please." A pause ensued. "Central Energy Station? This is the professor of history at the University of Terra speaking. One of my students informs me that the North Pole region was out of communication with the Visaphone System this morning. Is that statement true? I would—"

A voice, apparently from nowhere, spoke into the professor's ear. "Quite true, Professor. A train of our ether waves accidentally fell into parallelism with a train of waves from the Venus Substation. By the most peculiar mischance, the two trains happened to be displaced, with reference to each other, one half of a wave length, with the unfortunate result that the negative points of one coincided with the positive points of maximum amplitude of the other. Hence the two wave trains nullified each other and communication ceased for one hundred and eighty-five seconds—until the earth had revolved far enough to throw them out of parallelism."

"Ah! Thank you," replied the professor. He dropped his instrument into his coat pocket and gazed in the direction of the glass square whose image had so aroused his ire. "I apologize, B262H72476Male, for my suspicions as to your veracity—but I had in mind several former experiences." He shook a warning forefinger. "I will now resume my talk."

"A moment ago, gentlemen, I mentioned the John Jones Dollar. Some of you who have just enrolled with the class will undoubtedly say to yourselves: 'What is a John Jones? What is a Dollar?'

"In the early days, before the present scientific registration of human beings was instituted by the National Eugenics Society, man went around under a crude multi-reduplicative system of nomenclature. Under this system, there were actually more John Joneses than there are calories in the British Thermal Unit. But there was one John Jones, in particular, living in the twentieth century, to whom I shall refer in my lecture. Not much is known of his personal life except that he was an ardent socialist—a bitter enemy, in fact, of the private ownership of wealth.

"Now as to the Dollar. At this day, when the Psycho-Erg, a combination of the Psych, the unit of esthetic satisfaction, and the Erg, the unit of mechanical energy, is recognized as the true unit of value, it seems difficult to believe that in the twentieth century and for more than ten centuries thereafter, the Dollar, a metallic circular disk, was being passed from hand to hand in exchange for the essentials of life.

"But nevertheless, such was the case. Man exchanged his mental or physical energy for these Dollars. He then re-exchanged the Dollars for sustenance, raiment, pleasure, and operations for the removal of the vermiform appendix.

"A great many individuals, however, deposited their Dollars in a stronghold called a bank. These banks invested the Dollars in loans and commercial enterprises, with the result that, every time the earth traversed the solar ecliptic, the banks compelled each borrower to repay, or to acknowledge as due, the original loan, plus six one-hundredths of that loan. And to the depositor, the banks paid three one-hundredths of the deposited Dollars for the use of the disks. This was known as three per cent, or bank interest.

"Now, the safety of Dollars, when deposited in banks, was not absolutely assured to the depositor. At times the custodians of these Dollars were wont to appropriate them and proceed to portions of the earth sparsely inhabited and accessible with difficulty. And at other times, nomadic groups known as 'yeggmen' visited the banks, opened the vaults by force, and departed, carrying with them the contents.

"But to return to our subject. In the year 1914, one of these numerous John Joneses performed an apparently inconsequential action which caused the name of John Jones to go down in history. What did he do?

"He proceeded to one of these banks, known at that time as 'The First National Bank of Chicago,' and deposited there one of these disks—a silver Dollar—to the credit of a certain individual. And this individual to whose credit the Dollar was deposited was no other person than the fortieth descendant of John Jones, who stipulated in a paper which was placed in the files of the bank that the descendancy was to take place along the oldest child of each of the generations which would constitute his posterity.

"The bank accepted the Dollar under that understanding, together with another condition imposed by this John Jones, namely, that the interest was to be compounded annually. That meant that at the close of each year, the bank was to credit the account of John Jones's fortieth descendant with three one-hundredths of the account as it stood at the beginning of the year.

"History tells us little more concerning this John Jones—only that he died in the year 1924, or ten years afterward, leaving several children.

"Now you gentlemen who are taking mathematics under Professor L127M72421Male, of the University of Mars, will remember that where any number such as X, in passing through a progressive cycle of change, grows at the end of that cycle by a proportion p, then the value of the original X, after n cycles, becomes $X(1 + p)^n$.

"Obviously, in this case, X equaled one Dollar; p equaled three one-hundredths; and n will depend upon any number of years which we care to consider following the date of deposit. By a simple calculation, those of you who are today mentally alert can check up the results that I shall set forth in my lecture.

"At the time that John Jones died, the amount in the First National Bank of Chicago to the credit of John Jones the fortieth was as follows."

The professor seized the chalk and wrote rapidly upon the oblong space:

1924   10 years elapsed $1.34

"The peculiar sinuous hieroglyphic," he explained, "is an ideograph representing the Dollar.

"Well, gentlemen, time went on as time will, until a hundred years had passed by. The First National Bank of Chicago still existed, and the locality, Chicago, had become the largest center of population upon the earth. Through the investments which had taken place, and the yearly compounding of interest, the status of John Jones's deposit was now as follows." He wrote:

2014   100 years elapsed $19.10

"In the following century, many minor changes, of course, took place in man's mode of living; but the so-called socialists still agitated widely for the cessation of private ownership of wealth; the First National Bank still accepted Dollars for safe keeping, and the John Jones Dollar still continued to grow. With about thirty-four generations yet to come, the account now stood:

2114   200 years elapsed $364

"And by the end of the succeeding hundred years, it had grown to what constituted an appreciable bit of exchange value in those days—thus:

2214   300 years $6,920

"Now the century which followed contains an important date. The date I am referring to is the year 2292 A.D., or the year in which every human being born upon the globe was registered under a numerical name at the central bureau of the National Eugenics Society. In our future lessons which will treat with that period in detail, I shall ask you to memorize that date.

"The socialists still agitated, fruitlessly, but the First National Bank of Chicago was now the First National Bank of the Earth. And how great had John Jones's Dollar grown? Let us examine the account, both on that important historical date, and also at the close of the 400th year since it was deposited. Look:

2292   378 years $68,900

2314   400 years $132,000

"But, gentlemen, it had not reached the point where it could be termed an unusually large accumulation of wealth. For larger ac-

cumulations existed upon earth. A descendant of a man once
known as John D. Rockefeller possessed an accumulation of great
size, but as a matter of fact, it was rapidly dwindling as it passed
from generation to generation. So, let us travel ahead another one
hundred years. During this time, as we learn from our historical
and political archives, the socialists began to die out, since they at
last realized the futility of combating the balance of power. The
account, though, now stood:

2414   500 years $2,520,000

"It is hardly necessary for me to make any comment. Those of
you who are most astute, and others of you who flunked my
course before and are now taking it the second time, of course
know what is coming.

"During the age in which this John Jones lived, there lived also
a man, a so-called scientist called Metchnikoff. We know, from a
study of our vast collection of Egyptian Papyri and Carnegie Library books, that this Metchnikoff promulgated the theory that old
age—or rather senility—was caused by a colon-bacillus. This fact
was later verified. But while he was correct in the etiology of senility, he was crudely primeval in the therapeutics of it.

"He proposed, gentlemen, to combat and kill this bacillus by
utilizing the fermented lacteal fluid from a now extinct animal
called the cow, models of which you can see at any time at the
Solaris Museum."

A chorus of shrill, piping laughter emanated from the brass cylinder. The professor waited until the merriment had subsided and
then continued:

"I beg of you, gentlemen, do not smile. This was merely one of
the many similar quaint superstitions existing in that age.

"But a real scientist, Professor K122B62411Male, again at-
tacked the problem in the twenty-fifth century. Since the cow was
now extinct, he could not waste his valuable time experimenting
with fermented cow lacteal fluid. He discovered that the old
gamma rays of Radium—the rays which you physicists will remember are not deflected by a magnetic field—were really composed of two sets of rays, which he termed the *delta* rays and the
epsilon rays. These last named rays—only when isolated—
completely devitalized all colon-bacilli which lay in their path,
without in the least affecting the integrity of any interposed or-
ganic cells. The great result, as many of you already know, was

that the life of man was extended to nearly two hundred years. That, I state unequivocally, was a great century for the human race.

"But I spoke of another happening—one, perhaps, of more interest than importance. I referred to the bank account of John Jones the fortieth. It, gentlemen, had grown to such a prodigious sum that a special bank and board of directors had to be created in order to care for and reinvest it. By scanning the following notation, you will perceive the truth of my statement:

2514   600 years $47,900,000

"By the year 2614 A.D., two events of stupendous importance took place. There is scarcely a man in this class who has not heard of how Professor P222D29333Male accidentally stumbled upon the scientific fact that the effect of gravity is reversed upon any body which vibrates perpendicularly to the plane of the ecliptic with a frequency which is an even multiple of the logarithm of two to the Naperian base 'e.' At once, special vibrating cars were constructed which carried mankind to all the planets. That discovery of Professor P222D29333Male did nothing less than open up seven new territories to our inhabitants; namely: Mercury, Venus, Mars, Jupiter, Saturn, Uranus, and Neptune. In the great land rush that ensued, thousands who were previously poor became rich.

"But, gentlemen, land, which so far had constituted one of the main sources of wealth, was shortly to become valuable for individual golf links only, as it is today, on account of another scientific discovery.

"This second discovery was, in reality, not a discovery, but the perfection of a chemical process, the principles of which had been known for many centuries. I am alluding to the construction of the vast reducing factories, one upon each planet, to which the bodies of all persons who have died on their respective planets are at once shipped by Aerial Express. Since this process is used today, all of you understand the methods employed; how each body is reduced by heat to its component constituents: hydrogen, oxygen, nitrogen, carbon, calcium, phosphorus, and so forth; how these separated constituents are stored in special reservoirs together with the components from thousands of other corpses; how these elements are then synthetically combined into food tablets for those of us who are yet alive—thus completing an endless chain from the dead to the living. Naturally, then, agriculture and stock-raising ceased,

since the food problem, with which man had coped from time im-
memorial, was solved. The two direct results were, first—that land
lost the inflated values it had possessed when it was necessary for
tillage, and second—that men were at last given enough leisure to
enter the fields of science and art.

"And as to the John Jones Dollar, which now embraced count-
less industries and vast territory on the earth, it stood, in value:

2614   700 years $912,000,000

"In truth, gentlemen, it now constituted the largest private fortune on the terrestrial globe. And in that year, 2614 A.D., there
were thirteen generations yet to come before John Jones the fortieth would arrive.

"To continue. In the year 2714 A.D., an important political battle was concluded in the Solar System Senate and House of Repre-
sentatives. I am referring to the great controversy as to whether the
earth's moon was a sufficient menace to interplanetary navigation
to warrant its removal. The outcome of the wrangle was that the
question was decided in the affirmative. Consequently—

"But I beg your pardon, young men. I occasionally lose sight of
the fact that you are not so well informed upon historical matters
as myself. Here I am, talking to you about the moon, totally forgetful that many of you are puzzled as to my meaning. I advise all
of you who have not yet attended the Solaris Museum on Jupiter to
take a trip there some Sunday afternoon. The Interplanetary Suburban Line runs trains every half hour on that day. You will find
there a complete working model of the old satellite of the Earth,
which, before it was destroyed, furnished this planet light at night
through the crude medium of reflection.

"On account of this decision as to the inadvisability of allowing
the moon to remain where it was, engineers commenced its removal in the year 2714. Piece by piece, it was chipped away and
brought to the Earth in Interplanetary freight cars. These pieces
were then propelled by Zoodolite explosive, in the direction of the
Milky Way, with a velocity of 11,217 meters per second. This velocity, of course, gave each departing fragment exactly the amount
of kinetic energy it required to enable it to overcome the backward
pull of the Earth from here to infinity. I dare say those moon-
hunks are going yet.

"At the start of the removal of the moon in 2714 A.D., the accumulated wealth of John Jones the fortieth stood:

2714   800 years $17,400,000,000

"Of course, with such a colossal sum at their command, the directors of the fund had made extensive investments on Mars and Venus.

"By the end of the twenty-eighth century, or the year 2800 A.D., the moon had been completely hacked away and sent piecemeal into space, the job having required 86 years. I give, herewith, the result of John Jones's Dollar, both at the date when the moon was completely removed and also at the close of the 900th year after its deposit:

2800   886 years $219,000,000,000

2814   900 years $332,000,000,000

"The meaning of those figures, gentlemen, as stated in simple language, was that the John Jones Dollar now comprised practically all the wealth on Earth, Mars, and Venus -- with the exception of one university site on each planet, which was, of course, school property.

"And now I will ask you to advance with me to the year 2899 A.D. In this year the directors of the John Jones fund awoke to the fact that they were in a dreadful predicament. According to the agreement under which John Jones deposited his Dollar away back in the year 1914, interest was to be compounded annually at three per cent. In the year 2899 A.D., the thirty-ninth generation of John Jones was alive, being represented by a man named J664M42721Male, who was thirty years of age and engaged to be married to a young lady named T246M42652Female.

"Doubtless you will ask, what was the predicament in which the directors found themselves? Simply this:

"A careful appraisement of the wealth on Neptune, Uranus, Saturn, Jupiter, Mars, Venus, Mercury, and likewise Earth, together with an accurate calculation of the remaining heat in the Sun and an appraisement of that heat at a very decent valuation per calorie, demonstrated that the total wealth of the Solar System amounted to $6,309,525,241,362.15.

"But unfortunately, a simple computation showed that if Mr. J664M42721Male married Miss T246M42652Female, and was blessed by a child by the year 2914, which year marked the thousandth year since the deposit of the John Jones Dollar, then in that year there would be due the child the following amount:

2914   1,000 years $6,310,000,000,000

"It simply showed beyond all possibility of argument that by 2914 A.D. we would be $474,758,637.85 shy—that we would be unable to meet the debt to John Jones the fortieth.

"I tell you, gentlemen, the Board of Directors was frantic. Such wild suggestions were put forth as the sending of an expeditionary force to the nearest star in order to capture some other Solar System and thus obtain more territory to make up the deficit. But that project was impossible on account of the number of years that it would have required.

"Visions of immense lawsuits disturbed the slumber of those unfortunate individuals who formed the John Jones Dollar Directorship. But on the brink of one of the biggest civil actions the courts had ever known, something occurred that altered everything."

The professor again withdrew the tiny instrument from his vest pocket, held it to his ear and adjusted the switch. A metallic voice rasped: "Fifteen o'clock and fifty-two minutes—fifteen o'clock and fifty-two minutes—fift—" He replaced the instrument and went on with his talk.

"I must hasten to the conclusion of my lecture, gentlemen, as I have an engagement with Professor C122B24999Male of the University of Saturn at sixteen o'clock. Now, let me see; I was discussing the big civil action that was hanging over the heads of the John Jones Dollar directors.

"Well, this Mr. J664M42721Male, the thirty-ninth descendant of the original John Jones, had a lover's quarrel with Miss T246M42652Female, which immediately destroyed the probability of their marriage. Neither gave in to the other. Neither ever married. And when Mr. J664M42721Male died in 2940 A.D., of a broken heart, as it was claimed, he was single and childless.

"As a result, there was no one to turn the Solar System over to. Immediately, the Interplanetary Government stepped in and took possession of it. At that instant, of course, private property ceased. In the twinkling of an eye almost, we reached the true socialistic and democratic condition for which man had futilely hoped throughout the ages.

"That is all today, gentlemen. Class is dismissed."

One by one, the faces faded from the Visaphone.

For a moment, the professor stood ruminating.

"A wonderful man, that old socialist John Jones the first," he said softly to himself, "a far-seeing man, a bright man, considering that he lived in such a dark era as the twentieth century. But how nearly his well-contrived scheme went wrong. Suppose the fortieth descendant had been born?"

BILL'S BILL

T HE FIRST THOUGHT that came into Bill Carston's mind after unfolding the crisp yellow slip of paper which he found at his feet was:

"Great whizzimus—a hundred dollars! Now I've got enough money to buy that Red Dart motorcycle!"

But directly at the heels of this first thought came others which were awfully puzzling. Some, indeed, presented unpleasant possibilities. Every boy who has just found a hundred dollar bill knows just how Bill Carston felt about it.

For a whole year, with almost painful longing, Bill had been looking forward to the day when he should own a motorcycle. Unlike many other boys, the moment that he had thought of owning and had obtained his father's permission, he taken steps to accumulate the sum necessary for its purchase.

After looking over and considering all the motorcycles in the field, he had decided that the Red Dart machine, priced at $190, was the one that had the most up-to-date appearance, seemed to be most popular, and which appeared to endure more hard usage than any other.

But the price! Only ten dollars under two hundred—an immense sum of money, it seemed, for a boy of sixteen, and in school at that, to amass. From the very beginning there had been no chance whatever of getting help from Dad, whose business had been seriously affected by the great war in Europe.

So Bill, his courage bolstered up by the mental picture of a motorcycle, had called on Jerry O'Brien, the man who apparently owned all the newspaper routes on the North Side. Let's go back to that important interview—the beginning of his working out of his problems.

"Jerry," said Bill, on that occasion, "I've known several fellows that have carried papers for you. Any chance for me to get a job on one of the morning routes?"

Jerry looked him over critically for a full minute.

"Well, now," he drawled, as was his habit of speech. "I'm

needin' a kid just now for the Dearborn Avenue route in th' mornin's—and th' Clark Street route in th' afternoons. Each one pays a dollar a week. But think it over well, youngster. That mornin' route means that you got to git up at about four-thirty so's to start out at five—and it'll take you nearly till seven to finish. Th' afternoon route'll take from four to five-thirty. And don't forgit for a minute—it's awful cold some of these here winter mornin's. You got to git warmed up now an' then in th' hallways. An' you got to cover all th' space from Chicago Avenue to North Avenue. Takes some hustlin'. Think it over. Don't want to teach you the routes—an' then see you back out in a week 'r two."

Bill, however, didn't require much "thinking it over." The idea of owning a trim Red Dart made it seem almost easy to climb out of bed before daylight on winter mornings, to wade through snow-drifts and to lose the play of his afternoons after school.

"Take me on, Jerry," he begged. "Honest, I won't back out. I want to save my money for something that'll cost a whole lot— and the only way I can get it is to earn it."

So Jerry, with misgivings, began teaching him the route next morning, since Dad not only had shown no opposition to the project but even helped to argue Mother out of her objections.

It wasn't any "soft snap." In October, when he started, the mornings were warm, but slowly winter crept nearer, and it called for the exercise of all his will power to step out of bed in a cold room, to stand shivering while he drew on, among other things, his flannel shirt and two sweaters, and to make his way in the teeth of a driving gale, or perhaps a sleety rain, down Dearborn Avenue to the alley where his stack of 120 morning papers was left an hour before by the delivery wagon. Heavy indeed was the load when he started out, and, oddly enough, as his load decreased in weight, the heavier it seemed to become, so that, after all, the end of the route was almost as tiring as at the beginning.

The morning's work completed, there followed in quick succession—home, breakfast and school. After school, his homework; after the homework, the afternoon paper route instead of the usual football or baseball or skating, as in the past; the afternoon papers delivered, it was nearly supper time; after supper, to bed early, in order to get sufficient sleep for an early rising next morning. That was his diurnal round.

But there was always the great consolation. Each day brought him closer to the coveted motorcycle.

At the end of his first week in Jerry's employ he received $2. That, of course, meant that only $188 remained to be saved. At the end of his second week, this amount had decreased to $186. Thus, using for his own requirements only the small spending money that he received from Dad, and putting away untouched the money he had earned, he crept, week by week, newspaper by newspaper almost, toward the Red Dart.

The last snow melted and the warm spring mornings returned. Spring gave way to summer and summer proved to be not nearly so bad after all, since in addition to his three and a half hours a day in delivering papers, he had plenty of vacation time for baseball, swimming and other pleasures. But soon only a few weeks remained before school must reopen, and then the grind would begin again—papers, school, papers, bed—papers, school, papers, bed.

That was the thing he tried to keep out of his mind. What he preferred to think about was: "Ninety dollars laid away. One more year—or fifty weeks—a hundred dollars—and then I'll have the motorcycle for my very own."

Then came the astonishing discovery—a $100 bill. It happened this way:

One evening he saw in a paper a full-page advertisement of the Red Dart Motorcycle Company. It contained an announcement that a new booklet had been printed about the Red Dart, and that copies would be given out free or mailed on request of anybody interested in motorcycles. So Bill walked all the way downtown the next afternoon to get one of the little books. After feasting his eyes on the various models on exhibition in the salesrooms of the Red Dart Motorcycle Company, he asked for a booklet, got it and left the store.

In his eagerness to look it over, before starting back on the long walk to the North Side—for, be it understood, there was no sense in spending carfare when one has yet to save $100—he stepped out to the curbstone and opened the pamphlet. He "just happened" (there was no other explanation for it) to glance downward to the street at his feet. A folded yellow slip was moving in the wind; he stooped to pick it up; the wind whirled it under a wagon standing at the curb in the crowded street. Reaching out quickly the boy grasped it. There was a peculiar crackle as he unfolded it. One long look—and a strange tingling feeling passed over him.

A hundred dollars!

No one in the crowds that passed paid the least attention to him—and he felt as though all the eyes of Chicago were upon him.

At last . . . why, it made up what he needed to buy the motorcycle!—it saved fifty weeks' work!

As he trudged homeward, his mind was in a whirl. Every now and then he drew the banknote from his pocket and read each side with care, as though to assure himself that his experience was real and not a dream. What luck!

Then came the other thoughts—reasonable, troublesome. The loser might advertise for it. He knew that in such an event he could do nothing but return it. But maybe he wouldn't see the "ad." Or the owner might believe the bill was lost beyond hope of recovery, and so never make any effort to regain it. In that case . . .

As Bill, delivering his afternoon papers, thought the thing over he reasoned that if he didn't look in the lost-and-found columns for several weeks, he wouldn't see any "ad" for the $100 bill he had found, even if an "ad" were published, and therefore he need never have any arguments with his conscience on the score of retaining someone's else property. Then he could have his motorcycle and could give up the two newspaper routes which left him no time for himself.

As he staggered along the street with a bundle which was unusually heavy on account of the presence of sixty war-picture supplements, a small voice, coming from nowhere in particular, seemed to keep repeating, "Stay away from the lost-and-found advertisements—stay away from the lost-and-found advertisements—stay away . . ." He made more mistakes that afternoon than he had ever made before. Where he should have left copies of the *Evening News*, he left copies of the *Post*; and where *Posts* were wanted, many subscribers that night found the *Evening News*. Every now and then he rested his bundle on his knee and felt to make sure that the big bill was still in his pocket, and all the time his mind worked ceaselessly on the peculiar problem.

"Now if I don't look in the lost-and-found columns tomorrow, I can't see any advertisement for the bill, if there is one, and I'll have enough money for a gas bike—and I can turn over my routes to Jimmie O'Rourke, who lives back in our alley—he's awful poor—and I can ride 'way out in the country every afternoon—but maybe a poor woman lost it—and maybe it's all the money she had in the world; but no, a poor woman would never have a $100 bill . . . But I wish I knew who lost it—no, I don't; I hope I never find out."

That night at the supper table he ate abstractedly. His mother felt at once that something was troubling him. Dad showed no sign that he perceived anything was amiss, but after supper, when Mrs. Carston was washing the dishes, he drew Bill over to him.

"Well, Bill," he asked, "getting worried because vacation's nearly over? Or has Jerry O'Brien decided to give one of your routes to some other boy?"

"Well, I'm kinda sorry that vacation's nearly gone, Dad, but—"

"But what?"

"You aren't too busy reading your paper to answer an imaginary question, are you, Dad?"

"No, Bill. Go ahead. What's your question?"

"Well," began Bill slowly, "suppose you found something— something valuable—say money—would you look in the papers to see if it was advertised as lost; even if—that is, Dad, would you believe that 'finders was keepers'?"

"It is not polite," replied his father, "to answer one question with another, but that's what I am going to do. Here's my 'question-answer.' Now, Dad's business is not very good at present, although he manages to make enough to take care of you and your mother—and to keep you in school—and to let you have for your own use whatever money you earn outside of school hours. Now if Dad lost some money—no matter how little—would you feel that the finder should keep it—or that he should return it?"

"I guess your question answers mine," said Bill solemnly. "When you lose anything, you feel that it ought to be returned— and when you find anything, the loser is certainly going to feel the same." He stood up. "I'm going to bed, Dad. Got to take the paper route a quarter of an hour earlier tomorrow on account of a lot of new customers that Jerry traded in from another newsdealer."

As a rule, Bill slept too soundly to dream, but that night he saw himself handing over the counter of the grocery store a folded slip of paper with the numerals "100" in the corner, together with a suitcase full of silver dollars. And he saw himself receiving a bright crimson and green Red Dart motorcycle with wheels that kept going and going, making an awful noise. A little later he found that he was riding swiftly alongside a thundering express train and rapidly leaving the latter behind until it had become a mere speck and then he came to another railroad, and the crossing bell was ringing and ringing, and he couldn't stop the motorcycle, and a train was coming right toward him—and the bell rang louder and louder—and then he awoke with the sharp jangle of the alarm clock in his ears.

He dressed slowly and tiptoed from the house. After fifteen minutes he reached the spot where he got the papers he had to distribute—half of them *Tribunes*, which carried the city's classified advertising, and the other half *Heralds*.

For several minutes he stared at the *Tribunes*. All that he need do, he reflected, was to open one of them quickly, locate the lost-and-found column and run his eye down the printed page. Then he pictured to himself the yellow $100 bill which he had hidden under the paper of his bureau drawer. He might come across the owner's name. If he did, he would never be able to rest until he had restored the money. Perhaps, after all, it was best that he should not look. If people were careless enough to lose things, they didn't deserve to have them back again. Surely it would be foolish to look. Then, again, perhaps the loser had been a bank messenger and would have to make good the loss. Or—

He raised his papers up, swung his shoulder strap around them and started out on his route. Whenever he rolled a *Tribune*, preparatory to tossing it from the sidewalk to a vestibule, his hand involuntarily stopped for a second in its motion. But he managed always to throw it from him—and to pass on to the house of the next customer. Thus, *Tribune* after *Tribune*, *Herald* after *Herald* left his bundle; finally but one paper remained—a *Tribune*.

For a long while he hesitated in front of the last house on his route. Several times he tried to throw the paper from him—and each time managed to restrain himself from doing so. At last, however, he seated himself on the small iron railing doorstep and slowly unfolded the paper.

Part II

Soon he found the lost-and-found column. Then his heart seemed to drop clear to his toes. His visions of a motorcycle—a precious Red Dart—vanished into thin air, for his eyes were staring at an advertisement which read:

Lost: Yesterday; a bill of large denomination; can identify by giving serial number; reasonable reward if returned between 7 and 9 P.M. to John Bennet, 1400 Lake Shore Drive.

Bill went home to breakfast. His heart felt unusually light, considering the fact that he had come across information which now prevented his keeping the bill. He realized now that the tussle he had had with himself, when he stood with the last *Tribune* in his hand, had been a hard one. But after all, he reflected, he would never in future years have to consider himself a thief so far as the piece of paper money was concerned. That was some satisfaction. The coming year couldn't pass more slowly than the one just ended, and at the end of it he would have the Red Dart anyhow. Perhaps the reward would be as much as $10; that would shorten the next year's work by five weeks.

That day he read his motorcycle booklet from cover to cover, and then read it through again. Once during the afternoon he counted over the money he had saved. It was all there—$90. Perhaps Mr. Bennet might offer him as much as $20; in all fairness he could accept it. Then he would have $110. So there was a bright side to everything.

At seven o'clock that evening he was walking along Lake Shore Drive. After traversing a number of long blocks he reached "1400". He was rather surprised at first, for he saw a splendid mansion with a well-kept lawn, a drive-way, and other evidences of the owner's wealth. After fumbling nervously for a moment at the ornamental iron gate, he mustered up courage enough to walk up the steps and ring the bell. A man in gray livery—apparently a butler—came in answer to the summons.

"I'd—I'd—I'd like to speak to Mr. John Bennet," said Bill, utterly forgetting for a second the object of his visit.

"Step this w'y," said the servant. "hand hI'll see hif 'e's busy."

The servant rapped on the door of a room at the end of the hall. The door opened slightly. In the opening, Bill caught sight of a little sharp-featured man, with iron-gray hair and gold-rimmed eyeglasses which framed eyes that seemed to be unusually small and piercing.

"Young gentleman to see you, Mr. Bennet."

"Walk in," grunted Mr. Bennet. "Sit down."

Bill did so. The little man closed the door and took up a seat not far from Bill's chair. "What can I do for you?" he asked, glowering.

"I've found your money," blurted out Bill.

"Humph!" returned Mr. Bennet. "So you found it—hey?" He paused. "Well, I'm the one that lost it and my wife's the one who inserted the advertisement. She's got some old fashioned notions that everybody's honest. 'Sall nonsense! 'Sall nonsense! No such thing, of course. It was a hundred dollar bill that lost. Was that the one you found?"

"Yes," replied Bill, "that's the one, all right. Now you said—or your wife said—in the advertisement that you had the number of it. If you'll give me the number so's I can be sure it's yours, I'll turn it over."

Mr. Bennet jerked a small note-book from his pocket. He thumbed over the leaves. "Always put down the numbers of your big bills, boy. 'Swhat I always do. You'll find it pays—case they get lost. Hm—hm—hm—here it is—number M17472442, Series 1902. It was—"

"It's your money, then," interrupted Bill. "Here it is."

He thrust out his hand and laid the crisp yellow note on the stand near the older man.

"Humph—humph—" snorted Mr. Bennet, staring at Bill as if he were some new curiosity. "How'dja happen to find it? Where'dja come across it? What time o' day didja see it? Didn't know I'd lost it till last night when I told my wife about it. Didja find it near your home? Where do y' live? D'you work downtown? Whatcher name?"

At all these questions Bill caught his breath. Then he collected his wits.

"No, I go to school," he explained. "My name is Bill Cars— that is—William Carston. I live at 124 West Center Street—an' that's a mighty long ways from downtown. It wouldn't 'a' happened that I'd 'a' been downtown, only I've been saving to buy a Red Dart motorcycle—and I saw their advertisement in the paper about their giving away booklets about the Red Dart—so I walked downtown yesterday afternoon and got a booklet to read about the motorcycle I'm going to have later on. Well, I got the booklet at their main office on Madison Street and stepped out to the curb to read it—and found the bill—and—"

"Motorcycle!" exploded Mr. Bennet suddenly, as though the full import of Bill's words was just beginning to filter into his mind. "Motorcycle! Humph! 'Sall nonsense—'sall nonsense. D'you wanta get blown up clear over the moon? I wouldn't ride one of the pesky things myself for a million dollars. 'Sall nonsense—'sall nonsense. Why, if I—"

He was interrupted by a sharp rapping on the door. He crossed the floor of the room quickly and opened it. The butler was standing in the hall.

"Mr. Smith from New York to see you, Mr. Bennet," he said politely.

With a quick motion of his wrist, Mr. Bennet jerked out his watch and snapped it open. "Hm—hm—hm," he mumbled. "Forgot all about appointment with Smith. Hawkins, show Master William Carston out." A big figure loomed up behind the butler. "Ah, there, Smith, forgot all about you. 'Sall nonsense on my part, 'sall nonsense, o' course. Step in."

In a daze Bill found himself conducted through the hall. He heard the door close behind him. He found himself walking down the steps and along the cement path to the sidewalk.

"Well, I'll be whizzled," were his first words to himself, "maybe if a poor woman had lost the bill, I'd 'a' never got up enough courage to look in the lost-and-found column, so's I could give it back to her, but because I did, it turns out to be a swell feller on 'Millionaires' Row' who managed to forget all about the reward that the advertisement spoke of."

He hurried home. When he got near his house he discovered with a feeling of vexation that he had been unconsciously whistling a cheerful tune. So he at once put a stop to the music. When he entered the front door, his father caught sight of him.

"Well, Bill," he inquired, "any more imaginary questions tonight?"

"No, Dad, I've got a good story to tell you and Mother—but if I start now we'll all be talking about it for an hour or more and I'll lose my sleep. So I'll keep it till breakfast time—and tell you the whole thing then from beginning to end. I'm pretty tired now and I'm going to bed."

Once in the night he awoke and began wondering what Dad and Mother would say about Mr. Bennet's brusque dismissal of him after he had returned the lost $100 bill. But he soon fell asleep again and managed to spring out of bed at the first sound of his alarm clock in the morning. After he had returned from his route,

washed, and changed his clothes, he marched into the dining room
and took his usual chair at the table. His father and mother both
looked up.

"Letter for you, Bill," said Dad with a look of curiosity on his
face. "Better read it first. Then you can tell us the story you mentioned last night."

Bill looked wonderingly at the inscription on the envelope:

Master William Carston,
124 W. Center St.,
City

There was a return address on the reverse side, but he did not
see it. The writing, so he perceived, was small and cramped—not
at all like Aunt Mollie's writing; and Aunt Mollie was the only
one who ever sent him letters. Bewildered, he tore open the end
and looked within.

At first he saw nothing; then he caught sight of a small white
card down in one corner. He shook it out and read with perplexity
the words which had been written in red ink on one side:

> *Sales Dep't : Credit bearer with $100*
> *on purchase of any motorcycle in*
> *stock.*
>
> J. B.

Quickly he turned the card over. The printed words on the other
side, read:

JOHN C. BENNET

Owner and General Manager
Red Dart Motorcycle Co.

CHICAGO   NEW YORK   LONDON

SUNBEAM'S CHILD

Gunton, you're an unnatural father," declared Payne, as the two sat smoking in Gunton's library. "Do you think that if I had a boy fifteen years of age I'd keep him marooned in the care of a private family in England? Not for an instant. I'd have my son with me. I'd take him around to the theaters and cafes. I'd be his companion and pal. At any rate, I'd act as a real father. All you've ever done, though, is to write out a check every three months. I repeat my assertion, Gunton. Your attitude is wholly abnormal."

The older man removed his cigar from his lips and regarded the younger contemplatively. His face bore a perplexed look which seemed to indicate that he was pondering over some exceedingly involved question. Finally after a full minute had passed, he broke the silence.

"Payne, you've made that same accusation against me on several occasions during our seven years of acquaintanceship. Often I've felt that I'd like to tell you more about the boy—and his mother—and other things as well. But it seems that something has invariably held me back." He paused and blew several smoke rings ceilingward. "Tonight, though, I'm going to explain things to you. You understand, of course, that my words are between the two of us only?"

"Have I ever violated your confidence in these seven years?" asked Payne.

"No, you haven't—and for that very reason I'm going to unburden myself." Gunton leaned forward and placed his hand on the other man's knee. "And the sole remaining reason," he added simply, "is because I've learned that you are my friend. Now listen."

"I've never mentioned Sunbeam—my wife—to you. The circumstances under which we met were quite ordinary. I wasn't as well-off in those days as today—yet made a very good living. Her father was a business acquaintance of my uncle. She was the only child. We were introduced one evening at a private dance. And the result for each of us, I daresay, was love at first sight. Yes, the whole affair was quite ordinary—so I'll pass quickly to other things.

"As to the name Sunbeam. Rather fanciful, even for a pet name, eh, Payne? But you should have seen her to have understood. I'm sure that you've noticed those fragile little flaxen-haired dolls in the windows of the big stores around Christmas time? Just such a living, breathing human doll was Sunbeam. She was dainty, small, delicately featured. Her hair, which fell about her temples in the most entrancing ringlets, was the sunniest yellow. Her cheeks would have reminded you ineffably of the pink roses we see in the old-fashioned flower gardens. And her eyes—big and blue and trustful like those of a child. In fact, Payne, she was a child with woman's years, a beautiful unspoiled child, and when I was first introduced to her by my uncle, my peace of mind left me instantly. After I had known her for but a few weeks, I realized that I could never, never adjust myself to a life which did not include her. But my lucky star must have been in the ascendancy, for she gave me her love—and herself as my wife.

"I don't believe, Payne, that I shall ever forget the four weeks of our honeymoon. For quite a number of years, I had been enjoying a splendid salary, and I had saved the greater part of it. So just before we were married, I erected a charming little bungalow out in Hyde Park; in the rear it I put up a small brick garage and purchased an expensive limousine. Then, after several wonderful days of shopping for furniture, we were quietly married and left for a leisurely tour of the East. We took in Pittsburgh, Washington New York, Buffalo and Cleveland. By the time we returned to Chicago, our little nest was all complete, every piece of furniture was in place, and in care of it was a motherly woman whom I had engaged as a housekeeper.

"But now came the unpleasant part. I was compelled by the exigencies of my work to leave Sunbeam, since it was necessary for me to continue traveling for at least a year longer. I tell you, Payne, if you have never had to leave the woman you love for periods of time averaging a month, you cannot realize what a soul-grilling experience it was for me. It meant that I must go bumping about the country, enduring all sorts of hardships and inconveniences instead of being able to sit at home evenings in my big overstuffed rocker with Sunbeam on my lap, her smooth pink cheek snug up against my own and her warm kisses coming at the most unexpected moments. But depart I must.

"Now at this point I must digress a bit in order to tell you about an individual who was connected with the events which followed. If only he had never existed, then . . . But, after all, things are as they are; none of us must cavil at the immutable law of cause and effect. At any rate, to continue, this man's name was Dyke. It seems that long before I had met Sunbeam, he had been a regular caller at her father's house and had shown in numerous ways that he was anxious to ingratiate himself into her good graces. He was a fairly good-looking chap in spite of the fact that there was a somewhat tricky look on his face. I have but one thing to tell about him. This I remark upon because you are always talking about the Laws of Heredity, the Mendelian theories and what not. This fact constituted an oddity of nature which should interest you.

"On his left temple, Payne, was a dark patch of red which had been there since his birth; it was a nearly perfect equilateral triangle and in size was perhaps that of a twenty-five cent piece. And the odd thing about it was that his father had borne the same peculiar mark in the same place. And, to add to the strangeness of the fact, his grandfather too had carried a triangular patch of reddish skin at the left temple. This was true beyond any doubt, since there were many who had known Dyke's father and had seen the tintype of his grandfather. So much for that. Explain as you wish.

"Well no sooner had I been out of town a week than Dyke made a social call on Sunbeam. By no means, Payne, do I wish to give you the impression that she concealed it from me. Almost as soon as I reached the house after my first trip, she met me in the hall, snuggled up to me on her tiptoes and said, 'Dear, do you remember Mr. Dyke? While you were gone, he made a visit. And he asked whether he might drop in again some time.'

"I tell you, Payne, a blind ungovernable rage seized me when I thought of that shifty-eyed, birth-marked Dyke daring to call upon my fairy-wife in my absence. Old stories that I had heard about him recurred suddenly to my memory. And then and there I mentally determined that if he ever repeated the action, he should receive a lesson which he would never forget.

"So after supper that evening I made my way alone down to an employment office in the black belt, that portion of Chicago's South State street lying between 18th and 35th streets; it was here that the city's negro population lived and moved. And I found just the specimen of a man I was looking for. His name was Skoko—Skoko something or other—I've quite forgotten now what. He was a gigantic, brawny ape-like negro, a veritable black Hercules. I'll

warrant that there wasn't a nigger wench in existence that could
have helped but go crazy over him. He was a typical African,
Payne, with carbon-black skin, flat nose, flaring nostrils, great
thick lips, and kinky hair. His long muscular arms, low forehead,
and sloping cranium put me in mind of the stuffed gorilla that
stands in the Academy of Sciences at Lincoln Park.

"Here was the man I wanted, I told myself, mentally calculating
what chance of defense Dyke would have if this black gorilla in
human form ever began a chastisement! So I called him to one
side and stated the details of the position for which I required a
man.

" 'Now, Skoko,' I said, 'the manager of this agency informs me
that you've been employed in the past as cook, chauffeur, and
general caretaker. I require a man for those duties at my residence
in Hyde Park. I should expect you to drive my wife out along
Michigan avenue on those afternoons when she wishes to take the
air or to shop in the stores of the downtown district. So far, so
good. There is one more duty—a very unusual one—and one
which will never have to be repeated. If a man'—and I described
Dyke very accurately in name and appearance—'ever comes up
my steps, rings my bell, and asks for my wife, I want you to beat
him within an inch of his life so that he'll never show his face
around there again. And in such an event, I'll see that you're fully
protected so far as the law is concerned.' Then I named a salary
that caused that nigger to enter my employment on the spot.

"Sunbeam did not seem to be very glad when she learned that I
had engaged a servant who could act as a combination chauffeur,
housekeeper, and cook. But she finally agreed with me that it
would perhaps be a more advantageous arrangement for her, since
the man who had been coming every day to wash up our car and
act as occasional chauffeur was proving to be extremely unreli-
able. So I discharged the woman housekeeper that night with two
weeks of advance wages. The following morning Skoko was duly
installed as general utility man and protector to Sunbeam. During
the week I remained in Chicago, he demonstrated that he was a
very efficient servant. Hence, at no time did I regret the generous
salary I was paying him. After that, while on the road, I was no
longer preyed upon by the dread fear that Dyke might come
around and worm his way into my household—as I felt instinctively he would if he could.

"Seven or eight months flew by. My trips on the road were now
averaging but two weeks apiece and my stays at home were of

about the same duration. Apparently, Dyke had made no further attempts to call upon Sunbeam at the house, for she never made any mention of him again, and, in addition, catechizing Skoko elicited the fact that the only time she was ever out of his sight was for the two or three hours that she spent inside the great downtown stores. And I, very sensibly, never brought up Dyke's name again.

"Well, Payne, after those eight months had elapsed, I learned something that set me beside myself with joy. I had been at home for about a week when the family doctor called me aside one morning and told me the news—that later on there were to be three in our family instead of two. My heart leaped with gladness. Oh, how I longed for a boy—a little tyke with the yellow hair of his doll-like mother. Immediately I secured a leave of absence of a year from my firm. Then I made all the necessary preparations for taking Sunbeam over to one of the Italian lakes where we could wait together in quietness and happiness for the great event to take place. Three days later I closed up the Hyde Park residence. I paid off my faithful black, giving him a one-hundred-dollar bill as a bonus. When he left the house to return to the agency from which I had hired him, I tried not to show that my heart was heavy at breaking off from the home ties; and Sunbeam must have felt it more deeply than I, for the tears glistened on her eyelashes. And so, all this gone through with, we sailed for Italy.

"I rented one of the numerous villas that lie along the eastern shore of Lake Como. Built on the front of it was a long porch, where we used to sit together and watch the glorious colors of the Italian sunset. In fact, she herself remained on the porch the livelong day, saying nothing, never moving, her face bearing the strangest, most baffling expression. And how that expression troubled me, Payne, for I knew that her heart must be worried. Then, as never before, did I do everything in my power to give her all the love and comfort I could.

" 'Dear heart,' I said to her one day, 'don't look so sad and forlorn. Am I not the same to you anymore—or is it the fear of the coming ordeal? You must not be afraid, my own. I promise you that we'll have the best medical attendants that the region affords, regardless of expense. And after it's all over with, we three will go back to our little Hyde Park nest, and everything shall be just as it used to be. I'll get a car exactly like the one we had; I'll see that each piece of furniture is placed in the same position it used to occupy; I'll look up Skoko and re-engage him. We'll resume life again just where we broke it off.'

"On hearing that, her face lighted up, and she smiled a wondrous little smile—a smile, though, which proved to me that she was fearfully homesick. Upon seeing the smile, I added:

" 'There—how good it seems to see you smile again. Everything, darling, will come out all right.'

"And to my intense surprise, she burst into tears and replied:

'Oh, I hope so, how I hope so, how I hope so—and yet—I'm afraid. I'm afraid of—of—of—just everything.' And she commenced weeping so passionately that I almost thought her heart was breaking.

"Well, Payne, the months slipped by, one by one—until finally the great time arrived. Long before, though, I had installed two nurses in our villa, both English-speaking. I had secured the services of an extra servant as well. A most able physician and his assistant were in almost constant attendance. But, Payne, God must have intended her to give her life for her child, for she never breathed again after it was born. And I swear to you that later, when she lay in her coffin, I observed on her face the same strange elusive expression—a half smile—that had hovered there during the last months of her life. But the child was a boy, Payne, a healthy, vigorous boy, just as I had hoped. But—but—but—how can I go on—?" His voice broke.

Payne leaned forward and placed his hand affectionately on the older man's shoulder.

"Dear old fellow," he said tenderly, "I feel that I know what you want to tell me. The boy—was there—a—a birthmark on his left temple?

The older man gave a short, bitter laugh.

"By no means," he replied. "Nothing like that. From head to foot the boy was a dark copper color, with flat nose and unusually thick lips."

THE SETTLEMENT

SLOWLY AND PAINSTAKINGLY, cane in hand, Kirkland made his way along the fifth floor corridor of the Columbia Building. After studying each transom in turn, he finally stopped in front of one which bore the number 505. Then he lowered his gaze and stood for a fraction of a second reading the sign painted on the ground glass panel of the door:

> AMOS TRIGG
> Attorney-At-Law

He turned the knob and walked in. An elderly man, with iron-grey hair and eyes framed in heavy, gold-rimmed spectacles, looked up from a desk where he was shuffling over several papers.

"Kirkland!" he exclaimed. "Phil Kirkland! Didn't expect to see you back in the land of walking people for at least a couple of days yet. Did you leave the hospital before my letter reached there?" He rose hastily and placed a chair for his visitor. "Here, boy, sit down. You don't look a bit strong yet."

"No, I'm not," admitted the younger man, sinking into the chair with a sigh of relief. "But regarding that letter, Trigg, it's worrying me. It reached me just as I was pulling out from the hospital. So, as soon as I could round up a cheap furnished room, I got down here as fast as a pair of hopelessly damaged legs could bring me. It's bad news, I'll warrant. I've been on my back for three months, and that—that—money was absolutely my last dependence."

For several minutes the lawyer stared from the window without speaking. Finally he reached into one of the pigeon-holes of his desk and withdrew a narrow packet of papers.

"Well, I'm afraid it is bad news," he stated, a look of pity lighting up his face for a bare instant as he caught sight of Kirkland's brown eyes staring at him so eagerly. "Not good news at any rate, my boy, not good news." He paused, studying the papers. "I'd better recount to you the facts just as they stand and carry you up to the occurrence of yesterday—which same occurrence caused me to drop that letter to you. Here they are, dates and all:

"Late in the evening of the fourth of May, according to this first slip, you were run down by an automobile at the corner of Michigan Avenue and 33rd Street. You were taken to the Wesley Hospital as soon as an ambulance could be telephoned for. And there they found that both of your legs had been broken above the knee."

Kirkland nodded unhappily, "Yes. And I sent for you next day to ask you to look into the case for me, since the machine that struck me had been running without lights."

"Exactly," assented the lawyer. "So I agreed to look into the case and see what I could do with it—at my usual terms, twenty per cent. Well, I've already told you how I rummaged around in the vicinity of Michigan Avenue and 33rd Street, and how I finally located a small cigar store whose owner had seen the whole accident—as well as several important features connected with it.

"According to his statement—which tallied with your own—the machine, with no lights whatever burning, had swept along at a terrific rate of speed, and, after knocking you down and passing over you, had flown on without even stopping to see if you were killed or not.

"The street was almost devoid of people and machines at this late hour, and so, since two men were already picking you up, he had watched the car after it struck you and had seen it come to a stop not more than a block and a half away. He turned the key in the lock of his shop and hurried down to the point where the machine had drawn up at the curb. There he had come across the owner, obviously drunk, cursing to beat the band and hastily cranking up the engine. This accomplished, the latter had lighted the two headlights and pulled away from the spot. But our cigar store man was foresighted enough to get a description of the car, the driver, and the license number.

"I tell you, Kirkland, matters did look rosy to me. It certainly appeared as though we had a clear case against somebody—and all the necessary details, as well, for finding out who that somebody was. And let me say right here that it's high time that someone landed hard on those devilish scorchers—for it's getting to be so now that a pedestrian's not safe anywhere in Chicago on the sidewalk. But to go back to the facts of the matter. You know how I looked up the license number at the City Hall and how I found that it had been issued to no less a person than Sam Hoggenheimer, the millionaire distillery man. And I didn't need any investigation to find out whether this Hoggenheimer's description tallied with the one given me by the cigar store dealer, for every lawyer at the Chicago bar knows Hoggenheimer. In litigation, Kirkland, he's a devil. He wins out in every law case with which he gets tangled up, simply because he's got the capital to carry his cases higher and higher; to buy off witnesses; in other words, to wear his opponent out.

"Well, the cigar store man promised faithfully that he'd go into court if necessary and testify as to Hoggenheimer's criminal negligence in running at a high rate of speed—if not exceeding the speed limit altogether—with no lights burning. So it looked as thought we had old S. H. backed in a corner this time, dead to rights. As far as I could see, we had a chance to sue for $5000—which could give us a compromised sum of $2500. And that amount, of course, would give you $2000 clear. And I don't doubt that you deserve every penny, Kirkland, lying on your back for three long months with the knowledge that your legs would never be quite the same again."

"It was fearful, Trigg," assented Kirkland, uneasily. "The only thing that made it endurable was the knowledge that the man who had run me down was rich, and that I could get at least enough out of it—$2000—to buy up some little business where I could sit down for the greater part of the day. But about this bad piece of news—you've got me worried. What is it?"

"Yes, I'm coming to that. Well, during the next two and a half months following your injury, we were at a standstill on account of Hoggenheimer's sojourn at some California health resort where he was taking treatment for a valvular affection of the heart. He's a big, fleshy man, Kirkland, and a life of ease combined with loose living has put him more or less to the bad. And so, as you'll remember, he returned two weeks ago—just as you'd nearly served your sentence in the ward of the hospital. Of course I immediately called on him in his office. I told him that we had the descriptions of himself, of his car, and of his license tag. And I added that we possessed an unimpeachable witness to testify to those three things. I practically informed him that we had him dead to rights. And then I played my trump card—a card which, between you and me, was only sheer bluff. I declared that the man he had injured, Phil Kirkland, had wealthy relatives who would carry the case to the highest court in the state, if that were necessary, to obtain justice.

"Well, that trump card of mine, that bluff, seemed to impress him as nothing else had. He hemmed and he hawed. He scratched his chin. He chewed on his cigar. But he was foxy enough not to admit or deny that he was the man who had run you down. Finally he asked me what I'd consider a fair settlement for this damage suit that I intended to bring against him.

" 'Twenty-five hundred dollars,' I snapped back. 'My client's legs will never be as good as they were before the accident. And he's spent three months on his back.'

" 'Um'! was all he said. He seemed to be thinking it over. From what I've heard of Hoggenheimer I imagine he was figuring whether those hypothetical rich relatives of yours were backing you up as much as I declared. But finally he broke the silence. 'Mr. Trigg,' he grunted, 'as soon as your client leaves the hospital—which'll be in about two weeks, you say—fetch him to my office and I'll have him sign a release for me. Then I'll pay over to you the amount you mentioned.'

"Well, Kirkland, as a lawyer, perhaps I should have suspected that he was merely playing for a delay. But my knowledge of that man's fortune, as compared to a paltry $2500, completely misled me. I can't understand how anyone could hold back on an amount which, in addition to being an entirely just debt, was nothing but a drop in the bucket to him. And so I left the office.

"Day before yesterday I called him up and told him I'd be in his office with you in three days. To my utter dumfoundment he jumped all over me, called me a shyster lawyer, told me that I could bring action and be damned—and that I had nothing on him.

"Quick as a flash, I suspected that he'd got hold of some inside information about you; that he had learned in some way that I had been bluffing absolutely on the subject of your financial backing; that he'd ascertained that you didn't have a relative or a soul who could help you out in a long court fight. But there was assuredly, assuredly I say, no way for Hoggenheimer to have suspected that—much less to have known it.

"At any rate, I grabbed my hat, caught a street car, and went down to see our star and only witness, the cigar store owner. To my chagrin the store was sold out to a new man—and the former owner had vanished without leaving even a forwarding address. I located the place where he had boarded. He'd left there also. Back I went to the new proprietor of the cigar store and commenced quizzing him. He admitted that he dimly remembered seeing a big, fleshy man—and Hoggenheimer's just such a person—talking to the former owner of the store on the day that bill of sale was signed.

"The inference is obvious—too obvious. Hoggenheimer got inside information, in some way, that you were penniless—and without relatives or influential friends. So he rummaged around too, located our sole witness, slipped him a hundred or two, and packed him out of the state—possibly to Canada. To boil my whole narrative down to a single sentence, Kirkland, we've lost our case. With our witness gone and our bluff punctured, we haven't a leg to stand on. It looks mighty bad."

For a full minute Kirkland said nothing. He was stunned, overwhelmed, panic-stricken at the sudden and unexpected turn of affairs for him. Just as he was on the verge of receiving $2000 as compensation for a pair of hopelessly stiff and crooked legs—which was poor compensation indeed—the amount was snatched from his hands on account of the cupidity of a man who had more wealth than he knew what to do with. Vainly Kirkland tired to brace up under the engulfing wave of bitterness and dejection that swept over him—but to no avail. He realized dimly that now he stood face to face with unemployment, very likely hunger, for how long could a man live on $7—and who would take an employee whose legs were incapacitated for protracted standing? Finally he pulled himself together and spoke.

"That news is worse than bad, Trigg; it's fierce. I've been counting all along on that money to buy out some little business. For years I've been standing on my feet as a clerk at Huntley and McGuire's big dry-goods store. I never had any education nor pull—and I've never expected to get anything better than that. But even that's knocked out for me now—and the $18 a week that was attached to it looks like a fortune to me. And now—now—" He stopped helplessly and tried to swallow the lump in his throat.

"I'm certainly sorry, Kirkland," said the attorney. "It's not the loss of my own $500 share of that compromise money that troubles me—for I can live. But I'm honestly worried about you. We're up against a well-defined case of crooked work—which we can't prove. Hoggenheimer simply rustled around, tumbled into some bona fide information that you had no one to back you up, went down and paid our witness to sell out and leave town, knowing that he could outbid us by waving some cold cash under the latter's nose.

"As a matter of fact, I've taken steps to bring action today—and I'll stand the small preliminary expense myself. But Hoggenheimer's word is as good as ours—and in conjunction with a phony alibi will knock us silly in a court of law." He paused, looking down at the roaring traffic. "At least, Kirkland, you have the consolation of knowing that there's only yourself to support. You've no wife—no child. You can surely get by in some way."

For a bare instant a rather bitter smile flashed across Kirkland's face.

"I once had the prettiest wife you could conceive of—and the most wonderful baby girl that ever lived," he said tenderly.

"A wife! A baby girl!" exclaimed Trigg. "Why, I've never heard you mention 'em. Dead—are they?"

"The little girl—yes; and the wife—dead to me. There wasn't much to it, Trigg. I married her five years ago. She was pretty—too pretty, I guess, to be contented on $18 per. Life in a stove-heated flat never quite satisfied her. Although I honestly never blamed her for that attitude, it surely worried me.

"After the little girl was born, I thought that perhaps she'd be more contented. But she wasn't. Later—much later—she got a chance to go on the stage in a chorus part. So she left me. Even at that I'd have stuck to her always, knowing that she might some day come back to me—and her own little daughter. But finally the little one took sick. I guess I'll never forget that last night when the doctor told me her chances for living were slim. With her tiny velvety cheeks flushed—and her little blue eyes bright with fever, she kept calling continually for her mother. 'Mama, mama,' she cried, over and over, 'p'ease tum back to me, mama.' God—how my heart seemed to be grinding slowly to pieces.

"I hurried to the nearest telegraph office and sent a wire to the one who had left me shortly before—and who was in the city at that very instant. It said: 'Dolly, come over to North Side at once; baby not expected to live; calls you continually. Phil.' An hour later her reply reached me: 'Can't come; rehearsing for leading part in the Star Burlesquers; probably the doctor exaggerates. Dolly.' And at dawn my poor little baby girl passed away. The last thing she did was to thrust out her tiny arms and whisper faintly: 'Mama, mama, why you don't tum back to me?' "

Kirkland stopped. He stared hard at the foot of the desk. Then his hand suddenly clenched and unclenched.

"Damn her, Trigg," he burst out. "I divorced her two weeks later. And to this day, I've never seen her—with the single exception that I was once told that she was playing in burlesque under the stage name of Dolly van Sutten."

"Heavens, boy," commented Trigg emphatically, "she was no woman—no mother at all. Why she—she—she was a beast, a brute." He sat for a moment thinking. Then he stood up and placed his hand on the other's shoulder, adding brusquely: "Well, Kirkland, you've had your share of life's digs, there's no doubt about that. But try not to take it to heart. Go home—and don't worry. Come in again day after tomorrow. I'll have action instituted before that time. And we never know what developments are going to enter into any case."

Slowly Kirkland made his way down the corridor. He descended in the elevator. Once out on the street, he mounted a car. For a long while he rode northward. Finally, however, he dismounted and walked stiffly and clumsily along a side street until he reached the steps of a dingy rooming-house. He opened the outer door with his latchkey, and, step by step, resting every five or six steps, he ascended a stairway covered with a faded and threadbare carpet. When he reached the third floor, he proceeded along the hall until he came to the door of a rear room. Here he thrust another key in the aperture of the lock and shortly swung open the door, displaying to his gaze the room he had rented several hours before. Its floor was covered with dusty, yellow matting. It was fitted with a narrow iron bed. Its only remaining articles of furniture were a straight wooden chair and a washstand on which stood a cracked yellow pitcher and a washbowl.

He closed the door quietly, tossed his hat on the chair, and stood for a few seconds gazing unseeingly out on a dirty back yard, littered with broken milk bottles and rusty tin cans. Then he spun suddenly around and despairingly flung himself face downward on the bed.

For a long time he lay without moving, trying unavailingly to grasp the fact that he was confronted with the oldest problem of life—the problem that concerned the means of existence itself; face to face with the necessity of finding employment, no matter how poorly paid, by which he could remain off his feet.

One thing was certain: he must replenish his capital soon, for at the very most it could last him but seven or eight days. Bitterly, he began to wonder why the man Hoggenheimer, rich even in the modern accepted sense of the word, should take such evident joy in saving the paltry sum that for him, Kirkland, meant the sole chance of a halfway happy future,

He shuddered involuntarily when the recollection recurred to him of how, on the night of May fourth, the great whirring ma-

chine had sprung swiftly and silently at him from the darkness,
unheralded by either the warning honk of the horn or the blaze of
even one headlight. In turn, the long, tedious days in the hospital
came back to him, with their consoling thoughts that the man who
had run him down would surely recompense him after returning
home from the Pacific coast.

Vividly he recalled the thrill of satisfaction that had shot
through him when Trigg walked into his hospital ward two weeks
before and announced that Hoggenheimer had agreed to compro-
mise matters for $2,500. From that time on, naturally, he had
ceased worrying altogether. And then—yesterday—had come the
note from Trigg with its peculiar tone that hinted of bad news. And
on top of this, the latter's statement that Hoggenheimer had
laughed the case to scorn, and that the sole witness had been spir-
ited away.

Truly, the ways of the rich were mysterious. What could have
caused that sudden change in Hoggenheimer? How could he have
learned, if such were really the case, that the man he had injured
was without money, relatives, or friends; that he was absolutely
unable to engage in legal battle?

Slowly the afternoon faded away, and the dusk came on, throwing a pall over every object in the room. And still Kirkland lay on
the bed thinking, pondering, brooding. And following the dusk
came darkness. In turn the old clock downstairs in the hallway of
the rooming-house toned forth the hour of six, of seven, of eight.

Suddenly an idea smote him with such intensity that he raised
himself up in the darkness and sat on the edge of the bed with his
heart beating wildly. Why not go straight to Hoggenheimer himself? Why not secure an interview with him in his own home and
show him the poor distorted limbs? Why not plead with him for
some exhibition of justice? Why not see whether the personal element could conquer the unreasoning attitude of a man who had
shown himself anxious only to conserve his own wealth?

Within five minutes Kirkland was making his way, cane in
hand, toward the corner drug store. Inside, he seized the directory
feverishly and turned rapidly to the H's. Finally he came across the
notation for which he was searching:

Hoggenheimer, Samuel; bachelor, res., 1250 Lake Shore Drive.

An hour later he was walking slowly along Lake Shore Drive,
carefully studying the numbers of the magnificent residences that

lined "Millionaires' Row." Soon he glimpsed the number 1250, showing plainly through the lighted transom of a splendid brownstone house which stood some distance from the street in a spacious yard.

As he looked dubiously at the number, wondering whether his contemplated procedure would be condemned by Trigg, a man clad in the blue livery of a servant came down the steps, walked along the path that led to the sidewalk, jerked open the ornamental iron gate, and proceeded leisurely up the street. With a curious glance at the latter's retreating figure, still visible in the radiance of a distant flaming arc lamp, Kirkland turned in at the gate and proceeded up the gravel path. Only for a moment did he hesitate in the vestibule with his finger on the electric button. Then he gave it an energetic push.

From where he stood he could hear a bell ring loudly. He waited—but no one answered the door. Again he pressed the button. And still no reply. Then for the third time he gave it a long ring. And after another short wait he reluctantly descended the front steps. At their foot he paused irresolutely, glancing upward. Then he detected a gleam of light showing forth in the darkness from a second floor window at the side of the house.

Wonderingly he crossed the lawn and peered upward. He found himself able to make out with ease the outlines of a fleshy man sitting at what appeared to be a small desk. For several long minutes Kirkland wavered, wondering whether, in the absence of the servant, it would be quite diplomatic for him to ring for the fourth time. But as he stood there, vacillating from one plan to another, he became conscious, with a shock, that the figure at the desk was unnaturally quiet. So he fixed his attention more closely on the lighted window. Now that he studied the man in the upper room more intently, he became aware of the fact that the latter's head hung down on his chest at a greater angle than the mere writing necessitated.

Kirkland glanced quickly about him. The street was deserted. He himself was shrouded in the darkness of the house. So he stooped and picked up a handful of pebbles, which he flung forcibly upward. They rained on the lighted window with a loud staccato noise and then dropped back upon the lawn.

And still the figure remained absolutely motionless, totally undisturbed!

With more speed than he believed possible for him to attain, Kirkland hurried clumsily to the front steps for the second time.

Once more he pressed the electric button, but this time he kept his finger on it for a full five minutes. Then he returned to the lawn. The figure had not moved by a quarter of an inch.

Hurriedly he glanced along the edge of the house. An open basement window caught his eye. Perplexed, he stood biting his lip.

"That man's not asleep," he muttered finally, half aloud. "He's sick—or else he's dead; one thing or the other." He glanced upward once more. "I guess it's up to me to do the 'phoning for the doctor. I'll risk it, anyway."

He stepped quietly across the stretch of dark grass to the open basement window. There he let himself slowly in, hanging from the stone sill by his arms. Swinging one leg back and forth, he stretched his foot until the toe scraped the floor. A second later he had let himself down to a standing position. He struck a match and located a doorway which led to an uncarpeted hall. Along the hall he walked and, by the light of another match, found a flight of stairs which he ascended slowly, leaning heavily on the banister at each step. After he had covered one flight, he felt underfoot a soft, thick carpet. Groping along the wall, he climbed on to the second floor. Then, confused in the darkness, he turned slowly around. At once he spied a tiny shaft of light emanating from a keyhole. Cautiously he felt his way over to it and, stooping, peered in.

Seated at a desk in a richly furnished room was the same figure he had seen from the outside lawn—and even yet it had not moved. On the desk itself was an envelope propped up against a paperweight, a narrow strip of colored paper, and a large sheet of business size paper. Close by was a steel contrivance which Kirkland recognized instantly as a check protector. On a small stand nearby was a typewriter. As his gaze shifted to the writing machine, he caught sight of a fountain pen lying on the floor directly below the pendant hand of the silent figure.

For Kirkland, that was enough. He flung the door open and walked boldly in. Immediately he laid his hand on the forehead of the man at the desk. His suspicions were verified at last. The forehead was stone cold.

As Kirkland stood there, dazed, wondering what step to take next, his attention was riveted by the inscription on the envelope. He snatched it up and stared unbelievingly at it. It read:

Dolly van Sutten,
The Star Burlesquers,
Folly Theatre,
Chicago.

With his thoughts in a mad whirl, totally forgetful of his surroundings, entirely oblivious to the dead man at his side, he leaned
over the desk and drank in every word of the letter—a letter which
had been cut short by the hand of the Grim Reaper. It ran:

Dear Dolly:—
  Your information regarding the fellow I wrote you about,
that Philip N. Kirkland, who got tangled up in the machine
three months ago, was certainly surprising to say the least. So
he's your ex hubby, eh? And a poor mutt who has to depend on
$18 per for his bread and cheese. And as to your added infor-
mation that he's absolutely without any relatives or any financial drag, that throws an entirely new light on matters. And so,
Dolly, I'll certainly follow your advice about lying low and
waving a couple of hundred under the nose of him and his shyster lawyer as soon as they see they're up against a 'caseless'
case. I guess you're right—they'll be glad to grab it. And to
think, Dolly, that that lawyer of his had me bluffed to a fare-
you-well with a lot of bunk talk. I nearly coughed up the whole
2500 simoleons.
  Now, Dear Girl, I note that your letter says I've forgotten
your birthday. No such a thing. The truth of the matter is that
I've been rushed to death the last few days with specialists,
consultations and what not else. They claim my heart is on the
blink (the truth is—you've got that heart!) and that I'll have to
go East to be thumped by still another specialist in New York.
Beastly nuisance, I call it. Honestly, I think they're all up in the
air about it—and that they're only out for my money.
  But now—as to that birthday of yours. I want to buy you a
little trinket—but I'm going to let you make the selection yourself. For that reason I'm enclosing a signed check, with the
spaces blank, so that you can fill in the jeweler's name and the
amount of your purchase. Before mailing it I'll limit it to $500
with the check protector; so get what your little heart desires—
up to that amount. And as soon as I get back from the East
we'll—

Here the letter stopped abruptly. Bewildered, Kirkland passed the back of his hand over his brow—and the sheet of paper fluttered to the floor. Suddenly he stiffened up and glanced with a sneer toward the figure that still sat huddled up in the chair.

Then he stepped to the window and drew down the shade. A moment later he was rolling the narrow signed slip of colored paper into the typewriter and was laboriously tapping the keys, using one finger of each hand.

"My dear Kirkland," exclaimed Trigg exultantly, "the most astounding thing occurred in the night while you were asleep. I've come straight to your room to tell you all about it. At one o'clock this morning, a special delivery letter was delivered to me at my house, marked 'urgent, open at once,' and 'special'—all on the typewriter. It was a short typewritten note—and confound it, Kirkland, signed on the typewriter, too—from our friend, Sam Hoggenheimer, himself. He told me briefly that he was going East today and that I should cash the enclosed check immediately the bank opened. And in it was a signed check—with my name as attorney, and the amount, $2,500, inserted with the typewriter. So I—"

"Did you cash it?" interrupted Kirkland, pale, tense, leaning half out of his chair.

"Eh?' Did I cash it? My boy, I've been a lawyer too long to let a check get cold on my hands. I was Johnny on the spot when the bank opened—my own bank, too, by the way—and got it all in yellowbacks. And say, Kirkland, I was just in time, for when I called up his place ten minutes later to thank him, I was informed that he'd passed over the great divide at some indefinite time between nine o'clock last night and nine o'clock this morning. And a dead man's check is worthless. Whew! Great mackerel—what a narrow escape for us!" He paused and his face lighted up suddenly. "And say, Kirkland, I've rounded you up a job making out bills and statements. Do you think you could learn to operate a typewriter?"

"Sure do," replied Kirkland, staring out of the window at a cloud, "I've had a—a—little experience on the—the machine. Some day, Trigg, I'll tell you about it."

And a year later, he did!

QUILLIGAN AND THE MAGIC COIN

EUPHEMISTICALLY SPEAKING, Quilligan was suffering from the toxic effects of a common grain derivative. Mechanically speaking, his condition was such that it required the expenditure of more than the usual number of ergs to maintain his center of gravity directly above his point of support. Geometrically speaking, he was traveling along the path composed of a series of horizontal curves, each of which was halfway between a catenary and hypocycloid.

For the ninety-ninth time, Quilligan was drunk!

Possibly Arabian Nights adventures happen only to those who are drunk. Perhaps not. Very likely there was nothing mysterious about Quilligan's peculiar adventure with the magic coin, considering its prosaic outcome. And, on the other hand—

But, we reiterate, Quilligan was drunk.

It was eight o'clock in the evening. Since five that afternoon he had been wandering aimlessly back and forth through the mazes of the Loop, vainly searching for one person. He had inquired in all-night drug stores and fly-by-night auction houses; in ten-cent stores and Salvation Army soup kitchens; in pawnshops and penny arcades; in photo-postal studios and chop-suey restaurants; from traffic cops and blind beggars; from shooting galleries and home-scurrying shop girls; from chauffeurs and newsboys; from nickel show cashiers and street-corner shoestring merchants; from—

But the only result so far achieved had been the taking on of a cargo of the aforesaid grain derivative, each increment of which had drowned its inciting rebuff.

With such a rigorous search as this going on before our very eyes, it behooves us to investigate it a little more closely. Perhaps we can be of assistance—and thus stem the flowing tide of bitterness and booze that threatens to engulf Quilligan.

The object of Quilligan's search, it seems, was one Augustus Heinze Shutenthaler, a friend of his boyhood days. Exactly forty-eight hours before, Quilligan received over the general delivery of the postoffice at Kokomo, Indiana, a postcard which proved to be from Augustus Heinze Shutenthaler himself. In it the latter an-

nounced that in two days he was opening up his new and glittering
palace of free lunch and fiery liquor, bowing bartenders and bottled beer, in Chicago's downtown district, and that he hoped to see
his boyhood friend, Quilligan, there on the opening night. In view
of the fact that the postal had eluded the argus-eyed
Mrs. Quilligan, Quilligan was in Chicago ready to greet his old
friend, Augustus Heinze Shutenthaler. But in view of the fact that
he had forgotten to bring the postal carrying the address of the new
and glittering palace of music boxes and matchless brew, brass
railings and bottled rum, there was no Shutenthaler to greet—
no Shutenthaler to find.

Earlier in the evening a sympathetic druggist had looked up the
name of Shutenthaler in the city and telephone directories for
Quilligan—and had found no entry whatever. So that trail, therefore, was nipped in the clue. Hence Quilligan was becoming discouraged. He longed to see Augustus Heinze Shutenthaler,
with whom he used to paddle in the old swimming hole. He
longed to see Augustus Heinze Shutenthaler's new and glittering
establishment, and to imbibe a convivial glass with him. To return to Kokomo without seeing Shutenthaler would be no less than
a—hic—crime.

For the ninety-ninth time, Quilligan perked up and approached
a blue-coated traffic cop who loomed up in front of him from an
alcoholic fog.

"'S this way, ossifer," he murmured. " 'S m' fren' Shutenthaler. Shutenthaler—bran new s'loon—roun' here somew'ere."
With a majestic sweep of his hand he indicated the whole
156 square miles of Chicago. "Here—somew'ere. Where'll I fin'
Shutenthaler?"

"Now f'r th' third and last time," said the cop testily, "I'm tel-
lin' ye it'll be roonin' ye in I will, do ye be troublin' me wid
annymore quistions about y'r friend Shoohootenthaler. As I told
ye wanst before, I know nahthing about anny Tootenshaler. If th'
name's not in ather a 'phone directory 'r a city directory, thin I do
be advisin' ye to consult a fortin-tiller—'r somethin' like that.
Now be aff wid ye."

Sadly Quilligan turned away and resumed his wanderings along
South State Street. Always the same. No one knew anything
about Shutenthaler and the new saloon. What a—hic—fool he had
been for forgetting to bring that postal with Shutenthaler's location
on it. What a shame to have to return to Kokomo without seeing
the old friend of his boyhood days. The cop had advised him to

consult a fortune teller. If he didn't get any better results than he
had so far, he might consider the idea and—

He brought himself gradually to a position of oscillating quies-
cence. He stared. In front of him was the entrance of a rusty looking building, placarded all over with dentists' signs advertising gold fillings for fifty cents—and up. And crowning all the
tooth scenery was a sign that held great potentialities for Quilligan. It announced that:

> MADAME ASTRO
> Revealer of the Hidden,
> Discloser of the Future, Crystal Gazer,
> Trance Medium,
> Is to be found in Room 202—Walk up.
> Special for today:
> Crystal reading with trance: 50¢.

Swaying back and forth like an inverted pendulum, Quilligan
read the sign from beginning to end. Then he dipped his hand into
his trousers pocket and brought up all that he found there: two ten-
dollar bills, a silver fifty-cent piece, and a return ticket to Kokomo.
So far, so good. With punctiliousness he returned the two tens and
the ticket to Kokomo. And with the fifty-cent piece clasped in his
fist, he ascended a long flight of creaky, wooden stairs to a land of
false teeth and gold fillings.

May heaven guard Quilligan and those two ten-dollar bills in
his mad journey through the jungles infested by the tooth vultures.
If he ever knocks at the wrong door he'll come out minus the two
tens and plus a diagnosis of nothing less than pyorrhoea alveolaris.
Ah—even heaven must be on the job, for he stops in front of
Room 202. He knocks. Once more we draw a long breath, and
pause while the story slides ahead out of the present tense.

A long delay followed Quilligan's knock. If he had been able to
see through a wooden door panel he might have observed a huge,
florid woman hastily hiding an ice-cold bottle of beer beneath a
stand which carried a long black cloth and a great crystal ball. At
the same time he would have seen her scrambling into a som-
bre robe covered here and there with white crescent moons. But
finally the door opened.

"Lookin' f'r a Madame Astro," said Quilligan, bowing through a small and safe angle.

She bowed in return.

"I am Madame Astro," she replied in clear, grave tones.

" 'S m' fren' Shutenthaler," he explained concisely. "Can't locate Shutenthaler. Augustus Heinze Shutenthaler. Been ever'wher'. Thought I'd—hic—try fortune teller. Last resort, you know."

"Be seated," she commanded, beckoning him to a chair which stood in front of the crystal sphere. He dropped into it. Whereupon she closed the door and seated herself opposite him.

"Already I perceive that you wish the hidden revealed. I, Madame Astro, seer into the far, student of occultism, unveiler of the mysteries of the Orient, stand ready to help you. Speak, layman, speak—and—er—cross my palm with the sum of fifty cents. What wouldst know?"

Quilligan dropped the half-dollar at the side of the crystal ball. Madame promptly performed the vanishing trick with it.

" 'S m' fren' Augustus Heinze Shutenthaler, " he elucidated. "Started new s'loon downtown. Jus' wan' fin' Shutenthaler. Thaz all. Thaz all."

Madame nodded understandingly and sympathetically. Madame realized that here was a victim who, properly handled, was good for a double or even a triple fee. She commenced staring fixedly at the crystal ball. After a full minute had passed she began to sway gently from side to side. The swaying became more violent and then subsided, leaving her sitting stiff and rigid, her eyes glued mechanically to the transparent object in front of her.

Quilligan, rapt, watched her every movement.

Suddenly she leaned forward a trifle and commenced speaking in a dull monotone.

"I see—I see—I see—a—a—man. He is tall—and thin. He is clad in a checked suit. He is seeking vainly for—for—for—something. Ah!—what that is—I cannot see. He asks everyone. They shake their heads. He stops. He appears discouraged. He stoops. He picks—picks up—picks up—ah, nothing less than the magic coin—the all-powerful coin of the four wishes. Ah, fortunate, fortunate mortal, to hold in his possession the magic coin itself. Does he know that four wishes shall that coin give to its owner before it loses its potency? Four wishes! Wishes for health, for fame, for riches, for love, for knowledge, for what not else. Does he realize that he holds in his hand a coin that a king's ransom could not buy? (Either that bottle of beer has gone to Madame's head—or else she's spreading herself.) Four wishes! Wishes to be used wisely. Wishes to be used foolishly. Ah, fortunate, fortunate mortal. But will he remember—will he remember the number 4? The magic number 4? Will he remember? Will he—"

Quilligan reached over and gently tapped Madame on the shoulder.

"All ver' nize—majick coin—four wizzes," he said thickly. "But how 'bout m' fren' Shutenthaler?"

Like a flash she relaxed. Her eyes opened wide. She stared stupidly about her. "Idiot," she exclaimed, "you broke my trance. You snapped the most wonderful uninterrupted chain of vision I've had for a week. I could have told you everything you desired to know. As it is, it'll cost you another fifty cents."

Quilligan rose and pushed back his chair to the wall.

In Madame's second demand for cash he detected the faint creakings of a follow-up system. She was like all the rest. No one could tell him the answer to his problem: Where was Shutenthaler located? Without a word he walked to the door, opened it, and made his way down the squeaky stairs to the street. As for Madame Astro, however, she merely doffed her black robe, deposited her fifty cents in the Woman's National Lisle Bank, and resumed her bottle of cold beer.

Quilligan proceeded gloomily down the street. The clock on the corner of Van Buren and State showed the time to be 8:30 in the evening. Undecidedly, he paused, figuring whom to ask next. As he swayed to and fro in the breeze from the lake, the glint of something shiny met his eye. With infinite patience he stooped and picked it up. The light from the show-window of a nearby clothing store fell full upon it. A brief inspection showed him that his unsteady fingers held a bright metal disk on which the words were stamped:

Odd that, Quilligan ruminated. The crystal gazer; her vision of a tall, thin man in a checked suit picking up a magic coin, her warning—"Remember the number 4"; her statement that the coin held exactly four wishes for its owner and then became value-less!

He scratched his head.

After which he clutched the metal disk in his hand and continued along the street, still picturing Madame Astro staring into the crystal sphere. All bunk, of course, he reflected. No such thing as a magic coin. No such thing as four wishes coming to a man in the twentieth century. And yet—well, he'd take a try at it.

"Lez see—lez see," he mumbled gravely to himself. "I wizz zat—zat—someone would—hic—walk up t' me and thrust a nize fat purse in my hand. Nize fat one. Nize fat one. Greenbacks—sparklers. Nize big one."

Scarcely had he covered thirty feet than a tall, thin young man with sandy complexion and a pair of steely blue eyes, stepped up behind him and apologetically tapped him on the shoulder.

"Beg pardon," he observed smoothly, "but—er—you must have dropped your purse. I came near holding on to it because of the hard times, but I've always—er—tried to be honest—so I want to hand it back."

Quilligan wheeled sharply. With amazement he looked down at the slim young man. His eyes travelled to the latter's outstretched hand. Then they bulged out, for the hand was tendering him a fat leather purse, open just barely enough to disclose a bulky roll and a string of sparkling brilliants.

Only for a second did Quilligan hesitate. Then his own hand shot down into his trousers pocket and immediately reappeared, the fingers holding one of the two ten-dollar bills. With the other he reached out for the purse.

"You're the—hic—honestest man in the city," he affirmed genially. "Don't see how I ever losht it. Ver' honest man, m' fren'!" He pressed the crisp ten into the slim young man's palm. The latter clinched it eagerly. "There's reward—small, triflin' reward—f' ver' honest young man." He jammed the bulging purse into his coat pocket and hurried around the corner.

As soon as he reached an alley he turned and made his way down it for a space of ten or twelve feet to a point directly beneath a hissing arc-lamp. Then he withdrew the purse and prepared to count the contents. But, to his dumfoundment, he found only a tight roll of narrow slips of green crepe paper—and a string of cutglass beads.

"Beau'fully, beau'fully stung," he murmured, after the explanation had gradually sifted in on him. "Stung beau'fully. Ol' game—and caught Quilligan from Kokomo al' ri'. Well, got my wizz anyway—nize fat purse—but cosht me $10. That a majick coin, all ri', all ri'. Jus' goin' t' watch that coin."

He threw the purse and its contents in a dark corner of the alley; then he returned to the street.

He covered another block. By degrees he began to forget about the magic coin and to ponder once more about the question that had engrossed him all the evening: How and where was he going to find Shutenthaler?

Finally he stopped. The fact had dawned on him that it was high time to buy another drink—for there was still $10 left in the bank roll. But as he reached a decision in the matter, he caught sight of a big black negro, leaning nonchalantly against a doorway close by. Since the latter appealed to him as a possible source of information, he stepped over to him.

" 'S m' fren' Shutenthaler," he explained. "Fren' Shutenthaler—"

"Shoot a dollah, sah?" interrupted the negro. "Yessuh." He peered carefully up and down South State Street. Then he leaned over and whispered in Quilligan's ear: "Go straight to the fo'th flo' an' rap fo' times on the fo'th do'. Jes' remembah the numbah fo', sah."

Quilligan began the long, wearisome climb. Evidently he was on the trail of Shutenthaler at last. In turn he came to the second, the third, and finally the fourth and top floor. There he paused and counted the doors from the top of the stairway: one, two, three, four. He went down the hallway and rapped exactly four times on the fourth door. Instantly it swung open as if operated by an invisible genie. And as he walked in, it closed noiselessly behind him.

He peered around, discovered that he was in an immense room. At the rear of it was a long, green baize table, presided over by a black mustached man. Around the edges twenty or thirty men were crowded, some sitting and some standing, but all watching intently the spinning of a roulette wheel. With a sinking heart Quilligan realized that the wires of fate had crossed once more—and that he was as far as ever from the trail which led to Augustus Heinze Shutenthaler.

As he stood there irresolutely, his attention was riveted by one of the spectators at the green baize table raking in a handful of silver and paper money. That was interesting. So he stepped over, wedged himself in the spellbound audience, and began to watch the ceaseless play on the black and the red, the odd and the even, the high and the low. Soon he caught sight of the great square which was painted on the green cloth and divided into thirty-six smaller squares, each of which was numbered with one of the numbers on the roulette wheel. He turned to a man at his side.

"Whaz nummers for?" he asked.

"Sh-h-h," whispered his companion. "Go easy, pal, on th' gab. They're runnin' under cover here. It's this way, friend. You lay your mazuma on any number. If that number comes up on the next spin of the wheel, you get thirty-six times your stake."

With an effort Quilligan steadied himself, for he suddenly remembered the magic coin in his pocket—the coin with three more unused wishes. And he recollected at the same time that his total wealth was reduced to a lone $10 bill and a return ticket to Kokomo. Since his mission to Chicago had failed, here was a heaven-sent opportunity to go back to Kokomo with a roll big enough to choke the postmaster's mare. So he turned to the man at his side once more and said,

" 'F I—hic—put $10 on the nummer—any nummer—" He paused. More and more he began to see that he had nothing less than a half-Nelson on the Blind Goddess, for he possessed three A. No. 1 wishes as well as the red-hot hunch: Remember the number four. " 'F I put $10 on th' nummer four—an' th' nummer four comes up—do I get $360, fren'?"

"Righto, pal," said the man addressed, watching with unconcealed admiration an individual who, drunk or sober, contemplated risking a ten spot on a thirty-six to one chance. "It's thirty-six times your stake on a number bet."

Majestically Quilligan reached down into his pocket. He gave the magic coin an admonitory pat. Then he drew up his last $10 bill. A number of the players were depositing their stakes on the colored squares. Quilligan leaned over and placed his piece of paper money on the square marked "4".

"I wizz," he said sternly, to no one in particular, "that the number four comes up."

The black moustached man looked around. All the bets were placed. So he gave the disk an energetic twirl. It spun swiftly, the black and red merging instantly into a hybrid color, and the ivory ball giving a sharp rattling noise like a machine gun on the banks of the Yser. The wheel ran with undiminished speed for a quarter of a minute. Then it began to slow down. Quilligan looked on fascinated, steadying himself on the shoulder of his companion. Still more slowly it turned. The ivory ball now began to bounce several spaces at a time. Slowly and slowly the wheel revolved. And finally, with a last saucy leap, the marble dropped squarely into the slot marked "4".

"Well, by Hectofer," said the black moustached man, smiling gamely. "Stranger, you win. The first number bet placed tonight. Gentlemen, didja ever see the beat of it for sheer—" Crash!

An axe blade shivered the panels of the door. The shrill sound of police whistles and men cursing began in the outside hallway. Instantly confusion reigned supreme inside the room. The black moustached man sprang to the electric switch and snapped it. In a trice the room was plunged into utter darkness. Blow after blow continued to smash in the door. Amid the sounds of splintering wood and falling plaster, some excited person tipped over the roulette table. Men shoved, fought, struck out, kicked and tripped over each other in their wild efforts to elude the gambling squad that was breaking in the doors.

Quilligan, entangled in a mass of cursing, stumbling figures, found himself pushed and shoved through a small doorway. At once he felt a cool draught of air on his face. A second later he discovered that he was on a gravelled roof in company with twenty or more fleeing men. He saw his companions speed across the roof in the moonlight and disappear down a rusty iron fire-escape. So he followed, panting and sweating, because he was the last man. He descended hurriedly, swaying dizzily at every rung; but he clung on like a fly until he reached a dark alley. Here he threaded his way through a number of barrels and packing boxes, and finally came out on the brilliantly lighted thoroughfare.

Five or six doorways down, he caught sight of a blue patrol wagon backed up to the sidewalk, and a big crowd lined up from the curb to the building line.

He walked hastily in a northerly direction and soon found himself a block away from the scene of the excitement. Whereupon he leaned up against an arc-lamp post and made an effort to collect his fuddled wits.

At once he remembered that he hadn't had time even to collect his $360 winnings on his $10 bet. So he ruefully thrust his hand down into his pocket and drew up the magic coin.

"Y'r some majick coin, all ri', all ri'," he groaned. "Got m' firsh wizz—an' cosh me $10. Got m' shecond wizz—an' losh $10 more. Now I'm broke entir'ly." He paused, frowning at the coin. "Y're a big fake. Thought sho all th' time. Jus' a big fake, thaz all. I wizz I had jus' price of a drink—an' wizz I knew where I could fin' m' fren' 'Gustus Heinze Shutenthaler."

He flipped the metal disk idly over on his palm. Its reverse side read:

SIDESTEPPING RYAN

by Harry Stephen Keeler and
Franklin Lee Stevenson

I HAD VERY LITTLE expectation that afternoon that Tim Waldo would show up at the appointed spot. For "The Flea," so far as I knew, had been on the "wanted" list of the Chicago detective bureau for the past five years. And having successfully wiggled out of the clutches of the law on the Ippstein robbery of five years before, it hardly seemed logical that he would ever again have the temerity to venture into the confines of a city that boasted as many plain-clothes men as Chicago. And the peculiar letter had stated very definitely: State and Van Buren, Southeast corner, 2 P. M.

So I continued to wait for him, even though the hands of my watch passed in turn two-fifteen, two-thirty, two-forty-five. And finally, just as I had about given up all hope of his putting in an appearance, a short, check-suited figure wearing a resplendent red necktie and equally resplendent patent leather shoes, as well as a derby hat cocked on one side of its head, detached itself from the hurrying downtown throng across the street and slipped over to where I was standing. For a second he hesitated. Then he asked:

"Were you lookin' f'r someone?"

I thrust out my hand. "Is it Tim Waldo? If it is, your letter reached me."

"So you come, Jerry!" he exclaimed, seizing my hand in the clutches of his own slim white fingers, and pumping my arm up and down. "Jerry—Dempsey," he repeated in a much lower tone of voice, taking me in from head to foot with a quick glance. "An' my letter reached you, eh, Jerry?" He leaned over a little closer although there was no one in hearing distance. "Five long years, pal, since you an' me met on th' porch roof of th' Ippstein bunga-low. An' I'll bet you're wonderin', Jerry, why I sent f'r ye?"

"I am that," I replied. "When your letter came into my hands I was some surprised. But I'm here, Tim, after almost five years to a day since we met."

He chuckled. "I'll bet you was surprised. An' you'll be more surprised—" He stopped suddenly and began looking about him, obviously ill at ease. He surveyed several harmless passers-by with manifest suspicion written on his face. Then he turned to me again. "You an' me can't take no chances gabbin' on the stem in

broad daylight, Jerry," he whispered. "Drop in behind me when I
beat it, an' I'll give you all the dope later." Loud enough so that
the passers-by could hear, he bellowed out: "Sorry, stranger, but I
ain't got no match." Then he turned on his heel and started up
South State Street in the direction of a row of cheap, transient hotels.

I fell in behind him exactly as he had instructed me to do, and
after a walk of about two blocks in which I took pains to keep
from thirty to forty feet in his rear he turned into a dingy passage-
way over which hung a weatherbeaten sign:

EAGLE HOTEL
ROOMS BY DAY, WEEK, MONTH OR YEAR

Without turning his head he went up the stairs to the third floor,
myself still following. At the end of the long dark hallway, however, he withdrew a key from his pocket and unlocked a creaking
door which he held open. I passed in without a word. With a long
drawn out sigh, a sigh of relief, he locked the door behind us and
hung his derby hat over the knob so that the keyhole was quite
obscured.

"Now, Jerry," he said, "we can talk all we please. I'm so busy
in this burg sidesteppin' a guy named Ryan that I'm getting nervous as a cat."

"Ryan?" I ventured. "And who's Ryan?"

"Which goes to show, Jerry," declared Tim, grinning, "that
you're a Noo York crook instead of a Chicago crook, or you'd be
wise to who Ryan was. But I'll tell you all about it."

The room we were in was one that typical of the usual cheap
hotels that abound in every big city near the main depot. It was
furnished only with a badly cracked, white enameled bed, a rickety
wooden table, and a pair of straight chairs, although in one corner,
contrasting violently with the dilapidated furnishings, stood a
leather suitcase that radiated the very atmosphere of brand new-
ness.

Tim first dragged the table well away from the wall. Then he
drew up the two chairs and dropped into one of them. I took up the
other and waited to hear what he had to say.

"I 'spose, Jerry," he began in a low voice, "that you're still
wonderin' why I sent f'r you clear to Noo York, eh?"

"I sure am. The only explanation I can forge is that you've rounded up a big job that needs a pair of clever men." I waited a moment. "Did I hit it right?"

"You did, Jerry. But it's no small change job." He looked uneasily about him for a few seconds. Then he leaned over close to me and whispered: "Forty thousand dollars—an' all waitin' to be carted off!"

I let slip a long, ruminative whistle.

"Yes," he went on in a low voice, "the biggest an' easiest job that two crooks ever yet tackled. An' that's what brung Timmy Waldo—th' Flea—into the danger lines of Chi"—a shadow crossed his face—"an' of this guy Ryan." Apparently thinking, he paused, for a long while, unconsciously chewing on his upper lip.

"Well, Tim, I'm waiting to hear all about it. And you might tell me, too, where you've been keeping yourself these five years. And how you ever happened to think of 26½ Mott Street in little old N'Yawk, when you needed a man."

He drew out two cheroots, and lighting one, tossed the other over to me.

"Now look here, Jerry," he began, "me an' you—the Flea an' the notorious Jerry Dempsey—met under pecooliar conditions, to say the least, especially since the last I seen of you you had a black strip over your peepers, same as me. It ain't happened, f'r instance, Jerry, that you've gone an' joined the Salvation Army since then, have you? In other words, you ain't changed none?"

"Not on your life, Tim," I said reassuringly. "On this one point you can be absolutely sure: I haven't altered by an eyelash or an idea since we met on the Ippstein job—five years ago. Does that answer your question?"

"It does—an' it's O. K. So now, Jerry, to eloocidate that pecooliar letter of mine an' to tell you somethin' about myself durin' them last five years.

"O' course you remember how you an' me gets acquainted with each other—on the porch roof of th' Ippstein bungalow out on Grand Boulevard. Both of us, it seems, was tryin' to hook our respective claws on Lena Ippstein's weddin' necklace. An', as Chance would have it, we has to select the same identical moment to meet on the roof of that porch."

I smiled at the remembrance of that unusual night.

"I confess, Jerry, that when I first seen your figger loomin' up over th' edge of that roof, I thought sure you was a bull. An' let me tell you this, pal: I come mighty near pokin' you a stiff one in the jaw and drivin' you to th' ground, fi'teen feet below. But when you turns your head in th' moonlight an' I sees you got a black strip across your peepers, I knows there's nothin' left to do but shake hands on th' job and pull it off together.

"You gets next to me crouchin' there, an' whispers in my ear to take the lookout while you does th' inside work. F'r a minute, Jerry, I was a little suspicious of you, but seein' what you done for me a week later when I was locked up in th' County Jail, I didn't have no right to be thinkin' that way. Howsomever—to get back to the story—you steps in Lena Ippstein's boodwar to get your fingers on them weddin' sparklers that the papers had been spoutin' about.

"In five minutes, Jerry, you comes out, holdin' up that little gold wristlet with the row of stones in it. But, just as I'm about to ask you if that was all they was in the jool box, hell itself breaks loose. Zing! A bullet sizzes past my nut and splinters the window back of me into a million pieces. On top o' that, we hears the whistle of a harness bull, an' sees the' bright reflections on the lawn when th' lights go on all over the house. An' so, Jerry, we has to jump for it, you from one end of that there porch roof an' me from the other. But me—cuss my luck!—has to go straight into the hands of that same harness bull what done the shootin' an' what now run in off the street.

"But when I jumps, Jerry, I don't forget to take with me that short steel jimmy that I fetched along. An' no sooner does this harness bull close in on me than I brings that jimmy down on his bean with a whang—an' lays him flat on th' sod. But then, as I'm stumblin' to my feet again to follow you, who's almost to the street by this time, about forty million hands an' arms tightens around me. Two minutes later old Ippstein an' his two sons has me trussed up for th' wagon.

"So I lays in the county jail, Jerry, f'r a long time. They tells me that this harness bull—Ryan was his name—is lingerin' between life and death, with his scalp laid open, camcussion of th' brain, an' frackered skull. An' the gran' jury refuses to indict me f'r the Ippstein job until this Ryan lives or dies. But if he croaks, Jerry, it's to be murder. Oh Lor', I tell you I was beginnin' to be scared. Night after night I sees myself swingin' for it if that guy passes out.

"But about that time I gets the pecooliar letter addressed to Tim Waldo, County Jail, Chicago.

"I'd often been wonderin', Jerry, what become of you after you disappeared in th' darkness of Grand Boulevard that night. But when I opens that there letter in my cell an' five yellow centuries comes tumblin' out, I knows that it's from you—an' that it's my end of that diamon' wristlet. But say, Jerry, the fence you went to stuck you for fair, if you only got a thousand for it. Howsomever, that's the hell of our game.

"But to get back to the story. I realizes, o' course, that you don't dare put no writin' in that letter. So all th' time I'm waitin' for this guy Ryan to live or croak, I'm wonderin' who you was, where you come from, whether you was a Chicago crook or some out of town guy.

"But it happens, Jerry, that I carries that envelope around in my back pocket, an' account of my pacin' up an' down in that two-by-four cell of mine an' sweatin' to beat th' band from thinkin' about swingin' for Ryan's death, the stamp fin'lly comes off. And then f'r the first time I learns who you was, for I sees where you had wrote in small letters under the stamp: 'From Jerry Dempsey, 26½ Mott Street, N. Y. You know who.'

"An' say—I'd heard a dozen times in my life about Jerry Dempsey, th' slickest second story worker in the East. But I tell you I cert'nly never suspected as I was goin' to meet up with him on the porch roof of the Ippstein bungalow in th' town of Chi. So, havin' heard about you before, Jerry, an' havin' got a straight, square deal from you on that little job, I always remembers your name an' address what you slipped me under the stamp with the five centuries. An' I—But again I'm gettin' away from the facts. Them, I takes it, you wants to hear?"

"Yes," I admitted, blowing a few smoke rings ceilingward. "Part of them were in the newspapers about that time. But I'd rather hear your own side of the story, Tim."

"Well," he continued, "this here Ryan lives. Believe me, it was a long three months f'r me while he was fightin' off death, but at th' end of that time th' screws in the county jail tells me that he's took a big turn for the better. An' he keeps gettin' better an' better, till fin'lly I hears that he's discharged from the hospital. Then next day I hear that he's been took out of his harness and made a fly cop on th' Chicago detective bureau, account of his quick work in the Ippstein case.

"But, after all, Jerry, it was lucky f'r me that I'd planted Ryan in the hospital for them three long months, for if I'd been tried right after the Ippstein robbery, I'd 'a' been over th' road long since and servin' a stretch in the Joliet Big House. An' my havin' to wait f'r Ryan to live or die brings me up to the day that the famous Chicago County Jail daylight delivery takes place. Did you read about that, Jerry, in the Noo York papers?"

"I read all about the affair, Tim," I answered. "It was in all the papers, I imagine, from coast to coast. As I remember it, some of you fellows on the third tier had been let out of your cells into the exercise corridor—the bull pen—one Sunday afternoon. One of you had a bunch of hacksaw blades that had been smuggled into him by his girl. I don't remember the details clearly, but another one of you, I believe, sawed away two of the bars, unnoticed by the passers-by on Illinois Street, three stories below. Then, by means of a rope made from sheets contributed by each one, five or six of you came down in broad daylight. And the few people on the street that Sunday afternoon were so dumbfounded that not one had presence of mind enough to notify the jail office."

"Righto," said Tim. "An' to cut the story short, Tim Waldo was one of them that skinned down that rope. Well, I breaks for an alley on Illinois Street and comes out on Michigan Street, where I makes tracks f'r the Chicago an' Northwestern freight yards. There I manages to board an out-goin' rattler. By hidin' in the woods by day an' travellin' by night on different roads, I makes the Western coast in a little over four weeks. An' it's out on th' Western coast that I been for them past five years.

"But now to tell you why I'm so leary o' settin' foot in Chi. Two days after I makes my getaway, I passes through Burlin'ton, Iowa. Near th' tracks I picks up a Chicago newspaper what somebody has thrun out of the car window, an' I reads all about that there famous jail delivery—the first ever known in this burg. An' as I reads on I learns how them other guys is gettin' picked up, one by one. But at the end of that account is a interview with the guy I'd knocked out on the Ippstein lawn—Ryan of the detective bureau. But by th' workin's of fate an' city politics he's not plain Ryan no more, Jerry. He's Sergeant Ryan! An' he tells th' newspaper guys that he'll never rest as long as he lives until he lands th' Flea behind the bars—and makes him serve time f'r the Ippstein robbery."

"I don't wonder you're leary of the big town, Tim. Strikes me that you're taking long chances in venturing back here again."

"I'm takin' some slight chances, to be sure," he admitted, "f'r the dream of Ryan's life would be to nab me hisself an' get square for them three months in horspital I give him. But—" He lifted up his coat tail and showed me the butt of a villainous looking revolver protruding from his hip pocket. "But neither th' honorable Sergeant Ryan nor no other dick is ever goin' to take me, Jerry. I been in th' West f'r five long years, where they shoot to kill." A venomous grin spread over his face. And he added meaningly: "An' I'm a Westerner now, Jerry. Do you get me?"

He paused for a moment, while I nodded slowly.

"But now," he went on, "to tell you about the biz on hand, why I wrote to you at 26½ Mott Street, an' why I'm back in Chi.

"Out near Los Angeles, Jerry, I been workin' for the last six months as hostler on a big estate there. Don't smile, 'bo. The best of us has to work now an' then f'r our livin'." He paused for a second. "This estate belonged to old Mortimer Dean. Do you know who I mean?"

"Not Dean, the baking powder man? The one whose name is riveted to the steps of every elevated railroad in the country?"

"The same," smiled Tim. "Mortimer Dean—multimillionaire— th' guy that piled up his coin by advertisin' ordinary bakin' powder. At any rate, Jerry, old Dean bein' a widower has a female housekeeper what takes care of both the Chicago house on th' Lake Shore Drive in th' summertime, an' the California home in th' wintertime. An' seein' that the old gal was kinda shinin' up to me, I gradually makes love to her, Jerry, thinkin' I might pick up a little information about where the old gent keeps his silver plate an' so forth.

"An' say—she falls for it. But she's too foxy to spill any information about that there Los Angeles home. Nevertheless, I makes love to her all the harder, an' bit by bit, piece by piece—it took me a long two months o' careful pumpin'—I manages to extract some mighty interestin'—not to say valooble—information about this here Chicago home.

"It seems, first of all, Jerry, that old Mortimer Dean is a Catholic. Now I got nothin' ag'in th' Catholics. In fact, far's religion goes, I'm a strict nooter. An' let me tell you, pal, that he's a real Catholic, for he's got a shrine—or altar—or whatever you call it— right in his own home. An' bein' rich in the kale, he ain't stinted himself, it seems, in the ornaments that stands in that there shrine. They're gold—all of 'm."

"Gold? And solid?"

"Righto. This here shrine, however, is hid in such a way that it don't never need to be disturbed when the old gink leaves the city. In fact, nobody but old Dean, the housekeeper, Tim Waldo, an' maybe Jerry Dempsey knows that it exists. But I'm a-goin' to tell you about the chief adornment of that shrine.

"It's a gold candlestick, Jerry, what he had made in mem'ry of his daughter's death, an' what ain't never supposed to be moved out of there. It stands about three feet high. It's got a base an inch thick an' a foot across, with little solid gold angels like you an' me around it. And its stem is three inches across, with a one inch hole bored f'r th' candle. To boil down the old gal's description, Jerry, it weighs close on to 150 pounds. It—"

"Great Scott!" I ejaculated. "Then it—" I made a hasty mental calculation. "At $15 an ounce, Tim, she'd certainly reach mighty close to your figure of $40,000. So that's what has brought you back to the danger lines of the big town, Tim?"

"Righto," he replied. "I sure done a lot of figurin' with a stub of pencil when I learned about that there gold candlestick from the lovesick dame that was stuck on me. An' when I finds how it's right here in town year in an' year out, hid in the slickest way you ever heard of, I seen that it's up to me to beat old Mortimer Dean back to Chi by at least a week. I knows exactly how to uncover that shrine. I know just how to take care of that 150-pound stick of gold after we gets it. An' with th' stout shoulders of Jerry Dempsey on th' job, we ought to raise our respective antes by $20,000 apiece."

He reached over and clapped me exuberantly on the shoulder.

"So you see, Jerry," he added, "I ain't never forgot your squareness to me in mailin' me them five centuries as my end of the Ippstein loot. When I gets all this valooble dope out in Los Angeles, an' knows that it's up to me to round up a pal f'r the heavy liftin' of the job, I think first of all of Jerry Dempsey an' the little Noo York address that he slips me five years back. Natur'lly, I knows there ain't no use of my tryin' to round up a pal in any of them old Chicago haunts of mine. For I never forgets, Jerry, about that interview with Ryan"—his voice took on a sneer—"Sergeant Ryan—who says he'll put me back of th' bars if it takes him a lifetime. Is it all plain now? If it is, we'll go into the plans for the stashin' of this here gold candlestick."

Till late that night we sat in Tim's room, discussing in turn notorious crooks with whom each of us had an acquaintance, and going fully into the plans that Tim had been laying on the way from California to Chicago. So far as our actual procedure in removing the gold candlestick was concerned, he was quite cool and collected; but otherwise he seemed to be in a most nervous and unstrung condition. Later in the evening he got into the habit of springing to his feet almost every little while, and, after jerking his hand quickly to his back pocket where that villainous looking revolver reposed, of flinging open the door of the room. But each time, of course, the outer hallway proved to be empty.

Tim's plans, which I did not venture to modify greatly, consisted of reaching Mortimer Dean's Lake Shore Drive residence shortly after midnight, and of securing entrance to the deserted house by the usual simple means. He was quite emphatic in his assertion that old Dean's housekeeper had declared that no caretaker was ever left there on account of the valuables having been removed. And it was certain that by working from the rear of the house and without lights, we could escape detection by any casual night patrolman. At any rate, after finding the window of the old man's library by means of a crude map which Tim had constructed, we were to uncover the hidden altar, whose secret, of course, was still locked in Tim's mind. The heavy gold candlestick we would have to carry quickly across Lake Shore Drive at such a moment when we should see that the street was utterly deserted, after which we would be safe in the darkness and gloom of the vacant prairie land that lines Lake Michigan for blocks and blocks. There we could bury it and mark the spot. And later we could return with hacksaws and cut the thing into chunks of convenient enough size to be carried away in valises.

So when ten o'clock came we sallied forth, Tim carrying under his coat a short jimmy, and in his pocket a ball of putty, a glass cutter, and a tiny electric flashlight. And I noticed too, that before we left he carefully inspected the workings of his revolver.

By means of a roundabout course we reached old Mortimer Dean's Lake Shore Drive residence at about eleven-fifteen. There we lay in the bushes at the rear of the place until about one o'clock in the morning, after which the street appeared to be utterly devoid of theatre-returning cabs. Then we set to work.

By means of Tim's crude map we located the old millionaire's library window. With myself on all fours and Tim standing on my back, he quickly pried off the boards one by one, stepping down each time to lay them in order upon the grass so that they could be replaced later. Then, by means of a circular cut in the curved pane, the ball of putty pasted on the inside of the cut, and a sharp blow, Tim made a wide opening in the glass. By successive cuts he reached the window lock, and finally, after I had begun to ache in every bone of my body from the pressure of his feet on my spine, he ran the window up to its full extent.

We lost no time in climbing up over the sill. Once on the inside of the room, Tim flashed on his pocket electric light. At first I saw only the elaborate furnishings of a library, with the chairs, desks, and tables all shrouded in ghostly white covers, and the walls and mantelpieces quite denuded of all ornaments, valuable or otherwise.

But as I continued to gaze around I noticed a large oil painting on one of the walls. The picture in its massive gilt frame, which measured almost six feet by four, was merely that of a child playing with a lamb. Tim, too, caught sight of it, and focusing his light on it, gave a chuckle of delight. Straight and firmly, without hesitation, he strode over to it, where he commenced fumbling over the ornamental surface of the left lower corner. His fingers must have come in contact with a hidden spring, for, with a sudden whirring noise, the whole oil canvas rolled up like a shade. And there, built in the wall itself, was a large aperture with all the concomitants of a shrine.

Almost instantly I caught sight of the gold candlestick that Tim had described.

Even to me—callused as my aesthetic senses are—it was a beautiful thing. Solid and massive, shining in its dull red-gold color, bearing in the top its single white candle, it seemed almost sacrilegious for us to lay a finger on it.

But there was no religion in Tim. By the faint light that reflected from the surface of the candlestick back to his own features, I could see the greed—the insatiable greed—spreading over his face. With a smothered oath he strode over to it and flung the candle clear across the room. He seized the top of the candlestick and tilted the whole object carefully to a horizontal position. Then he beckoned for me to take the other end.

I did so. It must surely have weighed 150 pounds, for the slight distance to the window started us both to puffing. When we reached the sill, we laid it carefully there, evenly balanced.

"Now, Jerry," directed Tim in a whisper, "while I keep her from tippin', climb out an' get on th' ground. As I tilt my end up, catch the lower end an' help me to let her down slow. Go easy an' don't put too much strain on me, for it's me that'll be leanin' out of the window."

I sprang out on the dark, dew-colored grass and followed his instructions to the letter. Inch by inch we lowered that gold candlestick, Tim leaning far out and grunting audibly. As its heavy base touched the ground I glanced quickly upward at him. To be sure, I could not make him out very well in the darkness, but his white hands, showing plainly in contrast to the drab stone of the building, were completely visible.

Opportunity, they say, knocks but once on every man's door. So I did not hesitate an instant. It seemed almost a shame to do it, it was so simple; but, after all, business is business. I reached into my back pocket, and from there up to his wrists, where I snapped on a pair of clean, cold bracelets.

"What the de—" he ejaculated out loud.

I climbed back through the open window and pushed an electric switch button whose location I had observed a few minutes earlier. A great chandelier above us burst into radiance, filling the room with light.

"What the—why, Jerry—" he began again. But I interrupted him.

"Sorry, Waldo," I said, "but that letter you sent from Los Angeles to 26½ Mott Street, New York, never reached Jerry Dempsey, for he's serving time in Sing Sing. Instead its contents were telegraphed back to Chicago detective headquarters. And—"

"An' you?" he interrupted feebly, staring at me wide-eyed.

"Yes," I said, as I took off my hat and pressed back the hair which covered the long irregular scar that had been there for the past five years. "I'm Sergeant Ryan."

30 SECONDS OF DARKNESS

"TOMORROW EVENING, my dear T. B.," DeLancey suddenly remarked, "I intend to be the cause of a little excitement at old Garrard Bascom's dinner party. In simpler language, my dear fellow, I propose to steal the Countess of Cordova's $100,000 diamond necklace. What do you think of the project?"

With surprise I stiffened up suddenly in my chair. My newspaper dropped from my fingers and I stared unbelievingly at the immaculately clad figure that was seated across from me. But his pair of brown eyes returned my gaze unflinchingly.

"Do you mean to assert, DeLancey," I managed finally to ask, "that you intend to try such a feat as that at a dinner table surrounded by thirty or more people—and the usual two or three Pinkerton detectives present?"

"Precisely," he smiled, blowing a few smoke rings ceilingward. "I've had the thing in mind ever since our invitations arrived. But, my dear fellow, you haven't yet given me your opinion."

"I think you are bereft of your senses. The chances that you take will land us both in a state penitentiary one of these days, if not in some European rat-infested dungeon."

But DeLancey only smiled more enigmatically, and commenced smoothing back the black hair that was turning slightly grey at his temples.

I confess that I invariably slumped into a feeling of profound dismay whenever DeLancey proposed to perform one of his apparently impossible exploits. Yet, time and again, he had achieved the seemingly unachievable—and I had been able to go my way rejoicing, knowing that liberty was ours for a while longer. But always, down in my heart, the dread feeling existed that sooner or later was to come the one mistake, the one misstep in DeLancey's almost perfect plans, that would carry us both inside the dull gray walls for many years.

Across Europe we had gone, DeLancey leaving in his wake a series of mystifying thefts—thefts that to this day are riddles to the Continental police. Petrograd, Berlin, Rome, Madrid, Paris, London, even New York, had contributed their toll to the man's super-cunning brain and his magnetic personality. So for the last few months, while we were living in our Chicago bachelor apartments, I felt that we were assuredly to refrain from any more of these feats—at least for an appreciable time to come. It seemed to me that in justice to ourselves, to the pleasure that we took in each other's company, to the joy of existence itself, we should continue to live quietly on the proceeds of DeLancey's last feat—the theft of Castor and Pollux, the famous red and green twin diamonds, from the vault of Simon et Cie in the Rue Royale, Paris. Success had crowned that performance, I had good reason to know, for it was into my hands that DeLancey had sent the stones in the custody of Von Berghem. And Von Berghem, traveling as an invalid in company with his small son from Paris to Calais, from Calais to Dover, from Dover to Liverpool, from Liverpool to New York, suspected finally of having had something to do with that inexplicable crime, arrested at the docks in New York and searched for three long hours, had come through unscathed, not an inspector nor a police officer discovering that he was blind and that the diamonds were concealed behind his spectacles—concealed back of his hollow glass eyes themselves.

True, that particular success had been due in a great measure to the skill and cunning of Von Berghem himself, yet it was DeLancey's genius that had first seen the possibilities that lay in the blind beggar whom he had found wandering in the Montmartre cemetery.

I pulled myself together with a start and turned to DeLancey, watching the inscrutable smile that still lingered on his face.

"Are you able to tell me, DeLancey, just how you expect to remove a $100,000 necklace at old Bascom's dinner table under the glare of that big electric chandelier? What do you intend to do if he orders a search? Who the Countess of Cordova is, and how you know she's going to be there? How you know this necklace is to be around her neck? What part I am to play in the affair? How—"

"Enough, T. B.," he chuckled. "Stop your restless pacing back and forth. If you'll sit down I'll answer your questions one at a time."

I dropped back on the edge of my chair and waited to hear what he had to say.

"Now," he began slowly, "it is only fair to tell you, my dear fellow, that our exchequer is low—extremely so. The amount paid over to us by old Moses Stein for Castor and Pollux a year and a half ago—was hopelessly out of proportion to the value of those two stones." He shrugged his shoulders and frowned for the first time. "But that, T. B., is the unfortunate part of this exciting game of ours. The legitimate profits are cut to a half—to a third—even to a fourth.

"And so," he went on, "the time has come for one last coup—one big coup; and then, lad, South Australia for you and me. What do you say?"

"Anything," I replied fervently, "is preferable to this continual living in fear of a slip-up of your plans. I like you, DeLancey, and I can't endure the thought of—" I stopped, for a picture of De-Lancey being dragged away to suffer the ignoble fate of a prison sentence began to swim before my eyes.

"No doubt you do," he returned, after a pause. "But, nevertheless, the fact remains that our scale of living, the exorbitant rent of this apartment, our club dues, theatres, bachelor dinners, taxicabs, the gifts to that little dark-eyed love of yours, have all helped to consume our capital far too swiftly. But I don't regret it, T. B., for it has been capital well invested, since it has secured us two invitations already to Garrard Bascom's home in Rogers Park."

"I'm inclined to credit that to your strange winning personality," I returned.

"Personality, bah!" he snorted. "We've put up a bluff—we've jingled the money—we've belonged to the best clubs in the city; and those are the stunts that have made us welcome in such circles. But tomorrow night," he added savagely, "we'll try to reap the profits."

He paused a moment, and the smile that had so suddenly left his face slowly reappeared. For DeLancey was always genial, always in good humor, seldom ruffled.

"So as I said before," he went on, "it is up to us to make what you native born Americans—you real Yankees—call a killing. But it must be a decent killing, lad, such as the Cordova necklace, for after that episode the name of DeLancey will always be looked upon with a very slight—perhaps an appreciable—degree of suspicion and distrust. But I'll explain.

"Among several questions you asked me was how I know that this Countess of Cordova is to be present at old Bascom's dinner tomorrow evening. That, T. B., is simplicity itself. The countess, before she married old Count Cordova of Madrid, was Amelie Bascom of Chicago. And her arrival in this city was chronicled in the Tribune four days ago. Quite elemental reasoning, is it not?

"Have I never told you, my dear fellow, that I met the countess when you and I were in Madrid a year and a half ago? That the good lady, married to that old crustacean, was not at all averse to a violent flirtation? That—if I may be pardoned for any seeming egotism in the statement—I made quite an impression on her?"

I nodded, for now I dimly remembered having heard him mention something about the matter at some obscure time in the past.

"Now," he continued, "when she glances over her estimable papa's list of guests invited to that dinner party, you may rest assured that she is going to arrange to have—er—DeLancey for a partner. Have I made this quite plain?"

"You have. You seem to have a genius for paving your way—months and years ahead."

"Specialization in crime, T. B., merely specialization such as characterizes success in any line of endeavor. But enough of that. I'll now step to another one of your questions: How do I expect to remove a $100,000 necklace at a dinner table under the glare of a huge electric chandelier?"

"Yes. How—"

"By the use of a tiny pair of well-sharpened manicure scissors which, replaced in their black leather case, will be tossed clear across the room and remain unnoticed till the servants are cleaning the dining room several hours afterward."

"But you haven't answer—"

He raised his hand. "Of course I haven't answered your question. It happens that I'm not going to perform that simple operation in the glare of any hanging electric lights. I have sent in an order for thirty seconds of darkness."

"Thirty seconds of darkness!"

"Exactly. You remember Tzhorka?"

I surely did. Tzhorka was the little dwarfed Russian electrician whom DeLancey had met in the great world of crookdom. On more than occasion the latter had vaguely hinted to me that Tzhorka had worked with him once before. And this instance, I felt certain, was the night that old Count Ivan Yarosloff's safe in his palace on the Nevski-Prospekt at St. Petersburg, was burned open by a pair of carbon electrodes and several thousand amperes of current stolen from the lighting feeders that led to the Russian Admiralty Building at the farther end of the Nevski-Prospekt. So since I, no doubt, had helped to spend part of old Yarosloff's 83,000 missing rubles, I became interested at once.

"Yes," he said, "Tzhorka has been in Chicago for some time on plans of his own. And he has agreed to supply me with thirty seconds of darkness at any time I shall indicate."

My face must have shown my bewilderment, for DeLancey hastened to explain his statement.

"Did you notice, the last time we were at the Bascom mansion, how the house was lighted?"

I shook my head.

"Which goes to show, T. B., that your faculties need considerable sharpening before you can stand alone on your legs in this game. If you had taken cognizance of this fact, however, you would have discovered that the current which lights up the mansion and outlying buildings at the center of that great estate is brought over the ground from the Commonwealth Edison Company's feeders which skirt the eastern edge of the property. And in saying that it is brought over the ground, I am referring, of course, to the line of poles which carry two thick cables tapped on the Commonwealth Edison's feeders."

This time I nodded, for I was dimly beginning to comprehend that DeLancey, through the help of Tzhorka, contemplated tampering with this pair of suspended cables, thus interfering with the light supply of the Bascom residence.

"Late last night," DeLancey went on, "Tzhorka, dressed in a complete lineman's outfit, went up the pole that stands on the outer edge of the Bascom estate and spliced on to one these cables a so-called single-pole, single-throw switch with carbon contacts. Then, after lashing the inner span to the crossarm by means of a small block-and-tackle and what he terms a come-along, Tzhorka cut the cable completely through with a hacksaw. The whole arrangement, quite inconspicuous in itself, is in addition hidden by the foliage of a nearby tree."

"Then the current that feeds the Bascom estate," I exclaimed triumphantly, "is now passing through this switch. But how—"

"Yes. And if you had used those latent—nay, dormant—faculties of observation that are in you, you would have noticed also that the great French latticed windows of the Bascom dining room are in direct line with that outermost pole. In other words, my dear fellow, if Tzhorka should be astride that cross-arm in the darkness of tomorrow night, watching our dinner table intently through a pair of high-power field glasses, and he should see—er—a certain individual, myself for instance, raise his hand to his head and pat down his hair—say—twice in succession, he might easily slip on a pair of blue goggles and pull the handles of that switch. The house, stable, garage, kitchens, and everything would be without electric light, instantly, until such time that—"

"For thirty seconds—"

"After which," DeLancey concluded coolly, "Tzhorka, consulting the second hand of his watch, would throw back the switch. Then the lights would go on and—"

"You idiot, you rash, foolhardy numbskull," I raged, rising up from my chair in agitation, "a search would be immediately ordered by Bascom when anywhere from one to twenty-nine of those guests, not counting the countess herself, discovers that this necklace that adorns her neck is missing. You can't—"

"Which brings us face to face with another one of your questions, T. B. What can I do if one or two of those guests prove to be the usual Pinkertons and lock the doors in order to make a thorough search? A neat problem, isn't it?"

"Far, far too neat," I replied bitterly. "DeLancey, get this project out of your mind. You can't do it, I tell you. If you kept the necklace on your person—they would get it sure. And even if you were able to hide it some place during the thirty seconds that Tzhorka, five hundred yards away, holds open the switch, everyone would be watched so closely that you could not dare to regain it." I stopped, disheartened. "And what part am I to play in this affair, as I asked you once?"

"Nothing, this time, lad. All that you need to do in the darkness is to draw back your chair and rise, as no doubt some of the men and most of the ladies will. You might rattle a dish or two, if handy. Just add to the general confusion, for beyond that I have no definite part for you to play."

I leaned forward and placed my hand on DeLancey's shoulder. "DeLancey, give up this mad idea. I tell you the thing is impossible. Your arrangements are characteristic of the thoroughness that always surrounds your work, and to a certain degree admirable. But I tell you frankly this particular feat cannot be accomplished. It cannot." I leaned forward still farther. "Listen to me, old man. Give it up. Why must you take these chances? Why—"

"Enough, T. B.," he calmly interrupted me. "I've been planning this for several days. When I first studied that Cordova necklace in Madrid, just after the old count parted with it for a wedding gift, I felt a strange desire—almost a hope—that I might place my fingers on it within another ten years. I tell you I counted every stone: I feasted my eyes on their pureness, their scintillations, their unusual brilliancy. I studied even the clasp, so obsessed did I become with the thing and the possibilities for removing it. Not content with that, I looked up the records and valuation of the necklace in the Spanish Royal Archives of the Library Madrid. And then and there I determined that the Cordova line—money lenders, interest sharks, blood suckers as they have been for the past five generations—should pay toll at least to the thousandth part of what they themselves have stolen."

I knew that DeLancey's decision was final, for there, in his last statement, was his whole philosophy of theft summed up. Never yet had I known him to lay a finger on the property of anyone except those scattered individuals who amassed their wealth by extortion and trickery. So I saw full well that all the arguments in the world would prove to be useless now.

I made no more attempts at dissuading him from his purpose. Instead, I tried with all my ability to induce him to tell me just what method he expected to follow in order to leave Bascom's house with this $100,000 necklace in his possession. Did he intend, perhaps, to toss it from the French window? No, he claimed, for the coolness of the late fall weather was too great to count on the possibility of those windows being open. More than that he refused to say. And yet it seemed that some scheme, some rational, logical procedure, was mapped out in his brain, if he had gone to the trouble of securing Tzhorka's services in tampering with the electric cables that fed the Bascom estate.

After a quarter of an hour of vain questioning, I gave it up, for he proved adamantine this time in his resolve not to allow me to enter his plans. He persisted in arguing that, since I could be of no assistance whatever in this instance, it was best that I remain in total ignorance of what was to take place. And finally he seized his silk hat and ordered me to drop the whole subject and come for a stroll along Michigan Boulevard.

I confess that I did not sleep very well that night, for something seemed to tell me that tomorrow was the last day that we should be together; that the following evening was to end disastrously for DeLancey. But as I slipped into a bathrobe in the morning, I met DeLancey himself, emerging from his cold plunge, pink cheeked, smiling, totally lacking the slightest shadow under his eyes. Truly, it seemed as though there was nothing in the world that could disturb the man's equanimity.

After finishing the breakfast that was brought up to our suite, DeLancey donned his cape, took up his hat and walking stick, and pressed the button that summoned a taxicab.

"Now, my dear fellow," he said, "I may be away all day today as I have been during the past two days. Can you exist without me?"

"I thought that perhaps we should have this last day together—a trip to the country, for instance. But here you go off again—on that mysterious business that's been keeping you for two days now. If something unusual should develop, where could I find you?"

He wrinkled up his brows. "Well—I may as well tell you my whereabouts are uncertain. But for the present I'm off to old Moses Stein's shop on Halsted Street, ostensibly to make a purchase, but in reality to conclude the details for disposing of this necklace before we leave for Australia. I may be gone for—"

"Old Stein, the jewel shark? The fence?"

"Yes."

"Then you're still confident that you are to have everything your own way in stealing this necklace? That you can deliberately walk out of the house with it? That you will not make a single mistake?"

"Not absolutely confident," he said simply. "But old Stein knows that necklace as he knows pretty nearly everything of value in the world of jewels, and he has agreed to pay over sixty per-cent of the intrinsic value of those stones. And I, in turn, have agreed to place it in his hands by midnight tonight. So you see, T. B., there is no re-crossing of the Rubicon." He paused a moment. "I may be gone the greater part of the day. Since we dare not employ a valet, you might, if you will, lay out my evening clothes, studs, and gloves at six o'clock tonight—and order the taxicab for seven-thirty. The dinner is scheduled for nine, and we must allow at least an hour and a half to reach Rogers Park."

And without even allowing me to put forth one last argument, he slipped from our apartment. A second later I heard the clang of the descending elevator in the outer hallway.

That day was surely an unpleasant one for me. It seemed as though the fear of a slip-up haunted me this time far more than it had in all DeLancey's previous affairs in which I had participated. I tried to read, but my attention failed utterly to stay with the printed page. I tried to smoke, but invariably my cigar grew cold in my fingers while I became lost in my own abstractions.

What plans DeLancey had contrived I could not imagine. Why had he been so rash as to take the old jewel fence, Moses Stein, into his confidence on the subject of the Cordova necklace? Yet I

knew, too, that on more than one occasion DeLancey had con-
sulted with the old man on various jobs. One thing, at least, was
certain. In dealing with old Stein he was dealing with an individual
who knew the exact value and description of every piece of jewelry in the world of any historical value. In fact, it was Stein who
outbid Ranseer, the mad gem collector, for possession of Castor
and Pollux, a year or more before, and that without ever having
seen the stones, so well did he know their size, color, shape, cut-
ting and purity. So no doubt he knew the Cordova necklace as
well, if he had agreed on a finite sum to be paid over for it.

The day dragged by interminably.

I spent the afternoon walking along Michigan Boulevard and
returning to the apartment at intervals of an hour, feverishly looking for DeLancey to put in an appearance. Came two o'clock,
three o'clock, four o'clock. At five o'clock the afternoon light
faded. As darkness came on, I laid out his evening clothes and his
studs. Then I ordered the taxicab for seven-thirty. And when this
was done, I heard six o'clock tinkle from the tiny onyx clock on
our mantel.

What in heaven's name, I wondered vaguely, could be keeping
him? Mysterious as his movements had been in the last two days,
he not yet remained away so late as this. Where had he gone after
leaving Moses Stein's? Or was he still lolling in the old man's
Halsted Street shop?

Came six-thirty o'clock—and DeLancey!

He bustled into the apartment and quickly locked the door behind him. I was making a poor attempt at dressing for the Bascom
dinner. He glanced hurriedly at his watch and slipped into his own
bedroom without a word, where I heard him splashing about in his
tub a few moments later.

But just as I looked from the boulevard window at seven-thirty
and saw the lights of our taxicab as it drew up to the curbing far
down in the darkness below, he emerged from his room, dressed in
his immaculate evening clothes, debonair as ever, smiling as
though the fortunes of the night meant nothing to him one way or
the other.

We descended to the taxicab and started out on the long journey to Rogers Park. DeLancey persisted, however, in chatting
about a host of trivial subjects, the very discussion of which required all my self-restraint and composure. But when I touched
ever so lightly on the subject of the Cordova necklace, he frowned
and quickly changed the subject.

It was a quarter to nine when we rolled up Sheridan Road and turned in between the two great ornamental iron fence posts that marked the entrance to the Bascom grounds. A short drive farther over a gravel road between two tall blackthorn hedges brought us to a grating stop at the steps of the mansion itself. A second later an obsequious footman was opening the door of the cab.

So now the die was cast, for no more that evening—perhaps forever—could I have even a single secret word with DeLancey.

As I mingled with the guests in the drawing room, I tried my best to appear composed and completely at ease. Old Garrard Bascom passed from group to group, and shortly catching sight of me, standing alone and forlorn, introduced me to a pretty debutante who was to be my partner at the table. And I confess that my conversation held forth little promise of an entertaining evening for her, for my attention persisted in straying around the great room, from one individual to another.

Jewels there were a-plenty. They flashed from the ear lobes of most of the women, and from the shirt bosoms of some of the men. Here and there a pearl necklace could be seen, and once I caught sight of a flashing diamond stomacher adorning the person of a huge, powdered, beruffled dowager. The Cordova necklace, however, was the one object which I seemed unable to locate.

But suddenly I caught sight of both it and its owner—and DeLancey as well, seated on a divan which was almost concealed from my view by a huge fern. Truly, there could be no doubt that the rather faded woman who sat looking up at DeLancey was the Countess of Cordova, for when she tossed her head coquettishly at his no doubt complimentary sallies, the sinuous coil around her white throat seemed to emit a veritable stream of colored fire. As for him, however, he seemed quite oblivious to it. All preliminaries, though, must come to an end. Yet, when the butler appeared in the wide doorway and announced dinner, my heart persisted in giving a strange leap. But I gave my arm to my partner and I followed the guests to the dining room.

Matters there were just as DeLancey had stated they would be. The French latticed windows were tightly shut. Plainly, then, he must carry the Cordova necklace out of the house himself if it were to be carried away at all. As I dropped into my chair I could see far, far off through the window the twinkling lights of a passing automobile on Sheridan Road, and I found myself wondering what thoughts were running through Tzhorka's head as he crouched on the wooden cross-arm at the outermost edge of the estate and surveyed this laughing, chatting assemblage through the field glasses that DeLancey had mentioned.

As chance would have it, I found myself seated across from DeLancey and the countess. Several times during the first few moments I tried to catch his eye, but his whole attention seemed to be concentrated on arousing the inherent vanity of the woman who sat at his side. And since I could not hear a word of what he was saying, so great was the babble of conversation and the chink of glasses, I determined to conceal my nervousness to the best of my ability and to pay more attention to my partner.

Course after course proceeded with clockwork regularity. That the preliminary cocktails had mounted to the heads of some of the younger members was plain, for their laughter grew stronger and more strident. Old Bascom, from his position at the head of the table, beamed in turn on everyone, and the servants passed mechanically and noiselessly from chair to chair. And as nothing happened, I commenced wondering whether DeLancey had changed his plans at the last moment.

My gaze kept up a rather rapid circuit from the chattering young woman at my side, to the top of DeLancey's smoothly brushed black hair, to the string of sparkling brilliants around the countess's neck, to two of the guests who sat at the very end of the long table. Somehow I felt instinctively that they were not of the same world as the rest of those people, for the man's jaws were too strong, and his close-cropped mustache seemed to proclaim the plain-clothes man to such an extent that his perfect evening dress was considerably out of keeping with the rest of him. As for the young woman at his side, she had too much of an alert, business-like air about her, and a complexion that showed too well the absence of the trained masseur—and the French maid.

Yet nothing happened.

The last course was brought to the table, and a few moments later its empty dishes were removed. Then the tinkling glasses of iced crème-de-menthe were carried in and distributed. And just as I had concluded with a sigh of relief that DeLancey had given up his scheme, he performed precisely the gesture that I had been seeing in my mind's eye for the past twenty-four hours.

He raised his right hand carelessly to the top of his head and patted his hair twice.

Almost automatically I turned my own head and gazed in the direction of the latticed window—only far out and beyond, into the darkness. It seemed that several long seconds elapsed. But when I detected a bright point of light breaking into being a quarter mile distant, I knew that Tzhorka was playing his part. Almost on the heels of this momentary flash, the lights on the chandelier above the table, as well as the tiny frosted bulbs along the fresco work on the walls, dimmed—and went completely dark.

In the profound blackness that ensued, only an intense stillness, the stillness of utter surprise, followed. Then came a chorus of exclamations, which, with a ripple or two of laughter, served to break the silence. On top of this, a number of chairs were drawn hastily back from the table, and I heard a rumble of anger from the direction of old Bascom's place.

At this juncture, a succession of peculiar, almost indistinguishable sounds struck my ear, for I, of all that assemblage, was expecting them. I heard a slight snip, then a sharp sound as though some light object had struck the opposite wall of the room. Following this came the faintest suggestion of a metallic tinkle. But on top of that a woman's alarming scream sounded forth: "My necklace—"

Almost instantly, it seemed, a match was struck on the under side of a chair, and as it flared up I saw with surprise that it was in DeLancey's hand, and that he was standing erect looking dumfoundedly down at the countess.

"Get matches—or lights—or something, some of you men," he commanded sharply. "The countess has fainted—and her necklace is gone from her throat. Bascom, lock the doors. Don't let a man—"

But his words were interrupted by the instantaneous bursting into radiance of the great chandelier above the table.

The thirty seconds were over.

And it was just as DeLancey had cleverly announced, for, as far as I could see, he had deliberately drawn suspicion to himself in order to bolster up his own unpleasant position. The countess sat slumped up in her chair, in a dead faint. DeLancey stood above her, still holding the blackened match stub. And every guest, without exception, was staring open-mouthed at her white throat, now utterly devoid of a single diamond.

This last tableau lasted for only an instant. Then the man with the close-cropped mustache, whom I had suspected all along of being an employee of the Pinkerton system, crossed the floor rapidly and planted his back to the door, at the same time throwing back his coat and displaying a shining steel badge. Almost as quickly, a young society man next to him crossed to the French latticed window and took up a position there.

Now we were in for it. Fool, fool, fool of a DeLancey, I reflected bitterly.

Old Bascom, who had been standing bewildered at the head of the table, looking stupidly from his daughter's crumpled-up form to the man posted at the door, ejaculated:

"God bless my soul, O'Rourke, what's the matter? What—"

"There's been crooked work pulled off here, Mr. Bascom," retorted that individual quickly. "Can't you see that your daughter's necklace is gone?" He turned to the group around the table. "Two of you ladies help to bring the countess out of her faint. Some of you men look under her chair. If that necklace isn't found, you'll have to step in the next room one by one and be searched." He looked down the table to the young woman who had been his partner. "Miss Kelly, I'll detail you to search the ladies if the necklace isn't on the floor."

A chorus of indignant protests arose from the ladies. The men gasped and looked from one to the other with manifest suspicion written on their faces. A number of the guests stared at DeLancey, who still stood where he was, passing his hand over his brow.

"I feel," he stammered feebly, "that this puts me in a rather peculiar light. If—if there's to be any search made, I suggest that it be made on me first. I—"

But he was interrupted by one of the male guests who pointed down the table and exclaimed: "The countess's glass of cre—"

That gentleman, however, had no opportunity to finish his statement, for the female detective suddenly broke in:

"Look, ladies and gentlemen." She, too, pointed at the countess's untouched glass of crème de menthe. "The lady's glass of cordial is the only one on the table that's been spilled all over the cloth. It might be that—"

"God bless my soul," said old Bascom again, still trying to collect his wits, "what are you all driving at?"

I lost no time in staring at the point which Miss Kelly was indicating, and I saw what she was trying to call everyone's attention to. Just as she had announced, the green cordial in the countess's glass had slopped down the side of the fragile vessel and had made a great sticky stain around the base. And I daresay that everyone else saw it at the same time. Miss Kelly, however, hurriedly crossed around the end of the long table and hooked a businesslike finger to the bottom of the glass. A fraction of a second later I found myself picturing DeLancey's inward rage when he saw that he had been outwitted by a woman.

For as she raised her hand, something was hanging from the crook of her finger; something that might once have held all the colors of the rainbow, but which now, covered as it was with sticky green syrup, hanging pendant with the clasp opened, covered from one end to the other with crème-de-menthe, dripping green drops that seemed like emeralds being born from more emeralds, showed plainly where the Cordova necklace had gone. With no regard for the white table cloth, she held it up so that everyone could see.

"The necklace," she stated slowly and triumphantly, "has not been stolen." She looked toward Bascom. "An apology is due your guests, Mr. Bascom."

"God bless my—" he started to say faintly for the third time. But suddenly he seemed to collect his senses. He snatched up a napkin and, unfolding it, leaned over and held it under Miss Kelly's outstretched hand. Without a word she dropped the necklace into it, and he hurriedly folded it up and placed it safely in the his breast pocket. Then he turned to the stupefied butler.

"Harkins, get the countess's maid and help her to her room." He then glanced angrily at O'Rourke. "O'Rourke, you've made a nasty mistake." He looked at the rest of the assemblage. "I trust, ladies and gentlemen, that you will pardon this affront to your honesty here tonight. This is surely a deplorable happening. Something seemed to have interrupted the city current supply, and in the excitement my daughter must have leaned over, with the result that the clasp of her necklace loosened and it dropped into her glass of cordial. I humbly ask the pardon of one and all of you for the whole occurrence."

With the sudden entrance of the countess's maid, the guests quickly adjourned to the drawing room, the gentlemen, apparently by mutual understanding, giving up the usual coffee and cigars. On the way out of the dining room I caught sight of DeLancey and his face appeared as black as a thundercloud. Perhaps the abrupt disclosure that Pinkerton employees were at the table, or else their crude methods in handling the situation aroused some ire among the ladies, for cabs were called for shortly after and one by one the guests melted away.

With DeLancey I climbed into our vehicle, but nothing was said by either of us until we were rolling out of the Bascom grounds and down Sheridan Road. Then he remarked glumly:

"Well?"

"Well, I consider that you were mighty lucky to escape with your liberty. Your deal proved a fiasco—just as I felt it would all the time. In fact, you might just as well have taken a megaphone and called the attention of the whole company to the countess's crème-de-menthe glass, for the stuff was slopped all over the cloth. But one thing I'd like to ask, DeLancey. Did you honestly intend to drop the necklace into the cordial glass—or was that an accident?"

He spoke fully for the first time since leaving the Bascom estate.

"My dear T. B.," he said slowly, "how very, very obtuse you are. Is it possible that you don't yet know that the necklace which was fished from the countess's crème-de-menthe glass, and held up dripping and covered with the green syrup for everyone to see, was a paste duplicate that was put together by old Stein and myself in the last three days? Is it—"

But there was no need of his explaining further, for as we passed an arc-lamp and its rays flashed into the carriage. I saw something gleaming and sparkling in the palm of his hand— something that seemed to hold in leash the colors of a thousand rainbows.

THE DISAPPEARANCE OF MRS. SNOOZLEWORTH

I N HIS OFFICE on the top floor of the Rutabaga Building, Mr. Jeremiah Snoozleworth was pacing distractedly up and down, pausing only long enough between laps to wipe away the beads of perspiration that sprang to the surface of his bald head. "Strange, confoundedly strange," he said, puffing, and loosening the buttons of his plaid vest that hemmed in a goodly paunch. "Never before in the twenty years we've been married was Delia away from the house at five-fifteen at night. And to-night's our wedding anniversary! Peculiar—that's what it is! I'll try it once more."

He sank into his swivel chair and rang a number on the desk telephone. The monotonous drone of an unanswered bell buzzed through the receiver, but that was all. So he gave it up in bewilderment.

"I wonder," he said to himself, settling back ill at ease, and linking two pudgy hands over the lower part of his vest, "why in Sam Hill she wanted a yellow fifty-dollar bill this morning for all those ones and twos? Queer that she wouldn't tell me the reason." He paused, thinking. "By the great horn spoon, there's something about the whole matter that I don't understand!" He creaked back and forth in the swivel chair. "I'll try once more to get Artie on long distance, and then I'll slip home a half hour earlier and surprise her."

He lifted the receiver from the hook. "Long distance? Connect me with Littleburg. Yes, same party—Littleburg Ornamental Glass Works."

Quite a protracted pause followed. Suddenly a faint feminine voice replied: "Littleburg Ornamental Glass Works talking."

"This is Mr. Jeremiah Snoozleworth speaking. Put my nephew, Artie Snoozleworth, manager of the retail department, on the wire."

"Sorry," said the faint feminine voice, "but Mr. Artie Snoozleworth left the factory at noon to-day to take part in a tennis tournament."

"Great Scott!" fumed old Snoozleworth. "Does anybody ever tend to business, I'd like to know? Well, see here, miss, can you tell me anything about a one-hundred-dollar parlor lamp that I ordered through him, to be delivered at my home on my wedding anniversary? That's Monday—to-day, too, confound it!"

"Sorry, Mr. Snoozleworth, but I can't. The factory's closed for the day—and Mr. Artie Snoozleworth ain't here."

"Bah!" exploded old Snoozleworth. With exasperation, he banged the receiver back on the hook. Why in thunderation couldn't Artie have let him know whether the parlor lamp was to reach the house or not in time for a surprise to Delia? It was just like the young harebrain to skip off to a pill-swatting tournament at Littleburg and forget the whole matter.

Grumpily he drew on his overcoat, his hat, and took up his blackthorn walking stick. On the way to the main floor, in the elevator, he fell to wondering again what strange cause could have arisen to prevent Delia from being home at five-fifteen o'clock— for the first time in twenty years.

II.

As Snoozleworth swung from the entrance of the Rutabaga Building to catch the first car that would bring him to No. 13 Carbuncle Court, a tall, lank man, with a silk hat cocked on one side of his head, and a pair of old-fashioned gray sideburns that waved jovially in the breeze, tapped him on the shoulder. "Ah, there, Snoozle, old boy," said the latter. "Just saw your missus."

Snoozleworth spun on his heel. "Witherspoon!" he exclaimed. "Saw my wife, eh? Say, I've been looking for you for a week— about the Oldboys' Lodge meetings. But about—my wife—where did you see her?"

"Threading her way through the crowds downtown, Snoozle, with a black traveling bag in her hand. Not twenty minutes ago."

"Jumping Jehosephat!" said Snoozleworth. "That's queer! I wonder if some of her relatives are sick? If they are, then that explains it. Good!" His red, rotund face commenced to beam on the world once more. "Now, see here, Witherspoon, what's the matter with you? You haven't been to the Oldboys' Lodge meetings for three weeks."

The man with the silk hat and sideburns gave a grimace and closed one eye dramatically. "The missus, Snoozle, the missus.

She's been keeping me in nights. That's the whole reason. Next week, though, she goes for a visit. I'll be with you sure then." He clapped his hand on Snoozleworth's shoulder. "Whoop! Be with you sure, old fellow! Same place, same time as before. Here's my car. Got to go. See you that night, Snoozle. So long!"

He hurried out in the street and swung aboard an eastbound car, his silk hat never losing by a degree its jaunty angle, his gray side-burns still waving over the land of the free. A second later, Snoozleworth was seated on a westbound car, on which he stayed till the conductor called: "Carbuncle Court!"

It was twenty minutes to six—the daylight just fading into dusk—when he opened the door of his flat and walked in. But the flat was quite deserted. Perplexed, he stamped from the parlor to the kitchen, and back to the parlor again, but not a sign whatever of Delia did he see. He repaired to the bedroom, where he scanned the dresser in search of an explanatory note; but explanatory note there was none.

Mystified, and making no attempt at taking off his hat or coat, he dropped into an oak rocker that had been presented to him by the members of the Oldboys' Lodge. As he sat there, in the fading light, his gaze traveled absent-mindedly to the wastebasket, which stood directly at the side of Mrs. Snoozleworth's writing desk. The yellowish glint of telegraph paper caught his eye.

He arose from the rocker and, thrusting his hand in the basket full of trash, drew out the torn half of a telegram. Snapping on the electric lights in the room, he read it:

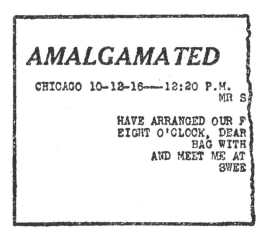

AMALGAMATED

CHICAGO 10-12-16——12:20 P.M.
MR S

HAVE ARRANGED OUR F
EIGHT O'CLOCK, DEAR
BAG WITH
AND MEET ME AT
SWEE

A sudden chill struck him. His blood pressure dropped in a second from one hundred and seventy to one hundred and thirty. Even under his hat, the perspiration sprang once more on his shiny head. He plunged his hand feverishly to the bottom of the waste basket, and succeeded in bringing up another portion of a telegram, almost similar to the first, except that it was the right half instead of the left.

With hands that trembled visibly, he placed the two halves in line with each other and read them—nay, devoured them:

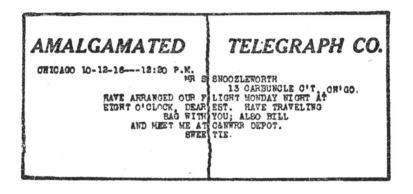

III.

In his anguish, Mr. Snoozleworth groaned aloud—the soul cry of a deserted man. Again he read the message, and again he comprehended its import. So—so Mrs. Snoozleworth was false—false after twenty years of married bliss! So false, so faithless, that she had selected their twentieth anniversary on which to elope—with—with the person who had signed himself Sweetie. Oh, it seemed impossible to believe! Yet the telegram, dated that very day, at twelve-twenty P.M., spoke mutely for itself. Line by line, he read it again, and, as he read, the whole explanation of the day's events became clear as the brew in Heinze's place.

"Have arranged our flight Monday night at eight o'clock, dearest." Dearest! So he, Sweetie—whoever he was—evidently appreciated Mrs. Snoozleworth to the extent of calling her dearest. Dumbly, Snoozleworth wondered how long it had been since he had addressed Delia by the name of dearest. "Have arranged our flight Monday night at eight o'clock." Well, that explained, in black and white, why Mrs. Snoozleworth had not been in the house at five-fifteen. She had sallied forth early to meet Sweetie—

whoever he might be—so that she might be out of the place before her poorer half returned.

He read on dazedly: "Have traveling bag with you." Ah, that, too, was plain—too plain. Witherspoon himself had mentioned, not an hour since, that he had seen Mrs. Snoozleworth threading her way through the downtown crowds with a black traveling bag in her hand. "Have traveling bag with you; also bill." Also bill! How plain now was her mysterious request, over that morning's breakfast table, for a fifty-dollar bill in exchange for all her ones and twos. That bill was needed by Sweetie to help out the expenses of their flight.

"And meet me at C. & N.W.R.R. depot. Sweetie." Oh, how he would like to fasten his fingers about Sweetie's neck and choke the very life out of him! Sweetie, despoiler of homes, breaker of noble hearts; Sweetie of the honeyed tongue, that had persuaded Mrs. Snoozleworth to flee the cozy domicile at No. 13 Carbuncle Court!

But, by tapioca, Snoozleworth swore grimly, Sweetie must be foiled; and he, Jeremiah Snoozleworth, wronged husband, must be the man to do the foiling. The foiling would be done on the strength of that one piece of information: "Meet me at C. & N.W.R.R. depot."

He jammed the two half telegrams in his pocket. There was no time to lose. He must reach the depot long before eight o'clock, and the sooner the better, lest the two elopers meet beforehand and board an earlier train. Oh, the injustice of it, the heartlessness of it, he told himself, as he hurried from the flat to start on the journey back to the Loop and the C. & N.W.R.R. depot. But as he boarded his car, a still small voice seemed to reproach him: "Jeremiah Snoozleworth, if you hadn't left your beloved wife every Wednesday night to traipse off to Heinze's place and the Oldboys' Lodge, she wouldn't be running away to-night with—with—Sweetie!"

On the ride to the city, he commenced wondering just who, of all their mutual acquaintances, Sweetie might be. He racked his brains and ran over the whole list of Mrs. Snoozleworth's friends, as well as his own enemies, but for the life of him could not fasten upon one who, under the saccharine cognomen of Sweetie, could be running away to-night at eight o'clock with Mrs. Snoozleworth.

It was six-forty when he reached the C. & N.W.R.R. depot. He immediately buttoned his long coat about his neck, drew down his hat over his ears, and proceeded at once to the train shed. There he took up a position at the side of the bulletin board, where he could watch the gates of every outgoing train.

As he stood there, his hand gripped tightly about the blackthorn walking stick that was ready to descend with a whack on Sweetie's cranium, he commenced wondering what kind of a man Sweetie would prove to be. Would he prove to be—er—a big, powerful brute with bulging muscles, or was he slim and young, dark and handsome and debonair like the usual type of villain that steals an innocent wife?

Seven o'clock came. Snoozleworth held his post. Eight o'clock came. He was all tense, gripping the blackthorn cane. It got to be eight-fifteen, eight-thirty, eight-forty-five. He was bewildered, and not a little chagrined. Nine o'clock came.

Then, with a long sigh, Jeremiah Snoozleworth woke up to the discomfiting fact that it was he himself who had been foiled; that the elopers must have met on the outside of the depot and changed their plans. Gad, he had lost beautifully! He made his way slowly from the train shed, through the waiting rooms, and back to the street car.

It was all over. Nothing remained now but to see Squiggles, the attorney, in the morning. After that the brief trial, the divorce—the publicity; and from that point on he would have to join a club, eat his meals there, depend for entertainment on the Dotty Burlesquers, like the other bachelors of his acquaintance, and attend the meetings of the Oldboys' Lodge.

He reached his flat for the second time that evening. Dejectedly he thrust his key in the front door and flung it open. Oh, the loneliness of the days to come—while Delia was flying with Sweetie across the continent!

IV.

As the door swung open, Mr. Snoozleworth stared down the front hall in amazement. The great dome light above the dining-room table was lighted. The table was set with immaculate white cloth, and—and their wedding silverware! Numerous dishes could be seen in place, tightly covered with silver hemispheres; and standing in the doorway between the dining room and the front hallway was the misguided, erring Mrs. Snoozleworth, her face, with its blond hair, the picture of despair and bewilderment, and her dress covered with a huge gingham apron. "Oh, Snoozie,

Snoozie!" she exclaimed, advancing toward him with open arms. "Where on earth were you, my dear?"

He hardly heard her. His eyes were staring fascinatedly at the end of a black leather traveling bag, which was barely peeping out from under the hall rack. His face grew stern. Striding forward, and pointing one finger at his spouse and one finger at the fatal piece of evidence under the hall rack, he thundered: "Mrs. Snoozleworth—woman—your perfidy is discovered! Where—where is your Sweetie?"

"Why, Snoozie—Jeremiah! What do you mean? Who is Sweetie? And why were you so late to-night—on our wedding anniversary?"

"Too late!" he roared. "Too late, Mrs. Snoozleworth—woman! I know all!"

"All?" she repeated wonderingly. She paused in perplexity. "Why, Jeremiah Snoozleworth, you've met that old Witherspoon, and you've been drinking in that Heinze's place again!"

Without a word, he strode to the brightly lighted dining-room table, and, digging up the crumpled halves of the telegram from his vest pocket, he laid them on the cloth.

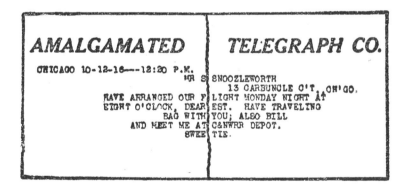

"There," he exclaimed dramatically, "is the proof of your perfidy, your treachery, Mrs. Snoozleworth—woman—you whom I promised to cherish, to love, to protect! You, for whom I purchased, through Artie, a one-hundred-dollar parlor lamp as an anniversary present. These, I tell you, are going to be exhibits A and B, signed by Sweetie himself."

She stared for a minute, and her face took on a look of intense surprise. Then suddenly she started to giggle. She slipped hurriedly into her bedroom and returned, a few seconds later, with the wastebasket that always stood under her desk, stooping as she passed the hall rack and bringing out the black leather traveling bag.

"You foolish, foolish old boy!" she tittered. She held up the traveling bag. "Here, Snoozie, is my present to you on our twentieth anniversary. It—it cost the whole fifty-dollar bill that I saved up, and I've been shopping for it all afternoon."

Mr. Snoozleworth shifted his center of gravity to the other foot, and pointed darkly to the telegram. "But—but—Sweetie. Who—what—why—"

His wife lowered her fingers into the trash of the wastebasket and withdrew two more half sheets of yellow paper. "Jeremiah Snoozleworth," she said, "you and I have both made a big mistake to-day. I, in opening two telegrams addressed to you—I was so, so curious, Snoozie—and you in matching up the wrong halves. Snoozie, you didn't get exhibits A 1/2 and B 1/2!"

Lifting up the left of the pair of yellow half sheets on the table, the remaining one read:

In the place of the half she removed she quickly set down one of the two half sheets she had withdrawn from the bottom of the wastebasket. It fit exactly, the infinitesimally serrated edges coming together in one single line. "You old dear," she murmured softly, "the beautiful lamp came at six o'clock, but—but I didn't want you to learn that I knew about it."

Snoozleworth didn't hear her. He was staring at the newly completed telegram:

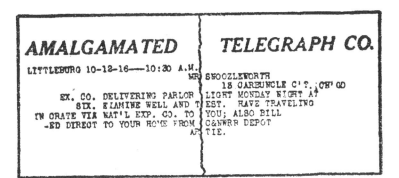

"Oh, Lord, Delia!" he said, with a groan, after the full significance of the words had crept in on him. "What a blithering fool I've been!"

"Yes, and you've been very naughty, Snoozie, to want to go to that old lodge. I thought I could keep you home by not giving you this message; but now, on account of the beautiful lamp, I'm going to forgive you."

She brushed off the two half telegrams and laid the remaining ones in place. They read:

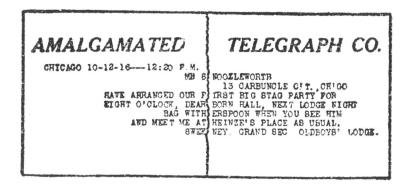

For several seconds Mr. Snoozleworth gazed at this second completed message that had so nearly been sidetracked, the deep red rising slowly to the very tips of his ears. Then he looked up. "Delia," he said humbly, "there's not going to be any stag next Wednesday night—for me. I'm going to a lollapaloozer of a swell dinner and then to the theater afterward, and you're coming right along with me, little girl!"

THE DEBUT OF SOAPY MULLIGAN

NOW, BOYS, may I have your closest attention? Burke, never mind rolling that cigarette for a few minutes yet. And each of you step a little closer, please. I don't want to see a hitch nor the shadow of a hitch tomorrow at sunrise. When that two-seated touring car back yonder plunges over the edge of this gorge and smashes into smithereens on the bottom, our work here in the Berkshires is done—and the big feature, 'The Dangers of Delia,' is ready to be cut and fitted for the final film. Any comments or questions? If not, I'll go over your final instructions for catching the big punch. Attention, please, Burke, McGreavy, Foxhall!"

Peasly, Eastern director for the Hexagon Feature Film Company, was speaking. Grouped about him in a small semi-circle were three younger men whose faces were far more genial than the rather crabbed, petulant physiognomy of the Hexagon Company's star director. On the ground near each one's feet was a camera and film box, and lying some distance away, strapped in a compact bundle, were two heavy tripods such as motion picture cameramen employ.

The place was a peculiar, almost deserted region in the foothills of the Berkshires. At a considerable distance in back of the four men, a deformed, sun-baked farmhouse could be seen, along the front of which ran a raised roadway, obviously in disuse, since tufts of grass and weeds had sprung up in profusion all along it. The road ran to where the four men and paraphernalia were stationed, then beyond them for ten feet—and there stopped abruptly.

The reason for its stoppage was quite a legitimate one: a giant gorge, apparently the bed of some path of the road. A casual visitor in the region, gazing downward from the edge or even back some distance from the point where Peasly, Burke, McGreavy and Foxhall were standing, would have been startled to the point of an unrepressible gasp by the sheer drop of a hundred feet to the bottom below, covered with jagged rocks and gnarled stumps.

That at some bygone day a railroad had existed at this point across the gorge, which itself was a full hundred feet wide, would have been suggested by the unusual height of the roadway that ran clear to the edge and stopped. In fact, the latter resembled nothing so much as an embankment. But this fact was furthermore borne out by the rotted remains of a great wooden trestlework which extended—nay, tottered—half-way across the chasm from the opposite side and then stopped in a tangle of splintered, protruding beams.

On a crudely constructed plank platform some distance below the top of the trestlework, but clear out to its very end, stood the third tripod, which evidently corresponded to the odd camera box at Burke's feet. And, judging from the mud and burrs and jagged tears in the latter's trousers, as well as the hammer thrust in his belt, he had just come across the rocky bottom from the other side after constructing it. Back in the blue haze near the farmhouse, stationed squarely in the center of the road, was a spick-and-span, two-seated, black touring car, standing alone without a driver.

Peasly opened his mouth to speak, but a deep rumbling interrupted him. A faint toot broke out on the still air, and a second later a long train of flying steam cars shot across a solid steel trestlework barely visible around a bend in the gorge a quarter of a mile from the old supplanted and caved-in wooden structure.

"Now, boys," began Peasly once more, as the unnatural silence of the Berkshires crept back upon them, "the situation is this: We caught Hamilton, taking the part of Audrey St. Clair, the villain, flying along the road at a fifty mile clip this morning at sunrise, in the car back yonder. We got the final scenes now clear up to the fall-in-my-arms effect of Delia, the heroine, and Donald West, the hero. So, since each one of you is familiar, I take it, with the scenario"—Peasly never called them scripts—"of the 'Dangers of Delia,' you realize that everything's finished but scene 304 to complete the five-reeler."

Burke, star cameraman of the Hexagon Company, rolled a cigarette deftly, still keeping his gaze fixed fast on his superior.

"Now," continued Peasly, glancing sourly at the paper tube in Burke's hands, "this scene 304, as you'll remember, consists of the mad plunge to death of the reckless driver, Audrey St. Clair, over the edge of this gorge." He waved his hand in the direction of the old river cut. "Now the exigencies of the plot, of course, demand that Audrey St. Clair's flight be made right after sunrise. Therefore, we've got to catch his plunge at the exact moment tomorrow morning that the sun is at the same height above the horizon as it was this morning when we flashed him shooting along that other road." He bowed slightly. "That, gentlemen, if you hold any aspirations toward becoming a director, is the kind of thing you must watch and guard against. The American public is not to be fooled. They notice the most trivial details of a picture that make or mar unity and continuity."

He paused a moment and then went on:

"So for that reason—on account of having to catch this thing so early tomorrow—I called you all out here this late afternoon to arrange your set-ups, to measure off your distances from the edge of the gorge, and to rehearse to a slight extent your work for early tomorrow morning.

"The wax dummy is already dressed in the clothing of Audrey St. Clair and is back there in the farmhouse, ready to be tied with coarse white thread to the steering wheel in the morning. The car, too, is now all in place and in direct line with the edge of the gorge here; and the old boy in the shack will keep his eye on it tonight. I myself will start it on low speed, jerk it up to high, and slip off the side. And then, boys, it's up to you to grind away until the crash comes." He turned to Burke. "How are you fixed, Burke?"

"I'm O. K.," grunted the latter. He flicked his thumb in the direction of the trestlework remains over the opposite half of the gorge. "My platform's all fixed and I'm going to leave the tripod in position all night. All I'll have to do at dawn is to set the camera on it. For a scene like that I've got what you might almost call a close-up, Mr. Peasly. It ought to make the audience gasp and rise up in their seats. Steep side of gorge in full view. Car shooting straight at 'em along road. Terrific plunge right in front of their eyes—down—down—off the screen entirely. It'll rouse 'em, all right. Only objection is the confounded dummy. They're next to these dummies nowadays."

Peasly shrugged his shoulders. "Yes, but you can't kill a man to make a thrill, Burke. The destruction of a good car, though, never fails to stir 'em up. It's still a winning stunt in the film game. And with your close focus and this pippin of a gorge that was introduced in the earlier scenes of the story, we've got as good a plunge as any film producer ever staged." He turned toward McGreavy. "McGreavy, have you marked your tripod base?"

The young fellow nodded. "All three legs marked, Mr. Peasly. It won't take me five minutes in the morning to set up. I'll catch the car shooting over from the rear end, at a closer focus than Burke; and if anything goes wrong with his film at the last moment, I'll have nearly as good a run. Of course," he added, with a sigh that marked the true artist, "I won't get the effect of the car shooting straight down toward the audience. On the other hand, I won't catch that waxy stare on the dummy."

Peasly drew out a massive gold watch and snapped open the cover. "Let's see—five P. M., isn't it?" He looked toward Foxhall. "O. K., Fox?"

Foxhall nodded. "O. K. and all marked. I'll catch it very much like McGreavy—only from the other side of the road. Can't see how we can lose the scene, Mr. Peasly. Burke's is the best set-up, though."

"Yes," admitted the director. Again he snapped open his watch. "Well, I guess that's all for today. Remember now—the sun rises at six-two tomorrow. At six-thirty goes a five-hundred dollar second-hand touring car into smithereens. So without fail now, all of you be on the job at six in the morning, ready to catch the big punch scene in 'The Dangers of Delia.' That's all. You can go."

II

At eleven o'clock that night the ragged figure of one Soapy Mulligan, knight of the road, radical socialist, traveler from coast to coast, and specialist in conservation of physical and psychical energy, detached itself from an empty boxcar of a Buffalo and North-Eastern Railroad freight train in the Berkshire Hills.

The eyelashes of his bleary eyes were full of cinders and grime; his crumpled brown felt hat was pulled tight down over his head till only a few tufts of unkempt gray hair peeped out; his face was covered with a five days' growth of scraggy beard—and his soul was full of wrath. The reason for the super-abundance of ire in his spiritual cosmos was the fact that his detachment from the previously empty boxcar had been quite involuntary, being expedited, as it were, by the thick soled shoe of an unfeeling brakeman.

The night was chilly, in spite of the fact that it was summer. Soapy stood back off the right-of-way for a few minutes, shivering and watching the long, indistinct train of cars some distance from him in the darkness, the puffing engine far up to the front and the red glare against the sky as the fireman jerked open the firebox to throw on more fuel. He also kept a wary eye on the form of the brakeman, partly invisible against the dark cars, yet plainly marked by the swinging yellow lantern. The latter, however, maintained such a perfect guard over the string of empties, that as the whole train started off with two faint, melancholy toots of the whistle and he swung himself upon the rear steps of the caboose,

Soapy was left stranded and alone in the silence of the Berkshire Hills.

A short glance and a few lighted matches showed him that the road—if road it were—was in disuse, and that it stopped abruptly at the edge of the same gorge that he had been following from the Buffalo and North-Eastern tracks, a quarter mile or so in the rear. But disused or not, a certain method of deductive reasoning had never failed: a road meant houses; houses meant barns; and barns either had hay in them or they didn't. And even a depleted hayloft was preferable to the open countryside for spending the rest of the night.

Without bothering to tack on a Q. E. D. to his proposition, he started up the road, leaving the gorge in back of him. Soon he caught the dim outlines of a house looming up a hundred feet ahead of him, and he cautiously allowed his whistle to die out in an instant. A second later he stopped squarely in his tracks, his breath shooting from him in a loud grunt. He had run straight into a vehicle of some sort, posted right in the center of the road.

At first, while he rubbed the pit of his stomach, he thought he had collided with a threshing machine; but, lighting another match, he discovered with amazement that it was a deserted automobile, maintaining a solitary vigil through the night.

He crept around to the back of it and struck another match. He wondered whether the gasoline had run out, and some unfortunate automobilist had been forced to tramp back to the nearest town, or whether the machine had broken down. He stepped along the side with the burning splinter of wood in his hand and peeped under the rear seat. What he saw there caused him to give a chuckle of delight.

The floor of the car, at some bygone day, had been covered by a soft, thick, green carpet, studded around the edge with shining brass nails. And folded up in a crumpled bundle under the rear seat was another piece of heavy carpet, much like the first, and evidently intended for a lap robe. So he clambered up on the car and felt over the two seats for the cushions. But the leather cushions, for some unknown cause, had been removed; and the hard, bare seats were not nearly so inviting for a night's slumber as the carpeted space beneath the rear seat itself.

Soapy had never been an individual to stand on ceremony, or to hold long colloquies with himself as to his modes of procedure in life. He crawled down in under the rear seat, drew up his knees slightly, opened out the generous piece of loose carpet, and drew it entirely over him for a coverlid. For a pillow he used his arm and crumpled brown felt hat. Then, with the celerity and indifference to surroundings that had come from years of experience, he dropped away into a warm blissful sleep.

III

Soapy's slumber was unusually sound that night. Much experience in sleeping under different conditions had given him the ability to adjust himself almost instantaneously to all sorts of varying circumstances. And, too, the night before he had secured but two hours' broken repose on account of his private car having suffered a derailment some ninety miles to the east. The loud, wrangling voices of the wrecking crew, their shouts and curses as they jacked up the empty freight and pried feverishly at it, the flash of their kerosene torches through the chinks of the car, had been very annoying. Soapy had made a resolve next morning never again to grace that particular line with his patronage.

Quite a while elapsed before he awoke for the first time. But when he did awake, he did so very suddenly and very abruptly, a somewhat calloused nervous system apprising him that all was not well. For several seconds he strove to determine just what was taking place, and suddenly struck upon the solution—his bed was moving.

An impulse told him to keep the green carpet well over his head and to travel until he was discovered by the occupant of the car. But the growing vibration and bumping beneath him showed plainly that all possibility of sleep was at an end.

He wondered what time it was. So he cautiously drew back his improvised cover-lid and craned his head first from under the seat, then over the edge of the machine. But one peep, both at the driver and at the road ahead of the car, caused him to struggle with a hoarse cry to get to his feet.

Morning had come, for the great red elliptical disk of the sun was some distance above the eastern horizon. But that wasn't what disturbed Soapy Mulligan's equanimity. It was the momentary glimpse he secured of a strange, waxen, rigid figure at the wheel— a figure, the color of whose flesh and whose unnatural stiff posture showed plainly that he was either dead, crazy, or drunk. But that was not all. Whoever was at the wheel—fool, lunatic, or corpse— was running, squarely, blindly, happily toward an open gorge over which there was nothing in the way of a bridge.

The whole thing had taken place so swiftly that Soapy had not even time to collect his wits. From the instant that he had first stumbled to his feet from under the seat to the present instant, not five seconds had passed. And it seemed to him after that that only the hundredth part of a second elapsed before the car, with a terrific swoop, whir, and rush, shot off the edge of the cliff-like structure.

But it was in that fifth, fiftieth, or five-hundredth of a second that Soapy Mulligan performed the quickest piece of action that he had ever yet performed. Even as the car sped like a bullet off the edge, he was crouched on the top of the rear seat for a mighty spring; and as it dropped away from under his feet, his body had leaped into the air with all its might.

With the great horizontal velocity of the vehicle, it was doubtful even whether he could have leaped back with much margin of safety from all engulfing, all suffocating space to solid land. But, starting as it was on its downward drop by the force of gravity, the base for his spring dropped away, and the force of his upward leap was reduced to one half or more, with the result that the only portions of him that touched the edge of the dried mud cliff were his outstretched arms.

But the hands on those outstretched arms clawed fiercely, and each grasped a bundle of tenacious weeds that had sprouted up. And as the crash and the roar of splintering wood and metal rose to his ears he struggled desperately to get one knee up and over the edge. His eyes were blinded with dust; he was choking and gasping for breath. He did not see two men, each of whom had been standing paralyzed at a tripod, their arms hanging helplessly at their side, suddenly awake to action and commence clambering up the side of the roadway to draw him to safety. All he saw, in fact—and he gave a great sob when he saw it—was a huge lump of dried earth break off from the impact of his knee, leaving him hanging again suspended between life and eternity by two handfuls of weeds.

The force of his leap had momentarily taken his strength. Now he was growing weaker. He did not attempt again to draw up either knee. The two clumps of weeds were slowly being uprooted, or else his grip was slipping. So with one mighty, heart-breaking effort he drew himself perpendicularly upward, with the result that he got himself over the edge as far as his chest, his waist, his knees. Then he stumbled to his feet and rushed madly, terror-stricken away from the place.

He was just in time, in fact, to run straight into the clenched fist of Peasly, who had arrived at the spot puffing and panting, and he dropped like a log from the impact against his jaw.

"Take that, you dirty bum," he heard the latter screaming from a point close to his ear, "for spoiling the whole scene. Now, confound you, we're out another day's time and the price of a new machine. Stand up, you blasted hobo, and I'll knock you down again!"

IV

Three months later, on a chill fall day, Soapy stepped out of a Lake Shore boxcar in the Illinois Central Railroad yards at Chicago. With undue haste he slipped out of the yards and into the city. Then he turned his footsteps toward Hinky Dink's famous bar and lodging house, where possible warmth and congenial companionship, at least, awaited him.

He was chilled through and through, having ridden continuously for two nights and a day—all the way from Pittsburgh. He was so hungry that his stomach seemed like a bottomless void comprising the greater part of his anatomy. On his way up Randolph Street he passed a restaurant where the odor of hot coffee steaming out in the chill, damp atmosphere assailed his nostrils, and for the space of two or three seconds he leaned up against a convenient lamppost, faint from the very suggestion of food.

He slipped up Randolph Street as far as State, the city's main and principal business street, where property sold for ten thousand dollars a front foot, and proceeded along it, keeping, as he phrased it, "an eye out along the main stem for a harness bull." His objective was Van Buren Street, where, by a turn westward and a walk of two blocks under the elevated road, he could reach Hinky Dink's. Unfortunately, though, considering the state of his exchequer, Hinky Dink's meant only temporary warmth, and food— not at all.

By the beard of the great Jeff Davis, the king of hoboes, but he was famished! Visions of great steaming boiled dinners, as well as platters containing luscious beefsteaks, persisted in floating in front of his eyes, taunting him, rousing him almost to a frenzy. Time and again, almost mechanically, he raised a red, chapped hand rimmed with a ragged coat sleeve and passed it over his brow to aid in dispelling the tantalizing mental pictures.

When he reached Monroe Street he noticed a long line of people, stretching endlessly, it seemed, up to the middle of the block, where the line appeared to terminate at a wide, open foyer, gaily lighted with hundreds of incandescents in spite of the bright gray sky. His first thought was that some careless restaurant waiter had accidentally left a tray of food out on the sidewalk, and that these people were all pressing on each other's heels in order to—But a shred of reason came to his rescue and told him that these people were all well fed and that even such a wonderful sight as a tray of food could not cause them to congregate in a long line.

He shuffled along the curbing, watching the line stretching straight down the middle of the sidewalk, and as he drew nearer to the lighted foyer he saw that another line stretched away in the opposite direction, clear to Adams Street.

A chill breeze came in suddenly from the lake. A number of the patiently waiting individuals turned up the storm-collars of their warm overcoats; a few women tucked their hands deeper in their muffs. Soapy drew his thin ragged coat a little tighter about him—but shivered perceptibly even at that.

Scarcely had he reached the lighted foyer, over which hung an illuminated sign reading, "Pantheon Theatre," than his attention was riveted by a green touring car, which shot up with a rush to the curbing in front of the place and stopped with a grinding and whining of the brakes. He watched it carefully with a feeling that was a judicious admixture of curiosity and shrewd speculation.

A corpulent man in a long fur overcoat, wearing a shiny silk hat and tan gloves, hopped out; and as the door of the car swung open, Soapy read the gold-lettered notice that was painted on the green enamel:

Hexagon Feature Film Co.
President's Car:
Mr. Simon Blumenthal

Something in the well-fed, sleek and warmly clad appearance of Mr. Simon Blumenthal caused a sudden determination in Soapy to do something the like of which he had always studiously avoided in the past, particularly upon the main business street of a big city, where so many police officers abounded. And that determination consisted of soliciting Mr. S. Blumenthal for a nickel; in other words, for the price of a bowl of nectar in the shape of a cup of coffee and three round, ambrosial articles known to the initiated as sinkers.

"Take a look, Wilkins," the big man was saying. "According to telegrams we're receiving, they're pulling the same crowds in all the big towns from New York to 'Frisco. Best film, I tell you, man, we've put out yet. And with the crowds lining up like sheep, you can bet we're soaking the theatre managers triple rent for the reels." Wilkins, one elbow on the steering wheel, stared curiously toward the lobby of the Pantheon. "I tell you, my boy, it merely proves that the American public isn't looking for literature. They're looking for thrills. They want their hair to stand up on their heads; they want to gasp. It's thrills, I tell you, and nothing el—"

"Mister," whined Soapy, "could you spare a hungry guy a nickel for a cup of coffee?"

Blumenthal spun on his heel.

"Why, the impudence!" he exclaimed sharply. "Panhandling on the public thoroughfare, eh? See here, my man, why don't you go out and earn your nickel? Such people as you are better off in—" He raised a gloved hand and beckoned over Soapy's shoulder to someone. "I say—officer—will you arrest this fellow? He just panhandled me in broad daylight."

Trapped as he saw he was—and he knew the penalty well—Soapy turned to flee. But too late. The long arms of the law, exemplified by the muscular, blue-sleeved members of a police officer, closed about him so tightly that he couldn't even wriggle. But he didn't want to wriggle, for he was quite paralyzed by the giant colored lithograph displayed over the entire front of the theatre. And so well did it burn itself in that few seconds on his dulled brain, that in the long six months that he spent within the drab stone walls of the Bridewell on the charge of begging, kicked around from one stone heap to another by the calloused guards, sleeping on a hard cot in company with cimeci lectularii galore, dining daily on thin stew whose nutriment had been removed by city graft, he was able to recall it complete to the last detail of color, picture and lettering:

MOST THRILLING SCENE
EVER FILMED!
A TRIUMPH IN DARE-DEVIL
ACTING!

Keeno, the world-famed detective, disguised as a tramp, tied hand and foot in the bottom of the counterfeiters' car, escapes certain death by leaping into the air while the car is plunging over hundred-foot gorge.

—Most Costly——Most Sensational—
—Most Hair-raising——Most Genuine—
Episode Ever Shown on the Screen
Exhibited Only in
"DETECTIVE KEENO AND THE
COUNTERFEITING GANG"
or
"TRACKED TO DOOM"
Hexagon Feature Film Company

THE HAND OF GOD

I

FOR SEVERAL WEEKS she had been appearing in Carew's dreams. In each instance she was short and slender, and dressed in Chinese costume; dressed ever, in fact, in richly embroidered blouse and pantaloons of brilliant orange silk. Her oblique eyes were as black, seemingly, as the neatly bobbed bang which fell across her saffron-tinted forehead, and from her shell-like ears swung green jade earrings carved in the form of tiny Buddhas.

Sometimes it seemed to him that she placed her soft cool arms—the silken sleeves of the loose Chinese jacket-blouse falling away from them as she raised them—around his neck, and pressed her little body voluptuously close to his; and to him it was almost as though they had known each other always.

But ever he would awaken suddenly, to find the morning sun streaming into the room through his wide-open window which looked down ten stories on the green park below, the slim Oriental figure vanishing away like a mist—leaving him only the elusive sensation that she always left in parting—the feeling of warm kisses imprinted upon his lips.

Once it was a whole week before she reappeared to him; indeed, her visits were irregular at the best. That night, as he dropped off into troubled sleep, he saw her come floating toward him out of nowhere; and all night long they walked on, hand in hand, through fields of gigantic purple pansies, barbaric in their splendor—pansies that actually eyed them jealously as they passed—and talking, as they roamed, the little nothings that lovers have talked since the far-off Paleolithic Age.

But, as before, morning came—and she disappeared abruptly.

Once, in his waking moments, he analyzed her fully—or, rather, his recollections of her! In spite of the undeviating appearance she always presented in his dreams, hers seemed to be a most composite individuality—made up of those characteristics that most stood out, in all the various Chinese girls whom he had loved—or, perhaps, dallied with—and by whom, in turn, he had been loved. Her costume was unmistakably that of Ah Sen—who had sat for his canvases in the long ago in Philadelphia. While her oblique jet eyes—with their lashes so long for a Chinese girl's—were, of course, those of Su Chung, who had sold him preserved ginger in her father's store in Frisco, and whom, when the old man wasn't looking, he had kissed across the worn wooden counter. The black bang hanging more than ordinarily low on the fore-head—touching, in fact, the crest of the eyebrows—and also the unusual jade earrings carved like tiny Buddhas, belonged all, of course, to O Lyra Weng who had lived with him in New Or-leans—and who had proudly tossed back to him the $500 with which he had attempted to assuage her despair at his departure. No, this girl was assuredly no particular Chinese girl—that was certain. She was just a fusion—of them all.

Odd, too, for the manner in which Chinese girls had always drawn his fancy—for a while, that is!

Tonight of all nights, he felt certain he was to meet her again. For while he lay in his bed, waiting for sleep to come, after all the cares of the long day in preparing for his marriage the following week with Laurine—dainty Laurine, with her china-blue eyes and her marigold yellow hair—he was oppressed by a peculiar medley of nervousness and weariness that told him he was sure to dream.

The light from the new air-beacon, across the park, reflected fitfully from the polished brass knob of his bed. Fitfully, because the illumination from the beacon rose and fell—rose and fell—as it threw first its millions of candlepowers forth—and then died, to show that it was just a signpost of the Air Age. And then flowered forth again. He watched the flickering gleams dreamily, wonder-ing whether the visionary Chinese maiden was to be part of the night's subconscious wanderings. Twice he yawned. Once he dozed off. Strange, those flickerings. An automatic message—to every plane—everywhere that one could see it—that this was goal post No. 49 on the National Airways Route No. 6! His eyes turned toward the brass candlestick on the mantel across the room. It came forth as a candlestick only as the light rose—but died al-ways, as such, whenever the light fell. Was a thing real, he won-dered dreamily, if it came into being only on account of another thing? Wasn't it, after all, just an "idea"—being "thought" into existence by the bigger thing? Wasn't everything in this room which came forth when the beacon flared up—just an idea? Take, for instance, the burnished copper shade of the reading lamp in the corner of the room. Flicker—here—flicker—gone! A lamp—no lamp—a lamp—no lamp! His eyes roamed without his head moving. Everywhere in the room—things of metal—polished objects—flicker—here—flicker—gone!—flicker—flicker—flick—but the flickerings were no longer now bringing candlesticks, bedposts, lampshades—they had coalesced—in fact the light was constant—enormous purple pansies—the slim figure in the little embroidered Chinese suit—great fields, stretching far and away!

II

"So, Moon-flower, you have come again? And you—but why do I call you Moon-Flower? Well—why not? You always come to me, don't you, when the moon is mistress of ceremonies? And not the sun? And—no, no, I don't mean here. For here we have always the sunlight—and our huge pansies—and the fields. I mean the moon in the other world, where things are re— . . . But let's not discuss it. It hasn't any bearing on things. And I'm waiting, dear. See? My arms just waiting to enfold you." He studied her face questioningly. "But why—that odd look on your face? Are we not to walk together across the lovely, fragrant fields again tonight? Tell me—what is wrong?"

Her lips did not move, but the conviction grew upon him that he understood as well as though a radio blared it into his ear.

"So-o-o! And that is it? That I am to be married—to Laurine?"

The view changed; a blood-red river flowed close by; the sun burned pinker, larger; some leaden thing seemed tugging at his heart.

"Can you not understand, Moon-Flower," his symbolic self pleaded on, "that she is real—while you are only a creature of my imagination? Truly—I swear to you that that is why I am marrying her—and not cleaving to you. It isn't because she is blonde and blue-eyed and all that—a Caucasian girl. You should know that. And you should know it, too, with the wisdom of many girls! For you are gazing bitterly at me with Su Chung's eyes—Su Chung, who always smiled at me across the counter. Gazing at me under the petite little bang that is no other than O Lyra Weng's. In fact, those jade earrings you wear are O Lyra's—proud little devil, too, the way *you*—that is, I mean *she!*—cast that five hundred back at me. And your costume—why, to the last silken thread—it's Ah Sen's. Yes, I know I told her I loved her—but I meant only—ahem!—in an artistic way. You should have—that is, *she* should have understood. Your lips, though, are none of any of theirs—

they are, as sure as anything, the lips of Kuan Ha—who pleaded to me that her Chinese lover had left her because of me—and that I should marry her therefore. See—all imagination, my dear! That is what *you* are. While Laurine—well—*she* is material, tangible, made of flesh and blood. Someone to love—and to be with. While you are but a phantasm, a nothing, an ephemeral thing existing only in my nocturnal fancy. That's why, Moon-Flower, she is to be my wife, while you—alas!—can never be anything but my little Chinee-gal dream sweetheart!"

The muscles of the hallucinatory face gazing upon him never relaxed from their cruel austerity. And a great unease filled him.

"What—what are you hiding behind you?" he queried. "Oh—I see! A Chinese dagger. It's beautiful. And for me, you say? Where did you get it? Did . . .

"Not—for me? Not—in the way I think—that is? Surely . . ." Now a great fear gripped him—a weird, night-born fear. "Oh—for shame! Surely—surely you would not transform our happy little dream into a common nightmare, would you? Surely you . . ."

His whole being stiffened. "Drop it, I tell you! Drop it, you little Chinese she-devil—or I'll twist that pretty wrist of yours till I break it. Drop it, I tell you. Or I'll . . . Ah God! Stop! Dream-Girl! Moon-Flower! Stop! You have plunged it into . . ."

III

"Oh, it's you, is it, Grogan?"

"Yes, Chief."

"Well—what did you find when you got there?"

"Well, Chief, the clerk at the Parkway took me up to the room. As he told you hisself on the phone, the hotel passkey would go into the lock all right—showin' that the key wasn't on the inside of the lock—but the passkey wouldn't open the door—showin' that the door was bolted from the inside. So, of course, after again gettin' no sign of an answer, we busted in the door. The key, incidentally, we found on the dresser. The one other opening to the room—the one window—looked down ten stories to the park below—no, no fire escape, Chief—the Parkway was built before the skyscraper laws in this burg. But le' me try to tell it all to you before you ask questions. I—what's that? Connecting doors—from other rooms? No, no, none! One door only—and from the hallway—and bolted; one window only—unlocked—and looking down ten stories into the street and the park. All right, I'll go on.

The papers in his bureau showed he was Donald Carew all right—same as he claimed to be at the Parkway—and not some racketeer using some phoney monicker. He's a high-up artist—in case you don't know nothing about art—and a letter in his coat pocket showed that he was to have been hitched next week to his high-society debbytante, Laurine Cassia Randell. And his bank statement, laying on the bureau, showed he had some 25,000 bucks in the cooler. And . . ."

"What's that? Where was he?"

"Oh—I thought I told you that when I commenced all this. He was laying across his bed, in his pyjammers—and deader'n a doornail. And . . ."

"Did you call a doctor?"

"Yes—on'y the one I called happens to be the coroner's physician! That is, Chief, I called the coroner—and he's out of town—so his doc's on his way over. The while I'm waiting here in the parlor of the Parkway, and Carew's rooms upstairs is locked up tight—and soon's the doc gets here, I'll start back for the office."

"But what induced you, Grogan, to call the coroner's physician—instead of some nearby one? People die of heart disease every day."

"Sure, Chief. Sure, I know they do. But this fellow didn't exactly die of heart disease! He evidently was a suicide. Though damned if I was going to marry a gal as pretty as Laurine Randell—and had twenty-five grand in the bank—would I bump myself off. But anyway, y'see, he had a Chinee dagger with a jeweled hilt stuck in his chest—well—not just stuck—no!—but driv to the hilt between two of his ribs. Here comes the coroner's doc now. I'll be right over."

IV

"Is this Hannah Burke?

"Yes, that's who I mean—the gal who cleans up Number 1056 each day.

"Well, this is Dennis Grogan—of the Detective Bureau speaking. Say, how long has that Chinee dagger been laying around Mr. Carew's room?

"What? You ain't never seen it before? And it ain't his?

"Well, it's gotta be his. It was in his room. And it's got his fingerprints on it—so if that don't show it was his—and was there, then nothing . . .

"I—see! You cleaned up his room at five o'clock last evening, and dusted everything, and changed the paper in his bureau drawers—and there wasn't no Chinee dagger there then? All—right!"

V

"Damn it, Bessie, gi' me the Criminal Identification Laboratory. I've been—oh, Filison? Grogan speaking. On the Carew case. Yes. Say, now about them fingerprints of Carew's on that dagg—

"What's 'at?

"You—did—not? You—you mean you found no fingerprints at all?

"Oh—you did? Well, who the hell's fingerprints are they? Listen, if . . .

"A single set of five fingerprints—from one small hand?

"And—and they're not Carew's at all?

"Then it can't be suic—

"For Cri— . . . Never mind. Good bye!"

VI

"Gentlemen of the Coroner's Jury, listen closely now to the evidence of Dr. Burkhalter, Coroner's physician for this county. He made an exhaustive examination of both the body of the deceased, and of the conditions and surroundings accompanying the latter's taking off—before anything was materially disturbed.

"As an alienist-detective he has made both a material and a psychological analysis of this case. And as he is a rising young authority in this new field of research. I believe I can promise you that his evidence—whatever it will consist of—and whatever its nature will be—will be interestingly constructive.

"Now, Doctor, we will proceed: First, what do you consider, to the best of your knowledge and information, to have been the immediate cause of Donald Carew's death?"

"An internal hemorrhage, Mr. Coroner, resulting from a lesion made by the forcible insertion of a very sharp dagger thrust between the third and fourth ribs of his left side."

"Well, we have here the weapon, drawn from the body; so there is no question, I guess, about that. But what, Doctor, is your theory as to how and by whom the deed could have been committed? You are aware, of course, since you were the first official examiner of the place—outside of Mr. Grogan of the Detective Bureau—that the only window of that particular room looks out upon space from ten stories up in the air—and is entirely lacking any fire escape; and that the one door of the room was found to be bolted on the inside—after, that is, Mr. Grogan and the hotel manager broke it down. Hence, it would seem practically impossible that any unknown person could have struck the fatal blow.

"And yet the man is dead—and from the thrust of a dagger found still lodged in his body. Now then, in order that these ten gentlemen assembled here may bring in one of the specific verdicts covering definitely both the mode of commission, and the cause or perpetrator thereof, which the law of this city provides *must* be rendered in the case of all violent deaths, may we have—in order to clarify things for them—your professional statement that it was a plain case of suicide?"

"No!"

"No? Ah—this is getting interesting! What then are your conclusions, Doctor? By which these gentlemen may bring in their verdict?"

"The man was murdered."

"Murdered? Well, that certainly makes for a clear-cut verdict. If true. But . . ."

"Though I regret to say, sir, that the manner in which he was murdered does not exactly make for one of the few specific verdicts permitted here under our laws. For he was murdered by his own imagination!"

"What? How—how could that be?"

"It was probably a case of dream auto-suggestion."

"I don't think I follow you quite. You say . . ."

"Well, it's just this way: I found the bedclothes tossed aside, a chair upset, the silken table-cover belonging to a low stand which sits ordinarily at the right side of the head of the bed—a stand containing a couple of books—pulled away, table-cover lying on the floor in one spot, books lying elsewhere on the floor. All the evidences, in short, of a surging, back-and-forth struggle between two persons. But, as we know positively, there could have been but one person—the deceased—in that room at that time; and so the natural and only thing for me to do was to, in some way, account for the struggle—which I proceeded to do.

"I found, by talking on the long-distance phone with the man most familiar with the life and habits of the deceased—his uncle, with whom he lived as a young boy—that he was at times somnambulistic—though only on the approach of momentous periods in his own affairs. Such as critical football matches in boyhood— graduations from elementary schools—visits from far-off relatives whom he admired. He was never told about his somnambulism, however, lest he brood about it. It was hoped by his uncle that it would wear off.

"I found also that he had had delivered to him just around six P.M. the evening of the night he met his death, by special-delivery parcel-post, a genuine Chinese dagger, brought up to the door of his room by the special-delivery man. And . . .

"How? Oh, the discarded wrapping paper from the package was still in his wastebasket. The return address 'Novar and Pavlun, Chicago,' almost told the story, since a Chicago directory reveals that Novar and Pavlun deal only in theatrical props. However, a telephone connection with them elicited the fact that Carew had ordered the dagger for use in some kind of a dramatic canvas he was outlining in his mind. A genuine thing it was, too, which they had obtained at some time in Chinatown. I only wish all cases were as simple as this—with respect, that is, to tracing ownership of a lethal weapon. And I—what was that latter question again? Oh, why his fingerprints were not on its brass handle? Well, it seems, from the story of the special-delivery boy, that Carew was just going out as the boy came—was dressed, in fact, in full dress suit and white cotton gloves—so it's evident that he undid the package, gloves still on hands, examined his acquisition well— gloves still on—and then set the dagger atop the little low table that stands at the side of the head of his bed. The fingerprints that *are* on it are undoubtedly those of the girl at Novar and Pavlun's who packed the dagger for mailing. She wiped it well off with a silk cloth, she said to me on the phone, before packing it—but seized it in her right hand before depositing it in its nest of torn tissue paper. And so—now what was that? That Carew didn't wear his gloves to bed? No, indeed! No—but I'm coming to that.

"Now he was, as we now know, about to be married—and un- doubtedly certain ones of his two million brain-cells were never quite at rest on that engrossing subject, but, by subconscious cere- bration, kept him, even in his sleep, susceptible to dreams.

"And his dreams in that room must have been unusually vivid things—pseudo-self-hypnotic affairs—rather, to be exact, mes- meric phenomena. The reason I say that is because the rise and fall of the air-beacon light just across the park makes every polished metal object in the room continuously flicker. No, actually pulse! I mighty near fell into a state of self-mesmerism myself, trying it out last night. And for a man like him, somnambulistic, the mechanics of his surroundings provided psychological territory for strange things to happen,

"And, getting back to the deceased himself again, it is fairly safe to deduce that, in his waking state, he feared and strove to guard against, as the day of his coming marriage approached, the jealousy of some earlier and now discarded sweetheart. I understand that he's had romances with a number of Chinese girls in his life. Romances which amused him—but left them scarred in one way or another. I wouldn't wonder but that he felt those Chinese girls now hostile, inimical—all of them—to his happiness. But, anyway, brooding over this, or something like this, in his half-conscious mind directly before deep sleep claimed him, his brain cells, both by auto-suggestion and by actual mesmerization due to flickerings somewhere in line with his eye, became liberated from all control of his will-power, and immediately composed and dramatized before his mental eye the imagined form of some sweetheart nemesis—and his conscience and fears attributed to that person the physical motion of a personal attack upon him.

"What I am trying to get at is that we cannot call the state he was in ordinary sleep—or ordinary self-hypnosis, either.

"But being a full-fledged somnambulist, at least at strenuous periods in his life, he tossed back the bed clothing with his left hand and arose and struggled to grasp the dagger held, pointed toward him, in the hand of his self-imposed phantom—which dagger, however, lay not in a real hand, but atop a little low table at the side of his bed. I wouldn't be surprised but that it was the flickerings in the dagger handle itself that caused the pseudo-mesmerism. Or the final stages of it. But, subsequently, in moving his hand defensively in unison with the hand of a pure apparition trying to thrust the weapon into him, there followed the very thrust he dreamed he was trying to turn aside.

"What I am trying to say is this: his eyes being open, as is always the case with somnambulists, he could ever see the actual dagger—for the air-beacon light, you know, never becomes quite completely extinguished. Always there is some light in that room. But his mind, being asleep, also saw the part of the picture that didn't exist; i.e., the visionary assailant holding this same dagger—and so, in closing his fingers tightly around the fingers of the phantom hand that presumably held that dagger, he actually closed them around the handle of the real dagger. Pointing, of course,

toward himself. The powerful energy with which the purely imagined assailant strove to drive the dagger into Carew's breast was
provided by his active somnambulistic self—that self which makes
it possible for somnambulists to climb roof parapets and do almost
impossible other things. The negligible and almost minus force
which Carew used to keep the dagger *from* being driven in was
provided by his impotent feeble dream-self—that illusive self
which makes us think, just after we have waked out of a nightmare, that we must have kicked our bed to pieces—only to find
out from our wives, who mayhap awakened us because we murmured a little, that only a muscle or two at best quivered. A
matched struggle, in Carew's dream, that struggle to stay the dagger. In actuality—a one-way affair!

"Fingerprints? Well, I find, myself, that lying in that bed, with
the low bedside table in its customary position, if one raises one's
right hand to seize the handle of a knife lying on that table and
pointed toward one, one's hand almost certainly sweeps around
against the inside edge of the low-hanging silken table-cover—
with the result that when one actually seizes the knife handle,
one's fingers and hand are canopied by a silk shroud. In short, it
was through that table-scarf—or the edge or corner of it—that
Carew's fingers closed on that brass dagger handle. The resistance
the scarf subsequently made, as it pulled from the table, scattering
its books, undoubtedly provided the initial stimulus to Carew's
illusion of a force pitted against his own hand. The scarf dropped
to the floor after his hand fell away from the dagger and plunged
into his breast—and he staggered back a few steps to fall prone
upon the bed.

"That is all, gentlemen. Though I can depict for you the general
physical and psychological mechanics of this death, I cannot in the
light of the circumstances I have outlined even suggest to you how
your verdict—under the laws of this city calling for very specific
verdicts as to commission and committor—would best be
phrased."

VII

"We, the jury in this case called, find that the deceased, Donald
G. Carew, came to his death from an internal hemorrhage, caused
by the thrust of a dagger held in the hand of God!"

"GOODBYE COPPERS!"

ENGLISH DICK," known back in gay, merry England as "King of the Safecrackers," thoughtfully surveyed the job as it stood at this second. Even spoke.

"Yeah, we're ready for the pop-off, Neddie-boy," he nodded complimentarily. "And this job'll go down in American crime history! Bill Brannon, King of the True Crime Story Writers, will be living off it for the rest of his life."

"English" was a red-faced man of about 53, with grey-touched sideburns, and wearing tweed knickers and a dark hunting jacket such as would be worn by a gentleman. His assistant, to whom he spoke, Liverpool Ned, was a saturnine, morose, pessimistic-looking individual of about 40, in a shiny black suit such as a pall-bearer would wear.

The rear section of the big jewelry store on the main street of this young city on the outskirts of Chicago was gloomy at this hour of 2 in the afternoon, being without windows, of course, but one could see the big safe with the putty-cup plastered right off the combination dial to the crack between the safe-door and its frame, and which had held the micrometrically measured "dinny-juice" or nitroglycerine boiled out of dynamite sticks, that would do exactly thus and not a bit more; the "oiled wedges" driven by padded hammers into the crack so that the "dinny juice" would seep down into the safe's interior; the "dinny-juice" stains all about the crack, the "quick-string" or fast fuse, hanging down from the "leak-in-point," and the "double-x's" or high-powered ignition caps plastered to the oily safe surface with Woolworth Stores Scotch tape.

"Now just a pep-talk to you, bloke," said "English" helpfully, "before we pop. And in the Queen's English, and not the Cockney I can talk when I want to and have to. That face of yours looks a mile long. Sure, sure, sure, that son-of-a bitch of a look-out there, Birmingham Basil, selling souvenirs, never brought the dinny-juice till an hour ago. But I thought he'd have some trouble in gettin' the dinny sticks, and be slow in boiling 'em up. And he was— on both. And was delayed. Just as I figured he might be while we kipped in here all night. But he got it, and did his job. He came. We got the juice. And I didn't care an owl's hoot. For—

"No, no, no," expostulated "English," "stop your mouthings. I know that the detective and police sub-chiefs and squad-car chieftains of Chi are holding their annual picnic here today, and are all right outside now liquoring up in the taverns, with blue squad-cars strung up and down the streets like pearls. Even did I see, when I peeked out the front last, Baldy Sam himself, Police Chief of Chi, who warned me when I came into that burg, 'No tricks now, English,' and who's going to give the grand spiel on crime prevention at 4 bells in some nearby field after they've fed their faces with their packed lunches. And the tacked-up, signed contract over on the wall yonder shows that the local county Burns Detective Agency, in possession of the key to the joint, inspects it on all holidays, Sundays, and 'closed days' like this, between 'not earlier than 4 P.M. nor later than 6 P.M.' bells; so we can't lay over with our junk and our sweet rig-up over yonder till that Congress of Cops has pulled out and started back for Chi where it belongs. It's now or not ever-never at all, not so? So now it is! But—

"Stop your facial contortions, will you?" demanded "English." "I got the floor now. I—but so all right. John Law is strung all over the street out there. But—so what? Outside there on the curb in front of this place we got that souped-up racing car, its blue-paint job all done over in quick-drying black, and fitted now with phony license plates, that Basil snitched from that garage in Chicago's Hyde Park, and that won't be hot for two days yet till that bachelor playboy-racing driver 'Rocket' van der Vere, reported in the hospital treating for housemaid's knee, comes out of the hospital and finds his doll-baby non-esty. So souped up is that interballistics missile, as Basil lovingly called it after having given it a sneak try-out on the third lane of the Congress Street freeway, it can outdo any car in the world today. All we got to do is to have one quarter-minute—oh, one half minute, to gun off in it, and nothing perched on wheels can overtake us. Every quarter-minute we fly, the distance between us and any pursuers increases by the cube root of X plus Y. You're the mathematician of our little mob. You figured it all out yourself back there, on paper. Just as I, the brains of our push, plucked this town out from a map of so-called 'Chicagoland,' and subsequently this store, off the railroad station a block or so, when I see the sign of it reading 'Closed a week because of illness of owner'. And—"

"But Christopher, Boss," interpolated Neddie-boy of Liverpool, "the minute we pop—and I think it'll be a super-perfect pop, the way you measured all the dimensions of that box and counted out the drops of dinny-juice even to the half-drop—the minute we pop—wowie!—them American police cars all over the region out-side—them gatted-up narks—oh all right, coppers then—they'll—"

"No, no, no!" almost yelled "English." "Not the *minute* we pop. The pop'll be loud, yes. It'll shake the town. Also the bang of that big safe door on the floor—and Uncle Genius here calculated this job, don't forget!—the bang of that big safe door on the floor'll rattle this shack. But people hafta collect their wits. First thing they'll all think is that a gas main exploded somewhere. There won't be no inkling of what's what till—

"But that's where you got to do *your* stuff fast. This slug-slowed right arm of mine—well, that's why I'm brains in this little quartette of English purloiners now starting a career in the Land of the Flea and the Home of the Slave. The minute she pops, heave into that black silk sack you're holding there all them tickers, sparklers and mazuma in there—don't stop to examine it—this ain't no counting-house. Heave it all in, and us out. It'll be *as* we 'out' that the first glimmerings'll hit 'em that there may have been a pete-job done. At first glimpse their fogged minds will be cert we're a couple of gas-main workers who are fleeing a blown up gas main in terror. But we're across the sidewalk before the glim-merings will have coalesced—naw, that ain't Cockney—I'm not talking Cockney today—before the glimmerings will have meshed together into something concrete—'twon't actually hit 'em till Birmingham Basil out there shucks his souvenir rack and flings in with us—we'll be in our souped-up car—yeah, our own interbal-listics missile as Birmingham will insist on calling it—before they've added 2 and 2 and 2 together and made a tentative 5-1/2 out of 'em. But long before, we're off. And once off," said "Eng-lish" triumphantly, "ain't nothing made on wheels today that can do anything but fall behind, behind, behind, behind, behind, the further we travel."

Neddie-boy opened his mouth to speak but "English" drove on with his pep-talk.

"We shoot straight north as the car is right now pointed. In 9-1/2 minutes, at *our* speed, we're just short of a spot called Penton Crossing, shown on the maps by our steel ruler as laying straight off here by that distance—yeah, 9-1/2 minutes of our speed—it'll be a crow's-flight run—every main street of an American town becomes the main county road when two places shown on a map lay right on the same steel ruler's edge—true, we haven't made a trial-run of the get-away route because Basil never lifted that car till night before last, and Lancaster Lou, camping in the thicket just ahead of Penton Crossing, with the transfer car, as exactly he wrote and confirmed but yesterday, is so hot, even in this country, because of that bump-off he made of that old Chink in Limehouse, that he's afraid to show his puss around in daylight till he gets a few face-changes—but it don't matter—if the county road between here and there turns into a caked-mud road instead of the concrete we leave on, and cuts our speed down a stinking 10 miles an hour, it'll slow the pursuers, running on Standard Oil of New Jersey synthetic tires, by 20!—so the make of the road'll be sauce for the gander as well as for the goose, but tougher on the gander—but all right—all right—all right—9-1/2 minutes ride, on our tickers—and we've reached where Lancaster Lou is. But now remember, we're 10 to 12 to even more full minutes separated from them rolling stage coaches barking along behind like he-dogs after a bitch in heat. Into the transfer car we dive, down the rocky lane he found, and into the never-before-discovered, evidently underground cave he also found what's now fixed up with A and P goods from the transfer car good for months and months of kipping if needs be, the transfer car itself tipped over into the abandoned water-filled stone quarry he told us about. And we've vanished—from the face of the earth!"

"My missus back in Liverpool will sure be worried," said Neddie-boy.

"Worried? She'll be proud as hell of her Neddie-boy. She'll—well, come on now. The more we talk, the more you'll get your bloody wind up. Pop!"

Neddie-boy, black silk sack in hand, stepped forward to the big safe. With an automatic cigarette lighter he lit the "quick string." Both men turned around, off the line of the "blow," facing the wall momentarily, fingers in ears.

"Bang!" It shook the neighborhood, all right. "Bang" again, as the big door fell forward onto the wooden floor, its bolt and its hinges riven as though by a giant shears. No wonder they called "English" the King of Safecrackers.

But Neddie-boy, choking a bit on the acrid whitish smoke pouring forth from the safe's now open maw, was shoving into his sack the contents, which consisted of watches, tied-up currency bills, trays of diamond rings. "All in," he said, jerking the string together that drew the sack-neck tight. "Let's dive!"

Through the rear of the shop frontward, through the front of the store with empty showcases, the two men raced. Out the door, sack on Neddie-boy's shoulder. A nebulous picture, revealed under an ominous grey sky from which the sun had vanished completely, of a suburban town main street of smooth concrete, studded with blue police cars each side, blue-jacketed policemen standing around, even Baldy Sam beaming vacuously from a kerb, was all that could be seen. Birmingham Basil, outside, accoutred with his rack of souvenirs, looked startled without any reason at all to be, since he knew, from many jobs done in Fleet Street, London, and elsewhere, the meaning of such sounds. "English" and Neddie-boy were in the souped-up black racing car in one bound—in the front seat, of course—Birmingham Basil, minus souvenirs, behind. Before one could say Jack Sprat, Jack Woodford, or Jack the Ripper, they were off like indeed a missile.

The houses and shops of that main street became almost immediately just a blur each side. If any pedestrians were crossing the street anywhere, they must have flown back in terror towards the kerb they'd started out from. "English," at the wheel, took only about 4 to 5 seconds gunning up to full speed. He cast a fleeting glance back to see whether anybody in blue police coats or blue caps had moved out of a position of deep-freeze, but the street bending slightly and gently prevented his seeing this. But he knew full well that back at the site of the job bluecoated figures were, at the most, shouting questions at each other, rubbing their fool chins, unable yet even to get organized, the while Baldy Sam, Chicago police chief, was at the most trying to choke out, "After 'em, boys—it's a job!"

They continued to fly like a missile, the blur each side of them. That precious quarter-minute—half-minute—that would make them forever uncatchable—was piling up. Indeed, all of two half-minutes were now in the limbo of the never-recoverable.

And then suddenly—suddenly!—they must have gone a full mile from where they'd missiled off—"English" saw it!—up ahead. Across the street were drawn blue squad cars in double rank—along the kerbs and sidewalks were more blue-coated figures—guns in hands—two tommy-guns, manned by blue-hatted figures—were pointed each side.

"Hell—damn!" raged "English." "A roadblock! Must—must have been two conventio—I mean picnics—one must have talked to the other by talkie-walkie—or else they jumped here by helicopt—"

He'd been pulling to a hopeless whining shrieking stop. Unflung the door. Was throwing his hands up in the air. Was stumbling out, hands up, followed by Neddie-boy behind him, hands up too, and Birmingham Basil the same.

None other than Baldy Sam, Chicago's police chief, with shining pate, stood there with handcuffs.

"Hell—fire, Baldy!" said "English" uncomplimentarily. "How'd you do it? You got here—with helicopters?"

"Helicopters?" snorted Baldy Sam. "If you wasn't from bonny England, 'English,' you'd have known that—but by the way, we'll run north leisurely in a little while and pick up your cohort somewhere where he's waiting with a transfer car—well, as I started to say, 'English,' if you wasn't from bonny England, you'd have known that this town of Norwood Park, situated just on the edge of Chi, was built on the site of a famous racetrack of the '90's—right!—the main street is the old oval track itself. You just went around the course, 'English'—and we just waited for you."

"Aeouw!" "English" moaned, in best Cockneyese.

SOURCES

Telescopic Romance, Chicago Ledger, 4 parts, August 14 – Sept. 4, 1920, as reprinted in Keeler News, No. 42, May 2003.

The Spender, 10 Story Book, October 1913.

When the Rivet Fell, 10 Story Book, October 1914.

Valley Express: On Time, 10 Story Book, February 1923 (original publication [1914] unknown)

Missing: One Diamond Salesman, Black Cat, August 1914.

Babes in the Wood, 10 Story Book, August 1914.

That Elusive Face, The Argosy, September 1914

The Services of an Expert—The Story, 10 Story Book, September 1914.

The Services of an Expert—The Play, Chicago Ledger, March 20, 1920

When Time Ran Backward, Black Cat, February 1915.

The Search, Black Cat, March 1915.

The Goddess in the Camera, 10 Story Book, February 1915

Victim Number 5, Chicago Ledger, September 16, 1922 (Original publication, Young's Magazine, September 1914)

A Check for a Thousand, 10 Story Book, May 1915

Package 22,227, 10 Story Book, August, 1915

Soapy's Trip to Mars, Chicago Ledger, March 13, 1920

The Rube, 10 Story Book, January 1915

John Jones's Dollar, Black Cat, August 1915

Bill's Bill, Boys Life, 2 parts, April & May, 1916

Sunbeam's Child, Keeler News, No. 28, September 2000 (Original publication [1918] unknown)

The Settlement, Black Cat, February 1916

Quilligan and the Magic Coin, Black Cat, November 1915

Sidestepping Ryan, 10 Story Book, May 1916

30 Seconds of Darkness, Black Cat, May 1916

The Disappearance of Mrs. Snoozleworth, Top Notch, May 1, 1916 as reprinted in Keeler News, No. 60, December 2006

The Debut of Soapy Mulligan, Philadelphia Inquirer Sunday Story Section, March 18, 1917 (Orginal publication, Short Stories, July 1916

The Hand of God, 20 Great Tales of Murder, edited by Helen McCloy and Brett Halliday, Random House, 1951

"Goodbye, Coppers!" Keeler News, No. 43, July 2003 (Original publication [1962] unknown)

UNFOUND AND UNPUBLISHED STORIES

The Eddy, written 1913, unsold.

The Elopement Extraordinary, written 1913, sold 1916.

Jack's Lucky Coin, written 1913, unsold (rewritten as *Quilligan and the Magic Coin*)

Dream-Girl, written 1913, unsold (probably rewritten as *The Hand of God*)

A Ten-Year Battle, written 1913, unsold.

The Bertillon System, written 1914, sold 1914.

Can Such Things Be?, written 1914, sold 1915.

REPRISALS

Harry Stephen Keeler reused many of the stories in this book by incorporating them into the novels he wrote. They could be important parts of the plot or wildly unrelated interludes. Some became considerably longer. Some were little changed, others completely changed in vantage point and characters. The following books all contain different versions of stories in this book. The dates are for the first American editions. Happily for the twenty-first century reader all of these books are in print and readily available from Ramble House.

The Face of the Man from Saturn (1933)
    "John Jones's Dollar"

The Five Silver Buddhas (1935)
    "Sidestepping Ryan"
    "Victim Number 5"

The Mystery of the Fiddling Cracksman (1934)
    "The Settlement"

The Skull of the Waltzing Clown (1935)
    'The Hand of God"

10 Hours (1937)
    "Missing: One Diamond Salesman"
    "That Elusive Face "

Thieves' Nights (1929)
    "The Rube"
    "The Search"
    "The Spender"
    "30 Seconds of Darkness"
    "When the Rivet Fell"

X. Jones of Scotland Yard (1936)
    "A Check for a Thousand"

Y. Cheung, Business Detective (1939)
    "A Telescopic Romance"

NOTES

Texts are based on earliest known publication unless otherwise noted. Inclusions in later novels are based on American editions — book dates are American publication dates.

"A Telescopic Romance"
Written 1910, unsold
    Published in editorial column of The Chicago Ledger in 4 parts August 14 — September 4, 1920 as "Wandering Willie's Life Story."
    Text based on Richard Polt's transcription for Keeler News #42, May 2003.
    The story was greatly expanded as "Strange Romance" (attributed to character André Marceau) in *Y. Cheung, Business Detective*, Chapters 16-29 (1939).
    Considered but not used for Futurama episode "Time Keeps on Slipping", Season 3, Episode 14, originally aired May 6, 2001.
    As "Strange Romance" a short film on YouTube (2008). Written by Graham Self. Directed by Nick Eades and Graham Self.
    Starring Grahams Self and Emily McMahon with narration by Lisa Waite. Filmed and edited by Nick Eades

"The Spender"
Written 1913, sold 1913.
    10 Story Book, October 1913
    Chicago Ledger, March 27, 1920
    1st story sold, 1st published story
    Beginning of 27 year relationship with 10 Story Book
    1st of three stories with a hobo named "Soapy"
    "Soapy" changed to DeLancey for *Thieves' Nights*, Chapter 16, "The Adventure of DeLancey After He Escaped San Quentin" (1929).

"Valley Express on Time"
Written 1913, sold 1914
    Original publication unknown.
    10 Story Book, February 1923

"When the Rivet Fell"
Written 1914, sold 1914
  10 Story Book, October 1914
  10 Story Book, April 1920 as "The Adventure of the Man Who
    Mislaid His Memory", a frame story inside a frame story in
    "The Arabian Nights of 1920"
  Thieves' Nights, Chapter 9, "The Episode of the Man Who
    Mislaid His Memory" and Chapter 17, "Winner Takes All"
    (1929)
  In each version there is a different woman's name on the
    birthday card. In the Arabian Nights version the name is
    "Hazel." (HSK married Hazel Goodwin in 1919.)
  The other course of action — being taken to an asylum — was
    used as the premise of *The Monocled Monster* (1947).

"Missing: One Diamond Salesman"
Written 1914, sold 1914
  The Black Cat, August 1914
  10 Story Book, March 1923 (as "The Man the Chief Called In")
  Weekly Ledger. September 20, 1924 (as "The Man the Chief
    Called In" by Don Lampton)
  THE BEST OF 10 STORY BOOK, edited by Chris Mikul,
    Ramble House, 2006 (as "The Man the Chief Called In")
  Rewritten as "The Strange Adventure of the Kidnapped
    Chinaman" in *10 Hours*, Chapters 11-15 (1937)

"Babes in the Wood"
Written 1914, sold 1914
  10 Story Book, August 1914
  10 Story Book, April 1920 (as "The Adventure of the Two
    Babes Who Toured the Tenderloin," contained in "The
    Arabian Nights of 1920" and containing "The Adventure of
    Peter Red-Light from the Land of the Hula Hula" by John P.
    Robinson (no, that's not Keeler))

"That Elusive Face"
Written 1914, sold 1914
  The Argosy, September 1914
  The Albany Evening Journal, October 14, 1915

Chicago Ledger, November 11, 1922 (as "The Story of the Infallible Memory System and the Elusive Face" contained within "The Strange Visitor")

10 Story Book, December 1922 (as "That Tantalizing Face")

THE BEST OF 10 STORY BOOK, edited by Chris Mikul, Ramble House, 2006 (as "That Tantalizing Face")

Expanded as "The Strange Adventure of the Elusive Face" in *10 Hours*, Chapters 19-27 (1937)

"The Services of an Expert" (story)
Written 1914, sold 1914

10 Story Book, September 1914

10 Story Book, May 1919

Unknown British publication 1923 (British)

Unknown British publication 1925 (British)

Keeler News #3, March 1997

Alfred Hitchcock's Mystery Magazine, December 1999

THE WORLD'S BEST ONE HUNDRED DETECTIVE STORIES, VOL. 1, edited by Eugene Thwing, Funk & Wagnalls, 1929

A TO IZZARD: A HARRY STEPHEN KEELER COMPANION, edited by Fender Tucker, Ramble House, 2002

Greatly expanded as *The Man with the Magic Eardrums* (1939)

"The Services of an Expert" (play)
Written 1914, unsold.

Chicago Ledger, March 20, 1920 (as by John Jones in "The Editor Demonstrates One-Act Play Construction")

Produced 1928 or 1929 by the Community Center Players as part of "An Evening of Short Plays." Directed by Alfred Stury with Alfred Stury and Laurence Brewer.

"When Time Ran Backward"
Written 1914, sold 1914

Black Cat, February 1915

Keeler News #34, October 2001

"The Search"
Written 1914, sold 1915

Black Cat, March 1915

Thieves' Nights, Chapter 10, "The Very Raffles-Like Episode of Castor and Pollux, Diamonds Deluxe" (1929)

"The Goddess in the Camera"
Written 1914, sold 1915
 10 Story Book, February 1915
 Chicago Ledger, March 13, 1920
 Keeler News #59, October 2006

"Victim Number 5"
Written 1914, sold 1914
 Young's Magazine, September 1914
 Chicago Ledger, September 16, 1922 (as "Fifth on the List" by
 Don Lampton)
 The Creasey Mystery Magazine, June 1957
 MAIDEN MURDERS, Mystery Writers of America, Harper &
 Brothers, 1952
 THE FOURTH BOOK OF CRIME-CRAFT, Mystery Writers of
 America, Corgi, 1959
 Included in an anthology of mystery writer's first stories. It
 wasn't Keeler's first and the version published had been
 rewritten to use within a novel.
 The Five Silver Buddhas, Chapter 3, "The Singular Case of One
 Ivan Kossakof, Professional Strangler Who Bought the
 Second Buddha!" (1935)

"A Check for a Thousand"
Written 1914, sold 1915
 10 Story Book, May 1915
 Chicago Ledger, November 27, 1920
 10 Story Book, January 1923
 Unknown British publication 1923
 X. Jones of Scotland Yard, Document XXXII, "A Cheque for
 200 Guineas" as by Andre Marceau (1936)

"Package 22,227"
Written 1914, sold 1915
 10 Story Book, August 1915
 Keeler News #50, December 2004

"Soapy's Trip to Mars"
Written 1914, never sold
 Chicago Ledger, March 13, 1920 (as "Soapy's Trip to Mars: A
 short photoplay burlesque on the modern 'South-sea-

adventure' tale" as by John Jones in "Editorial Advice to Motion Picture Aspirants")
Keeler News, #69, December 2008

"The Rube"
Written 1914, sold 1915
10 Story Book, January 1915
Chicago Ledger, March 6. 1920
Changed to DeLancey for *Thieves' Nights*, Chapter 12, "The Episode of DeLancey Among the Vultures" (1929)

"John Jones's Dollar"
Written 1914, sold 1915
The Black Cat, August 1915
10 Story Book, August 1922
Chicago Ledger, November 18, 1922 (as "The Story of the Remarkable Dollar of Mr. John Jones" contained inside "The Strange Visitor")
Amazing Stories, April 1927
Amazing Stories, April 1956
STRANGE PORTS OF CALL, edited by August Derleth, Pellegrini & Cudahy, 1948
FANTASIA MATHEMATICA, edited by Clifton Fadiman, Simon & Schuster, 1958
A TO IZZARD: A HARRY STEPHEN KEELER COMPANION, edited by Fender Tucker, Ramble House, 2002 (as "The Strange Story of John Jones Dollar")
The Face of the Man from Saturn, Chapter 12, "The Strange Story of John Jones Dollar" (1933)

"Bill's Bill"
Written 1914, sold 1915
Boy's Life, 2 parts, April, May 1916, illustrated by Norman Rockwell.
Keeler News #17, October 1998
THE CHILD'S WORLD: FIFTH READER, edited by W. K. Tate, Sarah Winters and Hetty S. Browne, Johnson Publishing Company, 1917; Project Gutenberg, 2005.
FLAGS UNFURLED, edited by Laurel Hicks, A Beka Book, Pensacola Christian College, 1st ed. 1974. 2nd ed. 1986, 3rd ed. 1998

"Sunbeam's Child"
Written 1914, sold 1918
  Probably 10 Story Book 1918 (The story sold for $6, the
    standard rate for all stories in 10 Story Book)
  10 Story Book, May 1922
  Keeler News #28, September 2000. Revised version considered
    for inclusion in novel *The Strange Will.*
  A TO IZZARD: A HARRY STEPHEN KEELER COMPAN-
    ION, edited by Fender Tucker, Ramble House, 2002

"The Settlement"
Written 1915, sold 1915
  Black Cat, February 1916
  Grit, September 2, 1917
  Chicago Ledger, December 20, 1919
  10 Story Book, April 1922
  The Mystery of the Fiddling Cracksman, Chapters 6, 15-17, 22
    (1934)

"Quilligan and the Magic Coin"
Written 1915, sold 1915
  Black Cat, November 1915
  The Canadian Magazine, April 1921
  10 Story Book, April 1923
  Boston Sunday Globe Magazine, June 24, 1923
  Keeler News #26, April 2000
  A TO IZZARD: A HARRY STEPHEN KEELER COMPAN-
    ION, edited by Fender Tucker, Ramble House, 2002
  Rewritten version of "Jack's Lucky coin" (1913)

"Sidestepping Ryan"
Written 1915, sold 1917
  10 Story Book, May, 1916 (by Harry Stephen Keeler and
    Franklin Lee Stevenson)
  The Five Silver Buddhas, Chapters 7-11, "The Strange Case of
    One Tim Waldo, Burglar — Who Bought the Fourth Buddha"
    (1935) (Stevenson not mentioned)

"30 Seconds of Darkness"
Written 1915, sold 1916
  The Black Cat, May, 1916 (as "Thirty Seconds of Darkness (The
    Adventure of the Cordova Necklace)")

The Black Cat, February 1920 (as "Thirty Seconds of Darkness (The Adventure of the Cordova Necklace)")

Chicago Ledger, November 11, 1922 (as "The Adventure of the Cordova Necklace, Or Raffles in America" contained within "The Strange Visitor") In this version de Lancey and T. B. are changed to E. W. Hornung's characters Raffles and Bunny.

Thieves' Nights, Chapter 14, "The Adventure of Delancey and the Cordova Necklace" (1929)

"The Disappearance of Mrs. Snoozleworth"
Written 1916, sold 1916
Top-Notch, May 1, 1916 (as "Wink the Other Eye")
Keeler News #60, December 2006 (as "Wink the Other Eye")

"The Debut of Soapy Mulligan"
Written 1916, sold 1916
Short Stories, July 1916
Philadelphia Inquirer Sunday Story Section, March 18, 1917

"The Hand of God"
writing date unknown
20 GREAT TALES OF MURDER, edited by Helen McCloy and Brett Halliday, Random House, 1951
MURDER, MURDER, MURDER: 10 TALES FROM 20 GREAT TALES OF MURDER, edited by Helen McCloy and Brett Halliday, Hillman Books, 1961
The Skull of the Waltzing Clown, Chapter 14 (1935)

"Goodbye Coppers"
Written 1961
The Thumb #4?, 1962
Keeler News #43, July 2003

RAMBLE HOUSE's

HARRY STEPHEN KEELER WEBWORK MYSTERIES

(RH) indicates the title is available ONLY in the **RAMBLE HOUSE** edition

The Ace of Spades Murder
The Affair of the Bottled Deuce (RH)
The Amazing Web
The Barking Clock
Behind That Mask
The Book with the Orange Leaves
The Bottle with the Green Wax Seal
The Box from Japan
The Case of the Canny Killer
The Case of the Crazy Corpse (RH)
The Case of the Flying Hands (RH)
The Case of the Ivory Arrow
The Case of the Jeweled Ragpicker
The Case of the Lavender Gripsack
The Case of the Mysterious Moll
The Case of the 16 Beans
The Case of the Transparent Nude (RH)
The Case of the Transposed Legs
The Case of the Two-Headed Idiot (RH)
The Case of the Two Strange Ladies
The Circus Stealers (RH)
Cleopatra's Tears
A Copy of Beowulf (RH)
The Crimson Cube (RH)
The Face of the Man From Saturn
Find the Clock
The Five Silver Buddhas
The 4th King
The Gallows Waits, My Lord! (RH)
The Green Jade Hand
Finger! Finger!
Hangman's Nights (RH)
I, Chameleon (RH)
I Killed Lincoln at 10:13! (RH)
The Iron Ring
The Man Who Changed His Skin (RH)
The Man with the Crimson Box
The Man with the Magic Eardrums
The Man with the Wooden Spectacles
The Marceau Case
The Matilda Hunter Murder
The Monocled Monster

The Murder of London Lew
The Murdered Mathematician
The Mysterious Card (RH)
The Mysterious Ivory Ball of Wong Shing Li (RH)
The Mystery of the Fiddling Cracksman
The Peacock Fan
The Photo of Lady X (RH)
The Portrait of Jirjohn Cobb
Report on Vanessa Hewstone (RH)
Riddle of the Travelling Skull
Riddle of the Wooden Parrakeet (RH)
The Scarlet Mummy (RH)
The Search for X-Y-Z
The Sharkskin Book
Sing Sing Nights
The Six From Nowhere (RH)
The Skull of the Waltzing Clown
The Spectacles of Mr. Cagliostro
Stand By—London Calling!
The Steeltown Strangler
The Stolen Gravestone (RH)
Strange Journey (RH)
The Strange Will
The Straw Hat Murders (RH)
The Street of 1000 Eyes (RH)
Thieves' Nights
Three Novellos (RH)
The Tiger Snake
The Trap (RH)
Vagabond Nights (Defrauded Yeggman)
Vagabond Nights 2 (10 Hours)
The Vanishing Gold Truck
The Voice of the Seven Sparrows
The Washington Square Enigma
When Thief Meets Thief
The White Circle (RH)
The Wonderful Scheme of Mr. Christopher Thorne
X. Jones—of Scotland Yard
Y. Cheung, Business Detective

Keeler Related Works

A To Izzard: A Harry Stephen Keeler Companion by Fender Tucker — Articles and stories about Harry, by Harry, and in his style. Included is a compleat bibliography.

Wild About Harry: Reviews of Keeler Novels — Edited by Richard Polt & Fender Tucker — 22 reviews of works by Harry Stephen Keeler from *Keeler News*. A perfect introduction to the author.

The Keeler Keyhole Collection: Annotated newsletter rants from Harry Stephen Keeler, edited by Francis M. Nevins. Over 400 pages of incredibly personal Keeleriana.

Fakealoo — Pastiches of the style of Harry Stephen Keeler by selected demented members of the HSK Society. Updated every year with the new winner.

RAMBLE HOUSE's OTHER LOONS

A Shot Rang Out — Three decades of reviews from Jon Breen
The Time Armada — Fox B. Holden's 1953 SF gem.
Sideslip — 1968 SF masterpiece by Ted White and Dave Van Arnam
The Triune Man — Mindscrambling science fiction from Richard A. Lupoff
Detective Duff Unravels It — Episodic mysteries by Harvey O'Higgins
Mysterious Martin, the Master of Murder — Two versions of a strange 1912 novel by Tod Robbins about a man who writes books that can kill.
The Master of Mysteries — 1912 novel of supernatural sleuthing by Gelett Burgess
Dago Red — 22 tales of dark suspense by Bill Pronzini
The Night Remembers — A 1991 Jack Walsh mystery from Ed Gorman
Rough Cut & New, Improved Murder — Ed Gorman's first two novels
Hollywood Dreams — A novel of the Depression by Richard O'Brien
Six Gelett Burgess Novels — *The Master of Mysteries, The White Cat, Two O'Clock Courage, Ladies in Boxes, Find the Woman, The Heart Line*
The Organ Reader — A huge compilation of just about everything published in the 1971-1972 radical bay-area newspaper, *THE ORGAN*.
A Clear Path to Cross — Sharon Knowles short mystery stories by Ed Lynskey
Old Times' Sake — Short stories by James Reasoner from Mike Shayne Magazine
Freaks and Fantasies — Eerie tales by Tod Robbins, collaborator of Tod Browning on the film FREAKS.
Five Jim Harmon Sleaze Double Novels — *Vixen Hollow/Celluloid Scandal, The Man Who Made Maniacs/Silent Siren, Ape Rape/Wanton Witch, Sex Burns Like Fire/Twist Session*, and *Sudden Lust/Passion Strip*. More doubles to come!
Marblehead: A Novel of H.P. Lovecraft — A long-lost masterpiece from Richard A. Lupoff. Published for the first time!
The Compleat Ova Hamlet — Parodies of SF authors by Richard A. Lupoff – New edition!
The Secret Adventures of Sherlock Holmes — Three Sherlockian pastiches by the Brooklyn author/publisher, Gary Lovisi.
The Universal Holmes — Richard A. Lupoff's 2007 collection of five Holmesian pastiches and a recipe for giant rat stew.
Four Joel Townsley Rogers Novels — By the author of *The Red Right Hand: Once In a Red Moon, Lady With the Dice, The Stopped Clock, Never Leave My Bed*
Two Joel Townsley Rogers Story Collections — Night of Horror and Killing Time
Twenty Norman Berrow Novels — *The Bishop's Sword, Ghost House, Don't Go Out After Dark, Claws of the Cougar, The Smokers of Hashish, The Secret Dancer, Don't Jump Mr. Boland!, The Footprints of Satan, Fingers for Ransom, The Three Tiers of Fantasy, The Spaniard's Thumb, The Eleventh Plague, Words Have Wings, One Thrilling Night, The Lady's in Danger, It Howls at Night, The Terror in the Fog, Oil Under the Window, Murder in the Melody, The Singing Room*
The N. R. De Mexico Novels — Robert Bragg presents *Marijuana Girl, Madman on a Drum, Private Chauffeur* in one volume.
Four Chelsea Quinn Yarbro Novels featuring Charlie Moon — *Ogilvie, Tallant and Moon, Music When the Sweet Voice Dies, Poisonous Fruit* and *Dead Mice*
Four Walter S. Masterman Mysteries — *The Green Toad, The Flying Beast, The Yellow Mistletoe* and *The Wrong Verdict*, fantastic impossible plots. More to come.
Two Hake Talbot Novels — *Rim of the Pit, The Hangman's Handyman*. Classic locked room mysteries.
Two Alexander Laing Novels — *The Motives of Nicholas Holtz* and *Dr. Scarlett*, stories of medical mayhem and intrigue from the 30s.
Four David Hume Novels — *Corpses Never Argue, Cemetery First Stop, Make Way for the Mourners, Eternity Here I Come*, and more to come.
Three Wade Wright Novels — *Echo of Fear, Death At Nostalgia Street* and *It Leads to Murder*, with more to come!
Four Rupert Penny Novels — *Policeman's Holiday, Policeman's Evidence, Lucky Policeman* and *Sealed Room Murder*, classic impossible mysteries.
Five Jack Mann Novels — Strange murder in the English countryside. *Gees' First Case, Nightmare Farm, Grey Shapes, The Ninth Life, The Glass Too Many.*
Seven Max Afford Novels — *Owl of Darkness, Death's Mannikins, Blood on His Hands, The Dead Are Blind, The Sheep and the Wolves, Sinners in Paradise* and *Two Locked Room Mysteries and a Ripping Yarn* by one of Australia's finest novelists.

Five Joseph Shallit Novels — *The Case of the Billion Dollar Body, Lady Don't Die on My Doorstep, Kiss the Killer, Yell Bloody Murder, Take Your Last Look.* One of America's best 50's authors.

Two Crimson Clown Novels — By Johnston McCulley, author of the Zorro novels, *The Crimson Clown* and *The Crimson Clown Again.*

The Best of 10-Story Book — edited by Chris Mikul, over 35 stories from the literary magazine Harry Stephen Keeler edited.

A Young Man's Heart — A forgotten early classic by Cornell Woolrich

The Anthony Boucher Chronicles — edited by Francis M. Nevins
Book reviews by Anthony Boucher written for the *San Francisco Chronicle,* 1942 – 1947. Essential and fascinating reading.

Muddled Mind: Complete Works of Ed Wood, Jr. — David Hayes and Hayden Davis deconstruct the life and works of a mad genius.

Gadsby — A lipogram (a novel without the letter E). Ernest Vincent Wright's last work, published in 1939 right before his death.

My First Time: The One Experience You Never Forget — Michael Birchwood — 64 true first-person narratives of how they lost it.

Automaton — Brilliant treatise on robotics: 1928-style! By H. Stafford Hatfield

The Incredible Adventures of Rowland Hern — Rousing 1928 impossible crimes by Nicholas Olde.

Slammer Days — Two full-length prison memoirs: *Men into Beasts* (1952) by George Sylvester Viereck and *Home Away From Home* (1962) by Jack Woodford

The Golden Dagger — 1951 Scotland Yard yarn by E. R. Punshon

Beat Books #1 — Two beatnik classics, *A Sea of Thighs* by Ray Kainen and *Village Hipster* by J.X. Williams

A Smell of Smoke — 1951 English countryside thriller by Miles Burton

Ruled By Radio — 1925 futuristic novel by Robert L. Hadfield & Frank E. Farncombe

Murder in Silk — A 1937 Yellow Peril novel of the silk trade by Ralph Trevor

The Case of the Withered Hand — 1936 potboiler by John G. Brandon

Finger-prints Never Lie — A 1939 classic detective novel by John G. Brandon

Inclination to Murder — 1966 thriller by New Zealand's Harriet Hunter

Invaders from the Dark — Classic werewolf tale from Greye La Spina

Fatal Accident — Murder by automobile, a 1936 mystery by Cecil M. Wills

The Devil Drives — A prison and lost treasure novel by Virgil Markham

Dr. Odin — Douglas Newton's 1933 potboiler comes back to life.

The Chinese Jar Mystery — Murder in the manor by John Stephen Strange, 1934

The Julius Caesar Murder Case — A classic 1935 re-telling of the assassination by Wallace Irwin that's much more fun than the Shakespeare version

West Texas War and Other Western Stories — by Gary Lovisi

The Contested Earth and Other SF Stories — A never-before published space opera and seven short stories by Jim Harmon.

Tales of the Macabre and Ordinary — Modern twisted horror by Chris Mikul, author of the *Bizarrism* series.

The Gold Star Line — Seaboard adventure from L.T. Reade and Robert Eustace.

The Werewolf vs the Vampire Woman — Hard to believe ultraviolence by either Arthur M. Scarm or Arthur M. Scram.

Black Hogan Strikes Again — Australia's Peter Renwick pens a tale of the outback.

Don Diablo: Book of a Lost Film — Two-volume treatment of a western by Paul Landres, with diagrams. Intro by Francis M. Nevins.

The Charlie Chaplin Murder Mystery — Movie hijinks by Wes D. Gehring

The Koky Comics — A collection of all of the 1978-1981 Sunday and daily comic strips by Richard O'Brien and Mort Gerberg, in two volumes.

Suzy — Another collection of comic strips from Richard O'Brien and Bob Vojtko

Dime Novels: Ramble House's 10-Cent Books — *Knife in the Dark* by Robert Leslie Bellem, *Hot Lead* and *Song of Death* by Ed Earl Repp, *A Hashish House in New York* by H.H. Kane, and five more.

Blood in a Snap — The *Finnegan's Wake* of the 21st century, by Jim Weiler and Al Gorithm

Stakeout on Millennium Drive — Award-winning Indianapolis Noir — Ian Woollen.

Dope Tales #1 — Two dope-riddled classics; *Dope Runners* by Gerald Grantham and *Death Takes the Joystick* by Phillip Condé.

Dope Tales #2 — Two more narco-classics; *The Invisible Hand* by Rex Dark and *The Smokers of Hashish* by Norman Berrow.

Dope Tales #3 — Two enchanting novels of opium by the master, Sax Rohmer. *Dope* and *The Yellow Claw.*

Tenebrae — Ernest G. Henham's 1898 horror tale brought back.

The Singular Problem of the Stygian House-Boat — Two classic tales by John Kendrick Bangs about the denizens of Hades.

Tiresias — Psychotic modern horror novel by Jonathan M. Sweet.

The One After Snelling — Kickass modern noir from Richard O'Brien.

The Sign of the Scorpion — 1935 Edmund Snell tale of oriental evil.

The House of the Vampire — 1907 poetic thriller by George S. Viereck.

An Angel in the Street — Modern hardboiled noir by Peter Genovese.

The Devil's Mistress — Scottish gothic tale by J. W. Brodie-Innes.

The Lord of Terror — 1925 mystery with master-criminal, Fantômas.

The Lady of the Terraces — 1925 adventure by E. Charles Vivian.

My Deadly Angel — 1955 Cold War drama by John Chelton

Prose Bowl — Futuristic satire — Bill Pronzini & Barry N. Malzberg .

Satan's Den Exposed — True crime in Truth or Consequences New Mexico — Award-winning journalism by the *Desert Journal*.

The Amorous Intrigues & Adventures of Aaron Burr — by Anonymous — Hot historical action.

I Stole $16,000,000 — A true story by cracksman Herbert E. Wilson.

The Black Dark Murders — Vintage 50s college murder yarn by Milt Ozaki, writing as Robert O. Saber.

Sex Slave — Potboiler of lust in the days of Cleopatra — Dion Leclerq.

You'll Die Laughing — Bruce Elliott's 1945 novel of murder at a practical joker's English countryside manor.

The Private Journal & Diary of John H. Surratt — The memoirs of the man who conspired to assassinate President Lincoln.

Dead Man Talks Too Much — Hollywood boozer by Weed Dickenson

Red Light — History of legal prostitution in Shreveport Louisiana by Eric Brock. Includes wonderful photos of the houses and the ladies.

A Snark Selection — Lewis Carroll's *The Hunting of the Snark* with two Snarkian chapters by Harry Stephen Keeler — Illustrated by Gavin L. O'Keefe.

Ripped from the Headlines! — The Jack the Ripper story as told in the newspaper articles in the *New York* and *London Times*.

Geronimo — S. M. Barrett's 1905 autobiography of a noble American.

The White Peril in the Far East — Sidney Lewis Gulick's 1905 indictment of the West and assurance that Japan would never attack the U.S.

The Compleat Calhoon — All of Fender Tucker's works: Includes *The Totah Trilogy, Weed, Women and Song* and *Tales from the Tower,* plus a CD of all of his songs.

RAMBLE HOUSE
Fender Tucker, Prop.
www.ramblehouse.com   fender@ramblehouse.com
318-455-6847   10329 Sheephead Drive, Vancleave MS 39565